Chronicles of th...

A PRIDE OF PRINCES

Jennifer Roberson

CORGI BOOKS

A PRIDE OF PRINCES
A CORGI BOOK 0 552 13122 9

First publication in Great Britain

PRINTING HISTORY
Corgi edition published 1989

Copyright © 1988 by Jennifer Roberson O'Green
Cheysuli Map by Liz Danforth

Corgi Books are published by Transworld Publishers
Ltd., 61–63 Uxbridge Road, Ealing, London W5 5SA, in
Australia by Transworld Publishers (Australia) Pty. Ltd.,
15–23 Helles Avenue, Moorebank, NSW 2170, and in New
Zealand by Transworld Publishers (N.Z.) Ltd., Cnr. Moselle
and Waipareira Avenues, Henderson, Auckland.

Printed and bound in Great Britain by
Cox & Wyman Ltd., Reading, Berks.

To Georgana and John, who read them all, and listened;

Mike, Liz, Tom, B.D. and Hilde, for Friday night critiques;

Amber-Eyes Underfoot, Scooter Hightops, Shiloh "Buckethead" and Big Bubba No Trubba, for comic relief (and hair);

Russ, who keeps on selling 'em;

And Mark, for keeping me sane.

Prologue

The cavern was dense with smoke. The woman stepped through and dutifully it followed, purling in her wake. It gathered along the hem of her skirts like puppies on a bitch, suckling at her feet.

She walked from shadow into glare, into the pure clean light of *godfire* as it leaped from a circular rent in the stone floor. A hole, like a wound in the earth itself, bleeding flame.

Sparks issued forth, fell, formed a glowing necklet on the nap of her velvet gown. But she did not flinch as they died; the fire—like the sparks—was cold.

Beyond the flame, she saw her brother. Standing as he stood so often, for hours on end, and days, at the rim of the netherworld. *Godfire* bathed his face in its lurid lavender glare, limning the magnificent planes of his bones. A beautiful man, her brother; she might have been jealous, once, but she knew she claimed more power.

He saw her. He smiled. In the light his eyes were mirrors.

Briefly the flame died back; was sucked down, withdrawn, like a tongue into a mouth. But the afterglow remained, shrouding him in light. A transcendent luminescence that made her want to squint.

Beneath her feet, the floor was hard and sharp. The entire cavern was formed of black, glassy basalt, faceted as a gemstone. There were no torches in deference to the *godfire*; there was no need for manmade light when the Seker lent them his.

All around her columns gleamed. Slow spirals mimicked blown glass, delicately fluted; twisted strands, oddly seductive, stretched from floor to ceiling. Light lost itself in endless glassy whorls. The world ran wet with fire.

She crossed, hearing the echoes of her steps and the chime of girdle, silver on black, nearly lost in the weight of velvet. As always, she smelled the breath of the god. But to her, it was not unpleasant. The promise of power was a heady scent that set her flesh to tingling.

She paused on the brink of the orifice. "How long has it been since you ate?"

He smiled. "Trust you to concern yourself with things such as food."

"How long, Strahan?"

He shrugged; smoke shrugged with him. "A day, two, three—what does it matter, Lillith? I will hardly waste away in the service of the god."

Briefly she glanced down. They stood but six feet apart; between them lay a world. The world of Asar-Suti.

They had only to open the Gate—

Not yet. There was time.

Time for the fruition of their plans.

"Come up," she said. "You should eat."

His hair, like hers, was black. And it flowed back from a brow as smooth and unlined as a girl's, though there was nothing girlish about him. It cloaked his shoulders and reached beyond, bound back by a silver fillet wrought with Ihlini runes. In the glare of the *godfire* his gray suede leathers were dyed an eerie lilac, glowing purple in the creases. The doublet hung open from throat and chest, and in the gap she saw the white edge of a linen tunic. Soft gray boots stretched to his thighs. His wide belt was clasped with a two-headed silver serpent.

Lillith sighed as he did not answer. She was his sister, not mother or father. But both parents were long dead, and so this fell to her. "Will you come up?"

"I am hungry," he admitted, "but for something more than food. And I am thirsty, also, but the wine I want is blood. The blood of Niall's sons."

His eyes were alight with something more than reflected glare. One brown, one blue; even *she* had difficulty looking past the mismatched pairing to the emotions in their depths. But she looked, and she saw, and knew his patience was nearly ended.

"A little longer," she said. "Surely you can wait."

"No. I *have* waited. I am *done* with waiting." He smiled his beautiful, beguiling smile. "Lillith—I am *hungry*."

"Time," she said. "We have all the years of our lives."

"*They* do not. They are human, even if Cheysuli. They die. They live seventy, eighty years, and they die. While *we* are still but children."

"*You* are still a child." Lillith laughed, and the girdle chimed. "The last time I counted *mine,* my years were nearly two hundred."

He grunted, unimpressed; he was young in years, compared to her, but his power grew every day. "I have need of them, Lillith. The sons are no longer infants, no longer boys. They are men. Warriors. If we wait much longer—"

"But we will." Lillith shrugged naked shoulders. "We will wait as long as we must, and longer. Until the time is right."

"Twenty years, Lillith!" His shout reverberated in the hidden shadows of the cavern. "Twenty years since Niall thwarted me."

"Twenty years is but half a day to us." But she saw his frustration and felt a measure of her own. "I know. I know, Strahan . . . I weary of it, also. But we are close. The game begins—all of the pieces are in place. As you say, now they are of an age to make a difference."

"Of an age to serve me well." In the light, his mismatched eyes were eerie. "I want them. I want them here, within the walls of Valgaard, so I may make them mine. Mine to rule, as I will have *them* rule." He laughed suddenly, and their eyes locked in perfect accordance across the Gate of Asar-Suti. "When they are mine, Niall's sons, I will set them on their thrones, all three of them . . . I will take their *lir* and take their minds, *all three of them,* making them faithful Ihlini minions—" He broke off a moment, considering his words; continued in quiet, abiding contentment, "—and then *I* shall rule through their empty bodies in the name of Asar-Suti."

Lillith smiled, nodded, sketched an idle rune in the air between them that pulsed with purple *godfire*. It spun, whirled, twisted; tied itself in knots, was gone. "Of course. It is to be expected; we have laid our plans." She paused. "*Now* will you come up?"

"Up," he echoed. "Aye. In a moment. There is something I must do."

And in the eerie lurid light, Strahan the Ihlini knelt in deep obeisance to the god of the netherworld.

PART I

One

The sun hung low in the west, painting the city rose-red, ocher-gold, russet-brown. Sunlight, trapped and multiplied by mullioned glass, made mirrors of countless windows. Mujhara was ablaze with gilded glory.

The one-eyed man stood alone upon the curtain wall surrounding the massive palace of Homana-Mujhar. Spilling in all directions from the battlements was the royal city, home of kings and queens; home of the Mujhars of Homana. Home to countless others of lesser birth as well; he could not even begin to estimate Mujhara's population. He knew only that the number had increased one hundredfold, perhaps one *thousandfold*, over the past two weeks. The festival was even larger than his brother had predicted.

"Everyone will come, Ian had said, *from everywhere, even the other realms. Scoff if you like, Niall, but it is past time the Homanans paid homage to their Mujhar. More than past time they showed their gratitude for twenty years of peaceful rule."*

Twenty years. It seemed longer than that. And then, at times, it seemed only days since he had assumed the Lion Throne from his Cheysuli father, Donal, who had given himself over to the death-ritual on the plague-born deaths of his *lir*. With Taj and Lorn gone, there had been nothing left for Donal, save madness. And no Cheysuli warrior willingly gave himself over to madness. Not when there was a choice. Not when there was the death-ritual, which was surely more merciful than madness.

Niall sighed deeply, frowning down at the street far below the curtain wall, and the smooth earthwork ridge that girded the lower portions of the thick wall. He could hear the distant sounds of celebration: faint ringing tambors of the street-dancers; cries of stall-merchants; shouts and screams of children in their finery, turned loose to play in crowded streets and alleys.

Dead so long, my jehan. He readily acknowledged the still familiar pain. There was grief. Regret. Even bitterness, that a man so strong and healthy as his father should throw his life away.

Homanan thinking, he told himself wryly, made aware yet again of the division in his attitudes; how pervasive that division could be. *Have you forgotten the oaths you made when you accepted the responsibilities of the lirbond before Clan Council?*

No. Of course he had not forgotten. But it was difficult to be two men at once: one, born of a Homanan mother, who was the daughter of a king; the other born of a Cheysuli shapechanger, a warrior with a *lir,* and claiming all the magic the gods had given the race.

Automatically he looked for Serri, but the wolf was not with him. His lips tightened in annoyance. How could he have forgotten Serri was in the royal apartments?

Because, he told himself ironically, in a spasm of defensiveness, *with all the toasting going on, it is fortunate you can remember your own* name, *let alone Serri's whereabouts.*

Still, it displeased him that he could forget for even a moment. A sign of age, he wondered?

Niall abruptly laughed aloud. Perhaps. No doubt his children would agree he was aging, but *he* thought not. At forty, there were decades ahead of him still.

And then he recalled that his own father had not been so much older than forty when the loss of his *lir* had ended his life. His mother as well was gone; Aislinn, Queen of Homana, had died ten years after Donal. Some said of grief that grew too strong.

He stopped the laughter. Memories welled up. Most of them Niall had believed buried too deeply to trouble him. The gods knew he had *tried* to bury them; with drink, with daily council sessions lasting from dawn till midnight, with abrupt departures—*escapes*—into the woodlands with Serri, seeking respite in his *lir*-shape. But Deirdre had made him realize none of those things held the answers; that he would have to find a place for each memory and let it live there, where he could look at it from time to time and know what was lost, was gained, was learned.

Deirdre. The memories of her were fresh, beloved, cherished, and very near the surface. But there were other ones as well, buried more deeply: of guilt, of fear, of self-hatred, because once he had believed her murdered by his own unintended instigation. No matter how helpless, how unknowing he had been, trapped within the Ihlini web of madness, deceit and sorcery, he could not think of that time in his life without experiencing a fresh burst of shame, guilt, pain.

"So." She approached from his right side, his blind side; he had not heard her, either. "With all your great palace in an uproar, you'll be coming out here to escape it." Deirdre smiled, glancing over the nearest crenel to look upon the crowded city. "Peace in turbulence, then?"

Though she had been with him twenty years in Homana, she had not lost the lilt of Erinn. He smiled. "Aye, escape, except there *is* no escape. Everywhere I turn there is a servant telling me I must go here, go there— even Ian. Even *you*."

Deirdre laughed, green eyes alight, and moved in close to his side. His arm settled around her shoulders automatically. She wore green, as she so often did, to play up the color of her eyes. It suited her, as did the torque of braided gold and carved green jade he had given her the night before. "But 'tis for *you* all of this is being done," she reminded him tartly. "D'ye wish to disappoint so many people who have come here to pay their respects?"

He grimaced. "You make it sound like I am dead."

Deirdre leaned her head against his chest. She was neither tall nor short, but he was head and shoulders above most men, even the Cheysuli. "No, not dead," she said calmly. "Very much alive—or so you would have *me* thinking; I who share your bed."

Niall laughed and hugged her against his chest. "Aye, well, there is that." His fingers smoothed the weave of her braided hair. A year younger than he, she looked no more her thirty-nine years than his daughters. The hair was still thick and brassy gold; the skin still fair and smooth, with only a shallow threading of lines by her eyes; her hips and breasts, respectively, still slender and firm as a girl's.

"What were you thinking?" she asked.

"Remembering," he answered. "The night I stood atop the dragon's skull in Atvia, and lit the beacon-fire."

Deirdre stiffened. "Why?" she asked. She pulled away and faced him. "*Why*, Niall—why that? 'Twas more than twenty years ago."

"*That* is why," he told her. "Twenty years. The Homanans are even now celebrating twenty years of my rule, and all *I* can see are the memories of what I nearly did that many years ago." His voice was unsteady; he steadied it. "I killed your father, Deirdre. And nearly the rest of the eagles."

His pain was reflected in her face. "You fool," she said softly. "Oh, ye great silly fool. Liam would be taking his fist to you, he would. I *should*." She shook her head and sighed. "Aye, Shea died, but he took the assassin with him. Else we *would* all be dead, and you could be blaming yourself for that." Firmly, she shook her head. "You lit the fire, 'tis true, but 'twas Alaric's doing. Thanks to his addled daughter."

Addled daughter. Gisella of Atvia, half Cheysuli herself, and Niall's full cousin. Poor mad Gisella, who had married the Prince of Homana; Niall, now called Mujhar. The Queen of Homana, who now resided in Atvia in permanent exile from the land of her mother's birth.

He sighed. "Aye. 'Tis done, as *you* would say. But I cannot forget it."

"Then don't. Come in, instead, where a bath is being poured." She took his hand. "Are you forgetting? There is to be a feast for you in the Great Hall."

"Oh, gods, not again," he blurted. "Who is host tonight?"

"Prince Einar, heir to the King of Caledon," Deirdre answered, smiling. "The one you want to make a new trade alliance with."

He strolled with her along the sentry-walk. "Aye, I do. The old one is far out of date; there are more concessions to be won. Without them, we lose more money than we make, which serves Homana not at all. What I *want* to get—"

"No," Deirdre said firmly. "No, don't be filling my ears with that. I've been hearing too much of it these past two weeks, and I'll hear more of it over my food. *No,* Niall—not now."

He laughed. "Well enough, *meijha*—not now. I am sick of it myself."

The sentry-walk was not wide enough for two to walk abreast comfortably, not when one was as large as Niall. He moved Deirdre away from the edge, closer to the wall, and assumed the risk himself. Below them, in the other bailey, men-at-arms in new crimson livery practiced a close-order drill. The shouted orders from the captain carried easily to the sentry-walk, though Deirdre and Niall were still some distance away. It was easiest to stay on the wall and follow it around than to go down into the baileys, which were thronged with royal escorts and honor guards from other realms.

Niall sighed. "I think Homana-Mujhar will burst before the month is through. Certainly Mujhara will."

Deirdre frowned absently. "Einar," she said. " 'Twas him, was it not, so dissatisfied with his chambers?"

Niall snorted inelegantly. "*You* are chatelaine of this great sprawl of red stone, *meijha*, not I."

Deirdre's face cleared. "Aye, 'twas him. He demanded better quarters."

"Well, he *is* a king's son—and the heir to Caledon."

"And what of the heir to Ellas?" Deirdre demanded. "Am I to put Diarmuid out just because Einar wants his room?"

"What *did* you do?" Niall asked curiously.

Deirdre grinned. "Homana-Mujhar is filled to bursting, my lord Mujhar. I made them share."

Niall's shout of laughter erased the lines of tension that had etched themselves into his face as a result of trying to juggle multiple princes, envoys, cousins and heirs without giving offense to any. Deirdre felt he needed no more lines at all, regardless of his responsibilities; Strahan's demon-hawk had already ruined enough of his face. A patch hid the empty right socket and most of the scarring, but the old talon weals still scored the bridge of his nose and much of his right cheek, as well as dividing one tawny eyebrow neatly in half.

She glanced up at his face. To her, it was familiar, beloved, unremarkable, save for the unmistakable stamp of Cheysuli pride, even if he lacked the coloring. But to others, unaccustomed to the disfigurement, he was noteworthy only in that respect. *She* had first known him as a young man, at eighteen, when the handsome looks of his maternal grandsire, Carillon, had been fresh, boyish, as yet unformed by adversity. But the demon-born hawk of Asar-Suti had robbed him of his boyhood in addition to his looks.

For that, if for nothing else, Deirdre hated Strahan.

Through the casements of the palace came the dim glow of new-lit candles. The rose-red hue of the stone deepened as the sun dropped down behind the massive walls, from pink to dull, bloodied gray. Deirdre suppressed a shiver; there were times, she thought, Homana-Mujhar resembled a monument to war and death, rather than the home of Homanan kings.

Niall took her off the sentry-walk into one of the exterior corner towers, then down a coil of stairs to the interior of the palace. Deirdre had always felt Homana-Mujhar more confusing than Kilore, the clifftop fortress her brother Liam ruled from in Erinn. Kilore, known as the Aerie of Erinn, was plainer, more functional, lacking the multitudinous staircases and tower chambers of Homana-Mujhar. But then perhaps it was only time and distance that made it seem so; Deirdre had not been home in eighteen years.

"We should go," she said abruptly, as Niall took her into his chamber. Protocol required they keep separate apartments, and so they did—even had they wed, it would have been the same—but more often they spent the nights in his. "We should go to visit Liam before we are old and gray."

Niall bent to greet the black-masked silver wolf who got up from his place in the huge draperied tester bed to lean against one thigh-booted, royal leg. Their brief communion was intensely private, intensely singular, but Deirdre was used to it. No one came between a warrior and his *lir*, not even the woman he loved.

Serri, his greeting complete, went back to the bed. Niall smiled, brushed back a lock of hair from his brow and looked at Deirdre in amusement. "The gray begins already, *meijha*—perhaps we should leave for Erinn tomorrow."

"Ah, ye *skilfin*, you're no more gray than I am!" But she put a hand to her heavy braid as if to reassure herself she bore no tainted strands. " 'Tis serious I am, Niall— how many times must Liam invite us? And I his own sister?"

"And still a princess of Erinn." Niall stopped abruptly as he shut the heavy door behind her. "Ah, Deirdre, will you forgive me for that? You deserve to be a queen."

Astonished, she stared up at him. One slim hand was locked in his plain brown doublet. "Niall . . ." Slowly she shook her head. "Ah, no—d'ye think 'tis what I want? No, no, my love—'tis nothing to me, I swear, this thing of titles." Her mouth flattened, then twisted scornfully. "Queen of Homana, indeed. Well, I say let Gisella keep it—'tis all she has. I have *you*."

"Not so much, I think," he said mildly, but bent his head to kiss her.

A knock at the door intruded. "My lord? My lord Mujhar? Taggart, my lord . . . are you there?"

Niall sighed. "A moment," he promised her, and went to open the door. "Aye, Taggart, I am. What is it?"

Taggart was a slim, wiry man of fifty, clad in Homanan colors: black tunic with a red rampant lion stitched over his left breast. His trews were also black, with a gilt-buckled red leather belt cinching his waist. Graying hair was trimmed neatly against his head. He bowed briefly. "My lord—it is the princes."

Niall looked past the man to the empty corridor. "Oh? Where?"

Taggart was clearly uncomfortable. "My lord—not *here*. That is why *I* am here." He paused. "Because they are *not*."

The Mujhar's tawny brows rose a trifle. "Taggart, what are you trying to tell me? And make haste—my bath is getting cold."

Taggart bowed again, eloquent apology. "My lord, I—well—" He paused. "They are missing."

"Missing?" Niall smiled indulgently. "For the moment, perhaps, but I am sure they are here somewhere. You might try the stables; Brennan has a new stallion. Or the guardroom, if Hart has coin enough left for a fortune-game." He shrugged negligently, patently unconcerned by the temporary disappearance of his three sons. "And only the *gods* know what Corin may have suggested as an afternoon's diversion."

"Or Keely," Deirdre added dryly.

"My lord, no," Taggart said plainly. "I have looked in all those places. They are not here. They are not in Homana-Mujhar."

Deirdre came up to Niall's left side, where he could see her clearly; it was a habit she encouraged in everyone so he would not be embarrassed unduly or caught off-guard. "They knew about the banquet," she said, though it sounded more question than statement. "I know they did; Brennan remarked on it. He said he did not think much of Einar, or Einar's cousin, Reynald." She nodded, frowning a little. " 'Tis what he said, did Brennan—about the Caledonese princes."

Niall heaved a weary sigh of distracted annoyance and scratched at the scars in his right cheek. "Well, if *Brennan* remarked on it, then it took Hart to persuade him to leave so soon before a banquet. And Hart, likely, was talked into it by Corin. Oh, gods—" he cast a long-suffered glance at the ceiling, "—when you saw fit to bless me with three sons, you might have given me proper ones. Ones who know how to respect their *jehan's* wishes." He shook his head. "How is it *I* have raised three rebels? I was never particularly rebellious, myself."

Deirdre laughed. "Were you not, my lord? But I think you *must* have been, because I'm seeing you in all of them. Though more, I'll own, in Brennan than in the others."

"He is the first-born," Niall said absently. "And he knows he will be Mujhar after me; it makes a difference."

"Keely probably knows where they are," Deirdre suggested, somewhat pointedly.

Niall cast her a disgusted glance. "For all we know, *Keely* might have encouraged their defection. She is as bad as any of them. There are times I think she is more a warrior than even myself."

"Shall I ask her, my lord?" Taggart inquired.

Niall waved the suggestion away. "No, no—Keely would never say. If Corin is involved, she'll say nothing simply to protect him, even if she had nothing to do with it. Even, I think, if *I* asked her." He shook his head, frowning again. "Brennan knows better. Hart and Corin may not, but *he* does."

"Aye," Deirdre said gently, "but he protects Hart and Corin *now* just as he did when they were children. D'ye think he'd be stopping simply because they're grown?"

"Are they?" Niall's tone was sour. He did not wait for her answer, but turned to Taggart. "You may go. I attach no blame to you. It is not your fault if the Mujhar cannot control his own unruly sons."

Taggart, smiling, bowed and took his leave. Niall shut the door and turned back to face Deirdre once more. "Well, then, what is there to do? There will be three empty chairs where there are *supposed* to be princes, and Einar will undoubtedly consider it a snub."

"Oh, *Einar!*" Deirdre's tone clearly signified her opinion of the Caledonese heir. "I'll set Maeve next to him, and he'll not be noticing absent princes. And I'll put Keely on the *other* side." Her widening smile was suspiciously devious. "Caught between *those* two, he'll not be knowing what has become of him."

"Oh, gods," Niall begged, "save me from a woman who dearly loves intrigue." And then, abruptly, he began to smile. "Einar will never recover."

"No," Deirdre agreed contentedly. " 'Tis why I'll be doing it."

"Still—" Niall moved past her to the nearest chair and dropped into it, propping his booted feet up on a table that bore a decanter of wine and two goblets, "—they might have picked a better night to play truant. I *do* want that trade alliance. And I *did* want Brennan to handle as much of the negotiation as he could. He needs the practice."

"Brennan knows enough of negotiations." Deirdre poured him wine, passed him the goblet. "He is a mature, responsible man, Niall, not a boy. Save your disgust for Corin's bad tempers, or Hart's gambling debts, or Keely's waywardness—but give none of it to Brennan. He's not deserving of it."

"Come here." He sipped from his goblet as she came to perch on the arm of his wooden chair. "Tell me what *you* are deserving of."

"Your love," she answered promptly. "Am I not generous with mine? And I have given you a lovely daughter."

"Maeve *is* lovely," Niall agreed immediately, paternal pride rearing its head. "And sweet-tempered, and soft-spoken, and eager to please . . . all the things Keely most decidedly is not."

"And do you love her the less for it?"

Niall, smiling, shook his head. "She is a proud, strong woman, Cheysuli to the bone. . . ." He grinned at Deirdre, slipping into the Erinnish lilt. "And I'd be wanting her no other way."

"And the boys?" Deirdre's green eyes, across the rim of her silver goblet, were demurely downcast, but Niall knew her far too well.

"Aye, and I know what you are trying to tell me, *meijha*—that I should want *them* no different, either. Mostly, I do not. But there are times. . . ."

"Times," she said. "Like now? The bathwater, I'm sure, is cold, and yet you sit here and drink your wine. You are no better than your sons, my lord Mujhar."

"But you see, I *am* Mujhar. The banquet must wait for me." His fingers were in the lacings of her gown. "The banquet must wait for us *both.*"

Deirdre smothered a giggle. She was, she thought, too old for giggles now. "And your sons?" she asked. "What about your sons?"

"At this particular moment, I am less concerned with my sons than with the knots you have tied in your laces. Have you taken up celibacy?"

The giggle broke free of her throat. "No. Very definitely, *no.*" She reached down, took his belt-knife from its sheath, presented it to him hilt-first. "My lord Mujhar, must I be plainer still?"

Niall, smiling, accepted the knife and deftly cut the first lace. "The banquet," he said calmly, "will be indefinitely delayed."

Deirdre sat very still. "To make certain your sons will be present, of course."

"Of course," he agreed equably, and cut the second knot.

Two

The tavern was one of Mujhara's finest. It lay in High Street, where business catered to the aristocracy of Homana; where boys with brooms swept the cobbles six times a day and poured water on the puddles of urine left by horses, sweeping again, so customers did not have to concern themselves with the condition of their boots. The Rampant Lion was clean, well-lighted, well-run, and enjoyed an excellent reputation, faring well even among stiff competition.

Rhiannon had not expected to get the job as wine-girl at The Lion. But she had paid six copper pennies for a bath two days before she applied, pinned up her hair in the way she had seen ladies do, and put on the cleanest dress she owned. Carefully, she had told the tavern-keeper in her best accent that she was of good family, but lacked means; was there a place for a young woman who needed to earn a living in a *respectable* establishment?

She was delighted when her looks and well-practiced refinement won her the position, and she worked very hard to keep it. She was born of poor people; she had thought to spend her years in poverty and whoredom. But the gods had blessed her with cream-fair skin, thick black hair and wide black eyes, and a form that would win any man's regard.

It did not fail her now. She passed easily among the tables, serving the fine wines The Rampant Lion special-ized in. The Falian white, considered by many to be the finest vintage available, sold best. But the sweet Caledonese red and the rich, dark vintage of Ellas did nearly as well. The ales and lagers found fewer throats; Homanan nobles had a taste for wine, rarely imbibing lesser brews, and almost never the common liquors, such as *usca*. It was considered too harsh among the nobles, who boasted more refined tastes.

Nonetheless, it was *usca* Rhiannon was instructed to bring to a rectangular table of polished hardwood near the wide-bolled trunk of the roof-tree in the middle of the common room. She set the stoneware jug in the precise center of the table, put down the pottery cups without the crude clacking sound heard in most taverns, where the wine-girls knew no better, and watched as the three young men poured the blue-glazed cups quite full. It was obvious, from the way they drank it down, *usca* was no stranger to their throats.

She curtsied as gracefully as she knew how, hoping for a generous tip. They could afford it, she knew; she had an eye for wealth. These three young lords dressed less ostentatiously than many others in the common room, clothed in subdued if rich velvet and soft-worked leather, but there was gold around their necks as well as in their ears. At least, in *one* ear. On them all, only the left bore ornamentation.

They were all fine looking men, she thought; the gods had blessed them with good bones and fine, clean lines in their handsome faces, accentuated by strong, straight noses and well-defined mouths. All men, she thought, if young still, lacking the hardening that years and experience would bring them. Rhiannon's taste ran to *men*, not pretty boys; these three were aesthetically satisfying as well as highborn, and more than comfortable in the belt-purse.

One, however, was clearly Cheysuli. Though he was the first shapechanger Rhiannon had ever seen, she knew. She had heard stories about them; how they slept with animals instead of women and so could shift their shapes, not being wholly human. A man could tell them by their color and their gold; Cheysuli were uniformly black-haired, dark-skinned, and their eyes, as his, were always a clear, uncanny yellow.

But where was his animal?

Rhiannon looked carefully, searching discreetly for the beast that was his other self. But the only thing visible beneath the table were their legs. Six of them, altogether, all knee-booted and thigh-muscled under taut, soft leather breeches of excellent cut and quality.

She glanced up, frowning, and saw his eyes on her. Rhiannon sucked in a startled breath. Yellow was not enough, she decided; not *nearly* enough to describe Cheysuli eyes. They were yellow, aye, and odd enough in that, but there was something about them that made her back away a step, clutching her linen apron.

He looked at her, and she froze, unable to take a step.

"Aye?" he asked, when she continued staring.

A human voice. No growl. No bark. No whine.

Transfixed, Rhiannon did not answer.

"Aye?" he asked again, and the slanted black brows drew down.

He was, she thought, a demon, all black and bronze and yellow.

"Are you a lackwit, Brennan?" one of the others asked. "She works for more than kind words and copper pennies." Almost absently, he rattled dice and rune-sticks in a wooden casket. A heavy sapphire signet ring glistened on one long finger. He had the hands of an artist, she thought; the hands of a musician.

"Of course." The shapechanger reached into his belt-purse and took out a silver piece. Without looking, he offered Rhiannon the coin.

When she did not take it, he looked at her again, turning away from the sticks and dice the other threw. The silver was quite bright against the dark flesh of his fingers.

"I think," drawled the man with the casket, "she has only just seen her first Cheysuli." He grinned and looked up at her. "Let alone three at once."

Three? Rhiannon looked at him quickly. He was black-haired, aye, and his skin was as sun-bronzed as the shapechanger's, but his eyes were decidedly blue. *Very* blue; the sort of blue that put her in mind of spring, and the richness of the sky. They made her think of love, his eyes; so did the smile he smiled.

Disconcerted, she looked away from him as well. To the third, where she knew herself safe at last. He was all Homanan, obviously, with tawny blond hair and dark blue eyes; his skin was Homanan fair. And when *he* looked at her it was not to frown as the shapechanger did, or to smile an invitation as the second one did; no, none of those things. When he looked at her it was to look at *her,* to find out what she wanted.

Well, what *did* she want?

Rhiannon put up her chin. "Aye," she agreed plainly. "I've not seen a shapechanger before."

"Cheysuli," The shapechanger put the coin on the table, where it glinted against polished wood. "Not 'shapechanger,' *meijhana* . . . unless you *mean* to insult us."

There it was again: us. She frowned, flicked a glance at the blue-eyed man with the fortune-game, looked quickly away as his smiled slowly widened. And the fair-haired man merely laughed.

"So much for believing the Homanans trust us," he said. "Well, Brennan, how does it feel to have a woman *afraid* of you, instead of trying to keep your favor for more than a single night?"

"Cruel, *cruel,* Corin," the man with the casket drawled, and yet his smile belied the words. "You will have me thinking you are jealous of your oldest *rujholli*."

Rhiannon thought the fair-haired man—Corin, the other had called him—was her age, which made him all of twenty. The other two, she was certain, were older yet, by at least a year. The shapechanger looked at her. "*Are* you afraid of me?"

Rhiannon swallowed. "Aye."

Somehow, she had hurt him. She saw it quite clearly, and instantly. There was little change in his expression, but the eyes were eloquent. Such an eloquent, eerie yellow.

"Well," he said, after a moment's thoughtful silence,

"perhaps you would do well to serve the other tables, and send some other girl to us."

Oh, gods, if that were to happen, she would lose her place for certain! "No," she said quickly. "No. I—I'll serve you." She nodded in the direction of the jug. "You have your *usca* now. You won't be needing more."

"Will we not?" Tawny Corin smiled and lifted his pottery cup. "You judge us too quickly, *meijhana*."

There it was again, the strange, foreign word. Shapechanger? Rhiannon thought it likely. No doubt when they were together, they spoke in growls and barks.

"Brennan frightens the girl, and now Corin *flirts* with her." The third young noble laughed. "What is left over for me?"

Yellow-eyed Brennan looked up at Rhiannon. "Do you wager?" he asked calmly, without the trace of a smile. And yet she saw one clearly in his eyes; it was meant for the man with the fortune-game. "Say aye, and you will make Hart's evening complete."

"No, no," the other—Hart—demurred. "You leave out what comes *after*, when a lady is involved."

That Rhiannon understood plainly enough. Shapechangers they might be, but obviously it was not true they only lay with beasts. She knew desire when she saw it, as well as the prelude to it.

"No, I don't wager," she told them curtly. "Not even with silver pennies." And she went away, leaving the coin upon the table.

As one, they looked at the spurned gratuity. In the light from hanging lanterns, the silver royal gleamed.

"Well," said the one called Hart, "I wonder if she would come back for it if she knew what it was worth. Silver penny indeed!"

As he made as if to pick it up, Brennan hid it beneath one palm. "Wager with your own coin," he said grimly. "Or have you none left?"

"None left," Hart said cheerfully. "A run of bad fortune." As if on cue, one of the rune-sticks rolled.

Corin's snort was eloquently condescending. "Only bad fortune because I was the better man when you tried to beat me this afternoon." He picked up the stick and dropped it back into the casket. "Which means Brennan and I must pay for the *usca*."

"*You* can," Brennan told him. "I came here because I knew better than to let you two go out alone, not because I wanted to go drinking."

"And yet you are." Hart indicated Brennan's full cup. "Hardly water, *rujho*—I can smell it from here."

Corin smiled. Brennan merely shrugged. "All men make sacrifices."

"And you more than most?" Corin demanded. "Oh, aye—when you will have Homana!"

Brennan sighed; it was an old bone of contention. "You will have Atvia."

"And I, Solinde." Cheerfully, Hart scooped the dice and sticks back into the wooden casket. "Three princes, we, with glory yet to come in addition to fine titles. But I think, right now, I could do with less glory and more wealth." He eyed the silver royal. "Are you certain you want the girl to have it, after what she said?"

"I want the girl to have it," Brennan agreed. "And if you so much as *try* to take it when I am not looking, I will cut a finger off."

"If you are not looking, how will you know?"

"Because I would tell him." Corin shrugged as Hart scowled darkly at him. "What would you expect?"

"A little support, *rujho*."

"Brennan is your twin, not I. Look to *him* for support." Corin downed more *usca*.

Hart's scowl deepened. "Why do you resent it, Corin? You have a twin in Keely."

"Who says I resent it?" Corin retorted. And then, grimly, "Keely is a girl. We are close, aye, as close as you and Brennan—but she is still a girl. It makes a difference, *rujho*."

"Keely is a *woman*," Brennan corrected absently.

Hart laughed. "Aye, she is. Or would you name yourself a boy, Corin, even now at twenty?"

"*She* does not see herself as a woman," Corin stated flatly.

"No." Hart's brows climbed beneath raven hair. "No, she sees herself as a warrior." His smile was amused. "The only trouble with *that* is, the gods saw fit to give her a woman's body."

Corin frowned. "She has no desire to be a *man*. She just prefers to be something other than a fragile thing like Maeve."

"Keely *is* nothing like Maeve," Brennan agreed.

Hart snorted indelicately. "No. And I will lay a wager on it that Sean of Erinn, when he claims our warrior-sister, will have a difficult time taming her."

"Keely will never be *tamed*," Corin said plainly, "and you will lay a wager on anything." He scowled blackly at Hart. "As to *that,* I would trust my life to Keely sooner than most men."

"Aye, aye, so would I." Hart set the casket down in front of Brennan. "Care for a game, *rujho*?"

Brennan's eyes narrowed. "I thought you had no coin."

"I have what Corin owes me." Hart looked at his astonished younger brother. "I won twenty-five crowns off you last week."

"When?"

When we wagered on how soon Brennan would be thrown from his new stallion." Hart grinned at his older brother. "The third jump, remember? I won the bet."

Brennan glared back. "You bet *against* me?"

"No. I bet *on* the horse."

Brennan slapped his hand down as Corin reached toward his belt-purse. "Do not put a penny on this table. You know better than to encourage him."

"But he *won*," Corin protested.

Brennan leaned toward him across the table. *"Not a penny,* Corin."

Hart patted the casket. "A suggestion, *rujho*—let the game decide. I win: Corin gives me the money. *You* win: Corin gives *you* the money." He grinned, blue eyes bright. "Surely a fair way to decide."

Brennan sighed and leaned his face into one hand. "One day," he muttered, mostly against his palm, *"one* day, Hart, you will regret ever learning how to play these games."

Hart rattled the casket. "Care to wager on that?"

"Care to wager on *that?*" Corin looked past them both to a table just beyond their own.

Accordingly, Hart and Brennan turned to see what had caught Corin's attention. It was Rhiannon, Rhiannon and a young aristocrat who obviously wanted more from her than wine.

As he grabbed her, pulling her onto his lap, Rhiannon cried out and tried to lurch away. The wine jug she carried slammed against the edge of the table and shattered, spilling gouts of blood-red liquor across the table and onto the young nobleman's fine clothes.

He shoved her away, swearing as he leaped to his feet. Rhiannon stumbled against the table and thrust out both hands to keep herself from falling. As she clutched at the wine-soaked wood, a shard of broken crockery cut her hand.

Even as Rhiannon, trembling, backed away from the furious lord, he followed her. He seemed not to notice that the hand she clutched against her breasts left blood smears on her apron, nor that she was plainly mortified by what had happened and terrified of him. He spoke to her angrily in a foreign tongue, then slapped her across the face so hard he sent her staggering into another table.

But his move had been anticipated.

Brennan caught her, steadied her, held her.

Rhiannon sucked in a frightened breath as she saw who had rescued her. And then she saw how she had smeared blood on his black velvet doublet. "Oh, my lord—I'm *sorry*—"

"You should not be. Not *you.*" Gently he set her aside and rose to tower over her. She had not thought he was so tall, but then she was quite petite. "It is *his* place to apologize."

Rhiannon shot a startled glance at the foreign lord. No, she thought, it was *her* place to say the words. "My lord—"

"No." The shapechanger shook his head and stirred black hair against his shoulders, against the nap of his matching doublet. His hands fell away from her waist and Rhiannon saw the black leather belt at his, weighted with plates of hammered gold. On his left hip a knife was sheathed. The gold hilt was smooth, shining and lovely; its shape was of a mountain cat. But even as she opened her mouth to protest yet again, he looked at the foreign lord. "Apologize to her."

The young man's hair was curly and dark, oiled with a scented pomade that turned it glossy black. His nose was slightly prominent, with a crooked set that made his brown eyes appear set too far apart. His fine silk-and-velvet clothes, once pale cream and jonquil, were now variegated a sickly purple-red.

Rhiannon nearly giggled.

The bent nose made it difficult for the foreigned to look down it in a straight line, but his attitude was made plain nonetheless. In accented Homanan, he said, "I apologize to no tavern-drab."

"Apologize," Brennan repeated. "You frightened her, struck her, hurt her. It is the least you should do."

"By Obram, I will not!" the other cried. "Do you think *I* am required to do such a thing? I am the nephew of the King of Caledon!"

"Prince Einar's cousin?" Brennan nodded as the other stared. "It means you are Reynald, then; I thought you looked familiar." His smile was neither friendly nor amused. "My lord, I suggest that while you remain in Homana, you subject yourself to Homanan custom. Apologize to the girl."

Reynald plainly was unintimidated. "I will not," he stated flatly in his accented Homanan, and made a gesture that brought the others at his table filing out to flank him. Knives and swords glittered with gems, but the weapons were clearly lethal even in their ceremonial flamboyance.

As one, Hart and Corin rose.

Reynald smiled. "You are three. We are eleven."

"He *counts*," Hart observed.

"He smells," Corin added. "What is that oil on his hair?"

At that, the tavern-keeper came out from behind a cask of wine. "Please," he said, "this is not necessary. I will recompense you for your clothing, my lord."

Reynald stared down his crooked nose. "And for the insults from this man?"

The tavern-keeper looked at Brennan helplessly. "My lord, please—"

"Please *what?*" Brennan asked irritably. "It was his fault; you saw it. He deserves no recompense."

"He deserves to be booted out of here and back to where he came from," Corin announced flatly. "Are you forgetting, my foreign lordling, that you are in *our* land?"

"Precisely," Reynald agreed coldly. "Is this the way you treat your guests? Is this the way you treat a man who is to play host to the Mujhar himself this very night? Is this the way you treat a member of the Caledonese royal family?"

Hart smiled. "Does Einar know you are here?"

"My tavern," the tavern-keeper moaned.

Brennan placed a hand on Rhiannon and thrust her gently toward the man. "Bind her wound, if you please. This should not take long."

Reynald snapped something in Caledonese to his nearest guardsman. The man drew a knife and lunged.

Brennan avoided the Caledonese smoothly enough and let the man's momentum carry him through his initial lunge. On the way by, Brennan planted clasped hands in the back of the guardsman's neck and smashed him to the floor. The man went down and did not move.

Brennan's brothers looked down on the body at their feet. Hart nodded sagely; Corin merely grinned.

A blood-red ruby set in gold glowed on Brennan's finger. He smiled at Reynald and hooked thumbs in the plated belt that clasped lean hips clad in raven velvet. He was considerably taller than Reynald. Behind him, Hart matched him in height and weight; Corin was shorter and slighter, but looked tenacious as a terrier.

"*Now* will you apologize?" Brennan calmly asked.

For answer, Reynald cried out angrily, snatched up a cup and hurled the contents in Brennan's face. As Brennan swore and wiped his eyes, the nine remaining Caledonese guardsmen spread out to encircle the three Homanan princes. Brennan abruptly found himself pressed back against his own table. As his eyes cleared, he found a knife blade at his throat and felt the prick of a sword tip in his spine.

"Still unconvinced?" he said in passing to Reynald, and lifted a wrist against the knife as he spun to dislodge the sword.

Corin, closest to the door, ducked yet another knife as it slashed toward his face, and quickly drew his own. Blades clashed, caught, were twisted; Corin's hilt remained in his hand while the other man's did not. The Caledonese stared in consternation at his empty hand.

Pleased, if a trifle surprised—it was his first encounter in anything other than practice—Corin grinned happily and turned to seek out another foe.

Hart, caught between Brennan and Corin, almost immediately found himself cut off from either of them, hemmed in on three sides by Caledonese. His indecision was quickly banished; Hart leaped up onto the table, cracking rune-sticks and scattering all the dice of his forgotten fortune-game. A swordblade darted toward his right leg, but he avoided it easily, skipping over yet another. Four of the enemy approached; Hart quickly acknowledged the folly in remaining on the table providing an easy target and sought a quick escape route. A glance upward showed him the only means.

Hart leaped for a low, thick limb of the massive rooftree. He caught it, swung his body out and over his attackers easily, and dropped on them like a mountain cat on its prey.

Tables overturned as the fighting spread to encompass the entire common room. Jugs and cups shattered, spilling rivers of wine across tables, benches, the hard-packed earthen floor with its carefully stamped insignia of the rampant Homanan lion.

Brennan, having dispatched the Caledonese whose sword

threatened his spine, abruptly somersaulted backward over a table to avoid another swipe and landed on his feet, knife in hand. He had not meant to draw it, preferring to avoid edged weapons in the midst of such a stupid, silly brawl, but it seemed he had no choice. And so, shrugging a little, he threw the knife in a glittering arc at an enemy, and saw the guardsman fall at Reynald's feet. He was not dead, Brennan knew, because the knife—though hilt-deep—was in a shoulder, not his heart. Accurate as always; he nodded in satisfaction.

The satisfaction did not last long. A second guardsman leaped for him, knife in hand. Brennan caught handfuls of the yellow Caledonese livery, ripping the tunic as he tried to thrust the guardsman against a table. But he lost his grip as the silk tore, slipped in spilled wine, and fell heavily to one knee.

The Caledonese knife blade sliced easily through velvet sleeve to flesh beneath, cut deeply, then caught on the heavy *lir*-band above Brennan's left elbow.

The guardsman tore the knife free to strike again, scraping steel against gold. The velvet, shredding, gave way; the rune-worked gold was suddenly clear for all to see, with its flowing mountain cat clawing its way free of metal.

Blood flowed freely to fill the incised runes. Brennan swore in the Old Tongue, forgoing his Homanan, and made himself ignore the pain. As the man thrust again, looking for flesh instead of gold, Brennan pushed himself up from the floor and slammed a shoulder into his chest.

"Brennan!" Hart called. "The knife—"

"—did little damage!" Brennan shouted back. "Look to yourself, *rujho*!"

Hart did, neatly avoiding a sword swung perilously close to his right hand. He immediately jammed the threatened hand against his ribs and kicked out with a booted foot. He stripped the sword from the enemy's grip.

Corin, outnumbered rather more quickly than he had imagined, dragged himself out from under a senseless Caledonese and slashed weakly at the closest yellow-clad leg he could find. The blade bit into the leather boot sluggishly, doing little damage, but it caught the attention of the wearer. Swearing in indecipherable Caledonese, the guardsman stomped down on Corin's bared wrist and knocked the knife from his hand.

Pain shot the length of Corin's arm. "*Ku'reshtin!*" he cried, outraged, "let me *up*—"

Just as outraged by Corin's attempt to stab through leather to his leg, the guardsman merely put more weight on the trapped limb.

Corin let out a string of Cheysuli obscenities, then— too proud to lose but not too proud to ask for help—he shouted for his brothers.

When neither answered, he realized abruptly they had their own battles to fight and *he* was solely responsible for his. It was not a pleasing thought; he had grown accustomed to shouting for one or the other of his brothers, if not both, whenever necessary. Now, unhappily, Corin came to the disturbing realization that occasionally there was no one to rely on save himself.

"By all the gods of Homana," he muttered to the floor so close to his face, "why did we leave the *lir* in Homana-Mujhar?"

The guardsman glared down at him. "What are you saying, Homanan? Begging my mercy already?"

Corin, sprawled belly-down with the trapped wrist stretched out in front of him, twisted his head to look up. "Mercy?" Astonished, he gaped at the Caledonese. "*I* will give you *mercy*—" Abruptly, putting the aching wrist out of his head entirely, Corin lurched up and locked his left arm around the heavy leather boot. Before the guardsman could retreat, Corin had ripped open his knee with a savage bite.

The Caledonese let out a howl of shock and pain and stumbled back, freeing the wrist, and nearly ripped Corin's teeth from his mouth. Corin, kneeling as he flexed his swelling wrist, was privately amazed at his success.

Then a hand came down, caught his russet velvet doublet and jerked him to his feet. "You cannot win battles on the *floor*," Hart said mildly.

"I won *that* one." Corin grinned at the cursing Cale-donese. And then he stopped grinning, because the man with the bitten knee lunged past Corin and upended Hart entirely. "*Ku'reshtin!*" Corin cried, and flung himself on the enemy.

Hart, squashed beneath both of them, tried ineffec-tively to wriggle free. At last he resorted to swearing at the enemy *and* his brother. "Corin—get—*off*—"

"I am *trying* . . ." Corin scrambled backward awk-wardly, planting a knee against Hart's left thigh, and dragged the Caledonese with him. Hart, wheezing, sat up slowly and clasped tender ribs.

The tavern door, so very close to Hart, slammed open. He winced instinctively, hunched his shoulders and hugged his ribs even harder. Boots thudded against the hard-packed floor and swords rattled out of sheaths. Hart, catching a glimpse of crimson silk and leather-and-mail, felt the beating of his heart abruptly stop.

He squinted up at the men hesitantly, then closed his eyes. Aye. It *was* the Royal Mujharan Guard. Part of it, anyway.

"*Jehan* will have our heads for this," he commented in cheerful resignation, and smiled innocently at the nearest of his father's men-at-arms.

Brennan, consumed with gaining a victory over a Caledonese who simply *would not* go down, felt the lance shaft across his throat. Gently it pressed, so gently, warn-ing him subtly, but firmly enough to threaten the fragility of his windpipe.

Slowly, Brennan let his hands drop back to his sides. In pleased surprise he watched his opponent stagger, straighten, collapse onto the floor. The Prince of Homana nodded, smiled, turned slowly within the cage of the lance to face his new opponent.

Abruptly he froze. Leaping out of the crimson tunic over the leather-and-mail was a black Homanan lion, rampant: his father's royal crest. It matched perfectly the black-etched lion in Brennan's ruby signet ring.

The Homanan guardsman recognized his prisoner at the same time. The lance fell away. "My lord!"

Corin, as yet unaware of the new arrivals, scrambled out from beneath two now-prone Caledonese guardsmen. His face was smeared with blood, but his eyes were suspiciously bright. He grinned, delighted. And then, as he stood up, the grin slipped away.

Brennan faced a guardsman in the Mujhar's black-and-scarlet livery. Hart, looking none too pleased with affairs, leaned against a table and clasped his ribs. His handsome face was bruised, and one eye—the right—was plainly swelling and would soon turn black.

Corin looked at his brothers. He looked at the sudden stillness in the tavern. He looked at the four Mujharan guardsmen flanking him. And then he sighed and sat down on a wine-stained bench to cradle his injured wrist.

Three

Reynald of Caledon strode stiffly through the center of the common room, stepping over the downed bodies of his royal escort and kicking aside fragments of broken crockery. His foreign face was set in an expression of distaste, irritation and arrogance; his dismay at the results of the fight was evident even as he tried to hide it.

He drew himself up before the Mujharan guardsman who had set the lance shaft at Brennan's throat. Pointedly, he ignored Brennan altogether. "Your name?" he demanded.

"Dion," the guardsman answered. "Captain of this contingent of the Royal Mujharan Guard."

Reynald's dark brown eyes narrowed. "The Mujhar's men?"

"Part of his personal guard," Dion answered. "Attached to the palace itself."

The foreign prince nodded. "I am Reynald, cousin to Prince Einar of Caledon," he said flatly. "I wish to press charges against these three Homanans—I want you to see to it they are put in chains and locked away until justice can be levied. I intend to ask the Mujhar himself to hear my testimony."

"My lord, it is your privilege to do so," Dion said quietly. "But may I suggest you reconsider—"

"No, you may not, and I *will* not," Reynald answered. "I came here with my escort to enjoy an evening's entertainment in what I was told was a fine establishment." He cast a withering glance around The Rampant Lion.

"These men intruded, provoking a fight, and I demand reparation for this affront to my honor, and that of my cousin, Prince Einar."

"Oh, is Einar here?" Brennan asked lightly. "I did not see him."

Reynald glared. "Because he is not present means nothing. You have injured my honor, and—as I am a member of the Caledonese party here to celebrate the Mujhar's reign—what insults me also insults my lord prince."

"Your pardon, my lord." It was Hart's turn. "But I fail to see how *you* were injured in any way. You let your escort do your fighting for you."

"Aye," Corin interposed before Reynald could answer. "You and Brennan *could* have settled it between you, but you provoked a fight. *You* gave the order to attack." He paused. "I think. It was in Caledonese, but it *did* serve to make your escort attack, whatever it was you said."

Color blazed in Reynald's saturnine face. "I was required to protect myself. This man meant to provoke *me*." His outflung hand indicated Brennan.

"My lord?" Dion looked at Brennan.

Brennan opened his mouth, but Reynald spoke before he could. " 'My lord,' " he mimicked, glaring at Dion. "You give him more honor than you give me."

"Aye," Dion answered smoothly; it was easy to see his opinion of the Caledonese lordling, regardless of his neutral expression and tone. "I mean you no disrespect, my lord, but this man will one day be my king."

Reynald shut his mouth with a snap. He looked sharply from Dion to Brennan. "King," he echoed. There was, suddenly, the faintest trace of doubt in his tone.

"One day," Brennan agreed. "Not for a long time yet; my father the Mujhar is, thank the gods, a spectacularly healthy man." The faintest of twitches jerked the corner of his mouth; he was purposely underplaying his hand, which served to make it all the more devastatingly effective.

Reynald looked first at Hart, then at Corin. And all of a sudden the color drained out of his face. "Obram save me," he whispered, "you are all the Mujhar's sons. I remember, now—"

"You remember, *now*." Hart grinned. "A bit slow, are you, Reynald? We met only yesterday, did we not? In the Great Hall before the Lion Throne?"

"Where you wished our father *the Mujhar* best wishes for continued health." Corin pointedly emphasized their link to royalty. Reynald was the sort of man to understand such arrogance, having his own fair share of it.

"Chains, I think he said," Brennan told Dion. "Did you bring any with you?"

"No, my lord. Should I fetch some?" Clearly, the captain was enjoying Reynald's discomfiture.

Hart felt his ribs. "Enough," he said. "I think Reynald sees our point. And I think it is time we returned to Homana-Mujhar, before our *jehan* sends men out looking for us." He stopped short and looked at Dion. "Who *did* send you?"

"*I* did." Rhiannon stepped forward. The linen apron still bore bloodstains, now darkening, and her hand was wrapped in a clean cloth. "It was my fault this nonsense began. I thought I should be the one to stop it, so I ran to the palace and fetched them." She looked at Brennan. Her eyes lingered a moment on the earring in his left ear, now exposed by hair pushed away from his face. "I—I was ungrateful before," she said in a low voice. "You did this for me." She wiggled fingers showing at the edges of the cloth wrapping. "I didn't want you to get hurt—*any* of you." Her eyes touched briefly on Hart and Corin, but moved back to Brennan almost immediately.

Hart laughed. Corin's mouth twisted wryly.

Brennan smiled slowly. "Then you have *my* thanks," he said, and looked at Reynald. "I think we have arrived at an impasse, my Caledonese lordling. You may, of course, press charges—we *did* extinguish most of your royal escort, three to ten—" he grinned, "—but perhaps we may simply let bygones be bygones, and meet over the banquet you and your cousin Prince Einar are supposed to host in my father's honor tonight." Brennan paused. "And if we do not go *now,* we shall be quite late."

Reynald looked at the remains of his royal escort. Several of the men were clearly unconscious. Others were merely stunned, beginning only now to pull their wits back together. Two were on their feet, unwounded; they scowled sullenly at their fallen comrades.

Their lord, in his wine-stained silks and velvets, summoned what dignity he could muster. "Come," he ordered the two men still on their feet, and immediately departed the tavern.

Corin watched him go, then turned back to Hart. "What about the others?"

Hart grinned his lopsided, charming grin. "He is nephew to the King of Caledon, *rujho,* and cousin to Prince Einar. It is not for *him* to concern himself with men wounded in his defense."

"Ah." Corin, duly enlightened, nodded.

Brennan sighed and untied his belt-purse. He handed it over to the tavern-keeper. "For the damages." And then he worked a ring from one of his fingers. It was not the ruby signet of his rank, but a smaller sapphire set in silver. When it was free of his finger, he put it into Rhiannon's hands. "To replace the 'silver penny.' " He smiled warmly. "You see," he said, "Cheysuli are not so bad."

She stared after him as he preceded his brothers out of The Rampant Lion. And then she kissed the ring.

The Mujhar, stepping into one of the soft gray-dyed kneeboots, looked up sharply as Taggart finished speaking. "They did *what?*"

Taggart's face was very stiff. He repeated his final statement. "They destroyed most of Reynald's escort, my lord."

" 'Destroyed.' " Niall straightened as a body-servant knelt to adjust the droop of soft leather. "Is anyone *dead?*"

"Not so far as we can tell, my lord. It appears several

of the Caledonese are wounded, but none seriously."
Taggart folded his hands behind his back and waited.

Niall stood stock still in the center of the antechamber
that held most of the clothing suitable for a Mujhar. He
preferred the soft leather jerkin and leggings of the
Cheysuli, but all too often he was forced to wear Homanan
apparel. Tonight was such a night.

"My lord . . ." The body-servant held up the other
boot.

Niall glanced down, frowning in distraction. "Ah. Aye."
He accepted the boot and pulled it on, then waited as it
was properly adjusted. "All three of them?" he asked.

Taggart nodded.

"Even Brennan," Niall murmured. "Oh, curse them
for fools, all of them. I do not *need* this tonight—*most of
all* tonight." He waved the body-servant away and paced
across the room to the doorway opening into his bedchamber. Serri was, yet again, asleep on the bed.

"My lord, Dion reported that it did not appear to be
entirely the fault of the princes. And if my lord Reynald
truly *did* provoke them, there must have been good
reason."

"Reason, perhaps, but not *good* reason," Niall said
grimly. He shook his head, still bare of its heavy circlet,
and swung back. "I cannot believe *Brennan* took part in
this idiocy. It is not like him. Hart and Corin, aye—they
would hardly balk at a fight, regardless of provocation—
but Brennan?"

Deirdre swept into the room from another entrance.
"My lord Mujhar, your favoritism is showing."

"Is it?" Niall absently admired the rich blue gown that
fit her slender body so snugly. Her brass-bright hair was
twisted up on her head in a knot secured with thick pins
of silver wire, and she wore yet another of his gifts, a
silver chain crusted with diamonds and dark blue sapphires. It glittered against her throat. "Aye, well . . .
even *you* must admit it is unlike Brennan."

"What have they done, your sons?" Deirdre smoothed
the fit of his black doublet, quilted with jet and seed
pearls.

"They have torn up a tavern—one of the *better* ones, I might add—and accounted for multiple casualties," Niall answered. "In short, they may have permanently destroyed any hope for a renewal of the trade alliance between Homana and Caledon."

"Have they, then?" She patted the silver chain of office that stretched from shoulder to shoulder, each wide link cleverly fashioned into a rampant lion. A remarkable distance from shoulder to shoulder; privately, Deirdre smiled.

"You do not seem to understand." Niall moved away from her to face Taggart again. "Where are they now?"

"In your private solar, my lord." Taggart paused. "I think they knew you would wish to say something to them. They went there on Prince Brennan's suggestion."

"Wise Brennan," Niall remarked darkly. "Aye, I wish to say something to them. Go and fetch them, Taggart. Fetch them *now*."

Taggart was clearly surprised. "*Here*, my lord?"

"Here."

"Aye, my lord." A bow, and he was gone.

"Niall," Deirdre said uneasily, "what it is you are meaning to say to them?"

"Whatever comes out of my mouth at the moment." He took her arm and escorted her into yet a third chamber, a private withdrawing room.

"You will be giving them a *chance*, then." But she did not sound at all convinced.

Niall indicated she was to sit down in one of the X-legged chairs. "Promise me, *meijha*, you will leave the punishment to me."

"In other words, you are wanting me to be silent." She scowled at him as she sat down, but it lacked the determination to have much of the desired affect. " 'Tis for you to do, then," she agreed. "They are your sons, not mine." And she folded her hands primly in her lap.

"Oh, gods," Brennan said when Taggart had told them where they must go. "He *is* angry."

"And are you a woman or a warrior?" Corin demanded crossly. "We are too big to *spank,* Brennan; why do you dread facing him so much?"

"Probably because only rarely have I had to be reprimanded. It is *you* who have spent so much of your time in his bad graces." Brennan turned on his heel and marched out of the solar.

"So has Hart," Corin said defensively, following. Still he cradled the sore wrist, wondering if it were cracked or merely badly bruised. "I am not the only one who has been sent before our *jehan*."

"Is that a point of pride?" Brennan asked acidly.

"Your arm hurts," Hart announced, bringing up the rear. "You are irritable, *rujho*."

"If I am irritable, it is because I am plagued with a young *rujholli* who lacks the wit to know when to humble himself," Brennan declared. "He will only make it worse, if he gives our *jehan* defiance instead of contrition."

Corin swore in disgust. "It was *Reynald's* fault, not mine. And I was the last to join the fight. *You,* Brennan, were first."

"Aye," Hart agreed. "And that is precisely why I think he will *not* be so angry. He is accustomed to our scrapes, Corin. But with Brennan involved in this one, I think he will believe it had merit."

Brennan sighed. "That is something, I suppose." And he swung into the open doorway to the Mujhar's royal apartments.

Niall watched them file in. Brennan first, of course; as always. The eldest was plainly out of sorts in clothing as well as temper, though he tried to hide both by forcing his face into a calm, neutral expression and attempting to straighten the fit of his velvet doublet. Niall saw wine stains, blood stains, gaping rents. Through the remains of the left sleeve, *lir*-gold gleamed faintly.

Hart, now second in line, looked much worse. His dark blue doublet was as stained and torn, but his face was badly bruised and already showed the beginnings of a black eye. There was no blood or wound visible, but he walked with the odd, stiffly upright posture of a man afraid to move anything above his waist. Ribs, then.

As for Corin, the youngest trailed the other two as if to defy his father, jaw jutting out to advertise his unwillingness to accept responsibility for his actions. It was a familiar posture to Niall, who murmured inwardly that one day, if it pleased the gods, Corin *might* grow up—and was relieved to see the son who looked so much like him showed no signs of serious physical discomfort. Even if he did favor his right wrist, which looked suspiciously swollen.

Brennan glanced briefly at Deirdre, so silent in her chair, and halted before his father. Niall stood before one of the casements, hands folded behind his back. He waited as Hart halted, and then Corin, who promptly sat down on the nearest stool.

Hart leaned a little in Corin's direction and hissed, "Stand up."

Corin stubbornly remained seated. He stared at his father with an unrepentant, unwavering gaze.

Inwardly, Niall sighed. "One at a time," he said aloud. "Who shall be first?"

Brennan opened his mouth to answer, as always, first, but Corin got there before him. "It was a girl," he said flatly, indelicately, and made both his brothers scowl their disapproval. He colored. "It *was*."

"A *girl*." Somehow, Niall had not quite expected that. Generally it was something more, or something else.

Hart wet his lips. "A wine-girl," he said. Then, as if hearing how ludicrous it sounded, he added, "But not a common sort of wine-girl, or a common sort of tavern."

"Far be it for my sons to frequent a *common* tavern with merely *common* wine-girls." The Mujhar's tone was deceptively mild.

Brennan was not deceived. His eyes narrowed as he tried to judge his father's mood; Niall was pleased to see none of them could do it. He smiled and outwaited them.

"There was also a Caledonese *ku'reshtin*," Corin added. "Anyone will tell you."

"Will *you*?" Niall asked.

"I just have."

"Corin—" Hart began, in warning.

Niall waved it away with a raised finger that silenced his middle son immediately. "Say on."

"He hit the girl," Corin told him seriously. "He nearly knocked her down, and she did not deserve it. She had already cut her hand on the broken winejug."

Hart nodded. "He refused to apologize."

Niall's left brow lifted; the right one, divided by the talon scar, was mostly hidden beneath the diagonal slash of leather strap that held the patch in place. "A wine-girl asked apology of a Caledonese prince?"

"No," Corin said lightly. "That took Brennan, of course."

"Ah." Niall's single eye flicked to his eldest son. "Then it was *you* who began it?"

Brennan did not flinch from the tone in his father's voice, which managed to express surprise, disappointment, disapproval, all at once. "Aye," he answered clearly.

"You."

"I," Brennan agreed. "*Jehan*—he was unnecessarily rude. He hurt her."

"So you stepped in and defended her honor, if such still exists."

Deirdre opened her mouth as if to protest, shut it, waited for the interview to be finished.

Brennan frowned at his father. "Are you saying that because she is a wine-girl, she is undeserving of aid when someone mistreats her?"

"No," Niall answered. "I am saying that I hope she was worth the loss of a trade alliance between Homana and Caledon."

Brennan grasped the implications more quickly than the others. *"Oh."*

"Aye. *Oh.*"

"Do you mean it?" Hart asked. "Prince Einar will refuse to negotiate because of this?"

"Possibly."

"But you do not *know* that," Corin observed shrewdly. "Do you, *jehan?*"

"There is a possibility the negotiations will be postponed, even canceled. There are certainly precedents for

such things, when princes meddle in politics even though
they are more suited to drinking wine in *un*common
taverns."

"*Usca*," Corin corrected quietly. Hart looked at him as
if he had lost his wits.

Niall nodded a little. "Perhaps you were correct to
defend the wine-girl's honor; I will not protest that. It is
good manners, if nothing else. But I *will* protest the
disregard you had for the delicacy of relationships between realms. I will also protest your inability to recall
that diplomacy is necessary in nearly every situation,
certainly this one. And I will most decidedly protest your
inability to remember that Cheysuli warriors *do not brawl
in taverns.*" He paused, marking their shocked faces.
"*Princes* do not brawl in taverns. *My sons* do not brawl
in taverns." Again he paused, and heard the echo of his
voice ringing in the chamber. "Do I make myself clear?"

Corin stared at him defiantly. "We have done it before."

Hart moved closer to Brennan, taking a definitive step
away from his younger brother.

Slowly Naill moved from the casement. He walked to
his youngest son and paused before the stool. And
abruptly, before Corin could speak or make any sort of
protest, Naill reached down and grasped the injured wrist,
snapping Corin to his feet.

"*Jehan*—" But Corin, though clearly in pain, broke off
his protest when he saw the expression on his father's
face.

"You have spent twenty years in Homana-Mujhar,
sharing in the bounty of your birth," Niall said in a tone
that, for all its gentleness, implied more displeasure than
shouting might have. "Your *jehana* was Princess of Atvia
in her own right, bred of Cheysuli warriors and Homanan
kings. I care little enough what you may think of me, or
what I do—but you *will* respect the blood that flows in
your veins." Niall drew in a breath that did nothing to
dispel the rising anger in his tone. "That blood you have
spilled all too often in petty tavern brawls. It must stop,
Corin. It *must.* Rid yourself of this resentment and hostility and conduct yourself as a prince and Cheysuli war-

rior should." He paused, looking for something in Corin's blue eyes. "It is not worthy of you," he said, more quietly.

Corin set his teeth. "And *I* am not worthy of *you*."

Niall released the injured wrist instantly. His jaw slackened momentarily and something odd glinted in his good eye; something that spoke of shock, of memories and unexpected pain, in addition to the sudden flaring of an intense, abiding regret.

Deirdre wanted to go to him at once, but refrained. It would undermine his authority completely if she showed his sons how much Corin's words had hurt him; now, at this moment, Niall needed all the strength and resolution he could find, if he were to command their respect and obedience.

The Mujhar turned away a moment, then swung back to face them all. He looked at Hart and Brennan, ignoring Corin as if he had nothing more to say to him. Or as if he could not bear to look at him and see the son who so closely resembled the young Niall in coloring as well as insecurity.

"What I have said to Corin applies equally to you," he told his twin-born sons. "I have raised none of you to behave as common soldiers on leave, fighting over petty slights and imagined insults, nor as crofters spending their few coins on liquor and wine-girls . . . *nor* on foolish wagers." His eye flicked to Hart, then returned to Brennan. "I expected such behavior out of *you* least of all."

Brennan stood very straight, but his shoulders lost their set.

Quickly Hart spoke up. "Blame him no more than me, *jehan*."

"No," Niall agreed. "But *less* than you, aye. It was your idea to go there, was it not?"

Hart opened his mouth, then shut it. After a moment, he nodded. "We meant only to drink a little, *jehan*. Not to fight. You know I would rather throw the dice and rune-sticks than fight."

"Reynald deserved it, *jehan*," Corin said flatly. "And

if the rest of the Caledonese royal house is like *him,* you do not wish to make an alliance with them anyway."

"Do I not?" Niall looked calmly at his youngest son. "I see—I am to base the future of Homanan economy solely on the personalities of Caledon's rulers. At least, so *you* say."

"*Jehan*—"

"Corin, I think you have very much to learn about dealing with other kingdoms," the Mujhar said gently. "And I suggest you begin now, because in two or three years you will be going to Atvia to take your rightful place as heir to Alaric's throne."

"Atvia," Corin said in disgust. "And if I would prefer to remain here?"

"Well, there is a choice," Niall said. "You may remain here as a dispossessed, disinherited son, or accept your *tahlmorra* and go to Atvia."

Corin's eyes narrowed. "I might also stay here with the clans, *jehan.* You cannot dispossess me of my heritage, nor disinherit me from my *lir.*"

"I would not need to dispossess you of your Cheysuli heritage," Niall told him quietly. "A warrior turning his back on his *tahlmorra* is solely to blame for his disinheritance, which also includes loss of the afterworld." He paused a moment. "Corin, this serves nothing and is not necessary. What *is* necessary, however, is for all of you to acknowledge that you have been immature and irresponsible, and to accept your punishment."

"That depends on what it is," Corin muttered beneath his breath, as Hart glared at him openly.

"It is that I forbid you to attend the banquet this evening."

"That is *all?*" Hart blurted, and winced as Brennan kicked him covertly.

"In not attending the banquet, you will keep yourselves to your respective chambers," Niall explained, "and you will remain in them until I give you leave to go out of them. No banquets, no taverns, no Clankeep." He fixed his eye on each of his sons individually. "No horses," he said to Brennan. "No wagering," he ordered Hart.

And lastly, to Corin, "No visits from any of Deirdre's ladies."

"For how *long?*" Brennan demanded indignantly, forgoing all the diplomacy he had so carefully cultivated. "If I leave Bane for even a day, all my progress will be undone and I will have to begin again."

Hart frowned. "And how am I expected to pass the time, *jehan*, while I wait for your leave to go?"

But Corin laughed. "Enforced celibacy, *jehan*? Well, it will only leave the ladies all the more eager for me when I *can* share their company again."

Deirdre smiled serenely. " 'Tis hard for my ladies to be eager when their positions are in jeopardy."

Corin stared at her in astonishment. "*You* would do that?"

"To support the Mujhar, I will do anything," she said calmly. "Just as all of his children should, sons and daughters alike."

That enforced silence among them as nothing else had.

Niall nodded. "You may go," he said quietly. "Meals will be sent up from the kitchens."

In silence, his three still proud but decidedly chastened sons filed slowly out of the chamber.

Four

Corin shut the door to his chambers with a resounding thud, knowing it childish, but satisfied with the action nonetheless. And then he regretted it almost instantly, because he had employed his right wrist in the motion and the wrist was less than pleased.

He cursed, examined it briefly, decided it was very sore and bruised, but not broken. Still, it would keep him from arms-practice for a week or more, and that he did not appreciate.

Have I only myself to blame?

Why? came the familiar liquid tone of his *lir* within the pattern of their link. *What have you done now?*

He looked for Kiri and found her lumped in the center of his draperied bed. She was little more than a knot of red fur, with sharp jet nose tucked firmly beneath a black-tipped tail.

Corin sighed and sat down on the edge of the bed, staring disconsolately at his wrist as she worked the fingers. *I have involved myself in a tavern brawl, which is beneath me—or so I am told by my jehan—and have drawn Caledonese blood, which may result in damaged trade ties between Homana and Caledon.* He paused. *I have also been incredibly rude and disrespectful to my jehan.*

Have you?

"Aye," he said aloud, with conviction. "Kiri, why is it I always say things I regret? *Especially* to my *jehan*?"

Because your mouth works independently of your brain.

The vixen rose, shook her glossy red pelt into order, came over to sit beside her *lir*. Her expression was made quizzical by black mask and slanted amber eyes. *Lir, one day you will learn.*

"Will I?" He sighed and flopped backward, stretching out on the huge bed. "He threatens to send me to Atvia in two or three years, *lir* . . . and the gods know I have no wish to go."

Atvia is your place, the fox said. *You will be its king. Is that not a fine thing, and worth much pride?*

"A fine thing, aye," Corin said on a deeper sigh, "and undoubtedly worth much pride. The trouble is, I have little enough of that. I look at Hart and Brennan and see real warriors and princes, while I am left to feel inferior."

All nonsense. Kiri settled her chin on his muscular thigh, slanted eyes closing. *You have a lir . . . you have me—how could you possibly feel inferior?*

"A habit that often happens when a warrior receives his *lir* late," Corin retorted. "I was sixteen, Kiri, as you should well recall—both my *rujholli* were thirteen. I had three years in which to fear I would never receive one, while Brennan flaunted Sleeta and Hart learned to fly with Rael."

And the Mujhar had nineteen years. Kiri's tone plainly said Corin's complaint had no foundation.

A fist banged on the door. Corin knew the sound extremely well. "Keely," he called, "now is not the time to gloat."

There came a muffled shout from the other side. "I am not here to gloat—" His sister's voice broke off a moment, then renewed itself. "What have you done *now*, Corin, that would cause me to gloat?" Without waiting for his leave to enter, she pushed open the heavy wooden door and slipped through, shutting it decisively. She stopped dead; elbows jutted out as she locked hands on hips. "Oh, *rujho* . . . not another fight."

"No." Corin struggled up. "I am in this state of disrepair because Deirdre's ladies could not keep themselves from me." He looked down at his torn, soiled russet doublet. He smelled of wine, smoke and lantern oil.

"Did you win?" Keely asked.

"All three of us won."

"Three . . ." Her blue eyes, so like his own, narrowed. "Hart, of course . . . and Brennan? *Brennan?*"

"Brennan." Corin began to work at his right boot, desiring to strip it off. "He came with us to keep us from trouble, he *said*—and then promptly began the fight with Reynald."

"Reynald? Einar's brother?"

"Cousin." A twinge of pain shot through his injured wrist, and he swore. "The *ku'reshtin* tried to force himself on a wine-girl, and then when she refused his attentions he slapped her. She broke a jug and cut her hand."

"And Brennan came to her rescue." Keely's tone was dry; her expression indicated she, as much as Corin, was less than enamored of Brennan's status as eldest—and favorite—son. "How like him."

Corin swore again as he wrestled with the recalcitrant boot. "Keely—come and help me with this."

She swept across the room, shaking her head, and bent to catch the heel and toe of the brown boot in both hands. Only then did he realize she wore a rich copper-colored gown of silk and velvet instead of customary leathers; her tawny hair was braided Cheysuli fashion, pinned against her head and all achime with golden bells. A topaz and garnet torque clasped a slender, elegant neck.

Keely grunted, tugging on the boot, then caught his eye. Instantly color flared in her face. "Must *you* stare, too?" She was clearly annoyed as well as flustered. "Deirdre *insisted*—she said I could not attend the banquet in leggings and jerkin."

"Well, no," he agreed. "Keely—" He grinned, shrugged, laughed aloud. "So much for the independent *rujholla* I know so well."

"*Ku'reshtin*," she muttered, tugging on the boot again. "They will have *you* bathed and oiled and perfumed before you know it, and where will you be then?"

His mouth twisted in a grimace of disgust. "No," he said. "I am banished to my chamber."

The boot came off. Keely straightened stiffly, gaping at him as she clutched the leather in both hands. "What? You—banished? *Who* has banished you?"

"The only one who can," he answered wryly.

"He did *not*." The bells chimed as she shook her head in disbelief. "Why?"

"I am in disgrace."

"Because of the tavern brawl?"

"Aye. He was—less than pleased." Corin sighed. "He has every right to be, I think. We *did* bruise Reynald's pride a little." He smiled. "We bruised it a *lot*."

"Reynald deserves it," she said flatly, bending to remove his other boot. "Einar as well—do you know *I* have to be his partner at the banquet?" In disgust she jerked on the boot, which elicited a curse from Corin because it jarred his wrist. "Let him have *Maeve*, if he requires a princess to prop up his foreign pride."

"I think his pride will be propped up enough when he sees three empty chairs," Corin muttered. "He will know why, and doubtless he will gloat."

"Then I will see to it he cannot," Keely said firmly. A final twist freed his foot. She dropped the boot to the floor and sat down at his right side, leaving his other to Kiri. "Let me see your wrist."

He held out his arm. Keely carefully peeled the sleeve of the velvet doublet and the silken undersleeve back, baring the swollen wrist. Her fingers were gentle but matter-of-fact; like a warrior, she had little patience with injuries.

"Not broken," she said, after a moment, and pushed the arm away.

Corin scowled. "And will you be so solicitous with Sean, when you are wed?"

"Sean will take me as he finds me; he is not marrying a nursemaid," she said darkly. Then she made fists of her hands and banged the air with them. "Oh, *gods,* Corin, I have no wish to go to Erinn! I have no wish to be *cheysula* to some Erinnish island princeling!"

"Aye, well, our *jehan* pays little enough mind to what we do and do not want," her brother said grimly. "I said

I had no desire to go to Atvia, and *he* said it was my choice if I went, or remained here and became a dispossessed, disinherited son."

Keely's mouth twisted in disgust. "But if *Brennan* were to ask. . . ."

"He has no need to ask; Homana will be his. He goes nowhere." Corin sighed and rose to undo the fastenings of his ruined doublet. After a moment of struggling with his left hand, he appealed to Keely once again. As she clucked her tongue over his helplessness and undid the fastenings, Corin craned his head out of her way. "But at least Brennan was banished to his chambers, too."

Keely's fingers paused. "Brennan was?"

"All three of us."

"He *was* displeased, then."

"As he will be if I keep you here longer." Corin pushed her hands away. "I will call a body-servant—Keely, you must go. Give Einar a taste of your wit."

"With sweet Maeve on his other side?" Keely shook her head. "He will think me a waspish shrew."

Corin merely raised eloquent tawny eyebrows.

"*Ku'reshtin,*" she muttered, and took herself out of the room.

Hart soaked in a hot bath, drank half a decanter of wine, then suffered his ribs to be strapped by his body-servant. Once the man was done and dismissed, Hart went over to the polished silver plate hung on one of his bedchamber walls, and stared somberly at the bandages that made it so difficult to breathe. But the linen strapping did not draw his attention so much as the black eye. He fingered the bruising gingerly.

"You," he said somberly, "are a poor son. A poor son and a poorer prince. You know better."

Almost at once he felt restored. There. He had admitted his shortcomings; now he could get on with his life without excess guilt. He tried a smile at the battered face in the plate, found it did not hurt as much as he thought it might, and turned away.

You know better, but it does not stop you, chimed the

voice that served as his conscience. All Cheysuli had them. They were known as *lir*.

"No," Hart agreed lightly. "Why should it?"

The hawk shifted on his perch in the corner nearest the big tester bed. Rael was white save for the jet black edging on each individual feather, and his eyes, which were the color of palest ale.

It should if it is wrong, the hawk pointed out.

"Was I wrong?" Hart, still nude from his bath, plucked the clean leather leggings from his bed and very carefully pulled them on. He grunted, swore, cast aspersions upon the parentage of the Caledonese who had so squashed him. And then he recalled that Corin had had as much to do with it as the foreign guardsman, and promptly included his brother in his deprecations. "How could I be wrong, Rael; I was only defending myself."

It would be redundant to say you should not have been in the position to have *to defend yourself,* Rael commented, having said it regardless of redundancy; it was often necessary with Hart.

"Enough," Hart said succinctly. He rubbed his hands through heavy black hair still damp from washing. In the candlelight the *lir*-gold on his arms, now bared, gleamed. The light lingered on incised lines of intricate feathering; on the exultation of a hawk in flight, wings spread to curve around the wide, rune-bordered armband. In honor of the *lir* Hart now attempted to silence.

"Do you reprove your own *lir*?" asked Ian from the doorway. "A distinct admission of guilt, *harani* . . . you are slipping. And if you tell me you deserve this exile from the banquet, I shall *know* you have gone mad."

Hart grimaced. Before his uncle, all his new-found contentment fled. "No, no—I will save you from insanity, *su'fali*. What I did was necessary, and certainly not deserving of punishment."

"Ah, I am set at ease." Ian grinned. He was five years older than his brother, the Mujhar, but like most Cheysuli he did not show his age. His hair was still black, save for a single silver forelock that fell to hide his left eyebrow, and his flesh still taut over pronounced musculature, with only the faintest of creases fanning out from yellow eyes. In blue-dyed leggings, boots and jerkin, as well as *lir*-gold at left ear and on his bare arms, Ian was all Cheysuli physically, though he claimed a splash or two of Homanan blood.

"You have seen my *jehan*, then." Hart sighed. "He told you it was my idea to go to the tavern, I am sure."

"No." Ian shut the door and leaned against it, folding his arms. "He did not *need* to tell me—when I heard a tavern was involved, I knew it was your idea." He smiled in response to Hart's grimace. "Corin may be the impulsive one, rebelling against this or that, but he follows more than he leads. Brennan, of course, knows better than to leave Homana-Mujhar when his *jehan* has asked him expressly not to, unless given a very good reason for disobedience. And Keely was *here*; had it been her idea, she would have gone." He shrugged. "Whom does it leave, Hart? Maeve?"

Hart's response was a snort of derisive amusement. Then he sighed and scratched absently at his bandages. "I am so obvious, then."

"To me, aye," Ian agreed. "To others, no. You have the odd ability to hide yourself even as you stand before numerous people. I think it is something you enjoy."

"No, no, not always." Hart shook his head. "I do not hide myself from you, *su'fali*."

"Only because I have watched you do it, and know *how* you do it." Ian smiled. "Even Niall does not see it."

"Because he sees little of any of us."

"You discredit him, *harani*. He sees Brennan, because Brennan is his heir, and he must. He sees Corin because Corin is frequently contentious, often purposely. And Keely, of course, because Keely stubbornly refuses to acknowledge that others perceive her as a woman, when she would rather be perceived as a Cheysuli."

"And in Maeve he sees Deirdre." Hart sighed. "Favorite son, favorite daughter."

"I did not think it bothered you."

Hart looked at him in surprise. "It does not, *su'fali*. I

am content enough with my lot—*more* than content with it. I only meant he makes no secret of his prejudice."

"When you are a *jehan*—and a king—you will see why it is difficult for him to reconcile affection with authority," Ian told him. "It was so with your grandsire, and now your *jehan*."

"I do not see *you* reconciling such things with children, *su'fali*," Hart shot back. "Where is your *cheysula*? Where is your *meijha*? Are you so inspired by your *rujholli* that you neglect your own responsibilities?"

Ian, unoffended, merely smiled. "I am not dead yet, *harani*. There may well come a time I bestow a *lir*-torque on one particular woman. But until then—"

"—*until then*, you leave half the women in Clankeep yearning for you." Hart grinned. "Not to mention a few of Deirdre's ladies."

"That, I think, is Corin's province rather than mine."

"Not all of them, *su'fali*. I am not blind."

"No. Only distracted by the lure of the fortune-game, and other such profitless time-wasters." Ian shook his head. "Do you wonder why the Mujhar grows impatient with you? You act as though you have no concern for the blood in your veins. You are as much a part of the prophecy as the Mujhar, my young *harani*; as much as Brennan, Corin, and Keely. If you think to shrug it off with games, you will soon learn that a *tahlmorra* can make itself known at a very inopportune time."

"As with you?" Hart faced Ian squarely, all the levity banished from his bruised face. "As it did with you, when the Ihlini witch took your *lir* and your will and forced you to lie with her?"

At once he regretted the words. The story was one few people knew of, and fewer spoke about. No Cheysuli warrior—least of all the Mujhar's brother and loyal liege man—wished to admit he had been ensorcelled by an Ihlini. Knowing that the ensorcellment had involved sharing Lillith's *bed*—against his will, made powerless through temporary *lirless*ness—was a wound that did not heal. Even a yearly *i'toshaa-ni* ritual had failed to cleanse him of the humiliation.

And now his favorite nephew had thrown it in his face.

"*Su'fali*—" Hart took a step toward Ian, then stopped. "*Su'fali*—forgive me. I should not have spoken." In disgust, he scraped a splay-fingered hand through drying hair. "There are so *many* things I should not say or do."

"Aye," Ian agreed grimly. "And one day, perhaps, you will learn to say and do none of them."

Hart watched his uncle go. And then he roundly cursed himself, with elaborate eloquence.

The Prince of Homana stood by his great bed and looked down on the sleek black mountain cat sprawled across it with an elegance only her kind knew. The heavy rope of tail curved around one haunch. It did not twitch, nor did her tufted ears, but Brennan knew she was awake. He had sensed it within the link the moment he entered the room.

"I should have taken you with me," he said in weary disgust. "I should have taken you to keep me from trouble, even as I went with my *rujholli* to keep *them* from trouble." He sighed again. "As you see, the results were less than spectacular." He reconsidered. "No. They *were* spectacular. I should say, less than satisfactory."

The cat opened one golden eye. *It was not you, lir. It was your rujholli.*

"That changes nothing. *I* started the brawl."

With reason?

"Of *course* I had a reason." Brennan scowled at her. "I am not Hart, who does it out of ignorance while in the heat of greed. I am not Corin, who does it out of perversity. I am *me*, rememer? The eldest, the maturest, the most trustworthy of all the Mujhar's sons." He paused. And then he swore. "I should have let them go alone."

And if you had?

"Oh, there would have been a fight regardless, I think. Which is precisely why I *did* go with them." Brennan sat down on the bed. "Gods, Sleeta, I sometimes think I will go mad."

It is not your responsibility to be jehan to your rujholli, she pointed out. *They have one already.*

"Aye, aye, I know." Brennan picked at the ruined sleeve of his black velvet doublet. Beneath the blood-crusted fabric, his arm stung. He could not tell how deep the knife wound was. One-handed, he tried to undo the fastenings and found he could not. He went to the door and shouted for his body-servant.

The man came quickly enough, but so did Maeve. She dismissed him at once, even when Brennan protested, and declared she would tend her wounded brother herself. The body-servant accordingly brought hot water, clean cloths and salve, and Maeve set about stripping the doublet from Brennan.

He helped her as best he could, shouldering out of the velvet once she peeled it from the silken undertunic, and perched on the three-legged stool when she told him to. Deftly, she washed the wound with soft cloth and gentle fingers.

"You should remove this gold." Maeve tapped a fingernail against the *lir*-band.

"No."

"I think you will hardly give up your rank or warrior status if you do," she said absently, dabbing carefully at the crusted wound. " 'Tis only one, Brennan."

He smiled as he heard the faint Erinnish lilt in her voice. The oldest of them all at twenty-three, Maeve had spent all but two years in Homana, but the close relationship between mother and daughter had resulted in an occasional hint of Erinn in her speech.

"You will soil your gown," he told her, trying to pull the heavy yellow velvet away from leather breeches stained with blood and dirt and wine.

"I can change it. Wait—forgive me!—" as he hissed in pain, "—there. Only a little blood."

He craned his head to inspect the wound. The slice divided his flesh with neat precision, ending somewhere beneath the armband. He recalled the scrape of steel on gold.

Brennan flexed the muscle. It hurt, but seemed unimpaired. "Just tie it up, Maeve. I will be well enough."

"Patience, patience, my lord prince." She smiled and

slanted him a glance out of green eyes. "How can you go to a banquet with an arm left to bleed all over the guests?"

"Easily, as I am not invited." He worked at the heavy armband a moment; tugged it from its customary place above his elbow and slid it onto his forearm, where it dangled like a bracelet. The candlelight caught gold, flashed, washed the bronzed flesh with an ocher tinge. The flesh that was usually hidden under the band was lighter, though hardly fair; Brennan frowned and touched it, disliking the nakedness.

Maeve stopped sponging the wound. "Not invited!"

"Let us say—*un*invited." He scratched at the pale flesh above his elbow. "*Jehan* has decreed we are to remain in our respective chambers until he decrees otherwise."

"Hart and Corin, again," she said darkly, and sighed. "Brennan, one day you will come to their aid and they will get you slain."

"Is that a reason to ignore them, then?" He winced. "Maeve, that is living human skin, not the tanned hide of an animal."

"They take advantage of you, Brennan. And they always have. Especially Hart." Her lips were pressed flat as she carefully rubbed salve around the wound, pressed the flesh together, wrapped it snugly with linen. He thought the grim expression ruined the symmetry of her features. Like her mother, Maeve was green-eyed, blonde, attractive in a bold, handsome way. There was no mark of Niall upon her. Maeve personified the Erinnish side of her heritage, lacking even the faintest trace of Cheysuli gifts or coloring.

And that is one thing Keely can gloat over, he reflected. *My proud Cheysuli rujholla may lack the color, but none of the gifts. The Old Blood gives her a distinct advantage.*

"Well," he said aloud, "I can hardly let Hart go out by himself when I know he is likely to get into trouble."

"Aye, you can," she demurred. "He is not your *lir,* that you have to attend him always."

"No, not my *lir.* But twin-born, which is a link at least as binding as what I have with Sleeta." Brennan watched her face. "I mean no offense, *rujholla,* but you cannot begin to understand what is between children of the same birth."

Her fingers, tying off the linen, stopped moving. Stiffly, Maeve moved away to stand directly in front of him. "No," she agreed in an odd, flat voice. "No, I cannot. No more than I can understand why two of my brothers *and* my sister resent me so, simply because I had the great good fortune to be the only child born of the union between the Mujhar and his light woman."

"You cannot accuse *Hart* of resenting you," Brennan told her. "He resents no one. All he thinks about is how best to win his wagers."

Her mouth twisted. "Such consolation, Brennan—that you do not leap to deny the resentment on Corin's and Keely's part."

He sighed and reached out to catch one of her hands. It was stiff, and very cold. "Maeve, you know them. Corin resents the world, I think, for making him third-born instead of first; Keely resents that she has no voice in her disposition." He pulled her more closely to him, until a fold of her skirts brushed against one knee. "You are free of a cradle-betrothal. You are free of the responsibilities of helping to fulfill the prophecy. You are free of the need to prove yourself able to live up to self-expectations. But mostly, you are free to be yourself, which is what Keely wants more than anything."

"She *is* herself!"

"No. Corin understands this better than I—Keely and I do not agree on much, as you know—but I think Keely desires to be more than *cheysula,* princess, *jehana* . . . I think she wants to know the freedom most men have, to be whatever they choose to be, and do what they wish to do."

"*You* do not. *You* were cradle-betrothed. By the gods, Brennan, you will marry Liam of Erinn's daughter just as Keely will wed his son! How can she say you have more freedom than she does? How can she resent *me* simply because I am not discontented by my place in this life?" Maeve pulled her hand out of his and turned her back, skirts swirling. And then she swung around to face him once again, brass-bright hair whipping in its loose net of gold wire and glittering topaz gemstones. "Would she trade places with me, I wonder, in her desire for contentment, if she knew she would be called the *bastard* daughter of the Mujhar and his Erinnish whore?"

"*Who* calls you that?" Brennan was abruptly on his feet. The tears that glittered briefly in Maeve's eyes were enough to make him long to take his sword from its rack upon the wall.

"No one. Everyone." Maeve gestured sharply with both hands, expressing helplessness. "No one to my face, of course. They value their lives too much, knowing better than to say it near members of the House of Homana. But—I have heard it. Muttered. Whispered. Sometimes said quite clearly, when I go to Market Square."

"Maeve, you know he would wed her if he could. You *know* he would make her Queen of Homana, and you legitimate. And he will—when Gisella no longer lives."

"You speak of your mother, Brennan."

"I speak of the half-breed Cheysuli witch he married," Brennan said plainly. "I speak of the madwoman who bore him children, then tried to give them over to Strahan the Ihlini—and *would* have, had *jehan* not caught her at it, preventing the travesty." He shivered in distaste. "Gods—when I think of what I might have become had she succeeded. . . ."

"Dead," she said hollowly.

"Or worse." Brennan wanted to spit.

"Worse?" Maeve stared at him. "What could be *worse?*"

"We would be made minions," he said flatly. "Minions of Strahan; of Asar-Suti, the Seker, who made and dwells in darkness." He could not help the instinctive movement of his hand toward his knife. "He would cause us to be *minions,* Maeve, and to sit as puppets upon our respective thrones, allowing Strahan to rule in our places. To rule—and to destroy."

Five

"Two days," Hart said emphatically. "How much longer do you think I can last, mewed up in my chamber like a disobedient child?"

Corin, seated cross-legged on the floor of his chamber with Kiri in his lap, upside down so her belly could be properly scratched, looked at his brother expressionlessly. "For one, you are not *in* your chamber, you are in mine—and I think the idea was that you *were* a disobedient child."

"Aye, well, enough is enough," Hart said crossly. "I think he has forgotten us. Surely he could not expect us to remain night and day in our chambers."

"Sure he *could*," Corin corrected. "I am no fonder of my chamber than you of yours, but there appears to be no solution—" He stopped short. "I know that expression, Hart—what are you thinking?"

Hart grinned. "That we are Cheysuli warriors, and there is indeed a solution. That it is time we employed it." He scratched idly at his sleeveless Cheysuli jerkin, dyed a soft amber brown; the bound flesh beneath it itched. "That it is time I found a game before I lose my wits."

"I thought you had no money."

"There are the twenty-five crowns you owe me."

Corin grimaced. "Aye, that again." He waved a hand. "There, in the brass-bound casket—I think there are twenty-five."

Hart crossed to a table. He tipped the lid of the casket

and nodded, eyebrows raised; there were considerably more than twenty-five. Supple fingers dipped in, deftly counted out twenty-five pieces of gold, tucked them into a leather belt-purse already tied at his right hip. "Thank the gods for a thrifty *rujholli.*"

"No more thrifty than the next man," Corin retorted, scrubbing affectionately at Kiri's belly fur. "It is only that I avoid the games you thrive on."

"Aye, well . . . shall we go find one?"

Corin's hand stopped moving. "You are serious."

"Aye." Hart nodded. "Shall we go?"

"Now?" Corin glanced out the nearest casement and saw the sun was already down. "Our *jehan* has expressly forbidden this sort of thing, Hart."

"Aye."

Corin studied him. "That does not bother you in the least."

"Aye, it does. But not enough to gainsay me." Hart grinned and patted the now-filled belt-purse. "How will he know, *rujho*? We will go out like thieves and come back like thieves. Only wealthier."

Corin scratched slowly at his jaw, considering. "What of Brennan?"

"I asked." Hart shrugged. "He swore, called me a fool and every other name he could think of, Homanan and Old Tongue alike—and said he would leave us to our folly."

"Us." Corin scowled. "He was so certain I would go?"

"Quite certain."

"Ku'reshtin," Corin commented without heat. "Well, I think he has the right of it." He let Kiri get out of his lap, then stood. "Where do we go, *rujho*? Not The Rampant Lion again."

Hart laughed. "No, no, even I am not so foolish. No, I think we should go to a different part of the city, just to be safe in case our absence is discovered, and *jehan* sends the Guard again." One finger caressed the heavy knife hilt at his left hip. "I thought we might try the Midden."

"The Midden!" Corin, aghast, stared at him. "That is hardly our part of Mujhara, Hart. The Midden is infested with thieves, cutpurses, assassins. . . ." He shook his head. "No wonder Brennan said you were a fool."

Hart grinned his lopsided grin. "I did not precisely tell him that is where we are going."

Corin grunted. "The Midden is dangerous."

"Aye, it is." Hart merely continued to grin, and caressed his knife again.

After a moment, Corin's answering grin banished the scowl. He nodded. "But let me shed these useless velvets, *rujho*. If I go to the Midden with you, I go as a Cheysuli." He stopped short of the nearest clothing trunk. "You *do* intend to take Rael."

"Of course. He is even now perched on the curtain wall, awaiting our arrival."

Corin glanced at Kiri. For a moment his eyes were oddly detached, as he went into the link. Then he sighed. "Kiri says we are every bit the fools Brennan claims, but she will come. If only to protect me from myself."

"Rael said something very similar," Hart reflected. The *lir*-gold gleamed on his arms. "Hurry, *rujho*. I need a game."

Hart and Corin slipped down the spiraling stairs in a tower near the back of Homana-Mujhar. The staircase was only rarely used by any member of the family, being primarily intended for the household staff; Hart was certain if they met anyone, they could bluff their way past.

It might have worked, except Corin—in the lead—ran smack into a shadow-shrouded body at the bottom, near the door that would pass them out of the palace proper into the inner bailey.

Corin swore, fell back a step; Hart bumped him and jostled him forward.

"I knew you would come this way." Brennan's voice; he opened the door partway and let the diffused light of bailey torches spill into the tower. Corin blinked. Kiri's eyes reflected oddly in the distorted light. Sleeta was a plush velvet shadow in the darkness, golden eyes staring fixedly at Hart and Corin.

"Are you here to try and gainsay us?" Hart demanded. "*Rujho*—"

"No," Brennan said clearly. "Have I ever been able to stop you before?"

"Once," Hart said. "You tripped me; I hit my head and was knocked half senseless."

Corin snickered. Brennan nodded reminiscently. "But I caught you off-guard then, and I have not been able to do it since. We are too well-matched, now, in size *and* experience." He peered out the door. "I think the way is clear."

"You are *coming?*" Corin was patently astonished.

"*Lir* or no *lir*, I can trust neither of you to look out for your welfare. Aye, I am coming."

"And if *jehan* catches us?"

"He will no doubt have us executed," Brennan said lightly. "Now, where is it we are going?"

Corin glanced over his shoulder to Hart, who shrugged a little.

"*Where?*" Brennan asked suspiciously.

"The Midden," Corin said. Hastily, he added, "Hart's idea."

Brennan looked at his blue-eyed twin in silence a moment. And then he said, very quietly, "You are even a greater fool than I thought."

"I need a *game,*" Hart said. When Brennan only stared at him, he slipped past both brothers and stalked outside, *lir*-gold agleam in the torchlight.

They went horseback to the edges of the Midden, the border between lesser and greater Mujhara in attitude as well as advantages. The mounts they left at a small livery, then went ahead on foot. They walked the narrow, night-blackened streets like shadow-wraiths, moving through the depths of the moonless night. Sleeta padded silently at Brennan's side, only her great golden eyes betraying her presence. Rael was a faint shimmering blur overhead; Kiri, quick, delicate Kiri, trotted at their backs.

Others moved in the darkness as well, soft-footed,

silent, silk-smooth; men well-versed in the art of decep-
tion and subterfuge. No one spoke a word.

The cobbles under their boots were muffled beneath
layers of dirt and the remains of old droppings, packed
into the seams and hollows formed by rounded, time-
worn bricks. The winding street smelled of old ale, urine,
the close confinement of people unused to washing. In
corners they heard scuttling and squeaking; occasionally
the yowl of a tom cat protecting his territory.

The dwellings themselves were all of wood, set cheek-
by-jowl in crooked corners and dogleg turnings. Candles
glowed here and there, a lantern, occasionally a torch.
But the night held dominance.

Corin twitched his wrist experimentally. A shiver of
anticipation coursed down his spine; he felt the sting in
his armpits. "Where do we go?" he asked quietly.

Hart shrugged. "A tavern—any tavern. No place in
particular."

"Well-planned," Brennan muttered. "*Jehan* would be
so proud."

"Perhaps we should have brought Keely instead of
you," Hart retorted. "The gods know she has more willingness than *you* to explore the unknown."

"Perhaps you should have," Brennan agreed. "Then
there would be four fools in place of three."

"Leave Keely out of it," Corin warned.

"She *would* have come," Hart said.

"Aye," Corin agreed. "And then we would have to
concern ourselves with how many rude-speaking men she
would be likely to cut, to teach them better manners."

"There," Hart said abruptly, stopping short. "A tavern."

Corin and Brennan also stopped, keeping to the shadows. "There?" Brennan asked in disbelief.

"Why not?" Hart returned. "See you the sign-plate?"

The sign-plate in question dangled crookedly from a
length of leather thong. There was no wind; it did not
creak or spin or swing. It seemed to swallow what little
light there was in the street, and throw it back toward the
three Cheysuli princes.

"I see it," Brennan agreed grimly. "I think I can *smell* it, also."

" 'The Pig in the Poke,' " Corin read aloud. "How appropriate."

Brennan shook his head. "I am not taking Sleeta in there."

"Then leave her outside to wait with Kiri and Rael," Corin said. "They will be close enough if we need them."

"Come," Hart said impatiently, and stepped out to lead the way across the street.

Brennan brought him up short by catching one bare arm. "Wait you, *rujho*—I think we would do well, before we go, to agree to one thing."

"Aye, aye, what?" Hart's impatience was manifest.

"That we leave our knives sheathed," Brennan said clearly, catching Corin's eyes as well. "In this sort of place, if we show steel we will likely have it fed to us."

"By the gods, Brennan, you will have me thinking you *are* a woman instead of warrior!" Corin exclaimed in disgust. "Have it fed to us, indeed—we are *Cheysuli*, Brennan."

"We are also in a part of Mujhara where I doubt very much anyone will be much impressed by our rank or race," Brennan answered grimly.

Hart sighed and glanced over at the tavern. "I have no intention of showing steel, *rujho*—only enough gold to buy my way into a game."

"And I am willing to wager the game will be much different here than at The Rampant Lion."

"Wagering, are you?" Hart grinned. "Come, *rujho* . . . let us go in where your willingness to wager may be translated into *winning*." Without waiting for an answer, he headed across the street as the *lir* secreted themselves in the shadows.

The door caught on ridged dirt as Hart pushed it open; pushing harder, he knocked it off the uneven floor. His momentum carried it through to slam against the wooden wall, which served to stop all conversation in the common room and fasten everyone's attention on the new arrivals.

Brennan, just behind Hart, looked over the room, judging rapidly. And muttered beneath his breath, "We should have left the horses closer."

"And have them stolen?" Corin, last in, asked it very quietly as he shut the door, then turned back to face the room along with his brothers.

The Pig in the Poke was as unlike The Rampant Lion as could be. It was unlike any tavern the princes had ever been in before, and quite suddenly they came to the realization that their lives had been sheltered indeed. A few lanterns, stinking of cheap oil, depended from the roof-tree, which littered the floor liberally with debris and divots hacked out with knives and swords. The candles were tallow, not wax, and next to useless, giving off a smudged, greasy flame that burned only sluggishly. Thick smoke climbed up the limbs of the tree to hang in the air like a blanket. The common room stank of old ale, stale beer and unwashed bodies, as well as desperation and hostility.

Hart indicated an empty table not far from the door. It was stained dark from age and spilled liquor, sticky with wine residue, scarred from weapons and spurs. Hart caught hold of a bench and dragged it over the earthen floor made uneven and treacherous by divots and hardpacked ridges. He sat down and placed his hands on the table; his fingers twitched, as if needing the rune-sticks and dice.

Brennan and Corin followed a moment later. And when at last the tavern-keeper came over, silence still ruled the room.

He was not tall but incredibly broad, brown-haired and brown-eyed, with wide, spatulate fingers. His tunic and trews were spun of rough homemade yarn, nubbed with numerous flaws, and wine-stained. There was little fat on his body, save for a belly that overflowed trews and stretched the tunic tight.

He showed the resin-stained teeth in his mouth, but it was not precisely a smile. "You be far from your Keep."

"A man in search of a good game will go as far as necessary," Hart said calmly. "Have you one to offer?"

The tavern-keeper looked at each of them, one at a

time. His dark eyes were shrewd and judgmental. "Have I a game to offer? Well, I might. Have you *gold* to offer?" The eyes were on the *lir*-bands weighting three pairs of arms.

Hart wet his lips. "Oh, aye, you may say so, and safely. Enough to play. Now—the game?"

Brown eyes couched in creases stopped evaluating Brennan and Corin entirely, making Hart their sole subject. The tavern-keeper said nothing at all for several long moments, and then his unfriendly face loosened a bit. Not a smile, in no way, but an expression of comprehension as he saw how Hart's brown fingers tapped incessantly against the dirty tabletop.

"Your beasts," he said, in his lowborn dialect. "I'll not have any in here, where decent men are drinking."

Corin straightened almost imperceptibly on his stool. One hand dipped below the tabletop and stayed there, until an unwavering stare from Brennan, across the table, made Corin take his hand away from his knife.

Brennan looked up at the tavern-keeper. "They are *lir*, not beasts."

The man shrugged wide shoulders. "Beasts, *lir*—what do I care what you call those sorcerous things from the netherworld? All I know is, I won't have 'em in here."

"Then perhaps you should not have *us* in here." Brennan stood deliberately.

Corin looked up at his waiting brother, then shoved his bench back to rise. He stopped. He lingered there, halfway, and looked at Hart. *"Rujho—"*

Hart made no move to join them, and the tavern-keeper laughed. "Still wanting your game, are you?" He nodded a little. "Aye, I can see it. So, it touches even the wondrous Cheysuli." He turned. "Baram—this Cheysuli be wanting a *game.*"

"Hart," Brennan said quietly.

Hart shook his head. "Go, or stay. *I* stay."

Brennan watched the man cross the common room. "Hart—no. This place stinks of trouble. It stinks of *murder!*"

"Not so easy to murder a Cheysuli, I think." Corin sat down again.

Briefly Brennan touched the linen binding on his left arm, absently checking the knots Maeve had tied. Then, with a muttered imprecation, he sat down once more.

"Three to one?" Baram asked.

Brennan shook his head. Corin, seeing Hart's intensity, indicated he would stay out of it as well. He and Brennan both had seen their middle brother in such a state before; it was better to let him play alone, against one or more opponents. He had little time for those who merely dabbled.

"One to one," Hart said intently, and the tavern-keeper set down the house casket.

Baram touched the casket with a forefinger, then drew it away. He was black-eyed and gap-toothed, with a hideous scar on his chin. "You," he said gruffly.

Hart picked up the casket and upended it, pouring the dice into his left hand. There were no rune-sticks, only ivory dice now yellowed with age and dirt. The marks on them denoting a numerical system were mostly worn away.

Hart examined them, nodded briefly to himself, poured them back into the casket. Ivory rattled as he set the casket down. "The game," he said, and waited.

"Counting game," Baram answered. He paused. "Count?"

"I count."

"Throw thrice. Each. High two of three wins." He shrugged. "Simple enow."

"Simple enough." Hart nodded. "Throw."

They played through quickly, with nothing said past what had to be said. Brennan watched uneasily as other men in the tavern came closer to watch, leaving their own games behind. Corin drank wine and watched the dice as they rattled and danced on the table.

After some time spent trading coin back and forth between them—Hart's twenty-five gold crowns, Baram's inconvenient assortment of coppers and silver royals—

Hart leaned forward. "Not good enough," he said. "Shall we make it more interesting?"

Baram looked at the pile of coins glinting by Hart's elbow. Their winnings were evenly split, with neither man showing dominance over the dice. "Aye," he said at last.

Hart tapped his pile. "All."

Baram grunted. "Throw."

Hart threw tens, fives, twos; Baram twelves, eights, threes. Brennan watched the pile of coins in front of Hart go into Baram's pocket.

Hart frowned a little, tapped fingers on the table, nodded to himself. "Again," he said intently.

The Homanan slowly shook his head and pointed a crooked finger. "No gold, shapechanger. Nothing left to wager. Don't throw on promises.

Hart tapped his right forefinger on the table. The sapphire signet flashed in the smudgy light. "I have something left."

"No," Brennan said sharply.

Baram looked at the ring, at Brennan, at Hart. And he laughed. "Done," he said, and threw the dice.

Six throws, and the ring was forfeit. Baram put out his hand.

"No!" Brennan's own hand flashed down to catch Hart's, preventing him from stripping off the ring. "You are mad," he said flatly, "*mad* to think I will let you pay a debt with this. This ring signifies your title."

"I can get another." Hart tried to withdraw his hand from Brennan's grasp and did not succeed. "There must be hundreds of these stones in the treasury, Brennan; I can have another made."

"No." Brennan looked at Baram. "Will you take gold in place of this?"

"Gold?" Baram considered him silently a moment. "D'ye mean to make good his wager *for* him, then?"

"I do."

"Now?" Baram asked. "*Right* now?"

Grimly, Brennan nodded. "I have the coin."

"No." Baram's eyes went back to Hart, and he grinned his gap-toothed grin. "You said *gold*, shapechanger," he gestured toward the *lir*-bands on Hart's arms, "so I'll be taking those."

"*Ku'reshtin!*" Corin cried. "Do you think—"

"No." Brennan's sharp gesture cut him off. He sat very still on his stool. "I have gold crowns in my belt-purse, Homanan, and that is what I will pay you with. Nothing else."

Baram's determination was manifest. "I want those bracelets, shapechanger—and no man here can say I didn't win 'em *fairly*."

Hart's color was bad. "These—" he stopped, wet his lips, touched his left armband in something very like a caress. He started over. "These were never at stake," he said, "never. I owe you, aye, and you will be paid—but not with *these*."

Brennan unlaced his belt-purse and threw it onto the table. It landed with a heavy thump and a satisfying clink of gold. "There. More than enough to cover what he owes you."

Baram's hand shot out, scooped up the purse, hid it somewhere on his person. "Now," he said, "I'm paid. But I'm still waiting for *those*, and there're enough of us here to see that you give 'em to me."

"Try," Hart suggested, and before anyone else could move, including his brothers, he caught the table and overturned it.

Casket, cups and winejug flew in Baram's direction. Corin ducked, rolled off his stool, came up with knife in hand, knowing Brennan's ban on edged weapons no longer held true. Not at all; Corin saw the glint of a knife in *Brennan's* hand across the way. But he had no more time to watch for either brother; men were coming for him, and he saw steel in their hands.

Oh, gods, he thought, *I will have to slay a man.*

"Brennan—*behind you*—" Hart shouted, and then he had no more time to shout at his brother. Baram himself was on him with a long-knife in his hand.

A stool, on its side, rolled at Brennan's heels. He tripped, as he was meant to; staggered back, trying to plant his feet and regain his balance—a man, no *two*—reaching for him from behind—

Sleeta—he cried within the link, *gods, Sleeta, I never thought*—

Corin felt the wooden wall at his back. Shoulder blades, leather-clad, scraped; he pressed back, back, wishing he could somehow slide through the cracks in the boards. There was no more choice left to him, none at all; he bled from a cut across the back of one hand, and the two Homanans came at him again.

Hart twisted aside, caught Baram's wrist. As the Homanan struggled, cursing, Hart wrenched his arm back until the cords in Baram's neck stood up. Cords gave; the knife fell out of his hand.

The stench of spilled oil and greasy flame filled the common room. Someone cursed; another called that there was *fire*.

From outside the tavern came the scream of an angry mountain cat.

"Kill them, kill all of them!" the tavern-keeper shouted. "Kill them before they shift their shapes!"

Brennan, outnumbered, was slammed down against the floor. Beneath him, a wooden cup jammed against his spine, so that he writhed away from the pain; the knife was knocked out of his hand.

Defenseless, he kicked out and tried to twist away, but the two men had stretched him so that there was no leverage. All he could do was thrash helplessly as a faceless man bent down to slide the knife through leather, flesh, past muscle into the belly wall.

He dared not lurch upward. *Dared* not—gasping with effort, Brennan summoned everything he could of concentration, thrusting his consciousness out of the room, away, *away*, to somewhere deep in the heart of the earth.

Gods, gods— he cried in silent appeal, *let the magic come—let the power be tapped*—

Corin ducked a knife swipe; threw himself forward, beneath the arm . . . with all his strength he jammed his head into the belly of the Homanan. Breath expelled, the man fell backward, knees folding; Corin bore him down, braced quickly, shoved the knife deeply into the heaving belly. The Homanan cried out, thrashed futilely, cried out again.

Corin threw himself off, rolled, came up; blocked the second man's attack by catching the Homanan's wrist. Quickly, hardly knowing what he did, Corin sliced deeply into soft flesh of the underside of the outstretched arm. Blood flowed; flesh and tendons parted without a sound.

Hart bent, coughed, tried to breathe through the pain of sore ribs now doubly bruised. Smoke filled his throat as it filled the room, reaching cloying fingers into eyes, nostrils, mouths, even as it clogged the corners. Dimly he saw flames as they ran up the walls, danced along the roof-tree, dripped down to splatter on overturned tables and stools.

"Get out," he gasped. "Brennan—Corin—" He broke off as someone wrapped arms around his legs and pulled him down.

Hart struggled, felt hands insinuating themselves between his legs; groping, trying to grab, to wrench, to *rip,* using tactics of the sort Hart, honorably trained, had never, *ever* considered.

Outraged, he threw an elbow that caught the man in the face, smashed his nose; sent the Homanan tumbling backward, crying out.

Less beleaguered than Brennan and now twice as angry, Hart called up the earth magic and left behind his human form for the one with hooked beak and curving talons.

—the one that will lend me flight; that I can use to rake eyes from the enemy, to pluck them from their Homanan skulls—

Corin saw the flames, the smoke, the bodies. He saw the blurring of Hart's human form into the void that swallowed the space where he had stood a moment before; into the nothingness that was shed, replaced, made whole once again, only lacking the familiar shape of a man. Arms were wings, legs talons; the shout Hart began the shapechange with became the piercing cry of a hunting hawk—

—and was joined a moment later by the scream of a cat, as Brennan left behind *Brennan* to become an echo of his *lir,* tawny instead of black, but dangerous, so dangerous; so intent on his prey, as he raked claws across the nearest face, that Corin knew he had gone too far.

Too close, too close—oh, Brennan, no—not you—of all of us, not you—

Corin turned, stumbling, and reached for the door, for the latch, clawing it open; jerking open the door and thrusting it against the wall. Inwardly he called for Kiri. Aloud, he shouted for both his brothers' *lir,* and fell sideways, slamming a shoulder into the door; coughing, *coughing,* as smoke boiled out of the tavern into the darkness of the night.

Kiri, Corin said within the link, *Kiri, tell the lir to make them stop—tell them to stop—this place will become our pyre—*

The vixen understood at once, instantly passing the message to Sleeta and Rael. Corin knew better than to think he could talk sense into Brennan or Hart in the throes of the fight, especially as they were too angry, too blind to see the danger of remaining inside the tavern. Even with flame climbing the walls and running out along the roof to touch the dwelling next door, his brothers would not forgo the fight. Not now.

He heard screams from inside. He turned, saw someone afire. How the man danced; how the man screamed, as he tried to run and could not, trapped by the trunk of the burning rooftree.

Limbs, burned through, broke off, and parts of the roof began to rain down. Flame shot through the openings and engulfed the upper floor.

"Corin—" Hart, coughing, staggered out. Ash smeared his face; light from the flames set his *lir*-gold to gleaming. "Corin, is Brennan out?"

"No," Corin answered tersely. "Gods, Hart, this is *your* doing."

"*Mine*—" But Hart stopped the protest at once, swinging back toward the interior of the tavern. "Brennan!"

Rael flew out, followed closely by Kiri. Then Sleeta, unaccompanied.

Hart swore, plainly afraid. Corin caught his arm to prevent him from going back in, "No, *rujho*—no!" and Brennan stumbled out in human form.

Coughing, he nearly fell. "Dead," he gasped. "Dead, or dying—gods, *all of them*—"

"And most of the street." Hart's voice was clogged with phlegm. He coughed, spat; hugged aching ribs.

"No reason for us to mimic them *or* it," Corin said firmly. "We have ourselves and our *lir* . . . I suggest we go."

Brennan, moving out into the street, craned his neck to look over his shoulder. "They would have slain us . . . they would have had the gold off all our arms, planting steel in our bellies."

Hart tried to laugh and could not. But the sound was not one of humor. "Justifying their end?" he asked Brennan. "Do not bother, *rujho* . . . no more than anyone will when *we* are dead."

"If we do not go *now,* we may well end up that way." Corin's hand on Hart's wrist was not gentle. "Is it left to me, then? Well enough, the youngest to the oldest: *run*—"

They ran. And with them ran—and flew—their *lir*.

Six

They were lined up before the Lion Throne of Homana, his sons, in the Great Hall. Like little soldiers, Niall thought, all prepared to accept their punishment. Except he was quite certain they had not even considered the punishment he intended to levy on them.

The cushion beneath his buttocks did nothing to soften the confines of the Lion. The great wooden throne swallowed him up almost entirely, which was not a simple task considering his size; he reflected it must have been the same for Carillon, his grandsire, whom he so closely resembled.

He looked at his sons, standing three abreast before the Lion, in front of the firepit that began some six feet from the marble dais to stretch the length of the hall. He looked for guilt, regret, comprehension; he looked for some indication they understood how serious was the situation. But they had practiced for him, showing him stiff Cheysuli masks in place of faces, all of them, even blue-eyed, fair-haired Corin, who lacked the dark skin as well.

They had practiced, and he could not read their expressions. Until he told them how many were dead.

"At last count," the Mujhar said quietly, "there were more than twenty-eight bodies. It could be more; they are still searching in the rubble." He paused a moment, looking at his sons. "No one is quite sure; the entire block was destroyed."

Now the masks slipped. Now the faces were bared.

Shock, disbelief, denial; a profound, sudden and absolute comprehension of where the responsibility lay.

Niall shifted slightly, redistributing his weight within the embrace of the massive Lion. "I think the time for explanations is past. I think the assignment of guilt is unnecessary. Certainly apologies, however heartfelt, cannot begin to replace the lives and property lost. So I will request no explanations, no apologies, no admissions of guilt. I request only that you listen."

None of them said a word. Brennan, he saw, stood quite rigidly, staring blankly at an area somewhere in the vicinity of his father's left foot. Niall watched a moment as his eldest son tried to cope with the shock, the comprehension, the tremendous burden of responsibility he would, as always, try to assume. Even if it was only partially his.

Corin was plainly stunned. The color was gone from his face so that his tawny hair seemed a darker gold than normal. All the muscles stood up in his arms, flexing around the *lir*-bands; behind his back, Niall knew, Corin fisted his hands again and again, as hard as he could until all the muscles burned, protesting; inflicting discomfort to help the comprehension that what he now faced was real, and not some dream of his imagining. Niall had seen him do it before.

Lastly, he looked at Hart. Hart, whose insatiable taste—no, *need*—for gambling had, until two nights before, done little more than rob him of his allowance as Prince of Solinde; yet now it robbed people of their property. Of their *lives*.

Niall pushed himself out of the throne, bracing palms against the clawed armrests. He felt old, old and stiff, reluctant to rise and face them as a king, a Cheysuli, a father. And yet he knew he must.

He stood on the marble dais before the Lion Throne of Homana, personifying the strength and authority of his realm, and fixed his middle son with a single hard blue eyes. "I think it is time I stopped looking the other way. I think it is time I stopped rebuilding half the taverns in Mujhara with money from the Homanan treasury, and—

occasionally—my *personal* coffers. I think it is *past* time I forced you to become the man your *tahlmorra* intended you to be."

Hart did not flinch. "Aye, *jehan*," was all he said, and very quietly.

"I might wish you had been so acquiescent *before*, Hart."

The mouth flattened a little. "Aye, *jehan*."

"Well, then, as you are so acquiescent *now*, I must assume you will start for Solinde in the morning with good heart and good cheer."

The color slowly spilled out of Hart's face. "Solinde—?"

"Tomorrow," Niall confirmed, "where you will remain for the space of a year."

"*Jehan*—"

"You will be sent to Lestra, where you will—I hope, I *pray*—begin to learn what it is to be a prince . . . a man with responsibilities . . . a man who cannot afford to drink and dice and brawl." He paused. "Do I make myself clear?"

"Aye . . ." And then, in shock, "*But*—"

Yet again, Niall cut him off. "Your allowance will be strickly administered by the regent who now governs in my name. He will be advised that he is not to underwrite your gambling habit *in any fashion* . . . that if you some-how lose the last copper penny of your monthly allow-ance, you will bear the responsibility for repaying the debt. *You,* Hart. Not Brennan, not Corin, not Ian, Maeve, Keely or Deirdre. Certainly not me. And *certainly not* the Solindish treasury. Is that clear, also?"

"A *year* . . ." Hart's tone was hollow.

"Aye. You are hereby forbidden your homeland for the space of a twelve-month, unless I send for you myself."

"Exile." Bitterness, now, beginning to creep in. "First our *jehana*, now me."

"The circumstances are unrelated," Niall said coldly, "though I begin to wonder if there is more of Gisella in you than of myself." Abruptly, he stopped himself. "You will leave first thing in the morning."

Brennan took a single step forward. "*Jehan,*" he said, "no. I beg you. Say you will reconsider!"

"You are to hold your silence until given leave to speak," Niall said evenly. Brennan flinched visibly and did not move or speak again.

It was Corin's turn; Corin, who so rarely knew when not to defy his father. "And I am to go to Atvia, am I not?" he asked bitterly. "I am to be exiled too, like Hart. For a year."

"For a year," Niall confirmed. "The circumstances are much the same, I think, even if the individual problems differ; you need to learn to accept the responsibility for your own actions, *and* your manners, which can injure others. And if you think to deny me—as I see you intend already, judging by your expression—I suggest you think back to the deaths you caused only two nights ago."

"It was not entirely my fault," Corin said angrily. "Lay no blame, you say. Well, I *will*. You may blame the cutthroats who tried to slay us, *jehan*—the men who were willing to stick us and watch us bleed for the price of our *lir*-gold!"

"You will leave in the morning," Niall said quietly. "But before you arrive in Atvia, there is a task I would have you perform."

"Task?" Corin stared at his father. "You send me away, then ask me to perform a task?"

"One I think you will be pleased to do, as it concerns the Prince of Homana."

Corin frowned. "Brennan?"

"Did you think I would forgo punishing him because he is the oldest? Because he is the heir to Homana?" Niall shook his head. "No. I said I would assign no guilt, and I do not. Neither do I weigh it by the things you have done in the past, all of you. Brennan is equally responsible, and he will share equally in the punishment."

"Equally?" Corin demanded. "I think not. There is nowhere to *send* him. Homana is his to rule, one day; you cannot exile the man who will take your throne."

"I *send* him nowhere, that is true," Niall said quietly.

"But I can still make certain he begins to accept the responsibilities you and Hart must also accept. And it is up to you, Corin, to assist me." He paused. "I thought you might be willing to assume the task, once you realized it was within your province to alter the freedom of your oldest *rujholli*."

Corin glanced at Brennan, who stared stoically at the throne, avoiding his father's eye altogether. "How?" Corin asked finally, looking again at Niall.

The Mujhar turned to the Lion and resumed his seat, sitting back against the ancient wood. "You will stop at Erinn on the way to Atvia and deliver a message to Liam, Lord of the Idrian Isles. You will say to him the time has come for our realms to be formally united in marriage as well as in alliance." The single blue eye flicked to Brennan. "Liam's daughter is twenty-two, now. It is time the Prince of Homana secured the Lion with additional heirs."

Color rushed into Brennan's face. The yellow eyes were suddenly intent, and intensely feral. "You do not use a betrothal or marriage as *punishment!*" Brennan snapped angrily. "It does you little honor, *my lord Mujhar,* and gives none at all to Aileen."

"You have at least a six-month, if not more, in which to arrange your affairs and learn what it is to be a prince," Niall said. "Until Aileen arrives, you will attend me in all council sessions, at all trade negotiations, during the hearings when I entertain petitions put forth by Homanan citizens. I think you will be too busy to concern yourself with what does and does not constitute honor, in Mujhars or other people."

"After twenty years and more, you separate us so easily," Hart said blankly. "I cannot believe it."

"*Together,* you have done little more save drink and brawl and bring disgrace to your names as well as this House," Niall answered. "Apart, perhaps, you will learn what it is to be a man. To be a *Cheysuli warrior.*" As one, in stunned silence, they stared at him, Niall abruptly stood up from the throne. "I do not doubt there are things you wish to say to one another without benefit of my presence, so I will take it from you."

Niall's sons watched in silence as he strode stiffly from the Great Hall. But as the silver doors thudded closed, the silence was ended most distinctly.

"Did you hear him?" Corin asked in angry astonishment. "Did you *hear* him? 'I think the time for explanations is past.' " He swore loudly, with great eloquence. "We were given *no* chance to defend ourselves, *no* chance to tell him precisely what happened—he merely stands before that travesty of a lion and tells us what we are to do with our lives, as if *he* has the ordering of them?"

"He does," Hart said remotely. He walked to the dais, turned, sat down upon the top step, propping booted feet wide on the second one. "He is the Mujhar of Homana, and our *jehan*."

"Aye, he *is* Mujhar," Corin snapped, "and, *as Mujhar*, one of his responsibilities is to hear both sides of the story." He swore again and kicked at the gold-veined marble dais. "You would think we *planned* the fire, they way he talks."

Brennan stood at one of the stained-glass casements, staring blindly through colored glass to the bailey outside. He seemed oblivious to Corin's rantings.

"Gods," Hart murmured. "*Solinde*—"

"—and Atvia." Corin kicked marble again, as if he meant to dislodge a portion of his father's skull. "What do I want with a lump of rock in the middle of the Idrian Ocean?"

Brennan's hand traced the outline of one of the patterns in the glass. "Twenty-eight lives," he said. "*Twenty-eight.*"

"You would think he considers himself one of the *gods,* the way he stands before us and pronounces how we will spend the next twelve months of our lives," Corin said in disgust. "*I* think—"

"*Do you think I care what you think?*" Brennan abruptly spun from the casement and, before Corin could blurt a protest, crossed the hall to grab the front of his jerkin. "Do you think I care that you feel *inconvenienced* by having to accept your title in fact as well as name?" He pushed his brother back two steps, forced him up the dais, planted him solidly in the throne. "*Twenty-eight lives were lost, Corin* . . . it should not matter to you that those lives were spent in the Midden instead of Homana-Mujhar or Clankeep. It *should not matter!* They are *dead*, Corin . . . dead because of us!"

Corin inched back into the Lion, trying to escape Brennan's hands. "*Rujho*—"

"No," Brennan said tersely. "No explanations. No defense. In this I will be like our *jehan*." He took his hands from Corin's jerkin as if he could not bear to soil them. "We went there against our king's express orders, defying our *jehan* as well, and because of us an entire block was destroyed. Twenty-eight lives were lost, perhaps more. By the gods, Corin, how can you sit there and rail against our *jehan* with that guilt on your shoulders?"

"Let him be," Hart said wearily. "Oh, let him be, Brennan. I can think of better ways of spending our last day together than trying to levy even *more* guilt upon our youngest *rujholli*."

"Not more," Brennan shot back. "*Some* guilt . . . because I think otherwise he will dismiss this tragedy as not worthy of his time, his concern, simply because he has *more important* things to consider." Brennan's tone was filled with eloquent contempt. "Such as which of Deirdre's ladies should he seduce *next.*"

"I care!" Corin cried. "*I care,* Brennan—more than you can know. And *aye,* I do have something else to consider . . . something that may not have occurred to you. And even if it had, likely *you* would not consider it worth the worry."

"What?" Brennan demanded. "What else is there to consider?"

Corin's lips drew back briefly, baring teeth. In his anger, his ferocity, he was suddenly more animal than man, though he remained in human form. "I am afraid," he said through gritted teeth. "*Afraid.*"

"Afraid?" Brennan stared at him in astonishment. "Aye,

it will be different in Atvia, and will take time to adjust, but—afraid?"

"Aye, afraid!" Corin cried. "Are you forgetting, then, that our *jehana* is there? Mad Gisella, Queen of Homana, who tried to give her children to Strahan the Ihlini?" He had their full attention now, as he looked from one to the other. "Aye," he repeated, "afraid. because I will have to see her, to *face* her. . . ." He drew in an unsteady breath. "I will be required to breathe the same air as that half-breed, blood-tainted Atvian/Cheysuli witch, who *willingly* would have given us over to that Ihlini *ku'reshtin*, so he could twist us all—so he could turn us into minions for his amusement, to use as *puppets!*"

"Enough," Brennan said gently. "Enough, Corin—no more." His anger was banished, his contempt replaced with compassion. "Perhaps I judged you too hastily." He sighed and scrubbed at the lines of tension settling in the flesh of his brow. "Gods, save us from each other . . . save us from sword-sharp tongues."

"Save us from the Ihlini." Corin shut his eyes and leaned his head back against the throne. "Gods, *rujho*, I do not want to go. . . ."

"No," Brennan agreed. "Nor would I, in your place. Not even if you promised a casket of gold."

"For that much gold, I might." Hart's smile fell away almost at once. "No, no, forgive me for that . . . *I* am the one who put us in this position. Blame me, no matter what *jehan* says. Let me carry the guilt."

"Would you?" Brennan asked. "No, I think not. It is not in you to accept guilt, *rujho*, even if you comprehend that you are responsible for it."

Hart recoiled visibly from the comment.

"Well," Corin said in resignation, "for all I rail about it—and will—I think the distribution of sentences just. You go nowhere, Brennan; all you must do is wait for a *cheysula*. Not so bad, I think, but then it was not your idea to go to the Midden, and you did what you could to prevent us from becoming involved in an obviously dangerous situation. A wedding should not be so bad; the gods know Deirdre is bearable. Aileen is her *harana*, so if they are anything alike you should not find the marriage too onerous."

"No," Brennan agreed, "though I might wish the time to be of my own choosing."

"But he has taken that from you." Corin nodded. "He has taken it from us all." Abruptly he shoved himself out of the Lion. "I think I will defy him one last time, just so he does not forget me *too* easily—"

"Corin, *no!*" Brennan cried. "Why make it worse than it is?"

"Do you mean to refuse to go?" Hart asked in surprise.

"No." Corin straightened a jerkin still rumpled from Brennan's expression of anger and frustration. "I mean to go, because I must. But I mean to go *now,* rather than in the morning."

"Small defiance," Brennan said curtly. "You cut your nose to spite your face."

"Perhaps." Corin headed down the steps and toward the hammered silver doors at the end of the Great Hall. "But at least it is a decision I can make for myself. Besides," he swung around and walked backward, spreading his hands, "this way I will be home one day sooner." And he was gone, running from the hall.

Brennan said a sharp, brief obscenity in the Old Tongue that still, for all its brevity, managed to express his emotions very clearly.

"Three become two become one." Hart stood up from the dais. "Not a good wager, *rujho,* when the point of the game lies in *adding,* not subtracting." He sighed and walked aimlessly toward the silver doors. "No," he said wearily, "not a good wager at all."

"Hart." Brennan's voice stopped him at the doors, echoing in the vastness of the hall. "In a year, a *year*—we will be different people."

Hart leaned a shoulder against one of the heavy doors. "Aye," he agreed, "but still Cheysuli. Still *rujholli.* That is what counts, I think." He smiled sadly, pushed through, was gone.

After a moment Brennan turned to look at the empty Lion, all acrouch on the dais; the Lion of Homana, deprived of his Mujhar. Brennan looked at the old wood, the fading giltwork, the massive paws with their curving claws. He sighed. "You and I," he said, "will have to come to an agreement. You do not strip me of all my freedom, my good sense, my desire to be a man as well as Mujhar . . . and I will not bring dishonor to your name. To my House. Or to my people." He shook his head slowly. "And never again to my *jehan*."

But the Lion made no answer.

Deirdre was in her private solar, stitching on a tapestry with four of her ladies when Niall came in. She glanced up, saw his face, instantly dismissed the women. Before Niall could say a word, Deirdre was up and guiding him to a chair.

"I am well enough," he protested, as she pressed him down into the cushions.

"Are you, then?" she asked lightly. "I'm thinking not. I'm thinking you have, from the look of you, stared death in the eye, and lost." She made certain he was comfortable in the chair. "You'll be sitting here until *I* say you may rise."

Loose-limbed, he sat in the chair and stared blankly at the tapestry frame. "What is that?"

"Something I started a month ago. Something to go in the Great Hall, one day, when I am done." She knew very well his real interest did not lie in the tapestry; she knew also that Niall came around to things in his own way, in his own time. Prying would serve neither of them. "You see? Lions. Homanan lions, as you have told me; fierce, proud, loyal beasts, challenging all who *dare* to threaten their realm." Her voice wavered a moment as she looked at his ravaged face. "Niall—"

"Why so many?" he asked, staring at the tapestry. He bent forward to examine it more closely. "So many lions, Deirdre—and is this the Lion Throne?"

"Aye." She touched the design not yet fully stitched. "It seems to me some of the stories should be put down in yarn, and then hung up where all can see them. The recounting of the legends. Shaine, Carillon, Donal . . .

you and your sons. . . ." her voice trailed off. "All the Lions of Homana."

"My sons." And Niall sat back again, pressing one hand against his face. "Ah, *gods,* Deirdre—what am I to do? How am I to bear it? How will I last the year?"

She stood very still before him. "You have sent them away, then, Hart and Corin."

"I had no choice." The words were little more than pain, mumbled against his hand. "They gave me no choice, *meijha.* So many lives lost. So many *innocent* lives; not everyone in the Midden is thief or murderer. Some were little children." Abruptly he stripped off the patch that warded the empty socket and bent forward rigidly. "Ah, gods—it hurts—"

"Your head?" She moved forward, knelt, threaded fingers in his hair. She pressed his face against her breast. "Oh, Niall, I would be giving anything to take it from you, this pain. After all these years . . ."

His breath was loud in the chamber. "No—no—not just my head . . . when the old pain comes on me, it is generally bearable. But *this*—" He sighed. "This is more. This is what it is to be a *jehan*, regardless of rank or race."

"Aye," she said, "aye. There is pain with all the pleasure."

"A year," he said hollowly. "Gods, I said a *year*. Hart and Corbin banished . . . and Brennan made to wed."

She stiffened a little. "You'll be sending for Aileen."

"Aye. Corin is to stop at Erinn on his way to Atvia." Suddenly, he pulled away from her. "And perhaps I should have considered that *you* might want to go."

After a moment, she shook her head. "I'll not be denying that I want to see my homeland. But this is Corin's punishment; there is no place for me on board. Liam will understand."

He sat back again, asprawl, rubbing the ruined flesh near his empty socket. "They gave me no choice," he said wearily. "What was I to do?"

"What you did, I think," she answered, settling down at his feet in a puddle of pale green silk. " 'Tis not for me to say yea or nay on this—they are not *my* sons—but I will agree with you nonetheless. Boys must stop being boys. Even when they are men."

"If you had seen Brennan's face . . ."

"Aye, well, if 'twas anything like the other times, he was there for the others, not himself."

"No, not that . . . no, I mean when I banished Hart. I think that was a worse punishment for Brennan than telling him he must wed and take on more responsibilities."

Deirdre sighed a little, stroking his rigid hand. "Aye, aye, perhaps it was. They are so close, Hart and Brennan . . . the time apart will be hard on them."

"Hard on me," he said unevenly. "For all they have done a monstrous thing, I know I will hate myself every day I look at Brennan and Keely, and see their accusing eyes."

"Brennan and Keely must tend to Brennan and Keely," Deirdre told him firmly. "*You* must look to yourself."

"And you?" he asked, reaching out to clasp her fingers. "Gods, Deirdre . . . what would I do without *you?*"

She smiled and kissed the back of his hand. "*I'll* not be telling you. For if I did, you might find reason to be rid of an aging Erinnish spinster."

He smiled. "Aging, indeed. Not what *I* would say; I who share your bed."

But she saw the anguish in his eye, and knew it would last forever.

PART II

BRENNAN

One

On a night with no moon, men gathered. Light was conjured from torches, from lanterns; distorting faces that, by day, by good light, were simply *faces*; Homanan faces, some young, some old, some neither, being not yet fully formed, leaving youth behind while lingering yet on the doorstep, not quite ducking beneath the lintel to enter the common room of manhood.

But now, by torchlight, by lanternlight, the faces were leeched of humanity, of sanity, of the expressions that, everchanging, reflected happiness, sorrow, pride, regret, and all those subtleties lying between. Faces that were no longer *faces*, but aspects of dedication, fanaticism, and the desire to right a wrong.

Within the ring of looming trees stood stave torches, thrust into the ground to form a second circle, a ward against the darkness. Within the ring of torches, men clustered. And within the ring of men, a boy was made to lie down on cold, hard stone. No. *Not* a boy; no longer. A warrior, now; he had received his *lir*.

Against the stone, he shivered. They had stripped him, the Homanans. They had taken jerkin, leggings, boots, as well as his knife. They had taken it all, leaving him with nothing, save the knowledge that they could get no gold, because he had only just received his *lir*. There had been no Ceremony of Honors in Clankeep, to honor his name, his *lir*, his newfound warrior status.

And would be none, ever, now.

It was full dark, long past the time he should have

been back at Clankeep. But no one would come looking. He had left his father's pavilion four days earlier in search of his *lir*, knowing only he had to go, to assuage the craving that set his blood afire. No one would come looking, no matter how late it was, because it was a part of the ritual, to stay from home until the link was made.

Rings within rings: trees, torches, men. And in the center, himself. On an altar once serving as a part of sacred rituals, *Cheysuli* rituals, Firstborn rituals; now the altar, in its nook of towering trees, was forgotten by his people. Remembered only by Homanans, who meant to pervert its use.

Upon the stone he trembled, and shut his eyes against the darkness, the torchlight, the looming faces, with their aspects of fanaticism. He shut his eyes against the fear for himself, because another fear outweighed it. They would slay his *lir*, he knew. First. So they could see what it was for a Cheysuli warrior to lose his other self. And then, as he was consumed by grief for the loss of his *lir*, his newfound other self, they would slay the new warrior as well.

Beneath his naked back his flesh knew the touch of stone, and of blood. The altar reeked of it, stained black and red and brown, sticky with old and new.

Hands held wrists and ankles. Even his hair, so he could not thrash head against stone in a futile attempt at breaking free. Hands held him: Homanan hands. Deigning to touch his Cheysuli flesh, because soon enough his blood would wash them clean of taint.

"Bring the wolf," someone said. A man. Young, from the sound of it; the voice was cool, not deep, not high. Smooth as clover honey.

The boy on the stone jerked against human manacles. All held firm.

"Into the light," said the voice.

"No," the boy whispered; it was the first sound he had made.

The wolf was brought to the altar, into the ring of torchlight. A young male wolf, hardly more than a cub;

like the boy on the stone, he had not quite crossed the threshold between youth and adulthood. And, like the boy, now never would.

The jaws had been wired shut. A chain was wound about the ruddy throat, snugged taut. He struggled, whimpered, dug the air with hind claws even as the front ones reached for flesh. But the man who held the wolf was large and strong, and used to big dogs; the cub was no match for him.

"No," said the boy again. Begging now, forgoing all the pride of his people. Forgoing all save the need to see the cub made safe, unharmed, set free.

A hand touched the boy's brow, smoothing back damp hair. The palm was cool, almost soothing, like the voice. "We must," the voice said; the same one, the same voice, that had beckoned the wolf cub brought. That had beckoned the boy held down against the stone.

"There is a reason for what we do," the voice said. "A need. This is not idle whimsy, nor ignorant reprisal for the loss of the Homanan throne to a Cheysuli king. No. This is part and parcel of what must be done, in order to restore the balance of justice. To restore *rightness*." The voice paused. "Can you understand that? Can you understand that I do not hate *you*, boy, nor even hate your race? No. Hate is not what fuels me, other than using it when I must; in its place, hate has its uses. No. I do this because there is a need. Homana's need."

The hand was gentle against the boy's sweat-sheened brow. He tried not to listen, but he heard in spite of himself.

"There was a mistake made more than sixty-five years ago, when Carillon named Donal his heir," the voice continued. "Having no son of his queen, Solindish Electra, he turned to the closest male relative: a Cheysuli halfling got on his cousin, Alix, as much a halfling as her son. But there *was* a son, you see. There *was* a son . . . a wholly Homanan son, with no trace of Cheysuli blood."

The hand stopped moving; fell away. Fearfully, the boy waited, sensing a new tension in the air even though the voice remained calm, cool, quiet.

"Twenty years ago my father found Carillon's bastard. With the Homanan woman who bore the boy, my father went to face the Mujhar, Donal himself, to ask that the line of succession be restored to its proper path. And there within the walls of Homana-Mujhar, before Council, the woman was murdered by a man loyal to the Mujhar; my father was slain as well, by Niall, then Prince of Homana." The voice broke off. The boy heard only silence, but felt the thrumming of growing impatience that radiated from the others. And then the voice went on. "That man now rules, boy, the *royal murderer,* when it should be Carollan's place. And so there are those of us who will see to it Niall is deposed in favor of Carollan: the grandson replaced by the son." The voice paused again, then renewed itself. "That is how it should be, boy . . . *that* is how it should be. How my father, Elek, wanted it, before Niall murdered him."

The boy on the stone summoned all his courage. "Keep *me,*" he said, "keep me. But let my *lir* go free."

"The *lir* is an aspect of your power," Elek's son said. "A manifestation of the wrongness that plagues this land. You are bound in life, boy—that much I know of Cheysuli . . . now you will be bound in death."

"He is so *young*—" and the boy abruptly shut his mouth, bit his lip to seal it; no more would he beg Homanans.

"He is young, and so are you," said the clover honey voice. "But if we let you grow to manhood, and him to adulthood, you will be more difficult to overcome. I do not devalue the strength of the Cheysuli, nor the dedication of your warriors. Indeed, I salute your people, boy, well and truly. How could I not? Look what they have done . . . look how cleverly they have stolen the throne in the guise of recovering what once was theirs."

"Then I will take *lir*-shape," the boy threatened, "and you will *see* what I can do—"

"Now," said Elek's son, and the man with the cub in his arms drew his knife and swiftly cut open the ruddy throat.

As warm red blood rained down, the young Cheysuli cried out. And *cried*.

"Now." And another knife flashed in the torchlight.

The man who called himself Elek's son watched as the altar drank its fill. Blood spilled over the edge of the stone and was poured against the ground. The splatter was loud in the darkness.

After a moment, he nodded. "It is time," he said calmly, "we turned to larger prey."

"*Shansu, shansu,*" Brennan whispered tenderly, soothing her silk-soft shoulder with a gentle, beguiling hand. "Be easy, *meijhana* . . . be easy. . . ."

Her flesh quivered beneath his seductive hand, as if in answer to his tone.

"*Shansu,*" he whispered softly, stroking slowly, so slowly, "no need to be afraid. I swear it. I swear it. Any oath you choose . . ." Her flesh responded again. Brennan smiled slowly, warmly, in a manner of immensely patient desire and unconscious invitation. He was, in that moment, consumed utterly by the sole purpose of seduction. "Be easy . . . *be easy—*"

But the mare was not seduced. Without warning, she exploded in a flurry of activity that indicated *her* sole purpose was to rid her back of the man who sat astride it.

Brennan clamped legs against mare in an instinctive bid to maintain his seat. He had buckled on a Cheysuli saddle, lighter and less confining than Homanan gear, but also offering less latitude for error. With the mare in open revolt, the Cheysuli saddle—little more than a shallow pad of leather and sheepskin with wooden stirrups attached by strips of leather—was next to useless as a means of staying aboard.

The mare, gray as smoke, ducked delicate head between equally delicate forelegs and squealed in a decidedly unladylike fashion. Dark eyes rolled. Tipped ears flattened. Deceptively powerful rear legs elevated silken hindquarters like a ballista hurling a stone.

Brennan, flopped forward against his will, tried to scramble backward as she threw her head up, flinging it rearward. Pale mane whipped yellow eyes, bringing royal tears; by an inch only, Brennan missed having his nose smashed against his face, forever altering aristocratic good looks. As it was, a series of bone-jarring bucks served to twist his spine alarmingly, threatening to cripple him.

Dimly, he heard the clatter of hooves on stone, the grunts of equine rage, the shouts of running men as he tried to weather the storm. The squat buildings of the stableyard, built of the same rose-red stone that gave Homana-Mujhar its pastel patina, performed a dance of their own. He saw only bits and pieces of the curtain wall, the sentry-walk, the beamwork of stable roofs. Straw cushioned the yard, and dirt, but cobbles lay beneath both. Hard stone cobbles, promising a painful landing. He had seen it happen to others.

The mare sucked in another great breath and leaped sideways, lurched backward, lunged forward yet again. She wanted to run, but the snaffle in her mouth—for all its relative gentleness—prevented her; that, and Brennan's skilled grip upon the reins. It was a deadly dance: infuriated horse against determined warrior.

We each of us have too much to lose, Brennan thought briefly, as he lasted another of the mare's spine-twisting bucks. *Pride, too much pride . . . hers will be tarnished if I win, mine if she does—*

And abruptly, Brennan won. The mare stopped fighting the bit, the reins, the hands. She sidled uneasily a moment, first to the right, then to the left, scraping hooves against cobbles, and then quieted, snorting, long-lashed eyes half-shut as if to acknowledge defeat.

But Brennan, not daring to move as the mare slowly settled, knew better. It was too soon to trust the gray.

She shook her head. Swished her flax-pale tail. Snorted. Eyed the men gathered in the stableyard. Brennan could feel the mare's debate: *Do I throw the man now, or later?*

Later. As Brennan urged her gently into a walk, she circled the yard quietly.

Round and round. The buildings blurred together as the circling continued. With each revolution the mare grew calmer, more relaxed, and so did Brennan. He was aware of the eyes watching him and the gray, waiting for something to happen. Curious, expectant eyes, brown and blue and black, all of them, save for the single pair of green ones.

Maeve. She stood in the stableyard amid the grooms and sweepers and lads, clad in blue woolen skirts, close-fitting leather tabard belted snug, and soft house boots.

Carefully, he eased the mare in his sister's direction. With gentle persuasion, the gray tapped delicately across the cobbles and halted. Brennan looked down on Maeve, whose brass-bright hair, loosely braided, shone brilliantly in the sunlight. "Aye?"

She smiled, thumbs hooked into her belt in a distinctive imitation of Brennan's habitual stance. "I was sent to give you your freedom."

"Freedom?" He brightened. "*Jehan* sent you?"

"Aye." Maeve did not use the Old Tongue except on rare occasions. "He said I was to tell you he has rescinded his orders against you working your horses." She grinned. "Probably because he looked out a casement and saw you doing it anyway."

Brennan scowled. "This is not precisely *working*—at least, not when one trains a racing string. This was little more than making certain I would not be killed when *jehan* finally said I *could* start working them again." He sighed. "Thank the gods he has come to his senses . . . it has been four weeks since I *touched* any of them, let alone ridden them, and you just saw the result yourself. Now perhaps I can set my racing string back into order and begin winning again."

Blond brows rose. "I thought races were Hart's purvue."

"Wagering on races is," Brennan agreed. "Racing for purses is different. I do not bet. I ride." His face was grim; Hart had been gone a month, and the separation made Brennan irritable. "Gods, if only I could go to Clankeep—" He broke off and looked down at Maeve sharply. "I *will* go. I should have gone before. Even *jehan* cannot deny me a part of my heritage."

"No," Maeve agreed calmly. "Keely wondered how long it would take you to realize that."

Heat rose in his face. *Leave it to Keely*— "Aye, well, now I have. And so I go. The mare needs work." As if in answer the mare stirred; Brennan leaned forward to stroke the glossy smoke-pale neck. "*Shansu, shansu . . .*" He straightened as she settled once more. "Come with me, Maeve. How long has it been? A month? Two? Too *long*, whatever the length of time; you used to go all the time."

His sister's expression was curiously arrested, as if his suggestion and accompanying question had caught her entirely off guard. Then she twisted her mouth briefly, hiding most of her emotions behind a carefully blanked face, but Brennan saw the glint of something in her eyes. Regret? Resentment? Fear? He could not be certain, even as she answered.

"No, no—I think not," she said easily. "There is much here for me to do."

Brennan heard an underlying note of tension in her tone. He reacted accordingly, as he did without fail where Maeve was concerned. "What has Keely been saying?"

"Keely?" Maeve frowned briefly, then shook her head. "Oh, *no,* no, not Keely. 'Twas—" And abruptly, she snapped her mouth shut. "No more of it, Brennan. I'll be staying here."

"'What is so pressing that you willingly forgo a visit to Clankeep?" he asked in bafflement. "You used to nag me to go with you all the time."

"The tapestry," Maeve answered at once, too quickly. "The tapestry of lions my mother has begun. I promised I would help."

"Tapestry?" Brennan shrugged, bemused. "Maeve, I am sorry— "

"No, no, I do not expect you to know anything about it. It is a woman's thing, why would you? But, well . . . it will be beautiful, and glorious, and a thing our descendants will prize forever. . . ." She paused as her words trailed off and frowned a little, as if troubled by the faint forlorn note in her voice, then self-consciously tucked a loose strand of bright hair behind one ear. " 'Tis a thing of pride, Brennan, in race, heritage, tradition . . . a history woven of all the bright colors of our people: Cheysuli, Homanan, Solindish, Erinnish—"

Maeve stopped short, seemingly lacking the proper words. Brennan saw the turmoil in her face. And then, more quietly, controlled again, she went on. But he knew the lightness of her tone was little more than a well-practiced facade. "Well, 'tis a thing of magnificence, and I thought perhaps I should help. 'Tis nothing of the magic in me, but the pride is there regardless."

The mare tapped one hoof against a loose cobble. It rolled, clinking faintly; the mare bobbed her head and snorted down delicate, velvet nostrils. Brennan, tightening reins slightly in automatic response, looked down on his older sister and regretted more than ever that she had none of the gifts of their race. With them so evident in Keely, who took such great pride in her Old Blood that tact was nonexistent, it was harder than ever for Maeve to deal with her lack.

Perhaps if she did not live in a palace full of Cheysuli kin— But he let the thought die away. It would be no better at Clankeep, where only Cheysuli dwelled.

Brennan sighed. "Well enough, Maeve. Stay here and help Deirdre with her tapestry of lions. But I think you are a fool to turn your back on your heritage, no matter what the reason."

Brilliant color suddenly flamed in her face. "What would *you* know of it?" she cried. "You with your *lir* and your gold and your yellow eyes—you with honorable welcome wherever you go—" Maeve clapped hands over her mouth as the hectic color drained out of her face and left it strained and pallid. "Gods," she blurted, "I did not mean to say that. Oh, Brennan, you know I do not mean it. Not for you. Never—" And she turned so abruptly, skirts swirling, that she startled the mare into a sideways leap that nearly unseated Brennan.

By the time he had recovered his balance and had the mare settled again, Maeve was gone. He saw startled eyes and perfectly blank faces, knowing each stable lad busily tried to name what ailed the Mujhar's daughter. He would give them more to talk about if he hastened after Maeve. And so he did not. He soothed the mare carefully, summoned Sleeta through the link, and rode out of Homana-Mujhar.

But not without worrying.

Two

Home. The word reverberated through the link from
Sleeta to Brennan clearly. Equally clear was the big cat's
satisfaction and pleasure as she lashed her tail to and fro
and rubbed her jaw against his kneecap. *Home, lir . . . at
last.*

He had tethered the gray mare at the indigo pavilion
the Mujhar claimed, as Brennan had none of his own.
For a moment, he lost himself in the sensations of being
in Clankeep again, surrounded by folk who felt as he did,
thought as he did, believed as he did. In Mujhara, things
were different. There he was a prince, the heir to the
Lion Throne, and that knowledge altered perceptions of
him. Here he was nothing more than a fellow warrior,
though that was more than enough.

Pavilions surrounded them, huddled in clusters of dyed
and painted hides stretched over poles. Nearby a flank of
the gray granite wall curved its way through the wood,
bedecked in its ivy-and-lichen cloak. Smoke from cookfires
drifted, tendrils rising to catch on tree limbs, tangling,
like skeins of yarn; once freed, the tendrils were torn
into the hint of a haze that drifted on the breeze. Brennan smelled roasting venison, boar; the tang of honey
brew. His mouth watered in response.

Home. To Sleeta—to any *lir* perhaps—it was the closest thing to a home any of them claimed. And yet Brennan knew a brief inward stab of guilt. Clankeep was not
home to him. It was a place of dreams, of his past and his
future, the womb of his race, the security of his kin, and

yet it was not quite a home, because he had not made it so.

You could, Sleeta said. *It is not too late. There is much time for you to reacquaint yourself with our heritage.*

She was warmth engulfing his leg, one sleek shoulder pressed against a legging-clad knee. He could sense her anticipation singing through the link, nearly drowning him. If it pleased Sleeta so much, he would not deny himself the chance to spend time in his people's place.

Home, Sleeta purred.

"Well," said a quiet voice behind them, "which of the royal get *is* it? Corin? No—the color is wrong. Hart, perhaps—no, no, as you turn I see your eyes are yellow, not blue. Well, then, it must be—Brennan?" The tone was eloquently ironic, and yet it lacked the note of friendly raillery someone else might have used to underscore the words, if only to make certain Brennan understood it was a jest. "I see any of you so rarely, it is difficult to know which princeling is which."

Brennan knew better than to laugh or smile or clap the speaker on the back, accepting the jest in good-natured competition. Because the speaker was Teirnan, his cousin, and Teir's irony—as well as the competition—was meant in deadly earnest, if cloaked in velvet instead of steel.

Brennan sighed, turning to face his cousin, and heard Sleeta's low-pitched, throaty growl. Teirnan was without his *lir*, so the hostility was clearly directed at him, not at the small-eyed boar Sleeta abhorred. And Teirnan knew it.

His mocking smile altered, but only briefly. He made a rude gesture of dismissal that Sleeta ignored, as he knew she would, but he followed the ritual all the same. Sleeta hunched down, tail thumping the beaten ground, and stared at him out of implacable golden eyes. Watching. Waiting. As if she counted the hours until she could kill him with impunity.

Brennan drew in a weary breath. The confrontation was only the latest in a long series. "Teir—"

"What is it this time, cousin?" Teirnan forbore the Old Tongue, as if to emphasize Brennan's frequent separation from the clan. "Do you require additional assurances that you are indeed the man intended for the Lion?"

"No. *You* require those," Brennan said bluntly. "Teir, are you still convinced that you would do better than I? I thought the last time I came, when the *shar tahl* spoke to us both, we settled all this nonsense of bloodlines and legacies."

"I am no more convinced you should inherit than you believe *I* should," Teir answered flatly. "Why should I be? *Shar tahl* aside, facts are facts: I claim all of the rootstock bloodlines you do, but mine are untouched by Solindish or Atvian taint. There is Old Blood in me, and Cheysuli blood, and Homanan. Enough, I think, to fulfill that part of the prophecy pertaining to proper heritage."

"I think not," Brennan said gently. "Solindish and Atvian *taint* notwithstanding, it is required." Gritting his teeth, he managed to smile with infinite patience, though he was fast losing his share. "We have been through this time and time again, Teir—even when we were children! Look to the clan for your legacy. The Lion will be mine."

"My *jehan* says—"

"Your *jehan* is an empty, embittered man," Brennan declared shortly, forgoing his usual tact. "Ceinn worked against my *jehan* just as you work against me, and all out of a perverse desire to be someone he is not meant to be. Since he no longer has the option of thwarting my *jehan* through a disbanded group of Cheysuli zealots, he uses you. He twists you, Teir, like a green willow bough. And one day you will break."

"Disbanded, are we?" Teir retorted. "I think not, cousin. I think the *a'saii* live again!"

Brennan stared at him in astonishment. He thought first to charge Teirnan with a bluff, but Teir's tone was too thick with triumph, too assured. His pupils had shrunk so that his eyes were mostly yellow, intently cunning and feral as a wolf's; Brennan knew better than to discount him or his words. Not in something this important; something that could have an incredible impact upon the future of Homana.

Slowly, Brennan was able to pass words through the constriction of shock and growing anger in his throat. "You *ku'reshtin*," he said softly, "do you mean to say there are Cheysuli who work to bring down the prophecy?"

"Not bring it down. Serve it." Teir's face was shaped much like Brennan's, reflecting shared ancestry, but his bones were a trifle sharper, more predatory; his flesh was more accustomed to settling itself into expressions of calculation and ambition than anything more sanguine. "Only a fool foments rebellion out of simple greed," Teir said quietly. "My *jehan* and the *a'saii* desired Ian to hold the Lion. They still do—Ian lacks the Solindish and Atvian taint—but there is no more hope that he would assume the throne if the Mujhar were slain. So I tell you this, in preparation: we intend no harm to befall Niall *or* his sons, any of them, or his daughters, even his bastard girl." Something flickered faintly in his eyes, was gone. "Without bloodshed, we intend to take the Lion and give it over to the warrior whose blood best deserves to rule."

"Without bloodshed." Brennan wanted to spit. "Do you think any of us would politely step aside and let you have the Lion?"

"Aye," Teir said, "if Clan Council told you to."

"Clan Council—" Brennan stared. "Have you gone mad? Cheysuli Clan Council *supports* our right to rule!"

"Only so long as the members believe that right is yours," Teirnan said. "But if they no longer believed it, cousin, and bestowed that right upon another branch of the bloodline, what *would* you do? Fight? Become kinslayer in the name of greed and power?" Teir's voice was steady and quiet, lacking the fanaticism Brennan might have expected. In its place was a calm matter-of-factness as he spelled out the consequences of such an action. "You would divide the world, *cousin*, and make it a place of two races yet again. Cheysuli. Homanan. Set again at each other's throats."

"The Homanans would have nothing to do with it,"

Brennan threw back. "This is a thing between Cheysuli factions—"

"Is it?" Teir smiled. "So easily you dismiss the very people you intend to rule. Have you forgotten how we are outnumbered? We always were, always have been—and Strahan's Ihlini plague twenty years ago stole half our numbers again. It leaves the Homanans with a vast superiority, cousin. If we took to fighting for the Lion in the name of the prophecy, what is there to stop the Homanans from declaring a new *qu'mahlin* and stealing it back for themselves? Would you risk that?"

"Would *you?*" Brennan was so angry he wanted to knock Teirnan's teeth down his throat and make him choke on them. "If you throw down my *jehan*—even if you *set him aside* through action of Cheysuli Clan Council—you destroy the prophecy. You leave the Lion to the Ihlini."

Teirnan's eyes narrowed. "At this moment, we are less concerned with the Ihlini than with the proper disposition of the throne. Strahan has been in hiding for a very long time. Who is to say he is not dead?"

"Who is to say he *is?*" Brennan tried to steady his voice. "If you begin to discount the Ihlini, *cousin*, you are no warrior at all, but a fool. A *dead* fool; at least I will not have to concern myself with what idiocy you may yet attempt."

"You had best concern yourself with your future without a title," Teirnan retorted. "No more Prince of Homana. Just a man, like any other."

"Walk softly," Brennan warned. "You soil your own leathers with such words; we are cousins, Teir, and I am as Cheysuli as you. I am not 'like any other,' and never will be." He smiled as Sleeta rose, stretched, sat down to rest a part of her bulk against his left leg. " 'Just a man'? I think not. Not while I claim a *lir*."

Teirnan looked at the cat. Briefly hostility and acknowledgment warred in his face. And then he masked himself again, all civility. "I mean you no harm," he said. "We are bloodkin and more, being children of the gods, but you must understand that it is only a matter of time. While Niall sits on the Lion parceling out his children to this realm and to that, dividing Homana's strength, there are those who will come to see there are better ways of serving the Lion. Of serving the prophecy."

"You serve your own ambition," Brennan answered curtly. "Oh, I have no doubt there are others like you, desiring a change no matter what the consequences—there are always those who thrive on discontent—but you are in the minority."

"This year, aye," Teirnan agreed. "And probably next. But what of the year after that? Or the next after that?" He smiled. "The *a'saii* are very patient. That is the nature of our race."

And always had been. Brennan knew his history well enough: the Cheysuli, warrior-born and bred, were nonetheless cognizant of how carefully considered, meticulous change was used for the betterment of a realm. Once his people had given up their claim on the Lion to the very Homanans who feared them, because they wanted no civil war. And when Shaine's royal purge had nearly destroyed the race, the Cheysuli quietly, patiently waited out the *qu'mahlin* until Carillon united his newly-won realm. Slowly, so slowly the Old Blood emerged again, and was mixed with Homanan, Solindish, Atvian. The prophecy was nearly complete.

And now it was threatened again. From within as well as without.

"You are a fool." He spoke without heat, knowing only that he could not allow Teir to comprehend how very real was the threat of the *a'saii*. "A fool, and if I could do it, I would spill from my veins the blood that makes us kin until I was free of you."

"Would you?" Teirnan smiled. "And what would Maeve say, to lose me yet again?"

A chill washed through Brennan, followed by the heat of anger. "Maeve has nothing to do with this!"

"Does she not?" Teirnan laughed. "I thought she did. I thought you *knew*—"

"Knew *what*?"

"That the last time she came to Clankeep, she agreed to become my *meijha.*"

Impelled by rage, Brennan moved before Teirnan could. He was conscious only of clamping his hands around his cousin's throat and driving him to the ground, where he nearly crushed the fine bones beneath the flesh so like his own. *Ku'reshtin—*"

"Ask her!" Teirnan rasped through Brennan's assault. "*Ask* her, cousin! Do you think she would lie to *you?*"

Brennan pressed him against the ground. "She would never—she would *never*—not with you—not with such as *you—*"

"Ask her," Teirnan challenged. "But also ask her why she will not come to Clankeep. Ask her why she will not honor her vow."

"If she made one—*if* she made one—I will release her from it—I will *release* her from it—"

"Freely made—" Teirnan struggled, but fading breath robbed him of his strength. "—freely made, Brennan, and only she can break it. Only Maeve, or me. And I would never do it."

"Why not?" Brennan demanded.

"Because you want me to." Teirnan's laugh was torn from a badly bruised throat. "She never will. She is too honorable to do it. I am not. For a good enough reason, I will. But—for now it serves me . . . it serves me to see how angry and helpless you are—"

"By the gods—" Brennan choked. "By the gods, I swear if you ever harm her, by word or by deed, I will soil my hands with your blood. Kinslayer you may make me, but that is a burden I would gladly bear for the sake of my *rujholla—*"

"Bastard," Teirnan mocked. "The Homanans call her bastard."

Lir. It was Sleeta, quietly intruding. *Lir, if you mean to do it, do it. If you do not, then let him go. Do not be irresolute.*

You would like me to slay him, he said. *I can tell.*

No. But the tone was distinctly reluctant. *If you slay*

him, you take on the responsibility of a fool. And you deserve better than that.

Inwardly Brennan laughed, though it had little of humor in it. And then he released Teirnan and rose to stare down at the gasping warrior. "This will be settled," he said. "This thing between you and me and Maeve. It will be settled for all to know, regardless of the outcome."

Teirnan levered himself up on one elbow. "Ask her," he whispered. "Ask her if she was unwilling. Ask her if she was forced, when she came into my bed."

It cost Brennan dearly to shrug indifferently. "If she was," he said, "you are dead."

As Teirnan glared up at him from the ground, Brennan turned to fetch the mare, who fidgeted by the pavilion. *Sleeta,* he said, *we go home.*

The cat did not protest against leaving her own so soon. The cat said nothing at all.

Three

At sunset, the gray threw Brennan near the outskirts of Mujhara and left him to lie in the dirt, half-stunned, as she galloped toward the city. After a moment he sat up, spat out blood from a bitten lip, stared after her dazedly and cursed, if none too fluently; his tongue was also bitten.

Your fault. Sleeta sat not far away, tail curled fastidiously around one raven haunch. The tip flicked once, twice, was still. *You were paying more attention to your cousin's words and not enough to the mare.*

Brennan scowled and glared after the mare, massaging a sore shoulder. He did not look at the cat.

After a moment she flicked an ear. *Are you damaged?*

After a lengthier moment: "No." Grudgingly.

Embarrassed, then.

"Aye," he agreed morosely, staring toward the city that now hid the offending mare. From here he could not see the walls, for Mujhara had grown so much that the city proper—that portion that lay within the walls—had been swallowed by other dwellings huddling about the fringes, cluster upon cluster, until the new had nearly overtaken the old.

Well, what did you expect? She is horse, not lir. She has no understanding of such things as dignity and protocol.

Brennan slanted the mountain cat a glance of disgust mingled with amusement. Trust Sleeta to put things in perspective, though hers was often quite different from the views of others.

"Aye, well, she will have learned such understanding. When I am done with her."

If she goes back to Homana Mujhar.

That brought a frown. "Aye. She would be worth stealing."

But only if she can be caught first, Sleeta pointed out. *How many have your patience, your skill, your gentleness—*

Enough, he sent through the link, unable to suppress his laughter. *Enough, Sleeta—I know what you do. But I assure you, the only damage I have suffered is to my pride, and that will recover soon enough.*

Not if the Prince of Homana is discovered wallowing in the dust with a dirty, bloodied face.

That brought him to his feet faster than anything else, if a trifle painfully. He dusted leggings, straightened jerkin, attempted to clean his face, dabbled blood from his split lip, tried to ignore the sore shoulder, and sighed. "Prince or no, I deserved this. I know better than to trust the gray; still, Teir gave me cause to be distracted. That *ku'reshtin* . . ." Anger renewed itself. "If he *ever* harms Maeve—"

Sleeta sought to placate. *I think he would not be so foolish. Aside from you, there are other rujholli involved.*

"Aye. But one is gone to Solinde, the other to Atvia." A wave of loneliness suddenly swamped him. "Oh, gods, *lir*—without Hart I am half a man, and so alone—"

You have me.

He looked at her. She sat primly in the dirt, eyes half slitted against the setting sun. Outwardly she seemed unperturbed, but within the link he sensed her readiness. Sleeta waited for something.

Brennan smiled. "Aye. I have you. More than any man might ask for, even of the gods."

The tail flicked once; he had said what she wanted to hear. *Of course. I am Sleeta.*

Laughing, he thrust a hand into the firm plushness of her pelt and stroked her large, wedge-shaped head, losing himself in the silken velvet of her coat. He was a man for women above all things, but even a wondrously pleasing bedpartner could not fill him with such infinite satisfaction as his magnificent *lir*.

He sighed and tugged an upright ear. "Ah, Sleeta, what would I do without you. . . ?"

The mountain cat merely purred, as if the answer were implicit.

Brennan slapped one raven shoulder. "Onward, *lir*. Sitting out here will get us no closer to the palace. And I am hungry—it has been hours since I ate, and it is nearly time for dinner."

Sleeta licked one paw clean of dust, rose, stretched, padded toward the outskirts. Brennan matched his pace to hers.

The boots he wore were eminently unsuitable for walking any great distance, Brennan discovered quickly, particularly when one was already stiff and sore from an awkward enforced dismount. Hungry, footsore and decidedly out of temper, Brennan paused in one of the winding streets—now ablaze from new-lit torches—and bent to tug the offending folds out of his left boot. They were his favorite footgear for working horses, but only when he was *in* the saddle, not out of it. Already he had blisters.

You might have gone in lir-shape, Sleeta commented.

Brennan, braced against the wall of the nearest building, nodded briefly at the greeting of a passer-by. *Not within the city. You know Homanans never can tell the difference between lir and animals of the wild—likely they would slay us both before thinking to ask if we were human or animal.*

Sleeta was a blotch of darkness in the shadows, though the torchlight set the gloss of her coat agleam. She blinked, implacable as ever; though the link offered each of them an uncanny, unfettered means of communication, even to sensing emotions quite clearly, there were times Sleeta was shuttered against him. For all she was utterly devoted to him, she was also a very private animal

Brennan pressed a hand against his belly. "If I do not eat soon . . ."

Then eat, Sleeta suggested practically. *I am not one to deny my lir a meal when he is clearly so close to wasting away.*

Brennan grunted. It would take more than missing two meals to strip flesh from his frame. He lacked some of his father's sheer bulk, perhaps, but none of the height the Cheysuli habitually claimed, or the musculature. He was clearly a warrior: fit, firm, physically well-suited to the lifestyle of his fellow Cheysuli. But Brennan thought some of it came from frequent arms-practice and daily sessions with his horses in addition to simple bone and blood inheritance; Hart, so very much like him, generally appeared a trifle softer, though not precisely *soft.* And Corin—shorter, slighter than either of them—was built much more compactly.

A warbow, Brennan thought. *Hart and I are Homanan swords, long and lethal, while Corin's power is hidden in subtlety.*

A vision of his brothers rose before him and hung in the air as if to taunt him, to strip bare the thin skin hiding his loneliness. Hart, his other self, was now in Solinde; only the gods knew how he would hold his own in the land of the enemy. He would probably wager his life on it. And Corin, quick-tempered, quick-tongued Corin, would undoubtedly embroil himself in difficulties of his own unique design, in Erinn and Atvia.

"Erinn." Brennan spoke aloud. "Gods, Sleeta—Aileen will soon be on her way!"

"What did you say?"

For a moment Brennan thought he had gone mad; he could swear the cat had spoken aloud. And then he realized the question was from the young woman pausing by his side. She was wrapped in a thin dark cloak, but the hood slid from her head to display plaited black hair, glossy as Sleeta's pelt, and he saw a face he could not place at once, though he knew he had seen it before.

"No," he said, "I spoke to my *lir.*" He gestured to Sleeta, and saw the young woman's eyes widen as she looked at him more closely.

"You!" she said in surprise. "Oh—my lord—" And

she dropped into an awkward curtsy that puddled skirts and cloak in the dust of the cobbled street.

Startled by the unexpected homage, all Brennan could do was stare. And then as her upturned face was made clear by the torchlight, he recognized her.

"The girl from The Rampant Lion!" He reached down, caught a hand, pulled her up. "There is no need for that. . . ." He paused, though he did not release her hand. "Forgive me, *meijhana*, I have forgotten your name."

Her hand was cold in his. "Rhiannon," she answered softly. "Oh, my lord, I have dreamed—" Abruptly she broke off, snatching her hand out of his and yanking the hood up to hide most of her face. "I am sorry—I must go."

"Rhiannon—wait!" He caught a fold of her cloak to gainsay her, felt the thin cloth tear and cursed himself for being such a heavy-handed fool. He could well afford to buy her a hundred cloaks—and better ones than this—to replace the one he had torn, but he understood something of pride. The look in her eyes told him she had a fair share of what he himself claimed.

"I must go, my lord." She said nothing of the cloak that now gaped at her shoulder, where the hood had parted from the rest. "If I am late . . ."

"Then I will come with you, and if you are late because of me, I think the tavern-keeper will hold his tongue." He smiled at her and tried to pull the torn pieces of cloth together. "Have you food at The Rampant Lion?"

"Of course, my lord—though none so fine as you are accustomed to." She stood very still as he resettled the cloak. She did not look at him, keeping black eyes demurely averted; two gently insistent brown fingers beneath her chin drew her face up into the light where he could see it more clearly.

Something glittered against the fabric of her tunic. Brennan caught it, held it up: his ring. The sapphire set in silver he had given her in gratitude for bringing the

Mujharan Guard during the altercation with Reynald of Caledon, who had gone home weeks before.

"You want it back." She reached up to strip the thong over her head; he stopped her.

"No. No, it was freely given to you. It is yours, Rhiannon. For as long as you wish to keep it."

"As long—?" She laughed a little. "Forever, my lord. Of course."

"Of course." He grinned. "Come then, *meijhana*—or the tavern-keeper will rail at us both." And he tucked her arm into his elbow and escorted her to The Rampant Lion as if she were the finest lady of all the Mujhar's court, while Sleeta padded beside them.

It was the first time since he could remember that Brennan had crossed under the lintel branch of The Rampant Lion without one or both of his brothers. Rhiannon was lovely and sweet and struck almost speechless by the Prince of Homana's royal presence—but she was not Hart. She was not Corin. And he missed them both acutely.

The tavern, as always, enjoyed good custom, though Brennan had seen it busier. A few men huddled together at a corner table over some sort of dice game—*where is my rujho?* he wondered sadly—while others of a more solitary bent drank quietly at separate tables. Sleeta's presence among them garnered sharp looks and startled expressions, but it was no longer unheard of for a warrior and his *lir* to walk freely in Mujhara, and soon enough the men turned back to their business.

As they entered, a young man—black-haired, brown-eyed, of pleasant expression—came out from behind a curtain divider and fixed Rhiannon with a playfully displeased scowl. "Lady, lady," he chided, though without heat. "What am I to do when there are men who call for your efficient table service, and you are not here to please them?"

Color suffused her face instantly. "I—I am sorry, Jarek. I will stay late, to make up the time."

He laughed. "Aye, you will, if only to keep me company while I count the ale barrels." Jarek's good humor remained, but his smile did not quite extend to his eyes as he looked at Brennan. "Should I lay blame for your tardiness on this man?"

"You may," Brennan agreed, knowing full well—and understanding even better—why the tavern-keeper's manner bordered on unacknowledged hostility. "And rather than have Rhiannon remain later than she should, I will compensate you for her time." Fingers dipped into the plump belt-purse on his hip. "Name your price."

Jarek glanced at Sleeta, then back at Brennan. Red-faced, he smiled ruefully, shrugged, spread his hands. "What would I ask of a Cheysuli warrior save gold? But only in coin, of course; I would not presume to covet that you wear upon your arms." Still, he could not keep his eyes from the bands. "Be welcome in my tavern, warrior, and leave what you wish as a gift for Rhiannon when it comes time for your departure. That will be compensation enough."

"*Your* tavern?" Brennan took his hand away from his belt-purse. "I do not recall having seen your face before. And I am a frequent patron."

Jarek frowned a little. "Forgive me, warrior, but I do not recall *your* face. And this tavern has been mine these past six weeks."

Rhiannon's voice was quiet. "He bought it, my lord, not long after—the fight."

"Ah." Brennan shrugged. It did not please him to recall the battle with the Caledonese, since one thing had led to another, and now he was brotherless, even if only temporarily. "Well, blame me for her tardiness. I delayed her. And now—lest I perish—may I request a meal? And wine. Red wine. Fine Ellasian wine." Smiling, he moved to the closest empty table and sat down. Sleeta settled herself behind his bench and stretched out, a gleaming, breathing rug.

"At once," Jarek smiled, bowed, gestured. "Rhiannon will do the honors."

"Aye, aye, of course." Again she curtsied to Brennan,

with more grace this time, and hastened off to fetch the wine.

Jarek did not leave at once, though he watched Rhiannon depart even as Brennan did. Then he turned back, pale brown eyes assessive. He smiled; his tone was easy, carefully noncomittal, which was a story in itself. "She gives you great honor, warrior. I thought the Cheysuli did not put much weight in things such as curtsies and titles."

Brennan sensed Jarek's unspoken challenge clearly, though it lacked true hostility. Even if they were more than employer and employee, which seemed likely, Jarek no doubt knew Rhiannon would inspire much interest on the part of wealthier, high-ranking suitors. He believed his position within her regard precarious.

But Rhiannon did not strike Brennan as the sort of girl who would throw over one good man merely to stalk another with greater fortune.

"The Cheysuli do not," Brennan agreed easily. "The Homanans do. Rhiannon is Homanan, and therefore honors the title rather than the man." He smiled as Rhiannon came back with a jug of wine and a hastily-polished silver mug; he could see where she had spat upon it and rubbed it with a cloth.

"My lord," she said, filling the mug, "here is your wine—the best I could find." She glanced sidelong at Jarek. "Your private cask, Jarek, from the back of the cellar."

"*My* cask—"

"He is the Prince of Homana!" she hissed, and smiled self-consciously at Brennan. "My lord, what victuals can I bring you?"

Sipping wine, Brennan shook his head. "No matter," he answered when he had swallowed. "Fresh meat, new bread, some cheese . . . have you any fruit?"

"Raisins from Caledon," she said brightly, and then abruptly they shared the same vision: Reynald, cousin to Prince Einar, with his ruined escort around him. As one they laughed, and Jarek quickly took his leave, too quickly; his spine was stiff as iron.

Jealous, Sleeta remarked lazily from behind.

With cause, Brennan told her. *The girl is worth the jealousy.* And abruptly, thinking of Maeve trapped in Tiernan's web, he reached out and caught Rhiannon's hand before she could leave again. "*Meijhana*—" he lowered his voice to spare her embarrassment. "—is he good to you? Does he pay a fair wage? Does he have—expectations?"

She knew what the last meant clearly enough. Vivid color washed into her face, then fell away, leaving her pale and lily-fragile.

"Jarek is a good man," she said evenly. "As for expectations—aye, and why not? It *is* a good wage, and I am grateful for his generosity."

"How grateful?" he persisted. "And for how long?"

She jerked her hand away. "Why, my lord? Will you pay more? Will you keep me longer? Will you fulfill *my* expectations?"

He was aghast at her interpretation of his interest in her welfare. "Rhiannon—no. *No,* I swear, I do not ask because I want you for myself." And abruptly cursed himself; he told her the truth, but too bluntly. What woman *wanted* to hear a man did not desire her in his bed? "Wait you," he said clearly, aware of color rising in his own dark face. "I meant only to ask if he *forced* you. No more."

"Why?" Her heart-shaped face was stiffly set, but delicately proud.

He thought at first to lie for Maeve's sake, but did not. He felt Rhiannon worth the truth. "Because there are men in the world who will stoop to force a woman's will, and I would not want to see Jarek do it to you."

It took her by surprise. No doubt she had heard all manner of invitations in her employment, as well as crude suggestions; she did not expect a man to concern himself with her welfare outside of what she could do for him in bed.

"No," she said. "No, he does not force me. "It—it was wanted. . . ." She looked away from him, though her fingers crept up to touch the sapphire ring. He thought it unconsciously done. "He is a good man, Jarek, better than any other I have known."

Brennan nodded, releasing her hand. "Then I am pleased for you, *meijhana*."

"He is kind, and fair, and generous," she went on. "I am not made to work all night *and* day, like the girls in other taverns. I am given one day out of seven for myself. And all the meals I could wish for. He even gave me this—" She lifted a fold of the cloak, then blushed bright red as they both recalled how easily the cheap fabric had torn under Brennan's hand. "He is a *good man*," she declared desperately, clenching her hands in the cloak.

Brennan smiled a little. "I am convinced, *meijhana*. You are eloquent in your assertions."

"I must go," Rhiannon said in a muffled tone. "There is work to be done." Abruptly she swung to take her leave, and in doing so she knocked the winejug over. It spilled wine across the table to splatter on the floor, red as blood.

Brennan stood at once, avoiding the pungent torrent. He righted the jug even as Rhiannon tore off her ripped cloak to sop up what she could of the spillage. "Oh—*my lord*—"

"Stop fretting," he ordered firmly, seeing tears gathering in her eyes. "I am not wet, and there is more wine in the cellars. *Shansu, meijhana*—the world will turn again."

"*Clumsy,*" she said, half angrily, gathering jug and soaked cloth into her slender arms. And she was gone before he could speak again, dripping wine to mark an unintended path.

Flighty sort, commented Sleeta.

No, no, only overwhelmed by my title, Brennan explained, a trifle sadly, as he sat down again after checking his bench for wine puddles. *It happens so often, lir—too often for my taste. It seems I am never able to see the true person underneath all the awe and awkwardness.*

"My lord." It was Jarek, with a new winejug in his hands. "My lord, Rhiannon has explained her clumsiness. I beg you, spare her your anger. She is a good girl, and meant no harm."

The obsequious manner was new, ill-fitting, and unwanted. Brennan's mouth twisted in displeasure. "And do you think I want her beaten? Do you think I expect her to lose her place? It was an accident, tavern-keeper. Even if I were soaked, do you think I would want her punished?"

"How can I say, my lord?" Jarek returned stiffly. "Men who are princes often want things others might not." He jerked his head to indicate other patrons. "For a six-week now I have served the aristocracy and wealthy men of Mujhara. Do you think I have not seen all manner of retribution? Have I reason to expect you might want none taken?"

"Perhaps not," Brennan agreed coolly. "As it happens, you have no reason to expect anything of me. Except, perhaps, my custom, which The Rampant Lion has always enjoyed. Unless, of course, you choose not to serve me now."

"Do you want her?" Jarek demanded bluntly, forgoing anything approaching diplomacy or respect for a title; now they were merely men. "Do you intend to take her?"

Brennan sighed. "She named you a good man, Jarek. She named you a fair man. I am not disposed to argue it—she sounded quite convinced—but I *am* disposed to say you are a fool." He took the jug from Jarek's rigid hands and poured his mug full. "I am not in the habit of taking women from other men. Particularly if they are content where they are."

Jarek did not look away as Brennan drank. "You could offer her much more. And she is deserving of it."

Brennan drained half the mug, then set it down. "Every man and woman has a *tahlmorra,* Cheysuli and Homanan alike. If the gods intend better for her, she will have it. Otherwise, it will be none of my doing."

"She is—special." Jarek's tone was desperate. "My lord, I have no wish to lose her, not to any man . . . but I want what is best for her."

"It does you credit," Brennan told him after a moment. "But have you never thought that what is best for her may be the man she has?"

"It is *your* ring she wears around her neck."

"And your bed she warms." Brennan sat forward on the bench, resting forearms on the table. "If she wanted me in place of you, there are ways she could make it known. Ways she could make it happen." He shrugged. "She need only come to the palace and ask to see me on some pretext; I would receive her. Women have done it before. They do it every day." He held Jarek's eyes with his own. "When a man has wealth, power, rank, title— any or all—there are women who want to share it, even if for only a week, a night, an hour. They barter with their bodies in hopes of gaining favors. In hopes of gaining wealth. And some even dream of permanency." He poured more wine. "I am not celibate. I enjoy the courtship dance as much as any man. But neither am I a stud who likes the mares to force themselves upon him."

"Rhiannon—has not." Jarek's tone was harsh, strained.

"No. Do you think she ever would?"

Jarek looked away. "No. No. She is not a woman for that." He sighed heavily. "But—"

"Tend your custom, Jarek," Brennan said deliberately. "Rhiannon has need of you."

"And you?" Jarek asked.

He smiled. "I only have need of my *lir*."

Four

The food was excellent, the wine even better. Now, sated, content, drowsy, Brennan watched Rhiannon move smoothly around the common room tending Jarek's custom, and reflected that except for poor quality clothing and a certain naive innocence in her manner, the young woman could easily pass for one of Deirdre's ladies. She was well-spoken for an uneducated commoner and her courtesy was boundless, even with those men who chose to make sport of her or those who attempted to arrange a tryst. *Certainly she is lovely enough to grace Homana-Mujhar*— Abruptly he caught himself. He had pointedly told Jarek the Prince of Homana had no intentions of elevating Rhiannon out of her present circumstances, and here he was considering what it would be like. But he could not deny that he was attracted to her; for all Rhiannon's quiet, demure demeanor, he sensed she was also a passionate woman.

Who are you to contemplate bedding the girl when your Erinnish bride will soon be on her way? Sleeta asked, casually deliberate.

He sighed. *Who am I, indeed? Hypocrite, I think. Or merely befuddled by too much wine.* Brennan scrubbed his brow. *We should go home, Sleeta—there are questions I have for Maeve.*

He pushed himself up from the bench, recalled Jarek's solution to compensation for Rhiannon's tardiness, dug into his belt-purse and set a gold royal on the hardwood,

119

knowing it worth considerably more than a week's lodging and full meals.

Generous, Sleeta commented, rising to stretch all her elegant lean length in the glow of candlelight.

Worth it— He smiled as Rhiannon came to halt before him. "Jarek serves excellent wine and victuals, *meijhana*. And you provide most attractive table service."

"Oh, my lord—are you going so soon?" Color sprang up in her face, as if she felt her question too personal, or too revealing.

"I must," he told her, "but I will come again." *If my jehan allows me to*, he reflected wryly.

Slim fingers grasped the sapphire ring on the thong around her throat as her eyes locked on his, and understood what she saw there. "I—I am Jarek's woman, my lord—" She broke off, then went on, as if determined to make things very clear. "You—do understand. . . ."

"I understand." He smoothed a strand of loosened hair away from her cheek, slipping it gently behind an ear naked of adornment. "Let us be friends, then, *meijhana* . . . if you will allow it."

"*Allow it*—*!*" Rhiannon's laugh was half-swallowed. "Oh, my lord—whoever would deny you friendship?"

Brennan's smile was mocking. "My cousin," he told her wryly. "And I am assured there are others, as well." He looked past her to Jarek, watching them from beside the curtain divider. His face was a mask, but Brennan saw something in the eyes that spoke of many things a desperate man might know. "Tell Jarek I am not without honor," Brennan said. "Tell him I respect what others hold dear."

"Aye." Rhiannon nodded. "The gods go with you, my lord."

"*Cheysuli i'halla shansu*," he returned, smiling at her confusion. "A wish for Cheysuli peace."

Rhiannon nodded again, then abruptly turned away. Brennan walked out of The Rampant Lion.

He was but a street away from the gates of the palace when Sleeta growled a warning. Within the *lir*-link it was incoherent, more cat- than *lir*-like, as if the threat were something she might know in the world, and not a thing of men and women.

Brennan spun in place, hand to knife, and saw the cat crouch and hackle, ears flattened against her head. The growl issuing from her throat was a sound he had never heard from her, and it set the back of his neck to prickling.

Sleeta—

"*Lir—* That much was coherent. *Lir—lir—*

All he could think of were Ihlini.

"Sleeta—?" He backed up, pressed his spine against the nearest wall, tried to slow his racing heart. He thought of shouting—the watch could be just around the corner, and the Mujharan Guard was one twisting street over— but did not. It would have been lost in Sleeta's unnerving scream.

Dogs! It overwhelmed the link and flooded his senses with Sleeta's rage and fear. *Dogs—dogs—men—*

"Sleeta!" Her consuming emotions—visceral, primitive, little more than instinctive responses and reactions— nearly destroyed his own precarious balance. And he was in human form; if he assumed *lir*-shape he was almost certain to be overcome by Sleeta herself as well as the threat she sensed. *Lir, lir—* within the link, in hopes of reaching her—*lir, what is it? Where?*

The hounds—the hounds—

—and suddenly the hounds were on her, jaws agape . . . he could not count them all . . . grayish shapes in the darkness, legs and teeth and claws . . . baying, baying . . . biting . . . trying to take her down, trying to tear her throat—

"Now," commanded a voice. "Now, while he is distracted."

—and Brennan knew then they wanted *him*, not Sleeta, not Sleeta at all, except as a means to distract him, to turn his attention from *them*, who meant to catch him, hold him, rob him—

Or do they mean to slay me?

And all the while the hounds barked and growled and Sleeta screamed her anger and fear and hatred.

He tried to turn. He tried to defend himself. But his reflexes were curiously slowed. Only limply did his fingers clasp the knife hilt, offering no defense. Vision blurred. He cursed and thought to summon *lir*-shape regardless of Sleeta's straits, but hands fell on his arms, his wrists, his throat—fingers threaded themselves in his hair and knotted there—so much weight, so much power, all thrust against him, pressing him back against the wall.

"Sleeta—!" But hands closed his mouth, mashing lips against teeth.

—*Sleeta*—But he knew he could not touch her, could not reach her, not with all the hounds—

—failing: *Sleeta*—

"Strike him down," someone ordered. "One cat is threat enough; do you wish to contend with two?"

And he thought: *I know that voice*—

But the voice said nothing more. And if it had, he could not have heard it. With a club, they struck him down.

He did not know where he was. For one horrible moment, he did not know *who* he was; and then he knew, and recalled the attack, and realized he had not been robbed at all, or beaten, or slain. Instead, he had been *taken*.

Sleeta—?

He tried to move. Iron rattled. Darkness pressed down against his eyelids, blinding him entirely. There was no sound save his ragged breathing, and the scrape of his bootheels against the floor as his leg muscles bunched in panic.

Sleeta—?

But there was nothing within the link; no answer, no stirring within the pattern he knew as Sleeta.

Oh, gods—lir—

Nothing.

He lay flat on his back. The stone beneath him was cold, hard, unyielding. The stone around him was equally so; he was inside, then, not out. He could tell by the closeness that weighed him down, the faint echo of the iron as it chimed. Cuffed at wrists and ankles, all he could do was stare blindly at what he might name a roof, had he the light to see it.

"Sleeeetaaa—" The word was a sibilant hiss in a tone akin to panic.

There was nothing in return. No sound. No stirring in the *lir*-link.

Panic took his wits. He surged upward against the iron, trying to break cuffs and chain; fell back again when he thought his head might burst. Pain threatened to blind him, except he was blind already. His belly cramped, tried to spew out all the food and wine he had consumed at The Rampant Lion; would have, had he not clamped throat and teeth against it.

"*Lion* . . ." The gasp whispered in the darkness, running along the stone.

Jarek. *His* voice had given the order. Had he been so insanely jealous as to order his rival imprisoned?

Brennan bit back a groan. The blow had split open the flesh of his forehead and nearly cracked his skull. Even thinking of movement made his belly squirm.

Sleeta?

Again, the appeal went unanswered.

Oh, gods—not my lir . . . oh, gods, I beg you, let her be alive. . . . And he realized, to his surprise, the petition was born not of fear for his own death, but because he could not comprehend what the world would be like without Sleeta. She deserved to survive, even if he could not.

No light. Only darkness, and stone, and the weight of an unknown future.

Blood rolled into one eye, the right; his spasmodic lunge against iron had opened the wound again.

Spare my lir, he begged—

—and slipped again into nothingness.

He awakened shouting. The words he did not know, being little more than gibberish; he shouted, he *shouted,* and the sounds bounced back from the stone and beat against his ears.

He stank of his own sweat. And he knew the smell.
The stench filled up his nose and he knew it, he *knew* it,
recalling how once before he had been trapped, trapped
and completely terrified, so utterly *terrified* he had
screamed and cried and soiled himself, beating boy's
hands against naked walls—

*—the lir. All the lir, with beaks agape and claws un-
sheathed, all of them, beating wings against the air, against
his head, his face, his eyes—all of them trying to throw
him into the oubliette, the Womb of the Earth—to throw
him down and down and down, until he died of fear
alone, because everyone knew there was no bottom—*

Gods, he was afraid.

*—lir and lir and lir, shrouded in shadow, cloaked in
secrecy—he heard them . . . he knew they were there,
each and every one of them, speaking to one another,
telling one another he was not fit to be the Mujhar's son
because he was afraid, and Cheysuli feared nothing—*

But *this* Cheysuli did.

—so afraid, as the walls closed in. So AFRAID—

The memory washed up from the blackest depths of
Brennan's inner self, battering at his awareness until it
broke through to crash upon the cliffs of consciousness,
and he remembered it all. Once, and once only, he had
been enclosed as he was now, against his will, made
helpless. There had been no iron, no purposeful imprisonment, but the result had been the same. The *fear* had
been the same.

Then, there had been no *lir;* he was just a boy. Now,
there was no *lir;* Sleeta could not be found.

He caught his breath on something very much like a
sob. With no light, no world, no freedom, no *lir,* he
would surely go mad.

—so much weight—

Sinews stood up in ridges, twisting beneath his flesh.
Again and again he jerked limbs against the iron, until
his wrists ran wet with blood.

—out—out—OUT—

"*Sleeta—!*" he shouted, and the sound came back to
engulf him. To swallow him whole again.

* * *

Later, when he came back to himself: "—afraid." The voice was smooth as clover honey, but honestly surprised. "*Look* at him, Rhiannon!"

Brennan did not move, did not speak, did not open his eyes to look. He lay in absolute stillness, tensed and rigid, in iron manacles and blood, and thought himself gone quite mad.

It could not possibly be Rhiannon—

"You struck him too hard," she said.

Let it not be Rhiannon— And yet he knew it was.

"It needed doing," Jarek answered. "But that has nothing to do with *this*. He is terrified."

"Too hard," Rhiannon repeated. "You have knocked him out of his head."

—oh, gods, no—

Jarek's tone was thoughtful. "I have heard of it before, once or twice . . . a fear of being enclosed. But—in a Cheysuli warrior?"

"They are as human as the next man," she said sharply. "Do you think him a sorcerer? He is just a man."

"*Shapechanger*, Rhiannon. And—as the zealots would have it—pretender to the throne."

Rhiannon did not answer.

Lir—? he asked; he begged.

"He will be fit enough for the sacrifice," Jarek said. "Whether he is in his head or no, the gods will not care. Give them blood: they are content."

Brennan struggled to understand. *Pretender to the throne?*

"And you?" she asked. "Will *you* be content to know you have slain the Prince of Homana?"

"If it serves," Jarek answered, "and it will. Oh, it will."

"There are two other sons. The Mujhar is rich in sons."

Thinking: *I have been a fool—the woman has made me a fool*—

Jarek: "And poor when all are slain." Movement. The clink of iron links as Jarek tested the bonds. "Not so soft

a bed, is it? Cold, hard stone . . . iron for the bedclothes
. . ." He laughed. "What was it he called you?—*meijhana?*
Perhaps a bedding name . . . a sweet Cheysuli love-name."

"It means 'lovely one,' " Rhiannon said; then, laughing: "Do you know none of their Old Tongue? You,
Jarek, who claim to know them so well? Even *I* know a
little."

And I know less than nothing— Within the link, Brennan sent again to Sleeta. *Lir—lir—where are you?*

But nothing answered him.

"Go, Rhiannon. There are things to be said that do
not require your presence."

"No?" Her tone was bitter. "Are you done with me,
then, now that I have served your cause?"

"We may find use for you again," he said smoothly.
"Now go."

"He is in pain, Jarek. You struck him too hard."

"By this time tomorrow, he will never know pain again.
Now, *go.*" Movement. The susurration of cloth; bodies
moving. And then Jarek spoke again. "Well, my lord
prince, do you intend to pretend senselessness forever?
Have you no questions to ask?"

Brennan opened his eyes. A dish of oil with a twist of
wick filled his prison with smoky light. He saw squat
stone walls, very low, and a half-doorway barely large
enough to admit a man hunched over, with runes carved
around the opening. He had seen a similar place once
before, much younger, when the *shar tahl* had carefully
tutored the Mujhar's sons in clan history. He frowned,
then banished it at once as the expression pulled at the
wound in his hairline.

And then he knew. A cell. The sort of cell a priest
inhabited, not prisoner. But the runes around the low
door were Old Tongue, not Homanan; this place, then,
was of the Firstborn, and very old. Now freely profaned
by Homanan zealots.

Questions, Jarek had said. Oh, aye, he had one: *"Why?"*

Jarek nodded. "A good beginning, my lord." He shifted
his position, moving from a squat into a kneeling posture, and Brennan saw past him to the doorway. Seated

just outside was a Homanan, clearly on guard even with Jarek present. They took no chances. "There are many answers. One is that Cheysuli are demons and must be returned through death to the netherworld of Asar-Suti, from whence they issued." He smiled as his overdramatized voice echoed faintly. "Another is that the old gods of Homana have turned their eyes from us, requiring blood sacrifice to restore their favor." Jarek's grunt of laughter mocked the statement. "And yet a third requires the—*reduction*—of those now close to the throne, to make way for the rightful ruler." He glanced briefly toward the guard.

Brennan's head pounded. But for the moment astonishment kept the fear of enclosure at bay. "Have you gone mad? I can refute each of those ridiculous reasons!"

"Can you? The first two, perhaps—I no more believe you are a demon than I am myself, and the old gods perished long ago—but I do subscribe to the final reason for your assassination, my lord." The guttering flames from the oil lamp scribed shadows in Jarek's face. "I personally have nothing against your race. Cheysuli have as much right to live in this land as Homanans do, but—"

"Then *why*—"

"Why?" Jarek's tone was intent. "Because through a miscarriage of a twisted prophecy and the blind acquiescence of Homanans overcome by Carillon's legend, Cheysuli now hold the Lion Throne. And *that*, my lord Prince of Homana, is why you—and others of your kin—must die."

Brennan stared at him. "You *have* gone mad!"

"No," Jarek's demeanor remained unruffled. "There is a man in the world much better suited to rule Homana than your father."

"*I* have gone mad," Brennan muttered in disbelief. "This is nothing but a nightmare—"

Jarek merely smiled. His expression was oddly bland, as if he enjoyed giving nothing away except what he chose, and for specific reasons.

And suddenly, with ice-cold clarity, Brennan recalled

his cousin. "You are Cheysuli—?" It was question, statement and accusation all at once.

Jarek's brows jerked upward; something flickered briefly in pale eyes, then disappeared. He laughed. "Do I *look* Cheysuli, my lord?"

In the distorted shadows, his face was alien, full of planes and hollows. He was black-haired but brown-eyed, a pale ale brown; in poor light, around the rims, almost a yellow-gold. And though his skintones lacked the sunbronzing characteristic of most Cheysuli, so did Corin and Keely.

"Cheysuli," Brennan said, shivering once in shock, "and in league with Teirnan, with the *a'saii*—" He looked at the man waiting just outside the low door. "You use the Homanan zealots to mislead any who might work against you, who might suspect what you are doing. . . ." Iron chimed. "Everyone knows the story of Elek's murder—how he supposedly died by the hand of the Prince of Homana . . . and you use it. You use it and other lies to twist the trust, to twist the prophecy—you use the Homanan zealots to throw down the rightful House and replace it with your own."

"Do we?" Jarek shrugged. "No, my lord. I am in league only with those who believe Carillon bequeathed us a better living legacy than the one who now holds the Lion."

"*Living* legacy—" Brennan went very still. "Then if you are *not* Cheysuli, and you are not *a'saii*—" He stopped. "You mean Carillon's bastard son!"

"Carollan," Jarek affirmed. "Son of the last *Homanan* Mujhar, and dispossessed king."

"Dispossessed! He was never *acknowledged*—and even if he had been, he could not rule. He is deaf and dumb, Jarek!"

"That does not alter the fact he bears the proper blood. It does not alter the fact that he can sire sons who are *not* deaf and dumb."

Brennan rolled his head against the hard stone beneath his head. "This is madness, *madness* . . . this was settled twenty years ago, when my father and Caro met. There is no ambition in him. There is no desire for anything more than a peaceful life. And he has it, with Taliesin . . . do you mean to tear him away from it? To *force* the Lion on him, even if he does not desire it?"

Jarek's face and manner were not those of a madman, nor a zealot. He was quietly, wholeheartedly dedicated to his cause, lacking the fanaticism that might tip him into madness. He was utterly committed. Brennan saw in him the same quiet fire that burned in Teirnan, and wondered again if he was being purposely misled.

Jarek glanced over his shoulder at the Homanan guard, then turned back and wet his lips. "Twenty years ago my father was murdered by yours, my lord. Within the halls of Homana-Mujhar, before Cheysuli Council, Niall struck down my father to keep him from overturning the Cheysuli claim to kingship. For that cause, my father died. I swore an oath to carry out his commitment, and I mean to do it. No matter what the cost."

"Elek was sacrificed by his own people," Brennan said wearily. "My *jehan* held the knife, it is true, but only because in the crush of fighting someone put one into his hand and then forced him to stab Elek. It was carefully planned that way to implicate my *jehan*."

"I would expect Niall's son to say nothing else." Jarek smiled faintly. "It is old history, my lord, but history is a living thing, bequeathing life and knowledge to others, and the fuel to carry out ambitions and commitments. Time grows short—Carollan ages, and with each passing day Homanans forget the Lion belongs to them, not to the Cheysuli . . . not to Niall, nor to you, nor to the children you might sire upon your Erinnish queen." The light flickered, nearly died. "It is our *tahlmorra* to wash the Lion clean of Cheysuli claim, and give it to Homanans once again."

"*Tahlmorra*—" Brennan could not summon the means to spit. "If you do this—if you do this to me or to anyone else—the gods *will* turn their eyes from you!"

"Then all the better we appease them with blood sacrifice." Jarek picked up the dish of oil and told the other man to go.

Brennan tensed in his shackles. "You cannot simply slay me out of hand . . . in war, *aye,* but like this? In the name of *Carollan?*"

"But we can." The light was stark on Jarek's face. "You questioned if I could be Cheysuli, working with—*a'saii?*" He nodded, went on. "Perhaps this will convince you otherwise. For a six-month, now, we have been catching and slaying Cheysuli—not warriors, unless we are forced, because too many *lir* deaths would be remarked by other *lir*—but women and children. It is necessary." He bent closer, lowering his voice. "Now we reach higher, touching the royal family itself, to show no one is invulnerable. That even the highest can be overtaken." He paused. "Left to me, alone, I would devise another means. Death is death, but there should be dignity involved. Sacrifice is barbaric . . . but also useful. For those who thrive on such things, it serves to keep the fire burning. And we do need a fire, my lord—bright and hot and clean—if we are to burn the Cheysuli infection from the wound you have made in Homana."

"*Jarek—*"

But Jarek was gone, and he took the lamp with him.

Five

Eventually, Rhiannon came. She set the place alight with a single candle and knelt by him in shadows. Her palm was cool on his brow. Gently she parted sweat-stiff hair, pushed it back to bare the wound.

He jerked away from her.

She drew in a startled breath, twitching in shock. Abruptly she twisted to look over her shoulder toward the low entrance, as if she feared discovery.

Did she think he did not know?

He wanted to say: *leave me alone,* but he could not find the words. Thinking: *if I cannot be free of the place I am imprisoned, let someone share it with me.*

"Oh, my lord . . ." Her black eyes were blacker still in the shadows of his prison. "My lord—"

He cut her off. "Where is my *lir?* What have they done with my *lir?*"

"They have put her elsewhere. My lord—"

"Is she *alive?*"

"Aye. Of course." A smudge of dirt marred her face. "They want you whole. For the sacrifice. They will not slay her before the proper time."

He bared his teeth. "I cannot *touch* her. There is no Sleeta in the link!"

The flame danced, guttered, nearly went out; Rhiannon's hand was trembling. "I swear, she is alive. I *swear* it, my lord. Confined, as you are, but well enough."

"I cannot *touch* her!"

"Perhaps it is the drug." Plaited hair hung over her

shoulders, braided ropes of glossy hair, threaded with crimson ribbon. "The wine—Jarek's wine, the second jug—it was drugged, my lord. To dull your Cheysuli magic."

The candlelight was kind to her face. Black hair, fair skin, long-lashed eloquent eyes— Inwardly, the fear and fury rose. "By the gods, woman, you tricked me! You sucked me into this madness of Jarek's making."

"No! Oh, no, I swear . . ." Tears welled up into her eyes. "I knew noth—"

Brennan's mocking laughter cut her off. "Oh, aye, give me tears! No, no, woman, not again . . . I will not succumb to your posturing of innocence yet *again*."

"My lord—"

"I heard you," he accused. "You and Jarek, discussing my health and welfare, and the plans for my demise. Do you think I am a twice-born fool?" Iron chimed as he fisted grimy hands. "Go, woman. Hie yourself back to the man who is so kind, so generous, so—"

"Listen to me!" Her desperate hiss set the candleflame aguttering and cast distorted shapes upon the curving wall behind her. "Listen to me, my lord, when I deny knowledge of Jarek's plans . . . when I deny willing participation—"

"Oh, aye, you knew nothing." He writhed in his chains and knew again the helpless fear of a man entombed. "Oh, Rhiannon, I commend you; you played your part so well. I fell into the trap like a green boy sick for love of his first woman—"

"What do you want me to say?" she demanded. "Shall I swear by your gods? By the Mujhar? By *this*?" Light caught the sapphire ring dangling from its thong and set the gemstone aglow. "Then I will swear by *you*, my lord prince—by Brennan of Homana, firstborn of the Mujhar's sons, and destined one day to sit upon the Lion Throne."

"So glib," he retorted. "You spew out titles and destinies like a *shar tahl*, woman, but I will not be suborned by you again."

Rhiannon briefly bared small white teeth in a feral display of frustration. "You *fool*—I came here to give you what aid I can, and you spend your strength on insults!"

Brennan's laugh was a short bark of sound. "Fool, am I? No more 'my lord' this, 'my lord' that, now that the truth is out."

"At the moment, *my lord*, there is little in your state to recommend your heritage *or* your divinity!"

"Divinity . . ." This time the laugh was genuine. "Aye, not much of a man in this malodorous shell, is there?"

"I came to help," she said curtly. "Tell me what you would have me do."

He rattled his chains. "Set me free, Rhiannon. Prove you are innocent of my accusations." Thinking: *What lie will you tell me now?*

"Jarek has the key."

He wanted to strike the innocence from her face. "Are you not his whore, then? Have you no bed skill, that you cannot tease the key from him? Better yet, *steal* it!"

Color flamed in her face to rival the candlelight. "Jarek—is my first man," she said stiffly, with an odd integrity. "It has only been but a month . . . teasing is—not something I do very well." Her knuckles were white on the smoking candle.

He wanted to shout at her, to shake her, to force the truth from her. And yet, against all odds he believed her. "And if you do not try to tease, cajole, *steal,* Jarek will have me slain." He saw how her chin trembled convulsively. More quietly, he said: "Do you want that knowledge to compete with the memory of the ring I gave you?"

One hand closed over the ring and clenched it so hard the sinews stood up beneath the flesh. "If I am caught—" She stopped. "If I am caught, *three* will be sacrificed."

Brennan closed his eyes and felt the sweat sting the wound on his forehead. He would not deny the truth, even if he thought she might believe him when he told her Jarek would never consider such a thing. Jarek might.

Once again he tested his bonds and found them firm as ever, biting into weals and making them bleed again. He turned his head from her and ground his teeth, trying to keep himself from begging. If asking were not enough, begging would merely diminish what little pride he had left.

"My lord—" This time when she touched him, he did not pull away. "My lord, Jarek said you were afraid of places like this."

All the breath spilled out of his mouth. "I am." It was easier than he had believed; the fear did it for him. "This place—this *weight*—" He stopped short, shut his eyes, smelled the fear-stench again. "When—when I was but a boy, very small, I was trapped in a place not so different than this—all stone, cold stone, so much darkness and all the *weight*—" He swallowed, nearly gagged. "I had forgotten, thank the gods, *forgotten* . . . until now. . . ."

"Oh, my lord."

"Rhiannon—" He stopped, began again, not caring that this desperation was manifest; that the sound of his fear filled up his prison. "I beg you—*get me free!*"

Her fingers briefly squeezed the cold flesh of his arm. "I will do what I can do."

And she left him alone in darkness where he could cry in privacy.

Rhiannon did not come again. There was no freedom, no miracle that conjured a shackle key from the air to unlock his cuffs. There was no escape in sleep or unconsciousness. There was only the consuming knowledge that time passed too quickly, and that at the end of another day he would be dead, sacrificed in the name of Carollan, his great-grandsire's bastard son.

Curse you, Carillon . . . curse the loins that sired a son on some baseborn Homanan drudge instead of on Solindish Electra—

And yet he knew an insane amused irony in that curse, for without the loins that had sired Carollan—deaf, dumb Caro—there would have been no Niall. No Brennan. No need for Cheysuli rule at all, for there would have been a *Homanan* heir.

And no need for sacrifice. Uneven stone pitted his flesh through Cheysuli leathers. *Oh, Sleeta, give me the*

*strength to die as a warrior dies, not hating myself for
losing control in this fear of small, harmless places—*

Footsteps. Torchlight, reaching in through the low opening to set his prison aflame. And the shape of a man,
ducking down, bending to enter, to kneel at his side with
an iron key in his hand.

"My lord, your time is come upon you. The gods are
thirsty tonight."

"Put no hands on *me.*"

"What? And leave you here to go mad from close
confinement?" Jarek unlocked ankle shackles. "Lest you
forget, my lord, we have your *lir* as well. Try to escape,
and she shall surely die." His face was mostly hidden in
distorted shadows. "The drug was strong." Calmly, Jarek
set iron aside. It rang in the tiny cell. "An herbalist who
has knowledge of such things recommended a mixture of
ingredients deadly to most men, but merely temporarily—if
powerfully—discomfiting to a Cheysuli. One ingredient
you may recognize: the root called *tetsu.*"

Muscles spasmed. "*Tetsu* is deadly!"

"Does it matter?" Jarek laughed. "No, no, not when
used with certain other herbs—the root is dangerous, but
not deadly in proper proportion. Still, it exerts a powerful presence, does it not? Cut off from your *lir*, you are
no different from a Homanan." The wrist cuffs were
unlocked. "Come out, my lord. The gods await."

"And if I stay?" Brennan flexed painful wrists and set
his teeth against the cramping of his calves. "If I choose
to remain here, what will you do?"

"Brick up the door and leave you to die a madman."
Jarek shrugged. "It would discommode the gods briefly,
perhaps, to lose so princely a sacrifice, but there are
others. And who is to say the sacrifice be limited to the
Mujhar's *sons?* There are daughters, too—"

"No!" he cried, and heard it briefly echo. "No, not my
rujholla. Jarek—"

"Then come out, my lord. Come out into the air,
where you can breathe again, and know yourself *alive.*"

Alive. For how long? Still, he stood a better chance of
escape out of the cell than in.

Jarek moved aside and gestured Brennan to exit first.
He went, stooped and cramped, and felt fresh air upon
his face. No chains—he was *free*—

Flames were in his face. He thrust up a hand to ward
his eyes, felt heat and the lick of dripping oil. He staggered, thought to run, felt hands upon his arms; the
strength of Jarek's drug still lingered in his system.

Behind the flames, he saw faces. Strangers all, ten,
twenty, thirty or more of them, but he knew them. He
knew them by their avid eyes and feral expressions; their
commitment to Jarek's cause.

Nowhere did he see Rhiannon.

The men closed on him. "Come, my lord," Jarek said,
as they forced him to the altar.

It was old, dark stone, stained black with the blood of
murdered Cheysuli. Beyond the flames of the torches his
captors carried he saw other torches, ten of them, thrust
into the earth to form a ring around the stone. All the
earth was beaten into dust beneath the trees around the
altar; now his blood would muddy it.

He stiffened, tried to twist free, was shoved toward the
altar.

"Your *lir*, my lord," Jarek said quietly. "Do not forget
your *lir*."

They lifted him, even as he struggled; thrust him up
onto the stone; pinned him on his back.

"Justice," Jarek said.

"You are mad—*all* of you, mad!"

"The rightful line restored . . ."

"Carillon himself declared Donal heir in lieu of sons,"
Brennan appealed. "He wed Aislinn, Carillon's daughter, who bore him a son . . . whose *son* sired a son."

"The Lion shall have a *Homanan* Mujhar again . . ."

Brennan writhed; they held him down. "*I* am Homanan!" he shouted. "I am the Lion's get!" And he
thought in sudden, ice-cold clarity. *But if they succeed—if
I am slain—there is still my rujho . . . Hart can be
Mujhar. . .*

And the prophecy perpetuated.

Jarek still spoke, softly, calmly, as if he had practiced

it many times. "Elek's death shall be avenged . . . his memory replenished in the blood of his royal murderer's son."

Brennan cursed them all, but they understood none of it. They did not know the Old Tongue.

"Carillon's son shall have the Lion—"

"I am Carillon's great-grandson!"

"—and the Lion shall know the proper line again, the gods-blessed Homanan line. . . ." Jarek's smile was odd. And then he began to laugh, but the laughter was odder yet.

Brennan rolled his head against the stone. "Fools and madmen, *all*—"

Grinning, Jarek gave the order. "Strip him of his armbands."

He was stripped.

"Fetch the cat."

Sleeta—Sleeta—Sleeta—

Jarek stepped close. Torchlight glinted off the knife. "Your earring, my lord." And touched blade to ear as he took the lobe into his hand and stretched it down, as if he meant to cut the earring free.

Brennan spat at him. "In the name of the sun and the wind and the rivers, the earth and the sky and the seas—"

Jarek laughed.

"—name of the Hunter, the Weaver, the Cripple—"

And Jarek *laughed.*

"—I curse you, Jarek son of Elek—*I curse you to die the death of a lirless man, beneath the jaws and claws of a beast*— "

Jarek bent close, still laughing, and bared his teeth in a mocking challenge. "Levy all the curses you desire on *Jarek, son of Elek,* my lord. They will not touch *me.*" His eyes were black in the whipping torches, but the rims were a clear, eerie gold. "What I do, I do in the name of Asar-Suti, and *he* holds precedence over all your petty Cheysuli gods!"

"Ihlini!" Brennan cried.

"Now!" Jarek roared, overriding Brennan's shout.

Now, Sleeta echoed, as the *lir*-link blazed to life.

Brennan, tearing free of them all as out of the darkness the cry of a hunting cat rose, hardly noticed that Jarek's knife sliced through weighted flesh and severed his lobe. Pain was something he no longer acknowledged. Only anger. A terrible, burning anger that swallowed his knowledge of self and tipped him over the edge.

—down—

Rage fed the flames.

—down—

He did not know his name. He did not know *her* name, only that she was there, *here,* lending him needed strength, giving him what he needed; what he had to have, to use, to wield in the name of his anger.

Anger and something more. Something he knew as fear.

He reached out for the strength, the fear, the rage; touched it, snared it, hugged it to his breast.

—now—

Before an Ihlini, he knew, his Cheysuli gifts were muted nearly to nothingness, but now—oddly—he felt stronger than ever before.

—now—

Jarek no longer laughed. "Slay him!" he screamed.

—now— Brennan whispered. And within the webwork of the link, he tapped Sleeta and all the terrible heritage of his race.

In the guise of a tawny mountain cat, he shredded Jarek's throat.

Six

—run—run—run—
A litany in his head.
—run—run—
On four feet, curving claws raking divots of debris, the tawny cat ran. Running with him, Sleeta; black on black in the darkness of the night.
—run—
Deep in his chest, he coughed. Wreaths of vine and underbrush fouled his course, lacing his eyes with the whip-snag of tiny branches. Thorns caught at his pelt, breaking, clinging, burrowing into his flesh.

Still he ran. Flowing, like honey through a flame.

And then, unwanted, came the memory of what he had been, of what he had *done,* and he tumbled out of *lir*-shape into the man-shape known as Brennan.

He landed on one elbow; it gave, folding beneath his weight, and threw him over onto a shoulder, his left one, and then all the pain he had forgotten came rushing back again to set his bones afire.

Tangled in deadfall, he lay breathing heavily. His belly convulsed with it, until the grunting and gasping subsided, and he knew what he was again.

Man.

Brennan pressed himself up. Damp leaves formed a clammy cloak on naked arms against the night. He shuddered once, twice; gagged, and nearly spewed the contents of his belly onto the forest floor.

"Too fast," he croaked, touching his pounding head. "Too soon . . . agh, gods, my *head*—"

Sleeta's eyes were oil lamps in the darkness. *Lir—lir—* She pressed her chin against his shoulder, rubbing as if to offer strength and sympathy.

The pain of his abused head nearly took precedence over the *lir*-link, which frightened him. He tried to set it aside and think only of Sleeta, but the pain was so bad even his teeth hurt with it.

Lir. Sleeta leaned against him.

Forcing himself to ignore his own discomfort, Brennan tried to assuage hers, soothing her with gentle hands and tender words. Through the link they were reunited, reconfirming their need of one another; the cat's fear, shock and weariness were echoes of his own.

"Gods . . ." In human speech, it was the only word he could manage. He was disoriented, tangled up in the sensations of cat mixed with man, until for a moment he could not distinguish himself, being neither human nor feline, but *thing*.

An owl hooted from near by. Another answered; in the distance Brennan heard the rising howl of a wolf, the yapping of his pack. He drew up both knees and rested his forehead against them, willing the pain to fade.

Lir. Sleeta again, still pressed against him. His hand touched matted fur, sticky blood, fluid seeping from an open wound. And he was outraged at the sacrilege.

"Sleeta—" This time the words began to make sense. He knelt, gently examining her head, throat, shoulders, carefully fingering ribs and belly and haunches. In the darkness much of her disrepair was hidden, but he knew she was not unscathed. The dogs had taken their toll. "*Ku'reshtin*," he muttered. "Setting hounds upon a *lir*."

Effective. Sleeta licked at his neck. *They distracted me from you.* She paused. *Blood, lir. Did he set the hounds on you?*

Brennan carefully touched his left ear. No more lobe, no more earring. Only blood marked the place where he had borne the cat-shaped ornament.

No hounds, lir. This was done by man. This was done by Ihlini.

No! Sleeta's shocked response was immediate. *I would' have known an Ihlini.*

So I thought, he agreed grimly. *But in the past other Ihlini have walked unknown into Homana-Mujhar itself . . . who is to say what spell was cast to blind us to the truth?*

She was fretful from pain and incomprehension. *The gods set us to guard the Cheysuli, to know enemy from friend, to recognize ill intent.*

And to know Ihlini?

That more than anything else.

Brennan sat very still, not even daring to move his hand against her pelt. In but a few words Sleeta had said more of the purpose of the *lir* than he had ever heard from her before. As a child he had been taught that a *lir* was a gift of the gods, something incredibly special; the bond between warrior and animal was a blessing no one else could possibly comprehend, a thing to be cherished above all else. Such handing down of absolutes left little room for questions, even less for answers. The *lir* themselves had always been oddly secretive about so many things.

"Why?" He asked it aloud because somehow it made it more substantial; he asked it gently, casually, because he was afraid she would give him no answer if he sounded too intense. "Why are you to know Ihlini above all else?"

Having more power, they offer more threat. Sleeta licked his shoulder.

It was not the answer he wanted; it told him nothing he did not know already. "Surely anyone with power offers equal danger."

Her breath was warm. *Who is his own worst enemy?*

"*I* am my own, of course—that tells me nothing." And then he stopped speaking. His fingers dug deep into the thickness of her pelt. "Unless, of course, you are confirming my *jehan's* contention that Cheysuli and Ihlini are bloodkin."

Sleeta butted her head against his shoulder. *Lir, lir, enough . . . can we not go home?*

Home. Did she mean Clankeep or Homana-Mujhar? "Sleeta—" But he did not finish his question because he heard movement in the forest.

He thought at first it was the Homanans come to find him, to throw him down again on the altar to complete the sacrifice. He thrust himself to a crouch, legs drawn up to push himself into headlong flight, but he did not run. The world spun slowly out from under him, and he fell awkwardly over onto one hip, keeping himself upright only by dint of one rigid, outstretched arm.

No, Sleeta said. *Think before you run.*

He did as told, and understood what she meant him to understand. No, what he heard was not the noise of Homanans hunting him; not those fundamentalist fools. The unveiling of Jarek as Ihlini would be enough to send them fleeing. If there was one thing more horrifying to a Cheysuli-fearing Homanan than a warrior assuming *lir*-shape, it was an Ihlini sorcerer.

No wonder Jarek spouted all that nonsense about Carollan—he used it to cover his real intent, to hide himself in the others.

He crouched in the darkness with Sleeta crouched beside him. And then the cat gently butted an arm. *The girl, lir . . . the one who got me free.*

Rhiannon. So she *had* done as she had promised.

The noise came closer. No doubt she thought she moved quietly, using all the stealth she could, but to Brennan, warrior-bred and trained, her progress was easily followed. She had not learned to move randomly, to stutter-step, to wait, to move again, as if an animal. She rustled, snapped boughs, snagged vines and underbrush. He waited until she was close enough, and then he said her name.

Her startled reaction sent her crashing back two steps and then she was caught fast, clothing and hair snagged on twisted boughs. He heard her rapid breathing and the tearing of thin fabric as she sought to free herself.

"*Meijhana*—no. There is no need to flee *me.*" And he

rose out of his crouch to stand, one hand splayed against the trunk of a conifer to keep him from falling down.

"My lord?" All movement stopped. "Brennan?"

"Aye. And my *lir*, whom you were good enough to release."

He heard more cloth shredded, the clink of something metallic, the ragged eagerness in her breathing. And then she was free and stood before him. Debris littered her braids, clung to her clothing, marred her face. But she smiled, and laughed, and held out glowing gold.

"Yours, my lord. When all the others ran, I took them to give to you."

He had not thought to see the *lir*-bands again. Nor had he allowed himself the time to think on what the loss represented. Although the *lir*-gold did not make him a man or a warrior in place of a boy, it was still an integral part of who he was. The loss would have shamed him as much for his manner of death as wearing them honored his manner of living.

"*Leijhana tu'sai*," he whispered. "Oh *meijhana*, I owe you so much. For Sleeta . . . my life . . . for these. . . ."

Her eyes avoided his. "I could not find the earring, my lord. Perhaps—if we were to go back—"

"No. It does not matter. I lack the lobe in which to wear it." He smiled ruefully at her hiss of realization. "These are enough, *meijhana*. That I promise you." Slowly he slipped hands through the heavy gold circlets, one by one, and slid the bands up past his elbows until the gold was locked against living flesh. The bands were cool for only a moment, and then they warmed, remembering their customary place, and he was whole again. "*Leijhana tu'sai*," he said again, tracing the cat-shapes in the metal.

Rhiannon shrugged a little. "The return of your gold is still not enough to repay the pain I have caused you and your cat. If I had known what Jarek intended—" She stopped short, and tears welled into her eyes. "Oh, *gods*— how could I have been so blind, so *stupid* . . . how could I not have seen what he meant to do?"

He reached out and caught the back of her head against the palm of one hand and cradled it gently. Slowly he pulled her in until she pressed her face against his soiled jerkin, clinging to his arms. At first she held herself stiffly, plainly made uncomfortable by his rank if not by his compassion. Slowly he gentled her, as he had gentled so many fillies.

"*Shansu,*" he said softly. "Peace, *meijhana*—I think no less of you for your grief." Yet even as he said it, he wondered if he meant it. In the clans, grief was an exceptionally private thing. A Cheysuli showed none where others might see it.

Traditionally. *But traditions change . . .*

The tears did not last. Rhiannon moved back, out of his arms, and wiped her face, succeeding only in smearing grime across both cheeks. Twigs and leaves clung to her braids. But he thought he had never seen a woman who looked lovelier, even in disrepair.

"Oh, my lord—" She reached up and touched fingertips to his neck where the blood from his stolen lobe had crusted. "My lord, they have used you so cruelly. First your poor head, then the drug, the chains . . . now *this.*" She caught one of his arms as he wavered and tugged gently, urging him down. "Sit, my lord, I beg you. It is clear you are close to collapse."

"Is it?" Awkwardly, grateful for her assistance, Brennan sat down. Sleeta lent him warmth by pressing against one side; he wrapped an arm around her and gloried in her presence. "Gods, what I did—" He broke off as the world turned yet again, and bit back a curse as he tried to stay upright.

"Lie you down," Rhiannon said. "Here—I will help—" And she moved quickly as he toppled, taking his head into her lap. Tentatively she stroked sweat-stiffened hair back from his forehead. Her fingers were cool and light, and the pain was not so bad beneath her touch.

"Sleep, my lord," she said. "No more harm will come to you."

He smiled, though he did not open his eyes. "You sound so certain, *meijhana.*"

"I am. No harm, my lord Brennan—I promise. Your *lir* is here, and so am I."

For the moment, there was nothing more he wanted.

He dreamed of darkness and close confinement, and the knowledge of his fear. Weighed down, he could not move. Only his voice knew freedom, and even that was denied him. Muzzled by a deep, disturbing sleep, the only sound he emitted was a throttled wail, a muffled plea for release.

"My lord."

The woman's voice intruded. From a distance he heard it. He reached out for it, trying to catch it and cling to it like a babe to a mother's breast.

"My lord—" She paused. "Brennan . . . *Brennan*—wake up. I am here. I am here. I promise."

He struggled toward the voice. Something touched his face: a hand, warm and kind, offering him compassion. He reached out, caught it, clung, and the darkness began to recede.

"Brennan—"

And he came up out of the dream into reality again, and caught her against his chest, pulling her body beneath his, knowing only one way to banish such gods-cursed fear; how to prove he was alive, alive, *after coming so close to death.*

"Please—" he whispered, and then abruptly he was awake.

—oh, gods—

Even as he moved to relieve her of his weight, of his uncharacteristic *demand*, her hands pulled him back down. "No."

"But—you know what I meant to do—what I *would* have done, whether you wanted it or no. . . ."

"I know." She reached up to catch a lock of his hair. "Do you think I am unwilling?"

A dozen questions spilled into his mind. He wanted to speak of Jarek; of the line between lust and love; of the differences in gratification and gratitude. He could give her so many reasons for what he had so nearly done, and what his body still wanted him to do. But looking into her face, into her eloquent eyes, he saw no desire for explanation. She knew as well as he. She wanted as much as he.

She locked her hands into his hair and pulled his head down, down, until her breath caressed his face. "I did not love him, Brennan. That much I promise you."

For now, it was enough.

He gave Rhiannon into the care of serving women when they reached Homana-Mujhar. Sleeta he tended personally, as always. And, at last, he turned his attention to himself, tarrying in a hot bath even when his kinfolk came knocking at his chamber door with questions regarding his health, word of his battered appearance having been passed among the servants and so to his kinfolk. He sent them away with promises of a full explanation, and fell asleep in the cask.

At last he faced his kinfolk in Deirdre's airy tower solar, though now it was dark outside. He was more than willing to give an explanation now that he was clean again, clad in fresh leathers and smelling of cloves instead of fear and close confinement. But he did not begin at once, because Ian stepped close and stopped him short with a hand upon his arm.

He inspected Brennan's left ear attentively a moment. "A clean cut," he said after a moment. "You are lucky. You might have lost the entire ear."

Maeve, standing near one of the tripod braziers, grimaced and touched her own, as if sharing a measure of his pain. Keely, sitting crosswise in one of Deirdre's chairs, combed unbound hair away from her face with stiffened fingers. Her blue eyes were very thoughtful.

Deirdre, playing hostess, poured wine into a cluster of cups and began to hand them out. As she came to Brennan, he saw how tightly set was her mouth. She said nothing at first, giving Ian his portion, but he seemed to sense she intended to and moved away smoothly. It left Deirdre and Brennan confronting one another over a cup of blood-red wine.

He took it from her, but her fingers pressed his own. "Next time," she said quietly, "let the bath wait."

"I was *filthy*—"

"I know. And I am saying, let it wait." Her green eyes were steady, unyielding. "Think of your father instead of yourself."

He opened his mouth to protest, to repeat how badly he had needed the bath, but he shut it in silence instead. A glance at his father, waiting quietly in a chair near the fireplace, underscored the intent of Deirdre's words. Niall would say nothing, but there was suddenly acknowledgment in Brennan's mind that he had worried him deeply and unnecessarily, even if for only the brief length of time required by the bath.

He sighed. "Aye. Aye, I will." He touched Deirdre's shoulder briefly in thanks, then went to his father. The others would hear clearly enough, but it was to Niall he would speak. "I am well, *jehan*. I swear. There is—discomfort—" he shrugged "—but it will fade."

Niall looked up at him from the chair. "Who put you in irons?" he asked quietly.

"Irons!" Maeve stared. "What does he mean, Brennan?"

The others, clearly, had seen only the lobeless ear. The Mujhar had seen his wrists with their bracelets of flesh rubbed raw. And now everyone else did as well.

Keely abruptly swung her legs around, rose and crossed to him. Forthright as ever, she grabbed one of his hands and pulled it out where she could see it and his wrist clearly. He felt her fingers spasm briefly in shock, and then she let him go.

"Who *dared* to chain you up?" Her tone was level, on the surface unemotional, but he heard the truth beneath the sound. Anger. Outrage. An abiding disbelief.

"His name was Jarek," Rhiannon said, and shut the door behind her.

As one, all turned and stared at her. Even Brennan did not move to her at once, though he meant to, because he was too startled. He had known she was attractive, but the women had made her beautiful.

Awkwardly, she curtsied deeply. Heavy skirts—a deep, rich blue—draped on slate-gray stone. Her hair, bound back smoothly in a single braid, coiled like glossy black rope against soft wool. "My lord Mujhar—" And abruptly, she lost her balance.

It was Ian, closest, who caught her arm and raised her. Her face blazed with brilliant color. She allowed Ian to hold her stiff arm and did not attempt to move again, as if afraid she might embarrass herself further.

"Be easy, *meijhana*," Ian told her kindly, offering her his warmest smile. "There are times formality is required, but this is hardly one of them." His fingers squeezed her arm gently. "Be welcome among us, lady."

Brennan looked at his uncle instead of Rhiannon. It was no secret among Deirdre's ladies—and therefore the rest of the palace—that the Mujhar's brother was a man worth having, as friend or bedmate—or both—but Ian had never shown any indication of desiring permanency in feminine companionship. Certainly he did not now, but there was no mistaking his attentiveness to Rhiannon.

He would do the same for any woman . . . and then: *She must be twenty-five years younger than my su'fali!*

Smoothly Brennan moved forward and offered his hand to Rhiannon. She took it at once, and he could not hide the smile of subtle triumph as he turned her away from Ian.

He presented her to his father. "This is Rhiannon, *jehan*. Because of her courage, I am here to stand before you."

"You have my thanks," Niall said quietly. "*Leijhana tu'sai*, in the Old Tongue. But will you be more forthright in an explanation than my son? We still are woefully ignorant of circumstances."

"Why was he in irons?" Maeve demanded. "Do *you* know, Rhiannon?"

"Gently," Brennan suggested. "Rhiannon is ally, not enemy."

Rhiannon's hand was cold in his. "I know," she said, and proceeded to tell them in a quiet, steady voice.

When she was done, the silence was palpable. And then the Mujhar began to swear. Quietly. Calmly. Inventively. In perfect eloquence he levied every curse against the Ihlini he could think of.

"Well," Ian said dryly when Niall was done, "there is no need for *our* retribution. Surely this is enough."

"Track them down," Keely said tightly. "Track them *all* down, and slay them *all* as you slew Jarek."

"Jarek was Ihlini," Brennan reminded her. "For all we know, so were the others."

"How?" Maeve asked. "Could they *all* hide themselves behind Homanan faces? Even before the *lir?*"

Brennan shrugged. "Sleeta did not know him for Ihlini. It is clear Strahan has learned well the spell that shields Ihlini from the *lir*."

"And it makes them all the more dangerous," Ian said.

Niall shook his head. "I am not certain that is so. That Jarek was shielded, aye—but the others? I think not. It requires something tangible from a *lir*—a tooth, a claw, a talon, a feather . . . how many *lir* have died in Ihlini hands?" He sat forward in his chair. "Tynstar had Cai, my grandsire's hawk. Strahan had four teeth from Storr, Finn's wolf. But not enough, I think, for all of them."

"He might have had more than enough," Brennan said. "He told me that although they preferred to sacrifice women and children to avoid alarming the *lir,* they did kill a few warriors."

"An endless supply of *lir*." Ian, stark-faced, shook his head. "It is not impossible. It may be all *were* Ihlini, not Homanan at all. Jarek simply used the story of Elek as a ruse."

"But why?" Rhiannon asked. "If all were Ihlini, why act as Homanans at all?"

"Think," Ian said. "How better to infiltrate a realm than by portraying yourself as a *part* of that realm?"

"Even before people you intend to murder?" Keely asked. "That makes no sense at all, even for what I have heard of Strahan."

Ian shrugged. "I cannot say *why* Strahan does any of the things he does. But if he is true to himself—true to the Strahan *we* know—he will use every device in his ken to harm us." He nodded at Rhiannon. "Had she not freed Sleeta, thereby returning the power of *lir*-shape to

Brennan, Jarek and the others would not have been
unmasked. He would still be ignorant of the truth, because Strahan's allies take infinite care to keep us in
ignorance." He spread eloquent hands. "How best to do
that? By playing out the role."

Keely shook her head. "I still say it is senseless. I
cannot see why any of them bother to portray themselves
as Homanans when they mean to slay us regardless."

"Because you have no guile in you," Deirdre said.

Keely looked at her in surprise. "What?"

"No guile," Deirdre repeated. "You're a woman for
saying what you mean."

"Even when silence is preferable." Brennan smiled at
his scowling sister. "Admit it, *rujholla*—you would sooner
charge in shouting your name and intention for all to
hear, than to work in silence and subterfuge."

"So should everyone," she retorted. "What good is
there in crawling on your belly when there are legs to
carry you?"

"And what is wrong with waiting to move until all the
facts are known?" Maeve asked. "Keely, you are too
bold, too quick to say that you think when you would do
better to wait."

Niall silenced the brewing battle with a raised hand.
"Enough." The single word was sufficient.

Brennan made good use of the opportunity to put in
his own thoughts. "It is possible Jarek acted alone. Now
that I think on it, he seemed very aware of how the
others might preceive him, as if he had to think about
how he phrased things so as not to give himself away. To
me, he was always Homanan, in speech and attitude."
He paused. "At least—until he *chose* to divulge himself,
and then the others scattered."

Niall looked at Rhiannon. "It is for you to tell us what
you know of Jarek. Everything. Hold nothing back, or
you may deal us a blow Strahan would be proud of."

Rhiannon's face was pale as she stared at the Mujhar.
Her hand, in Brennan's, was still very cold. He squeezed
it to lend her reassurance; quickly she looked at him,

smiled faintly, then withdrew her hand entirely and nodded to the Mujhar.

Niall opened his mouth to speak again, but held his question as Deirdre touched his arm lightly. "A moment, my lord. Let the girl—and the rest of us—find a seat." She poured wine into the remaining cup and passed it to Rhiannon. "You're not to be holding us all in so much awe," Deirdre told her kindly, green eyes alight with humor. "Underneath all the gold and prickly pride, these Cheysuli are no different from you and me."

Rhiannon clutched the cup. "But—are *you* not?"

"Cheysuli?" Deirdre's brows rose. "No, no, not I. Erinnish, I am, no more. There is no magic in my bones."

"Nor in mine." Maeve did not smile, though her tone was even enough. "We are remiss in our gratitude. For what you did in Brennan's cause, all of us are grateful."

Rhiannon fixed her eyes on Brennan's face. What she felt was clear for all to see. "There was nothing else I *could* do."

Ian fetched a chair and brought it forward, thumping it down behind her. "Sit you down, *meijhana*." His smile was exceedingly charming; the glint in his eyes was clearly intended for Brennan's benefit. "Be at ease, as I insist—and tell us whatever you can of Jarek."

Slowly she sat down, clutching her cup of wine. She did not drink. She waited, watching as her hosts found places to sit, and then she drew in a breath so deep it made the sapphire glint in the candlelight. "He was a kind man—to *me*." Blood rushed into her face as clearly she heard the incongruity in her statement. "He said nothing to me of Elek, my lord Mujhar. He kept his affairs very private, aye . . . but how many men share such things with women? Even the women who share their beds?" Color deepened in her face; she glanced briefly at Brennan, then looked away. "He served Cheysuli willingly in the tavern. I heard no words of hatred or hostility."

"Nor did I," Brennan confirmed. "Even when he and the others threw me down on the altar, there was little of true *hatred* about it, and nothing of madness at all." He shrugged. "Again . . . up to the point he gave away his race by admitting he served Asar-Suti, Jarek was loyal, dedicated, openly commited to the bastard's cause . . . and I believed him. There was no reason not to."

Niall nodded. "I think you may have the right of it. He misled them purposely so he could, if he had to, blame *them* for your death. He would admit the truth of his identity to none who was not Ihlini." His eyes softened as he looked at Rhiannon. "Not even to you."

"What else?" Ian asked white-faced Rhiannon quietly. "Think of him in a new light, *meijhana,* and surely you will discover something in his conversation, his behavior . . . in the company he kept."

Rhiannon frowned thoughtfully. "Once, he said something of his birth. He said he was bastard-born." She shrugged. "I thought nothing of it—I too am bastard-born—but he said it mattered very much in the scheme of things. That in the end, the bastard blood would give him power no one else could hold." She glanced at Brennan. "It was not a claim I paid much attention to—until I heard him tell my lord he would bring down the House of Homana. And then I knew what I had to do."

"Thank the gods," Maeve murmured.

Niall shook his head slowly. "Power from his blood . . . for all we know, he may have been *Strahan's* son."

"Does it matter?" Keely asked. "He is dead."

Ian shrugged. "Dead, aye . . . but I will curse the nameless bitch who bore him anyway."

Rhiannon looked at him sharply. "But I *do* know her name," she said. "I thought it pretty, so I remember it easily." Rhiannon smiled a little. "His mother's name was Lillith."

As one, they looked at Ian.

Seven

"You cannot be certain," Niall declared. "*Rujho*—you cannot."

Ian's face was a peculiar chalky gray. "*How* not?" he asked hoarsely. "Am I to ignore the obvious?"

"What is obvious?" Niall demanded. "Do you think Lillith kept herself celibate before *or* after you?"

Ian looked blankly at Rhiannon, who stared back in growing alarm. "Have I said the wrong thing?" she asked. "Have I said something I should not?"

Brennan intended to speak, to calm her fears, but Ian moved to stand before her, neatly shouldering him out of the way.

"Rhiannon." For a moment Ian said nothing more, locked up within some private battle, and then he blew out a breath between constricted lips and knelt down in front of her. "*Meijhana*—" He took one of her hands into both of his. "Can you tell me how old he was?"

"How old?" She stared in bafflement at Ian, then glanced up at Brennan as if to ask instruction. But he could offer her nothing.

Ian was singularly intent. "How old was Jarek, Rhiannon?"

"My age," she answered. "Twenty."

"Twenty," Ian repeated blankly. He turned his head to look at Niall. "The age is right . . . and he was bastard-born of an Ihlini *jehana* whose name we know is Lillith. What other proof do you require?"

The Mujhar looked infinitely older. "Perhaps none,"

he said wearily, rubbing at the ruined flesh around the patch. "Perhaps we have all we need."

"Aye." Ian's face was oddly blank. "It was what she wanted. A child of us both, to mix the blood, the heritage, the *power*—"

"And now he is dead." Niall's voice was steady. "Why hate yourself the more when the need for it is passed?"

Ian's posture was incredibly rigid as he released Rhiannon's hand and rose. Brennan, watching him in growing alarm, thought he had never seen his uncle so shaken, or so vulnerable.

"Thank the gods," Ian said. He looked at Brennan. "*Leijhana tu'sai, harani,* for ridding us of another Ihlini—an Ihlini abomination!"

For all the words were brutal, Brennan heard the anguish in Ian's tone. He knew better than to believe it derived from grief, but there was more than dispassion as well.

How does a man deal with the death of a son he never knew? Brennan slowly shook his head. "*Su'fali*—"

"Surely you recall the story," Ian said harshly. The mask slipped from his face; Brennan saw the hostility that was so uncharacteristic of his uncle. "I was stud to Lillith's mare. She ensorcelled my *lir*, ensorcelled me . . . she *stole* the seed from me. Do you think I will grieve for that misbegotten spawn?"

Looking at him, Brennan saw an angry man who tasted the bitter fruit of shame. It was a new aspect of Ian, whose place in the household was one of abiding warmth and affection. He was *kinspirit* as well as kin.

It is as if he wishes to flagellate himself since we will not do it for him. "*Su'fali*—" Brennan began again, thinking to ease Ian's anguish, and realized there was himself to think of as well. Ian could not, for the moment, see past his own feelings to those of his nephew. "*Su'fali,* you are saying I killed a *kinsman.*"

For a brief arrested moment there was acknowledgment in Ian's eyes, and then it was quickly banished. "Ihlini. No more than that."

Slowly Brennan shook his head. "But he *was*. He was

an enemy, aye, but we shared blood. He was my cousin, just as Teirnan is. It does matter, *su'fali.*"

Ian's look was intense. "Then I will put it another way," he said with elaborate distinctness. "If you had known he was my son as he began to carve you to pieces on that perverted altar, would you have hesitated to kill him?"

A neat trap— But Brennan shook his head. "No, *su'fali.* No."

"Then do me the courtesy of attempting to understand my feelings," Ian said curtly. "I will not weep for a man who was born of my seed, but decidedly not of my beliefs and loyalties."

"Ihlini and Cheysuli," Keely said rigidly. "Gods, who is to say what arts he might have had? What magnitude his powers?"

"Firstborn," Maeve said tightly.

"No." Niall's answer was quick and definitive. "No, not a Firstborn. He lacked the other blood; therefore the prophecy was unfulfilled . . . and even if it *had* been, do you think the gods would countenance an accursed kinslayer on the Lion?"

Brennan's belly twisted. "Kinslayer," he said hoarsely. "Am *I* not accursed, then?"

He saw their eyes upon him. He could not read them, even as well as he knew them, because what they all considered was something entirely new. Killing enemy Ihlini, Homanans, Solindish and Atvians in service to the prophecy was one thing, and well accepted, but slaying kin? It carried a heavy weight.

Niall slowly shook his head. "Weigh yourself against Jarek, Brennan, and tell me which man deserved to die."

"Easy enough," Keely said sharply. "*Rujho,* you cannot doubt it. You are heir to the Lion Throne. Would you give it instead to Jarek?"

"No." He looked at his uncle, whose face was masked to them all, and yet the world was in his eyes. "No, I would not give the Lion to any man such as Jarek. But—" He paused, still looking at Ian. "*Su-fali,* surely

you must wonder what he might have been if *you* instead
of Lillith had had the raising of him."

"Must I?" Ian shook his head. "No, I must not. Else I
will begin to question my conviction that Ihlini and
Cheysuli cannot possibly coexist, within a realm or within
a conscience." His eyes were on the Mujhar. "You say
that once we were brother races, *rujho;* that the gods
sired us both. And I say they did not, being gods of
uncommon sense. But if you have the right of it . . . if
we *are* brother races, intended for cohabitation once
again when the prophecy is fulfilled . . . then how do I
live with it? How do I live with the knowledge that my
son tried to murder yours?"

Brennan saw clearly that a measure of Ian's pain was
his father's. Half-brothers only, sharing so little and yet
so much; he wondered if their bond was anything like the
one between himself and Hart.

"Then I will answer for you," Ian continued, as Niall
did not respond. "I could not live with it. And even if
you have the right of it after all, and one day we are
expected to lie down with Ihlini again . . . I would sooner
give myself over to the death-ritual than acknowledge
one as my kin." Ian looked at each of them, one by one:
Niall, Deirdre, Maeve, Keely and Rhiannon. Lastly he
looked at Brennan. "*Leijhana tu'sai,*" he said firmly, and
then he put down his cup of wine and walked silently out
of the solar.

The Mujhar sat down again and scrubbed at his rigid
face. "Ah, gods, spare my *rujho* this pain. . . ."

"My lord." It was Rhiannon, speaking softly, and Niall
turned his head to look at her. "My lord, is this true?
Jarek was his *son?*"

The Mujhar sighed. "It is an old story," he said gently,
"and a very private one. But aye, it seems likely Jarek
was Ian's son."

"Then he also was Cheysuli? Like you. Like the Prince
of Homana?"

"And one step closer to the Firstborn," Keely said
flatly, answering in place of her father. She tossed back a
gulp of wine, then shook her head in disgust. "So, the

Ihlini think to destroy the prophecy from *within* instead of without. A Cheysuli sire, an Ihlini dam, and children who do the bidding of the Seker."

"A formidable mixture," Niall agreed grimly.

Rhiannon frowned. "I do not understand."

Keely cast her an impatient glance, then looked at Brennan. "You would do well to tell her, *rujho*. Her ignorance is appalling."

"Keely, enough," Deirdre said quietly. "Are you thinking everyone knows what the Ihlini are to us?"

"Us?" Keely asked. "You are not Cheysuli."

"Keely, that *is* enough," Niall said sharply. "I will tolerate no insults to Deirdre *or* Rhiannon."

Keely recoiled, looking startled. "No! Oh, *no,* I meant no insult. Deirdre, I did *not.* I only meant you had less to fear, not being a part of the prophecy."

Deirdre's smile was crooked. "Aye, 'less to fear.' I'm only needing to worry myself over all of your father's children, as well as the father himself."

"Something *you* should think about," Maeve told her younger sister darkly.

"Aye, so I should." But Keely did not sound particularly repentant.

"Well," Deirdre said. "I'm thinking 'tis time I showed Rhiannon what there is to learn if she is to enter my service."

Rhiannon stared. "Your service?"

"My service," Deirdre repeated. " 'Tis hardly payment enough for saving the lives of the Prince of Homana and his *lir,* but I think 'twill be a beginning. If you are willing."

"Willing?" Rhiannon echoed. "Do you mean I am to stay here, with him—with *you?* I need not go back to the tavern?"

Deirdre smiled and slanted Brennan a bright, knowing glance. "There is a place for you here, if you want it," she told Rhiannon kindly. "You deserve better than serving wine to amorous young lordlings in tawdry taverns."

Brennan raised his brows. "*I* was always polite, and The Rampant Lion is not tawdry."

" 'Tis for Rhiannon to decide."

Keely grunted. "Even *Hart* would not lay a wager on that."

Brennan felt the familiar stab of loneliness.

Rhiannon looked at him directly a long moment. And then she rose and curtsied to Deirdre. She was slim and lissome in the rich blue gown. The rope of heavy hair swung against her hip. "Aye, lady, I will stay."

"Good." Deirdre's beckoning gestures encompassed Maeve and Keely as well. "Come then, there are things you must be learning. We'll be leaving the men to themselves."

Maeve and Rhiannon moved to the door at once. Keely, scowling darkly, finished her wine in a single gulp and then thumped the cup down on the nearest table. "Foolishness," she muttered, and was the last one out of the room.

Brennan smiled a little as the door thudded closed to punctuate Keely's temper. "Do you regret it, *jehan?* Siring such unruly children?"

Niall grinned. "There *are* times. . . ." He let it trail off and stretched out his legs, slumping back in the chair. Candlelight glinted off the cup still held in his hand. "If the gods are willing, you will know the same trials I do. But in the end it is worth it . . . too long was the House of Homana poor in children, poor in healthy sons." He shook his head. "Because of my unruly children, I am able to make just distribution of our holdings, and improve for our House the trusts held by other kings. Within one generation I am able to secure threefold the path of the prophecy. Believe me, that is something."

Brennan nodded. Idly he looked into his cup; his wine was untouched. He drank down half of it in two gulping swallows, then dropped into the nearest chair. His ear hurt, and his head, and the rest of him as well. "There is more," he said at last. "I saw Teir at Clankeep. He was his usual self."

Niall shook his head in disgust. "I thought Ceinn knew better than to raise his son on resentment and bitterness. It does no good—the *a'saii* are disbanded."

"Teirnan says they are not."

The Mujhar went very still. "Not," he echoed. "And do you say they again espouse a change in the succession?"

"With an *additional* change. Ceinn and the others may have wanted Ian to take your place, *once,* but this time Teir wants the Lion for himself."

"The fool. The young, arrogant fool!" Niall thrust himself out of the chair and paced to one of the casements. It was full night outside, but the glow from bailey torches banished total darkness. What he saw Brennan would not venture to guess, but then he was not certain his father looked at anything other than memories.

"He says they will appeal to Clan Council, charging that Teir's blood has precedence over ours, *jehan.*" Brennan shook his head. "He seems not to care that a division within the clans could well divide Homana."

"Teirnan never could see farther than his own immediate desires," Niall said in disgust. "Ceinn was shrewder . . . he said they wanted *Ian* on the Lion, or—when it was obvious Ian would never claim it—the first son 'Solde bore." He sighed and rubbed at ruined flesh, obviously troubled by old memories and grief. "Never did he claim it for himself. So—now he gives that son leave to win it—or steal it—however he can."

"*Jehan*—"

The Mujhar's tone was weary more than angry. "If he knew what it was to sit in the Lion Throne . . ." But he did not finish, turning instead to face his oldest son. "Well then, I think it is time to have him come to Homana-Mujhar."

"*Here?*" Brennan frowned. "Why?"

"I discounted the *a'saii* before, because I was foolish enough to believe my place secured," Niall said. "I was, after all, Cheysuli and Homanan, a part of the prophecy." He smiled in wry self-deprecation. "It nearly got me slain. I will not do it again . . . not when my son is at risk."

Brennan stared at his father thoughtfully for a long moment. Then he slowly shook his head as he understood the ramifications. "You are taking Teirnan hostage against the *a'saii*."

"Am I?" Niall's bland tone divulged nothing of his thoughts.

Brennan could not look away from the man. He had seen the Mujhar on many occasions dealing with all manner of circumstances, political and personal, but never had seen him so intently purposeful while seeming so unconcerned.

"He might not come, *jehan*."

"I think he will. If I know anything of Teirnan at all, he will come to prove himself. To prove what he is to *us*."

"I can *tell* you what he is," Brennan murmured darkly.

Niall smiled and walked slowly over to Deirdre's tapestry frame. He studied the pattern intently for a moment, then turned back to Brennan. "I cannot expect you to be boon companions any more than Ceinn and I were. But perhaps you can—*influence* him."

Brennan scowled. "I can think of better company."

"Doubtless so can he."

The scowl evaporated, replaced by a wry smile. "And if Ceinn objects? He *is* Teir's *jehan*."

Niall raised his tawny brows. "And I am Mujhar of Homana. On occasions such as this, there *is* some value in rank."

Brennan laughed aloud. "I think you *want* Ceinn to object."

"There is no pleasure in discord." Smiling, Niall lifted his cup and drank.

Son looked at father in detached appreciation. He did not much resemble Niall, being wholly Cheysuli in bones and color while the Mujhar was wholly Homanan, but they often thought alike, spoke alike, experienced similar feelings. There were times Brennan thought his father knew what he was thinking.

He scrubbed at his brow; weariness threatened to make him incoherent. He rose and set the cup down on the nearest table. "*Jehan*, if you will give me leave, I am for bed."

"Brennan."

At the door, Brennan glanced back. "Aye?"

"You have bedded the girl."

Brennan took his hand off the latch and turned to face his father more fully. "Aye." He felt a brief spasm of guilt as he recalled the initial circumstances, but it faded instantly. In the end, what he and Rhiannon had shared had not been a thing of force or mere gratification at all, but of entirely different dimensions.

The Mujhar's single eye was oddly opaque, but unwavering. "Perhaps I would do well to remind you that although *meijhas* are accepted in the clans, Aileen is not Cheysuli."

He thought he was too tired to be truly angry, but a trace of resentment flared. And was gone almost at once. He knew very well that if it were not in deference to Aileen's Erinnish sensibilities, his father would never interfere in his son's personal life.

"I have no intention of offering insult to Aileen," Brennan said quietly, "any more than I intend to make Rhiannon my *meijha*."

The Mujhar relaxed almost imperceptibly. He smiled. "Go and eat. And sleep. I intend to send men tomorrow to learn what they can of this Homanan idiocy concerning Caro—it may be nothing more than something created by Strahan for effect—but I will excuse you from it *and* from Council in the morning."

"*Leijhana tu'sai,*" Brennan said fervently, and pulled open the heavy door.

He slept heavily for part of the night and then awoke, sweating, as he felt himself slide toward the abyss. Sleep was banished. He sat up in bed and stared blankly at the draperies dripping from the framework of his bed and knew if he did not resolve his fear once and for all, he would never sleep well again.

Sleeta was a lump of warmth and blackness at the foot of his bed. Even in deepest winter he required no heating pans; Sleeta was more than enough. Through the link he felt her drowsy inquiry, and told her to go back to sleep.

What he intended to do required solitude, or the accomplishment—should there be any—would be tainted.

Brennan pulled on leggings, jerkin, soft houseboots. Moonlight slanted through casement slits, providing more than enough illumination for a man with Cheysuli vision. He went out of his room into the torchlit corridor and took the first down-winding staircase he came to.

In the Great Hall, the Lion crouched on the dais. Brennan hardly glanced at it; nocturnal visits in childhood had inured him to the eerie, lifelike stare of wooden eyes. And it was not the Lion that drew him now, but something else entirely.

Brennan kicked charred wood and ash from one end of the firepit, sweeping clean of debris the circular iron lid set flush against stained brick. He thought briefly of using a torch for a lever; dismissed it and bent to grasp the twisted handle. He muttered a plea for help, then braced himself and jerked upward.

The hinged lid yawned open and folded against the rim of the pit with a muffled clang. Ash rose; Brennan coughed. The exertion emphasized his need for rest and recovery. Raw wrists stung as other muscles clamored to protest abuse.

Brennan stood on the edge of the stairway leading deep into the earth. It had been sixteen years since he had descended the one hundred and two steps to the underground vault called the Womb of the Earth.

Aloud, he quoted a tenet of the clans: *"If one is afraid, one can only become unafraid by facing that which causes the fear."*

The words fell away into silence.

He sucked in a deep breath through a throat that threatened to close. "Prince of Homana? No. More like prince of cowards."

There was no disagreement.

Brennan swore. He caught up a torch from the rack and thrust it rigidly before him. It roared in the mouth of the stairway.

"Down," he said aloud, and made himself follow the order.

He counted. Each step took him nearer the Womb, farther from the Lion. Deeper. Until there was no light at all from the Great Hall, only the flames from the torch, and he knew it was not enough.

Brennan stopped. Sweat stung his armpits and dampened the hair against his face. The torch shook from the rigidity of his grip, distorting illumination. All he could see was blackness ahead and the promise of close confinement.

Down.

More steps. One by one, he descended them, until there were no more. He stood in a closet made of rune-worked stone. Slowly he put out one hand and pressed the keystone.

The wall fell inward, as he knew it would, and the vault revealed itself to him. The torch roared, spat flame, threatened briefly to snuff out. But it did not. And when he could, Brennan stepped into the vault.

The walls ran wet with torchlight. Gold veined the creamy marble and lent life to the *lir* imprisoned there. Brennan saw wings and claws and beaks and eyes, all frozen in the stone. Each wall, from floor to ceiling, was alive with marble *lir*.

"*Ja'hai,*" he muttered aloud. But the gods made no indication they heard his instinctive plea for acceptance.

Sixteen years . . . and I am no less afraid at twenty-one than I was at five.

Brennan took three steps forward, then two more. He stood at the edge of the oubliette. The torchlight did not begin to touch the darkness of the pit. He could see nothing past the rim.

There were stories about the Womb. Legends that said a man, meant to become Mujhar, was required to be born of the earth herself, of the *Jehana*, and this was the birthing place. No one knew if the stories were true, or merely imagery handed down by the *shar tahls* to make certain everyone would remember. Brennan himself could not say, although he had heard one story more than once; that Homanan Carillon, needing the blessing of the gods, had of his own accord gone into the oubliette. And come out again, whole, but with a greater understanding of what it meant to be Cheysuli, even though he was not.

"Homanan," Brennan said aloud. "But I am Cheysuli; is there really a need for such sacrifice?"

"Is there, my lord?"

He stood very still on the edge of the oubliette, taking great care to maintain his balance. When he could move again without fear of falling, he turned.

Rhiannon stood in the open doorway. She had exchanged gown for linen nightrail and woolen robe. Wrapped in deepest blue, cloaked in a mantle of raven hair, she blended into the shadows.

In her eyes was the knowledge of what they had shared the night before, and the desire to share it again. She was not a bold jade such as many of the court women, but neither was she a coy woman whose mouth was filled with innuendo. That she believed herself in love with him, he knew; perhaps she was. But he was not in love with her.

She did not move from the doorway, as if she understood quite well that to enter was to intrude upon something sacred, something of ancient and binding power. "I went to your chamber and saw you leave it, so intent you did not see me in the shadows. You looked so troubled—" she shrugged, excusing her boldness easily, "—I followed. I found the stairway in the firepit, and knew what you meant to do."

"Did you?"

"Aye." She raised her chin slightly. "Whatever you may think of yourself in the aftermath of what Jarek did, you remain a brave man. A man of pride and strength and determination, not one to let a thing like fear cripple his *tahlmorra*." She smiled. "Deirdre is a remarkable woman, my lord. She answered my questions before I asked them, and told me what it was to love a man so bound by a prophecy. She told me how to share a Cheysuli with his *tahlmorra*."

He would not spare her the truth. "And did she also tell you that within a matter of months there will be a

Princess of Homana who will share those things with me?"

"Aye," Rhiannon said.

He had expected tears, disappointment, resentment. She gave him none of those things. What she gave him was pride to match his own, and integrity, and an honesty he so rarely saw in Homana-Mujhar, except when he spoke with Cheysuli.

He smiled a trifle sadly. "Where is the innocence?"

A tinge of color entered her face. "Do not mistake me, Brennan. I want nothing more than what I had last night. You wanted it—*needed* it—then . . . and I think you want it now."

He did. For different reasons, perhaps, but he would not lie to himself any more than to her.

"Her name is Aileen." His words were brutal by design; he offered a final chance for withdrawal.

But it was not accepted. "I know," she said evenly. "*My* name is Rhiannon."

He took her hand. He led her out of the Womb of the Earth. He brought her to his chambers. To his bed.

To something he did not, could not regret.

Eight

Teirnan threw himself down in the Lion Throne. He grinned, caressing the ancient wood, then laughed aloud in joyous exultation. "Do you *know* how long I have wanted to do this? Can you guess?"

Brennan, who did not particularly care, merely shook his head.

"For as long as I can remember." Still Teirnan stroked the clawed armrests, glorying in the texture of age-polished oak. "Since my *jehan* first told me I was kin to the House of Homana."

Brennan's mouth twisted in irony. "And how carefully did he tend you, Teir? How subtle was he in impressing upon you his belief that you should rule in my place?"

Teirnan luxuriated in the throne, sitting back so that his head was shadowed by the gaping lion's mouth. "There was no subtlety at all, cousin. I am the son of dead Isolde, *rujholla* to the Mujhar . . . my blood cries out for the Lion."

Brennan, arms folded, paced slowly to the dais and climbed it, posting himself directly before the throne. "There are no *a'saii*, are there? Only you. And Ceinn, of course—but I think Ceinn's teeth were pulled many years ago, when my *jehan* named him *shu'maii* in his Ceremony of Honors."

Teirnan's hands clenched the claws of the Lion. "I have as much right to it as you."

"Do you?"

"My blood hearkens back to the days of the Old

Mujhars, the *Cheysuli* Mujhars, who had no need to marry unblessed foreigners in order to secure Homana. It was ours already, given us by the gods themselves." '

"And the Ihlini?" Brennan shrugged as Teirnan broke off to stare at him in shock. "I do not deny that through Ceinn your blood is purer than mine . . . that because of Ceinn, you count some of the oldest and *cleanest* blood in your heritage." He tipped his head to one side in a brief gesture of idle acknowledgment. "After all, even your *jehana*—kin to the Mujhar himself—had decidedly mixed blood, while yours is admittedly less so." Brennan was motionless, holding him with the understated gentleness of his tone. "But if you wish to sit here and prate about it how you are improved by such purity, recall that it was precisely *because* certain clans refused to marry out that this dynastic manipulation became necessary. This realm to that realm, this warrior to that woman . . ." He shook his head. "Perhaps you should also consider that it becomes more and more likely we *are* bloodkin to the Ihlini."

"No." Teirnan was deadly serious as he pulled himself out of the throne. "You speak heresy, Brennan."

Brennan shook his head. "I speak of probabilities."

"How can you *say* that?"

"Look at the *lir!*" Brennan said. "Will they attack the Ihlini? *No*—even though they will do their best to destroy anyone else who means us harm. Will they tell us why? *No*—all they ever say is that they follow the law of the gods." He drew in a breath, understanding things more clearly himself even as he spoke. "It does seem entirely possible, *cousin*, that the reason that law exists is to keep children from slaying children—"

"Children—?"

"The children of the gods." Brennan exhaled slowly. "I find it hard to believe the gods would give their children the weapons with which they might kill one another when what their parents desire is for them to live in accord."

"But Ihlini kill Cheysuli!"

"And Cheysuli kill Ihlini." Brennan drew in a breath

of dull acknowledgment, understanding it at last. "But without benefit of the *lir*. Without benefit of a full complement of powers . . . so that the battles are battles of *men,* and not the get of the gods, who have more power than perhaps they should to live in a world of men."

Teirnan's breath rasped loudly in the hall. "It cannot be," he said.

"How can it *not* be?" Brennan asked. "*You* know the prophecy, Teir. Its aim is to merge bloodlines and unite deadly enemies. We know the four realms: Homana, Solinde, Erinn and Atvia. Even now we are closer to fulfilling that portion of the prophecy. I will hold Homana. Hart will have Solinde, Corin Atvia, and Keely will wed into Erinn. As for the two magical races, who else can they be but Cheysuli and Ihlini?"

Teirnan's face was gray. "May the gods strike you down!"

"Why?" Brennan asked. "It was the gods who gave us the prophecy."

Teirnan backed up a step and ran into the throne. He stopped abruptly, rigidly, and stared blindly at his cousin. His face was a death-mask.

"Teir," Brennan said with abiding patience, "I do not advocate we go to Strahan with words of peace in our mouths. But I think perhaps my *jehan* has the right of it: the time is come for the Cheysuli to begin acknowledging *all* Ihlini are not dedicated to Asar-Suti. There are those who serve themselves because they believe in peaceful unification as much as our prophecy demands it."

"Unification," Teirnan echoed.

"Blood merged with blood," Brennan told him. "And a chance for lasting peace."

Teirnan looked at the Lion. He touched it again, exploring it with his fingers. His face was immobile in its intensity, the angles hard as stone. "What will happen when the prophecy is fulfilled?"

Brennan frowned; Teirnan was leading up to something. "Peace. Cohabitation. The Firstborn will live again."

"*Aye.*" Teirnan overrode his words. "Aye, they will—and do you know what will happen?"

Brennan raised his brows. "Who can say? Their power will be complete . . . there will be no weaknesses."

"And what of us?" His cousin asked intently. "What of the Cheysuli, who *do* have weaknesses?"

"Teir—"

"Blood merged with blood, until the new overtakes the old. Do you see what will happen? There will be no more need for us!"

Brennan started to put out a restraining hand, thought better of it. He could not predict what Teirnan might do. "The gods would hardly guide us to fulfillment only to discard us when we have reached it," he said dryly. "We have been such faithful children."

"Faithful, aye . . . perhaps *too* faithful." Teirnan frowned and fingered the hilt of his Cheysuli long-knife. "Aye, I have heard some of this heresy you spout. Niall has made it no secret for the last twenty years. Peace, he says, as *you* have said, with the coming of the Firstborn. But what else? What *else*, Brennan? Have you not heard that we are also to lose our *lir?*"

"I think that is exaggeration."

"Oh? It was the Mujhar who said it, and his loyal liege man, our *su'fali.*" Teirnan shook his head. "I think perhaps the heresy may hold a kernel of truth. For all I and others have continually denied it, including the *shar tahls,* I think perhaps we *are* to lose our *lir.* And for that—for that *alone*—I think we should reconsider what the prophecy really means."

Brennan sighed. "Is this nonsense compensation for your pride because you know you will never hold the Lion? Teir—"

But Teirnan shook his head and stepped abruptly away from the throne. "I renounce it."

After momentary astonishment, Brennan opened his mouth to compliment his cousin on recovering his senses, but said nothing as Teirnan spoke again.

"I renounce it. I renounce *you.* I renounce anything to do with the House of Homana, even Maeve."

The latter had already been settled; Maeve had admitted to making a vow to become Teirnan's *meijha,* but in

ignorance of his ambition. Discovery of it had driven a
wedge between them, and she had not returned to
Clankeep. Neither did she have, she said, any intention
of honoring her vow; Teirnan's declaration was therefore
an empty one.

Brennan sighed. "Teir—"

"Do you see?" Teirnan demanded. "We will be diminished. We will be *used up*. There will be no more need
for flawed children when the Firstborn live again."

"You *fool*." Brennan's disgust was manifest.

"Am I? No. I think I am the only one who understands fully what will happen." Teirnan moved away
from the throne again. "You have the right of it, Brennan; there were no *a'saii*. Only an overly ambitious cousin.
But now—*now* I think the need is come again. . . ."
Teirnan rubbed his face with both hands, as if to make
certain he fully understood the consequences of what he
intended to say. "I renounce the prophecy."

Shock turned Brennan icy. He shivered violently. "You
cannot!"

"Why? I am bound by nothing more than my willingness to serve it. Now I choose not to do so."

"If you renounce the prophecy you turn your back on
the clans, your race, your *tahlmorra*—"

"Then I will do so."

"*Teirnan!*" Emphatically, Brennan shook his head. "You
deny the afterworld."

"I begin to think *this* world is more than enough."
Teirnan moved past him and descended the dais steps to
the stone floor. Before the firepit, he turned to face his
cousin. "I thank you for your frankness, Brennan. For
explaining how necessary it is for us to breed Firstborn
on Ihlini, and how the results will change the world.
Because if you had not, I would still be blindly serving a
prophecy that will undoubtedly insure the destruction of
our race."

"I could gainsay you," Brennan told him angrily. "Here,
in this hall, we could settle this idiocy."

Teirnan swung to face him squarely, beckoning him on
with empty, eloquent hands. "Then come, cousin. But if

you do, be certain the fight will be to the death." Teirnan's eyes blazed with a feral light. "If you truly mean to gainsay me, then you will have to kill me."

They stared hard at one another. Teirnan's face was alight with some inner exultation, a kindling of new and abiding commitment. Brennan looked at him in disgust coupled with frustration, and considered calling his bluff.

But there is every chance Teirnan does not bluff. And if he does not, and I should kill him in some stupid, pointless battle, I become kinslayer yet again. He shook his head. *Teirnan is not worth it.*

"Go," Brennan said harshly. "But remember that you are now a clanless man. Your rune will be painted out of the birthlines. Your name will be struck from the histories. Your *jehan* will have no son."

It was a powerful inducement to make a warrior recant his renunciation. But Teirnan was not induced. "Unless he should come *with* me."

"Ceinn would not—" But Brennan broke off. It was possible Ceinn *would;* he had raised this rebel. It was also possible others would; Brennan was realistic enough to know there were warriors who might prefer the old order to the new.

Teirnan smiled a little. "Aye. I see you understand."

Brennan's mouth was dry. "You would willingly divide the clans?"

Teirnan shrugged. "I offer an alternative. It will be their choice."

"It will be *no* choice!" Brennan cried. "What kind of warrior are you?"

"*A'saii,*" Teirnan said evenly. "Clanless, runeless, and free—*free to serve myself.*"

It was all Brennan could do not to shout at him. "You profane this place," he said in a deadly tone. "You dishonor your *jehana.*"

"Isolde is dead," Teirnan said curtly. "As for profaning this place, I will take myself out of it."

Mute, Brennan watched his cousin go. He could find no protests in the face of such deadly determination. And when he was alone again, save for the massive throne, he went to it and sat down. It was not the first time. He and the Lion were on good terms.

"He will change his mind," Brennan told it, as much to reassure himself as to placate the Lion. "He will never leave his clan." But there was no answering reassurance from his conscience. Uneasily, he touched the lobeless ear. "Perhaps I should tell *jehan*."

Brennan did, over the Mujhar's evening meal, which Niall took alone in his private solar; Deirdre was otherwise occupied. His father pushed aside his platter of unfinished food so sharply his knife rattled against the silver. "I cannot *believe* you were so foolish as to incite Teir to such idiocy! You know what he is like."

Brennan sat slumped over the table, chin propped up on one hand. He was disgruntled enough; his father's displeasure made him feel worse. "Aye, well, I think we need not worry. Teir often says much but does very little."

Niall's tone was decidedly cool. "That is your opinion after carefully considering what would happen if he did precisely as he threatens?"

"How could he turn his back on so much?" Brennan asked in guilt-born exasperation. "His clan, his race, his *tahlmorra*—"

"Obviously he is willing to do so. For all he gives us impotent threats much of the time, *this* one may be real. How many warriors do you know even *jest* about such action?"

Brennan scowled. "None, but—"

"*But.*" Niall's tone was distinctly harsh. "I suggest you leave for Clankeep now and see if you can repair the damage."

"*Jehan*—"

"I myself will go in the morning. This sort of threat will be of concern to the clan-leader as well as the *shar tahl*." Niall scraped his stool back and rose, his meal unfinished. "Well?"

Belatedly, Brennan also rose. He was grateful they were alone so no one else could see his frustration. "Teir will do nothing tonight. Why not let me go with you in the morning?"

"Because I have told you to go *now*."

Brennan sighed and shoved the stool out of his way. "Aye, *jehan*—aye, *aye*," he muttered, and strode angrily toward the door.

"Even kings must take responsibility for the consequences of their own actions," Naill said as Brennan opened the door. "Begin now, and it will be that much easier when you are Mujhar."

His heir shot him a look of deep disgust and closed the door with a resounding thud as he stepped into the corridor. *Lir, we have been sent on a foolish errand.*

Sleeta was one floor up in his chambers, but the link dissolved the separation. *We?* she asked pointedly.

Do you berate me, too?

She sighed. *Where are we going, lir?*

Clankeep.

Her tone brightened. *Then I will bestir myself.*

Upon Brennan's orders his newest horse was brought, saddled and ready. It was late afternoon and the weather was cool; winter was not so far away. The stallion, all black save for a splash of white upon his nose, sidled and snorted, stomping noisily on the cobbles. His eyes rolled as he espied Sleeta, who waited on the steps.

"My lord, I can saddle another," the groom said as the stallion's lips peeled back to display large teeth.

Brennan avoided the bite. "No. I am in the mood for Bane." He caught the reins and swung up into the Cheysuli saddle, clamping legs against sleek sides as Bane laid his ears flat back and essayed a tentative sideways leap. "The Mujhar rides out in the morning."

"Aye, my lord." The groom stepped away quickly, dodging flying hooves as Bane commenced dancing across the bailey. Brennan rode out the worst of the stallion's customary protest, then signaled the gates open. "I cannot say when I will return," he called, and let the stallion go as Sleeta bounded through.

He was at the border dividing meadowlands from forest when Rhiannon caught up to him. After the first

short gallop across the plains to work out frustrations and
Bane's bad temper, Brennan had slowed the stallion to a
walk. Rhiannon clearly had kept her mount at a run; the
bay mare was lathered with sweat.

He waited until Rhiannon had caught up before reaching across to grab one rein. "You know better," he said
sternly. High color stood in her face. She was breathless,
black eyes alight with exhilaration; the wind had blown
tendrils of hair free of confining braid.

"I know better," she agreed, "but there was no help
for it. You did not heed my call to wait."

He frowned. "When did you call?"

She laughed. "When the horse tried to smash your
knee against the gatepost. You were swearing, my lord; I
am not surprised you did not hear me."

He smiled ruefully. "Aye, well, I am somewhat fond
of my knee, and the gods know I have more need of it
than Bane." He released her rein and jumped down from
his horse. "Dismount, *meijhana*—the mare should be
walked."

"Aye, of course." She slithered out of the saddle in a
tangle of tassled boots, blue skirts and midnight mantle.
The heavy rope of hair was lost in the folds of the
mantle, but he saw a glint of silver ribbon threaded
through the plait.

He reached out and caught one slim hand, pulling her
close. Rhiannon, laughing, stretched up for his kiss, then
locked hands around his neck to pull him closer yet.

"Do you mind?" she asked as he released her. "I
wanted to be with you. So often I must spend all my time
with Deirdre or the ladies, when I would rather be with
you."

He felt a twinge of guilt. It was no secret that Rhiannon
shared his bed, yet the Mujhar held his silence. Brennan
had no doubt Niall knew, but perhaps he knew also that
repeated reminders of Aileen's imminent arrival would
merely promote discord.

"I do not mind, *meijhana*, but you may find it tedious.
I am sent to Clankeep to settle things with my rebellious
cousin."

"Teir is a fool," Rhiannon declared. "Maeve loves him—had he any sense, he would try to gain the Mujhar's favor so he can take her for a wife."

"Then perhaps *Maeve* is the fool." He turned Rhiannon toward the wood. "Come, *meijhana*—the mare needs cooling."

She fell in beside him, leading the tired mare. "Where is Sleeta?"

"Gone ahead. Hungry, she says, but she will not be far."

Fingers twined. They walked in companionable silence, leaving behind the open plains for the shadows of the wood. The track was wide and beaten smooth; Clankeep was no longer closed to those who were not Cheysuli. Homanan goldsmiths came to trade for ornaments, and other craftsmen as well.

"There was another reason," Rhiannon said quietly. "The Mujhar meant to send a man to tell you, but I said *I* would go." She looked up at him gravely. "Word has come. Aileen's ship has sailed from Erinn."

Brennan nearly missed a step. Behind him, Bane nibbled irritably at his shoulder.

"I wanted to be the one to tell you."

He looked down at her. Her face was mostly averted, but he heard the merest trace of a waver in her voice. "*Meijhana*—"

"I know," she said. "I have always known. You will marry her."

"It was a cradle-betrothal." He sighed. "It was more than that, *meijhana*—it was agreed before I was born."

"I know." She shrugged, speaking brightly. "I am no one. I could bring you nothing. Nothing but—" She hesitated, then halted and turned to face him squarely. One hand was splayed across her belly. "Nothing but this child."

He caught her shoulders and held her firmly in place, ignoring the mare's snort of fright and Bane's rolling eye. "Are you certain?"

"Quite certain, my lord." Rhiannon's smile was odd. "Does it please you?"

"How *not?*" He was astonished that she could ask it. "A *child*, Rhiannon . . . how could I not be pleased?"

"A *bastard*, my lord."

"Do you think I care about that? A child is a child."

Rhiannon laughed. "And an *Ihlini-Cheysuli* child? What do you say to that?"

"His fingers locked in the folds of her woolen mantle. *"Ihlini—"*

One cool hand was a shackle on his wrist, clinging, pressing, *squeezing,* until the flesh began to protest. "Ihlini," she said distinctly, "Ihlini *and* Cheysuli. Why else do you think I wanted you?—why I made you want *me?"*

She was a woman, and weaker than he: angrily Brennan tried to break her grip, twisting sharply; to shock and dismay he found he could not. Because even as he moved, thinking to thrust her violently away, he felt the explosion of pain through the link.

Sleeta was nearly incoherent. *Lir—lir—lir—*

Even as Brennan tried to twist free again, meaning to run toward the source of Sleeta's anguish, Rhiannon prevented him. With one hand only, fingers spread rigidly against his breastbone, she coolly forced him off the track and against the nearest tree. "Back," she said only, supremely indifferent to his aborted bid for escape.

Lir— The cat's helplessness was his own, transmitting itself through the link with frightening ease and accuracy. Though Rhiannon exerted little pressure, Brennan was slammed against the tree.

"Sleeta—"

"She is ours." Deftly Rhiannon pulled the reins free of his clutching hand and freed both horses, sending them away with a burst of purple flame from negligent fingers. "I suggest you do not try to struggle, for Sleeta's sake if not your own. My servants hold her now."

He wanted to overpower her. He wanted to snap her elegant neck. But Sleeta's welfare was paramount in his mind, and there was no doubting Rhiannon's confidence. He dared not try to move, or risk his *lir's* life as well as his own.

Sleeta?

Lir—lir—Ihlini— And abruptly her pattern was broken, like a candle snuffed rudely out.

Rhiannon's hand still rested on his breastbone, promising violence. That she used some form of arcane force, he knew; she was strong, *too* strong. The rough bark of the tree ground against his spine, even through the leathers. Within he raged at her; without he made no effort to escape or attack.

"Good man," she said, "good warrior. Do not move and she will live."

"Slay her and you slay *me*."

"Empty threat," she answered. "*I* have what I want of you."

He tried to reach Sleeta through the privacy of the link, but nothing answered his frenzied search. There was emptiness in the pattern. "You have already killed her!"

"No, my lord. Not yet. She has been overcome by brutal force, but she lives. For now. Until we are through with you."

"How do you intend to kill me?" Bitterly. He could not believe he had been so gullible.

"Strahan wants you alive."

"*Strahan—*" He nearly gaped. "This is Strahan's doing?"

"Strahan's *suggestion*. My doing." Rhiannon smiled and reached up to caress his face even as he tried to jerk away. "It could have been worse, Brennan. Much worse. Seduction is better than force."

His lips peeled back from his teeth in an instinctive expression of feral disgust. He thought he might be ill.

"Lillith believed I could not do it," Rhiannon said quietly. "She feared I was too young, even by human standards. But then my mother forgets that Ihlini women are born to seduction as Cheysuli are born to the *lir*."

His muscles spasmed beneath her hand. "*Lillith—*"

"—is my mother. My *jehana,* you would say. As Ian is my *jehan*." Rhiannon laughed softly. "We are cousins, you and I—in addition to being bedmates."

"But—*Jarek—*" Brennan stopped. He required no explanation. In the face of her triumph and confidence, he knew she spoke the truth. "Not Jarek at all . . . nothing but misdirection, to make us believe ourselves safe . . . it was *you* all the while. . . ."

"It was me all the while." Rhiannon smiled. "Jarek was a fine diversion. Thinking *him* Ihlini, you did not look at me." She laughed. "A clever plot to take you . . . send Solindish Jarek into Homana as a *Homanan*, where he would pose as Elek's son to win Homanan aid. And then we would take you in the name of Carillon's deaf-mute bastard."

"Was it your idea to let Ian believe Jarek was his son?" he asked bitterly. "Your idea to let *me* believe I was kinslayer?"

She pursed her lips. "The first? No. It was my mother's idea; a gift, she said, for Ian." Rhiannon smiled. "As for allowing you to believe you were kinslayer, well . . . it made you more vulnerable to me. That was my idea."

He drew in a deep breath, longing to spit in her face, but knowing better. Ihlini held his *lir*. "A complex and clever plan."

"It took a great deal of time to lay this plan—more to execute." She shrugged. "But then *time* is nothing to us." Black eyes narrowed. "And now we go, my lord. Strahan grows impatient."

His struggles were futile, and he knew it; Rhiannon's power over Sleeta was too pronounced. But he ignored the pressure against his breastbone and caught her wrist, thinking to snap it in two, to shatter all the bones. Or to crack her fragile skull with a blow from his other hand.

And yet he could do none of those things. Even as he tried to move, he found his body would not answer. His hand fell away form her wrist; he slumped against the tree, pinned by slender fingers. In her eyes was triumph and the knowledge of burgeoning power.

Angrily he bared his teeth in a feral, mocking smile. "Valgaard is a long ride from here. If you think it will be *easy*—"

"Who said anything of riding?" Rhiannon pulled something from beneath her gown; he saw a glint of familiar silver. It was the ring he had given her, but the sapphire glowed an eerie purple instead of clear blue. "We Ihlini have better ways."

He manged to laugh, albeit was little more than an impotent bark of sound. "You forget; I am Cheysuli. Your sorcery will not work."

"*You* forget, my lord—I am Cheysuli also." She smiled. "Ask why Sleeta did not know me. Ask why I hold you so easily. Look into your mind and find the link I have forged through careful and subtle means, all done in the throes of passion, when you would not notice my intrusion."

He rolled his head against the tree in desperate denial. "You cannot. . . ."

"Can I not?" She was magnificent in her pride. "But I *can*, cousin . . . the merging of our blood gives me a new dimension of power altogether, when that blood is also joined with Asar-Suti."

Her serenity alarmed him. "But you are not a First-born—"

"No. Not yet. But closer. Closer even than you. Because in the end, it will be the blood of our child—of Ihlini-Cheysuli children—who will hold dominance in Homana. Dominance in the world."

Rhiannon unhooked the silver chain that had replaced the ring's original leather thong. And though he tried to twist his head away, she clasped it around his neck. The chain was ice against his throat.

One last time—

"Brennan." Calmly she interrupted his futile attempt at *lir*-shape. "I do not love you, but neither do I hate you. What I do, I do to serve my race, as much as you serve yours. We are kin, close kin, and I have no wish to spill your blood; I share more than a measure of it. Ian is in us both." She caught his hands and linked her fingers with his, even against his will. "But we cannot control the Firstborn unless we make our own."

"*Ihlini—*" He writhed against the tree.

Rhiannon kissed him. And then the world was gone.

Interlude

Where she walked, smoke followed. Disturbed by the motion of heavy skirts, it tore apart like a webwork of lilac lace, then repaired itself in her wake to renew its delicate dance.

Godfire hissed in the whorls of glasswork columns. Down and down, around and around; light glistened in the twisted strings of the Seker's magnificent harp. She thought once to touch the closest column to see if it would sing, but she did not. It was not for her to do.

She walked, and the smoke followed. All the way to the rent in the flesh of the earth, where flame instead of blood issued forth in a blinding glare. Beyond it, poised on the rim of the Gate, stood her mother and her uncle.

On the near side, Rhiannon halted. She folded her hands in her skirts.

Lillith smiled. In her daughter she saw herself, and took pride in the girl's loyalty as well as her loveliness. "How soon will the child be born?"

"Seven months. Brennan was—most accommodating."

"And you?"

"I?"

"You are young," Lillith said kindly. "Cheysuli and Ihlini are bloodkin, born of the same gods, and meant to lie together. It is understandable if this was—difficult. There is no shame in wishing it could be another way."

Rhiannon lifted her delicate chin. "Was it difficult for *you*, when you seduced my father? Was it hard to break that immense Cheysuli pride?"

"Ian's pride was never broken," Lillith answered. "*He*
may have thought so, but it was *lirlessness* he felt, nothing more." She paused. "When you speak of breaking
pride, remember that what is theirs is also ours."

"They will never accept it," Rhiannon said. "Never
will they accept us as anything more than enemies."

"Good," Strahan said coolly. "If the day ever comes
that an Ihlini and a completed Cheysuli lie down together
willingly, the Seker is defeated. The gate will be sealed
forever, and the Firstborn shall rule the world. We will no
longer exist."

Rhiannon frowned. "What is a 'completed' Cheysuli?"

"One with all the necessary blood, save our own." The
glare increased, leeching shadows from Strahan's face,
then faded away to a dull glow, as if the god listened.
"The prophecy is a true one, Rhiannon. The Cheysuli
weave it like a tapestry, and the pattern is nearly completed. But we can still alter it. We can tear away the
brightest yarns, as we have torn away Brennan, and use
them to fashion another."

Lillith nodded. "Link by link, we must shatter the
chain."

Godfire hissed; the flame rose, swelled, died away
again.

"What will you do to him?" Rhiannon asked.

"Break him," Strahan answered. "Then mend him
most carefully."

"How?" she asked intently.

Strahan's eyes narrowed. "Have you a suggestion?"

Rhiannon's laughter echoed amidst the columns and
set the glassy strings to thrumming. "Lock him away,"
she said. "Lock him away in a small stone place . . . with
no light, no *lir,* and no hope at all for escape."

PART III

HART

One

Solinde was an inhospitable, barren land, Hart thought, until he left behind the borderlands and entered wooded hills. The wide track leading out of Homana into Solinde traded plains for huddled hills, winding like a tunnel through heavy vegetation. Thick and deep, the shadows held dominance over sunlight.

He was thankful he had exchanged sleeveless jerkin for something a bit more substantial. The doublet, dyed a rich emerald green and belted with bronze-plated leather, was of stiffer leather than a Cheysuli jerkin and, though still immensely comfortable, its long sleeves provided warmth against the breath of a fall day. In the wood, in the shadows, the chill seemed to seep through flesh into his bones.

Hart shivered as the trees closed in, branches reaching for his face. The tunnel shrank and the shadows deepened, until he felt singularly oppressed. All around him were trunks and limbs and vines. The wood smelled of decay.

Lir, he said uneasily; Rael was out of sight.

Here. The hawk answered instantly. *Above you, lir, above the trees, where it is bright and warm in the sunlight.*

Hart tilted his head back and searched, but all he could see was the screen of limbs, a latticework thrown up by trees and vine and shadow. *Perhaps I should leave the horse behind and go on as a hawk.*

And then you would arrive without all your finery.

Hart laughed aloud, casually patting the saddlepacks

that clothed most of his stallion's rump. "Little enough of that, I fear. Aye, I *could* have brought every trunk, but what is the sense in that? I have leathers, food and a fortune-game . . . what else do I require?"

Good sense, Rael retorted. *Or am I expected to supply the wisdom while you supply the gold?*

"I intend to *win* the gold, not supply it," Hart explained. "Sweet Solindish gold . . . I hear it is red as copper, but with twice the weight and thrice the value of Homanan."

Then you will need thrice the amount of your allowance to make the games worthwhile, Rael countered. *Sooner wagered, sooner lost.*

"I win, *lir*. I win."

Tell it to the Mujhar.

Hart scowled blackly at the branches overhead, trying to see the hawk, but gave up after a fruitless search. Feeling oppressed yet again by the wood, he pulled up and held the stallion in place.

All was silence initially, as if the wood paused as he did, waiting to see what he would do. And then the impression passed and the wood was a wood again, full of familiar song. And even one Hart welcomed: the splash and gurgle of a stream.

"Water," he said aloud, then leaned forward to pat the stallion's chestnut shoulder. "Not as good as wine or ale, I'll wager, for *me,* but it will do for us both until we reach Lestra."

He guided the horse off the track into the thicker wood, tearing vines and bracken as they went, beating their way through brush. It gave way at last to spongy ground and the rocky bank of a wide, shallow stream. Hart swung off his sorrel and turned him free to pick his way through rocks into the water; he himself balanced precariously on a flattened boulder and bent to scoop up handfuls as he braced himself with one splay-fingered hand.

The water was cold and sweet. Hart lingered even as the stallion did, ignoring the chill of his fingers. He was weighted with bow and quiver in addition to his long-knife, but at least he wore no sword. Even though he had learned it in deference to his Homanan rank, he much preferred fighting with Cheysuli weapons.

Hart felt the vibration first even as the stallion did, transmitting itself through the water. And then the sound, close upon its heels; the splash of hooves in water, running, and the clop and clack of rocks torn free of their customary bed. He pressed himself up as the stallion stumbled through the rock-choked stream to the bank on the far side, to shy away into the shadows. Hart stood his ground silently, knowing a Cheysuli's very stillness was protection in itself.

Lir. He appealed to Rael for information.

A rider, the hawk answered. *In flight from yet another.* And then. *A woman, lir. In crimson, mounted on white.*

He saw her, then, come running out of the shadows. She was a palette of white and scarlet: hair white-blond, gown bright red, the mare unsullied white. She hunched in the saddle, bent low over the mare's neck, and the vivid mantle billowed behind as she urged the mare onward.

The mare would fail soon, Hart knew, or trip and fall, snapping slender forelegs, perhaps even her neck. The streambed was treacherous with rocks and deeps and shallows; it was only a matter of time.

She was by him. And then he stepped out into the center of the stream, water lapping just above booted ankles, and unstrapped his Cheysuli warbow.

Lir.

A single man, Rael answered. *Not far, not far, coming on.*

Coming on. Hart nocked an arrow, drew the black string back to his ear, and waited.

The rider came on, splashing through deeps and shallows. It was clear he did not see Hart, so intent was he on his prey. Hart waited, waited; watched the horse come closer, coming on, *coming on,* churning water into spray.

And when the man was close enough, Hart ordered him to hold.

The rider drew up in shock, brown-haired, brown-eyed, staring with mouth agape as he tried to control his mount. And then he shut his mouth, reaching for his sword, but did not unsheathe it, did not spur on as he saw the arrow was intended for his throat.

"Hold," Hart repeated.

The man spat out a spate of Solindish Hart could not decipher. But the emotions were clear: anger, astonishment, outrage.

"You tempt me," Hart said quietly.

It was plain the Solindishman understood Homanan. Color rose in his face. Impotently he raised a clenched fist, but it was conspicuously empty of knife or sword. In accented Homanan, he said, "It is my duty, my *task*—"

"And now your duty is failure," Hart answered. "I have no knowledge of the place you are from—Lestra, perhaps?—but I suggest you go back to it."

"Homanan!" the man cried. "It is my *responsibility*—"

"Go back," Hart said calmly. "Gods, but you do tempt me."

The Solindishman glared angrily past Hart toward the prey he had lost. Then he muttered an imprecation in throaty Solindish and jerked his horse into a rearing pivot and an awkward departure that splashed Hart liberally with water.

He returned the unused arrow to his quiver, hooked the bow over a shoulder and turned to face the woman.

She had not gone far past him, or else she had come back. The white mare stood in the center of the stream, sucking water gratefully; the woman sat erect in the saddle with crimson skirts and mantle all tangled on equipage, while her hair came free of its braid. Her expression was serious, yet it did not hide the flawlessness of the delicate bones of her face.

Fragility personified. But Hart thought he might be wrong. He had seen her ride.

"My thanks," she said gravely, gathering up her reins. For all her fingers were slender, they handled the mare competently. And tightened, wary, as he splashed through the water toward her.

The mare eyed him in alarm and shied two steps, until the young woman checked her with a rein. Hart halted at once. From closer range, the incandescence of her beauty was incredible. It unfolded like a lily in the sun, then dominated its surroundings. Ice-white hair, ice-blue eyes, with glorious, flawless skin.

"You have done me a service." Her accented Homanan only attracted him the more.

Hart grinned. "Saving your life, or your virtue? Aye, you might say so."

"No." Her long-lidded eyes were gray-blue. "No, he meant me no harm. What he said of his duty, his task, his *responsibility*—all was true. But not as you believed. He was bodyguard, not ravager. Certainly not assassin."

He stared up at her. *Gods, but this woman is enough to charm the teeth out of the Lion, and he would give them willingly*— He smiled. "Lady—he was not? Then what service did I do you?"

Her laughter set the world ablaze. "Freedom—you give me *freedom* . . . at least until the others come searching for me." Some of her gaiety was banished. "And they will. They will."

He could well imagine they would. *He* would. "So, you allowed me to chase away the man who guarded you." He laughed out loud in genuine amusement, appreciating her wit. "The man must now be cursing me for a fool, or himself."

Her eyes were full of laughter. "Aye, cursing us all—or cursing those who set him to his task." Almost abruptly, the humor spilled out of her face. An odd grimness replaced it. "But do they expect me to do nothing, meekly accepting their will?"

He heard a trace of bitterness in her tone and wondered if perhaps she *had* intended to use him to rid herself of her hound. "You said nothing, lady," he told her quietly. "And if I had slain him, what would you have told those who gave him his duty to ward you against enemies?"

She shook her head decisively. "No. No. I would not have let it go so far." She tightened reins and prepared to go. "My thanks, Homanan. But my business is better left to me."

He caught one of the reins, stepping closer. "And what do you give me for your freedom?"

She frowned. "Give?"

He shrugged. "I have done you a service. Now I ask payment, lady."

"If *you* think—"

"I do." He pulled the mare closer. "A kiss, lady. Small token of your gratitude, payment for my service." He grinned, arching suggestive brows. "Not so much, I think."

"More than you *know*, from me." One booted foot kicked out and caught him flush on the jaw.

He staggered back, swearing, and lost his grip on her reins. By the time he could see clearly again, the woman had spurred the mare on and was gone.

Rael, he said. "Rael!"

Not so far, lir. Mount your horse and catch up.

He whistled the stallion out of the trees and splashed through the stream to the bank, swearing all the while. She had caught him squarely, snapping his head sideways toward his right shoulder; neck muscles protested in unison with the jaw. Had she been man instead of woman, she might have broken his neck.

Were she man instead of woman, you would never have asked a kiss.

Hart, swinging up into his saddle, laughed aloud as he heard the hawk's tone. *No, I would wager not.* He urged the chestnut through the water onto the bank on the other side. *Where, lir? Which way?*

Westward, along the track. Riding toward Lestra.

The mare, he knew, was tired, and had drunk too much water to sustain a comfortable gallop for long. His own mount was rested; he would be on them soon enough.

He was. Rounding a curve in the tunneled track, he saw a flash of white tail ahead. Closer, closer yet; divots of dirt and turf were thrown up into his face. He ducked down and let the stallion shield him even as he ran.

The girl looked back once, then again. Her face was lost in the tangle of unbound hair; like the mare's tail it streamed out behind, a whipping pennon in the wind. Hart, grinning as the stallion closed, saw the girl reach up swiftly and catch her hair at the nape of her neck, winding it swiftly into a single plume. And then she stuffed it beneath the neck of her gown with both hands, the mare running free, and caught reins again to pull the mare off the track into the shadows of the wood.

Hart nearly rode by the broken opening in the vines. A decisive hand on the reins checked the stallion into an abrupt slide on his haunches, and then Hart spun him and sent him crashing after the mare.

Lir? he asked.

Hard to see, Rael answered. *She twists and turns, but still heads westward.*

"Lestra," Hart muttered, and swore as vine leaves slapped mouth and eyes.

No more track, save for what he could break open in her wake. No more headlong run, but leaps and stumbles instead, as the stallion tried to negotiate bracken and fallen trees. The world was a maze of green and brown and black, all shadows in the daylight, with little or no sun to illuminate their passing. The sound of his own mount obliterated hers. It was only when he saw a flash of white and crimson that he knew he drew closer again.

A quick glance over her shoulder; the curve of one fair cheek. And grim determination in the line of her lovely mouth. He saw her jerk the mare offstride and then turned her northward instead of west.

She will kill the mare yet— But the thought was never finished. The mare's passing startled a hare from cover and he broke. The stallion, startled, leaped sideways, stumbled, ran directly into a huge felled tree and, in trying to leap it off-balance, merely succeeded in snapping front legs. His rider was thrown headlong out of the saddle into the nearest tree.

Lir— But the light of the world was snuffed out.

*   *   *

A sound. A voice: a woman's, with desperation in her tone. Telling him in accented Homanan to wake up, and then when he did not, pleading something else in indecipherable Solindish.

Solindish.

His eyes snapped open. He was conscious almost at once of extreme discomfort, all tangled in vine and bracken and clawed by boughs and limbs. His head throbbed unmercifully; he recalled, dimly, that it had collided with a tree trunk.

He shut his eyes again. *Gods, but my head hurts. . . .*

He heard a rustle in deadfall and underbrush. Through his lashes he saw the bright colors of her clothing, now dulled by debris and mudstains. That she meant to come to his side was plain; equally plain was that Rael, a flurry of wings and talons, would not allow her to.

"Oh, wake up," she begged. "Wake up and call off this hawk!"

Rael swept down again from the tree and slapped a wingtip across her raised arm, driving her away once more.

Enough, Hart said dryly. *Have you no eyes, lir? The girl is magnificent—let her come as close as she wants.*

Rael's relief was tangible as it thrummed throughout the link. But his tone belied the truth. *Was this a ruse, then, to trick her into giving you your payment?*

Have you ever known me to willingly suffer so much pain in the name of a woman?

Rael lighted on a tree limb. *No,* he said dryly, and folded his wings away.

Hart opened his eyes again. "If I try to move, lady, will my head fall off? Or is it still attached?"

She twitched in surprise, then shifted a trifle closer. "Alive, then," she said in relief. "Oh, I thought I had killed you."

"No." He levered himself carefully up on one arm and wished he had not; his head throbbed alarmingly and a bough stabbed him in the ribs. "Well, perhaps you did." Tentatively he fingered his forehead. "Gods, lady, I would say you need no bodyguard, nor even *my* protection."

She said something in Solindish, then shook her head. "I meant no harm to you. I wanted to *escape* you, aye, but not at the cost of your life."

"And my horse?" Hart looked over to where the chestnut lay. The stallion's breathing was labored. That he had exhausted himself trying to rise with his shattered legs was plain; Hart cursed aloud in the Old Tongue with as much eloquence as he could muster. "You acquit youself well," he said shortly, and pushed himself out of the underbrush with another bitten off curse. He wavered and clutched the tree for support. But the stallion's plight was more imperative than pain; grimly he unhooked his bow and jerked an arrow from his quiver, walking unsteadily to the chestnut.

"The hawk—" she began.

Hart did not so much as glance at her. "Rael will not harm you." He nocked the arrow.

She rose, skirts tangled on her boots, and came to stand beside him. "Had I the strength, I would do it myself."

Mocking: "Aye, lady. Of course." He raised the bow and drew back the string.

Released. It sang briefly, so briefly, and then the stallion was dead.

He hooked an arm through the bow, settling it across his back, and bent to unfasten the saddlepacks. The horse was slack in death, and very heavy; Hart had to expend more energy than he had left to free the saddlepacks. His head ached, and he sat abruptly to avoid falling down.

"Give them to me. I will put them on my mare." Slender hands beckoned him to comply. "Where do you go, Homanan?"

"Lestra. Lady—there is no need for that."

She took the packs anyway and slung them across her mare's white rump, buckling them onto the saddle. Then she brought a skin of wine and knelt beside him. "She is not accustomed to carrying two. You will ride, and I will lead."

"Nor is there need for *that*." He drank, returned the skin, rose unsteadily.

She swept the glorious hair away from her face and showed him lifted brows. "And do you intend to *fly?*"

Hart laughed. "Aye, lady, I do."

She nodded calmly, plainly doubting him. "Even *Ihlini* cannot do that."

He looked at her sharply and recalled this was Solinde, the realm the Ihlini called home. Here they lived with impunity. "Thank the gods," he said curtly. "No, such things are for the Cheysuli."

"Aye, but—" She broke off. The color ran out of her face, leaving her wan as death. She looked quickly at Rael, then back at Hart. In silence she asked the question.

"Aye," he told her, "I am. Rael is my *lir*."

She pulled her mantle more closely around her slender body, as if to ward off a chill. "I thought—I thought him merely well-trained, when he would not let me near."

"*Lir* are not trainable; they do what they will do." He resettled his bow and quiver. "And now, lady, I suggest—"

But she did not allow him to finish. "I have heard they have *yellow* eyes. Yours are decidedly blue."

He raised his brows. "Doubtless you have heard many things . . . *some* of them may be true." He smiled as he saw her frown of indecision. "Aye, most Cheysuli have yellow eyes. I do not because I am also Homanan. But the rest of me is Cheysuli."

She looked at Rael again. "You become *him*."

"No. I become another. Rael remains Rael."

She looked at his hands, at his fingers, at the shape of the bones of his face. As if she searched for some clue that would make him bird instead of human. Raptor in place of man. "The Ihlini have said—"

He overrode her. "Do you traffic with Ihlini?"

She stiffened. "This is Solinde, not Homana! The Ihlini have freedom here."

"Freedom to raise a rebellion? To rule this realm in place of those who should?"

"What is it to *you?*" she asked angrily. "You are a

Homanan, a *Cheysuli* . . . what is Solinde to you? You have no stake in what happens in my land!"

"Do I not?" He smiled. "Oh, but lady, I think I do . . . because one day I will rule it."

"*Will* you?" She faced him squarely, tangled hair hanging to knees, skirts caught high on her boots. "You say so, to *me?*"

"I will say so to anyone, because it is the truth." That she was genuinely angry, he knew, because it was shouted from her posture and the expression in her eyes. He had seen such anger before, such cold, controlled anger, born of a true hostility shaped by war and heritage. He had seen it in the clans, in the older warriors who had come through Shaine's *qu'mahlin* and decades of Solindish-Ihlini wars. But he had not thought to see it in her. "Lady, I do not lie in hopes of impressing you—"

"Oh, no?" she asked. "Men have done it before. *Homanans* have done it before. Why should I believe you are any different?" Icy eyes swept him from head to toe; contempt was implicit in her posture. "I think your sincerity requires practice, Homanan. You are not particularly convincing."

Hart stared at her. She was either completely unaware of her disarray, or else so angry she did not care. *Or else she realizes that nothing could dull her beauty.*

He wet his lips. "Lady—" he began patiently.

"No one rules Solinde," she said coldly. "No one. A regent sits in Lestra claiming right of authority from Homana's Cheysuli Mujhar." One arm gestured toward the city and a rigid finger divided the air. "But is that a ruler?—*no.* A travesty, no more. We are a proud land, shapechanger, and unused to kowtowing to a foreign Mujhar who rules out of ignorance, holding Solinde in trust for a man we do not—*cannot*—know. So, shapechanger, when you tell me lies for your own amusement, to impress me or otherwise, it bears no fruit at all. I am impervious to such things."

"Impervious to the truth?" Without waiting for an answer he moved past her to the mare and dug into his saddlepacks. When he had found the thing he sought, he turned back again and put it into her hands. "There, lady—the truth."

She stared at the thing in her hands. It was small for a thing of so much significance, and yet the shocked tears that sprang to her eyes belied the seeming worthlessness of it. "This is the seal," she said, "the Third Seal of Solinde!"

"Aye."

She stared at him; all the color had left her face. "The Trey was broken when the war with Carillon was lost. When Bellam was slain." Her heavy swallow was visible against the fragile flesh of her throat. "The regent has one seal, the Mujhar the other two. But—*this* is the Third Seal!"

He had not expected her to know it so precisely, only to know the cipher. Nor had he expected the seal to have such an effect on her, that she would stare at him in shocked discovery. He had every intention of telling her who he was, if only to prove he was not a liar, but it seemed she already knew.

She clasped the seal against her chest, shielded by pride and hair. "So." Her voice was cool, dulled by shock and hostility. "*So*, the Mujhar at last sends his wastrel son to sit in judgment on Solinde."

Wastrel son. It hurt. Worse than he had expected. "Lady—"

She backed away a step, edging toward the mare. "If I took this . . . if I took this with me and sent men back to murder you—"

"—you would be executed." He moved too swiftly for her, catching her hands in his own. "Aye, lady, wastrel son that I am, I am also the Prince of Solinde."

She laughed. She laughed so hard she cried, and then thrust the seal at him. "Take it! *Take* it! Without the other two it is nothing. Even in *my* hands!"

"Lady—"

But she was free of him, shedding his hands easily as she leaped for the mare and scrambled into the saddle.

Curtained by hair, there was little of her face he could see. But he heard her words all too clearly.

"Hart, *Prince of Solinde,* know you that battle has been joined!"

And before he could speak, she was gone.

Two

Oil braziers burned in every corner of the room, casting
a pall of clean bright light that obliterated the shadows of
early evening. It glittered off the silver and crystal wine
decanter, off the fine-mesh ceremonial mail shirt showing
at hem and sleeves of his rich blue Solindish overtunic,
off the polished silver plate that conjured his reflection:
black hair, still damp from the bath, starting to curl
against his shoulders; bright blue eyes in an angular face
of burnished bronze, not even remotely Solindish; and a
somewhat rueful set to the mouth as he pushed hair aside
and studied the swelling on his forehead. The pattern of
the tree bark was impressed in his flesh.

Hart sighed, turned from the plate and faced the man
who waited so quietly, so patiently, by the table near the
fireplace. "I *will* survive," he said mildly as he saw the
man's expression. "I promise."

The pale brown eyes watching him narrowed minutely,
fanning outward a webwork of tiny creases. Tarron, regent of Solinde by authority of Niall the Mujhar, was not
a man who gave up his thoughts without careful deliberation. But neither was the newly arrived Prince of Solinde
ignorant in the ways of reading men, even lifelong politi-
cians; Hart had learned to discern the inner man in
dozens of dicing games.

Tarron inclined his head slightly. "As you say, my
lord—surely you would know better than I."

Surely I should . . . Hart agreed inwardly. *As surely as
I know my head is likely to fall off.*

198

Rael, settled on his óaken perch in a corner of the royal chambers, remained eloquently silent. Hart ignored him altogether and smiled blandly at the regent, hoping to turn Tarron's irritation into good humor. His abrupt arrival in *lir*-shape had ruffled feathers other than his own, figuratively speaking; Tarron, he felt, was displeased more by the lack of pageantry associated with the arrival than by the sudden usurpation of his own authority. Hart knew a messenger from Homana must have arrived before him, if only to prepare Tarron, because his father would have seen to it.

Jehan would know better than to spring me on Solinde—or on Tarron—unannounced. Hart's smile widened to a crooked grin of wry humor as he recalled what the girl had named him. *But I wonder what the regent thinks now that the* wastrel son *has arrived?* He gestured toward the polished table and two padded chairs. "Sit you down, regent," Hart suggested, and did so himself.

What Tarron thought of his lord's wastrel son remained unspoken as he seated himself at the table and accepted the wine Hart poured. The regent's ascetic face was smooth and serene again, a polite, politic mask. He was older than the Mujhar himself, Hart knew, having served as councillor to Donal before Niall's ascension and Tarron's subsequent appointment to Solinde. He was well experienced in dealing with men of all ranks and races. Even Cheysuli.

"Is all to your liking, my lord?" Tarron inquired.

Hart laughed, amused by his attitude. They faced one another like two men in a fortune-game, seated across the table with nothing at all to bind them together save a royal command. They did not play with dice, they did not wager, but the game was surely on. "Aye, and how not? Since my somewhat unusual arrival less than two hours ago, I have been bathed, clothed, fed, examined by a chirurgeon, and ensconced within royal apartments as luxurious as my own in Homana-Mujhar." A gesture encompassed the chambers. "The servants have been so thick around me I can scarce move my elbows for fear of blacking an eye or knocking loose a tooth. Only *now* am

I given room to breathe, and I find myself attended by no less than the Mujhar's regent himself, when I would do well enough on my own." His mouth twisted wryly. "If I said no, you would have it all done over again, and *that* I could not bear."

Tarron did not smile. "You *are* the Prince of Solinde."

Hart laughed aloud. "Aye. But even *you* must know my reputation; it is what puts me here instead of Homana-Mujhar." He leaned forward, looming across the table. "I am Hart, the second son, the *wastrel* son, who spends his gold and wits in taverns, dicing his life away. I am the man responsible for setting the Midden aflame, though unintentionally, and for killing thirty-two people—men, women, children. And I am punished for it: I am sent to rule Solinde." He sat back again, all humor banished, flopping against the chair. "But where does that leave Solinde, regent? Where does it leave *you*?"

Tarron did not hesitate. "It leaves me in fear for the future of this realm," he said quietly. "It leaves me wondering if the Mujhar's prejudice interferes with his intellect. And most certainly, in these past two hours, I have seen nothing in you that assuages my fear, and *everything* that leaves me wondering how I can possibly do what my lord has commanded, and teach a hopeless reprobate how to govern." He paused. "Even a *royal* one."

Hart stared at him a long, rigid moment. He had expected anything but censure from the man; Tarron was too well-versed in the delicacy of politics and the exigencies of rank to ever be so blunt and risk his entire career. But Hart knew better than to believe he had misheard, asking to have them repeated; the words had been explicitly distinct, displaying neither malice nor bitterness, only heartfelt sincerity.

That kind of honesty was a thing Cheysuli honored. But Hart was more than Cheysuli. He was also Prince of Solinde.

"*Ku'reshtin*," he said without heat, more surprised than offended. "Is this how you spoke to Donal?"

"Your grandsire never required it," Tarron answered quietly.

Hart gazed at him thoughtfully. The regent wore understated clothing of plain, unrelieved black, as if to downplay the importance of his rank. His dark brown hair was graying at the temples and brushed back from a face almost stark in its severity of expression, but it was derived of sharp bones rather than of nature. And yet Hart sensed little or no humor in the regent; he wondered if Tarron recalled the follies of his own youth.

Unless there were *no follies.* He sighed a little and tapped fingertips against the wood of the table. "No doubt you feel I deserve it; perhaps I do. Perhaps this is why my *jehan* sent me to you. Perhaps I am to develop some sense of guilt for past indiscretions, merely by seeing the condemnation in your eyes." Hart sat up and pushed the chair back to rise, scraping wooden legs against marble floor. "And perhaps I *will,* one day—but not just yet."

Belatedly Tarron rose as Hart moved to open the door. "My lord—where are you going?"

"Out," Hart said succinctly. "The urge for a game is upon me, and the sweet perfume of a smoky tavern."

"My lord—"

Rael, Hart summoned, ignoring the regent's protest; the hawk flew out of the open casement even as Hart walked out of the room.

He went out of the palace and into the bailey, following blurted directions he had asked of a Solindish servant. Lestra's royal palace was enough like Homana-Mujhar that he had no difficulty finding the bailey and hence the guardroom; when he paused by several off-duty soldiers lounging by the entrance, he saw they assessed him indifferently, not knowing who he was. Anonymity suited him well enough, at least for the moment.

"I am looking for a game," he told them, tapping his heavy belt-purse significantly. "Not here—undoubtedly

your captains prohibit wagering within the castle walls—
but elsewhere. In the city. Can you suggest a tavern?"

They were Solindish, not Homanan, for their woolen
tunics were indigo banded with silver braid, not the crimson and black livery of the Homanan Guard. Four pairs
of eyes reassessed him, noting the richness of silken
overtunic, the glitter of costly mail, the quality of leather
trews, silver-buckled belt, polished kneeboots. To them,
Hart knew, he was an enigma: a Homanan garbed Solindish. It altered their responses.

And if they knew I was Cheysuli? He smiled; Rael had
perched himself on the roof of the guardroom.

"Homanan tavern, or Solindish?" one of the soldiers
asked in accented Homanan.

Hart shrugged. "Does it matter?"

The Solindishman, red-headed and green-eyed, showed
his teeth briefly in a humorless smile. "It matters. Lestra
is a Solindish city, for all the Mujhar might have it
otherwise; the Homanans cluster together like chicks about
a hen."

"Avoiding the fox, no doubt." Hart smiled benignly
and spread upturned hands. "By all means, let it be a
Solindish tavern. Wagering has a tongue all its own."

The four men exchanged glances, murmuring among
themselves in low-pitched voices. Finally the spokesman
shrugged and looked back at Hart. "The White Swan,"
he said. "Not so far from here. Do you require escort?"

"Is it customary?" Hart asked evenly. "Without one,
is a Homanan likely to be accosted?"

Again they exchanged glances. The red-haired man
smiled. "In the shadows, one man is very much like
another."

Hart grinned back. "A chance I might have to take
. . . but I know a little Solindish. Perhaps this phrase
might be enough?" And, though the accent was horren-
dous, he told them, in their own tongue: *"A Cheysuli
never walks alone."*

On their benches, they straightened. "Cheysuli—"
blurted one, staring. Two of his comrades muttered in

Solindish; amidst the mostly alien words Hart heard his own name twice.

The fourth man, the redhead, slowly rose and faced him. They were of a like height and similar build, though the shapes of their faces and coloring was entirely different.

"My lord," the redhead said formally, "word of your arrival has been given out. But I think we expected another sort of man. The animals . . . all the gold—" He broke off, shrugging awkwardly. "There are stories, my lord."

Hart laughed. "My things were misplaced earlier today. Fine as it is, Solindish clothing is somewhat more elaborate than Cheysuli leathers." He tapped his left arm. "Beneath all this silk and mail and linen lies the gold you refer to. As for my *lir*—" he gestured "—Rael is always with me."

All four craned their heads and saw the hawk, little more than a silvered shape upon the edge of the roof.

The redhead looked back. "Shall we escort you, my lord?"

"No, Rael is escort enough. Simply give me directions to The White Swan."

"You might do better at another tavern, my lord."

"A tavern catering to the chicks clustered around the hen?" Hart grinned as the other man reddened. "The White Swan, soldier."

He was given explicit directions, and a warning.

"The White Swan is a supremely *Solindish* place, my lord," the redhead told him. His discomfort was quite plain. "You may not find the welcome to your taste."

Hart grinned. "I am Cheysuli, soldier; even in Homana, even *sixty years* after the ending of the royal purge that nearly destroyed us, we know the taste of hatred and prejudice. But I have learned that where a man may not be welcomed, his wealth always is."

After a moment, the Solindishman smiled. "Aye. The custom is no different in Solinde."

Hart thanked him, saluted him, left the palace entirely and entered Lestra proper with a winged shadow overhead.

*   *   *

The White Swan was, he thought, one of the finest taverns he had ever entered, certainly as nicely appointed as Mujhara's own Rampant Lion. Good wax candles in clay saucers stood on every table, lighting food or play. The beamwork of the ceiling was higher than most, which pleased Hart immensely. Cheysuli height often resulted in the need for constant ducking, for Homanans were almost uniformly shorter, and built taverns accordingly. But here he could stand and move with impunity. He admired the clean, sweeping lines of the blond beams; whitewashed walls made the tavern look large and airy instead of cramped and dark.

Rael he left outside perched atop the roof, knowing better than to invite immediate trouble by taking the hawk inside. The window were of thin, costly glass; had he need of Rael, he could summon the bird easily through either one.

If I am to judge the stakes of the games by the richness of my surroundings, the winnings will be well worth any rudeness I may encounter.

But he encountered none at all, save the curiosity extended any stranger entering a tavern patronized by friends and comrades. The cut and quality of his clothing, particularly the ceremonial mail, marked him a wealthy Solindishman, obviously a noble, and worthy of attention because of that alone. The hawk-shaped earring was mostly hidden in his hair, but Hart believed that even had his eyes been as yellow as Brennan's, no one would have named him Cheysuli. This was Solinde, even though ruled by Homana; no one expected to see a Cheysuli in the heartland of Ihlini.

The tables were mostly full. None was entirely open, though not all boasted a full complement of gamblers or other patrons. But Hart knew he could not very well invite himself into a game; his lack of Solindish—and command of flawless Homanan—would instantly mark him an enemy to those men who chose to regard the Homanans as such.

One of the wine-girls came up to him and curtsied briefly in deference to his obvious wealth. What she said he could barely discern, for he spoke very little Solindish even after childhood tutoring—he had been a supremely indifferent student—and only very slowly; she chattered at him like a magpie. He knew better than to attempt an answer in her tongue. Instead, he drew from his belt-purse a heavy coin: the gold royal of Homana. He placed it in her hand and shut her fingers over it. "There is more," he said distinctly, "much more, for the man who gives me a game."

The Homanan words silenced the tavern instantly. As one, shocked faces looked up from games and drink to stare at him, and then the shock turned slowly to hostility.

The girl tore her hand from his. The falling coin rang dully against the hardwood floor. She backed away from him, wiping her hands on her skirts, and stopped only when she fetched up against a table. She was black-haired, black-eyed, pretty; she reminded him vaguely of the girl from The Rampant Lion, who had been so impressed with Brennan. But that girl had been Homanan, and this one was clearly Solindish, with all attendant resentment of her foreign overlord.

Hart was imperturbed. It was no more, no less than he had expected, after what the soldier had said of the Swan. Calmly he untied his belt-purse and dangled it before them all. He shook it once, twice; the clash of gold and silver was plain for all to hear.

"A game," he said, "not a war."

They stared, did Solindish eyes. Out of hard, eloquent faces, full of hatred, full of anger; of a burning, brilliant resentment that seemed to intensify as he waited.

Supremely Solindish, the soldier had said. Aye. That was one way of putting it.

Perhaps I have misjudged them . . . perhaps something is stronger than the lure of gold or gems. Disappointed, he began to tie his belt-purse back on his belt.

"*I* will give you a game," said a voice in accented Homanan.

Hart brightened even as there was murmuring from the others. He heard one word mentioned more than once, and thought it might be a name.

It was. The man rose, scraping his stool against the hardwood floor, and gestured Hart to join him. "I am Dar," he said. "I give you no welcome to the Swan, for it it is *ours,* and only ours, but I will give you the opportunity to buy your life back."

Hart paused. "Buy my life back?" he echoed.

Dar did not smile. "It was forfeit the moment you asked for a game."

Hart looked at the others. All remained clustered at their tables, but no games were played, no wagers laid, no food and drink consumed. The atmosphere of the place was decidedly unfriendly, but he smelled the tang of anticipation as well. They waited for something, the Solindish. They *wanted* something specific, just as he desired a game.

He looked back at Dar. "I said a game, not a war. I am not here to rehash old battles, nor discuss political things. I have no interest in either. I am here to wager, nothing more."

The other studied him briefly, marking height, weight, strength, and the indefinable self-confidence of a Cheysuli that others called arrogance.

The Solindishman nodded slightly, as if his decision were made. "You asked for a game without knowing the stakes," he said coolly. "Know them now, and clearly: for a Homanan, what he wagers is nothing less than his life."

Hart looked at him closely. Dar was perhaps a year or two older than himself, sandy-haired, brown-eyed, with strong, bold features that marked him a singularly dedicated man, no matter what the cause. Like the others in the tavern, he wore clothing and appointments of good quality—tawny leather trews, russet quilted velvet doublet, a belt-knife hilted with gold. Obviously, The White Swan catered to the wealthy and high-ranking. Just as obviously, Homanans were unwelcome regardless of wealth or rank.

His own assessment finished, Hart nodded a little. "A good way of winnowing out the undesirables," he said lightly. "How many men did it cost before the Homanans learned to go elsewhere?"

Dar did not smile. Neither did he hesitate. "Two," he said, with deliberate clarity and succinctness.

He was not a man much intimidated by others, particularly when a game was in the offing. Hart knew the type well, relishing their eagerness for play as much as his own. The Solindishman's baiting bothered him not in the least; if anything, it added a fillip to the game.

Hart shrugged negligently, aware of the familiar flutter in his belly. It spoke of risk and danger, of success and failure. It sang a song of possibilities; of hope and need and desire. But he showed none of it to Dar, knowing better. "And so it shall remain," he said lightly, striding to the table to hook out a stool and plop his belt-purse down upon the table. Pouring out a stream of gold and silver, he sat down and looked at Dar. "Match it," he said gently, "with red Solindish gold." He paused as the other slowly sat down. "Unless, of course, you stake your own life as well as mine."

For a moment the other hesitated, arrested in mid-motion. There was a brief flash of recognition in his eyes, and then it was gone. "Oh, no," Dar said quietly. "I am Solindish, not Homanan; I am of the *occupied* race, not of the oppressor. My life is not required." The irony was subtle and yet exceedingly clear to Hart, who chose to ignore it altogether.

"Let us play man to man, not soldier to soldier; wagerer to wagerer, not oppressor to occupied," he suggested. "The game is all that matters."

Dar's sandy brows rose to disappear beneath thick hair. "The game? Well, since it is *your* life we wager, you may choose the game."

"Considerate." Hart looked at the wine-girl, standing so close to his shoulder. The others had drawn near as well, clustered in ranks around the table. He had seen it happen before in games of high stakes; men who could not or would not risk so much preferred instead to watch, gaining a measure of the pleasure without the threat of loss. He smiled at the girl. "Have you a fortune-game?"

She was patently unimpressed by his charming smile, which might have perturbed him had he not been more caught up in the need for the risk, the chance to play the odds and win. Her lips drew back. *"Homanan!"* was all she said.

Dar laughed. "Translation: the Swan has no Homanan games."

"Then I will play a Solindish one," Hart said evenly. He studied the other without bothering to hide it, knowing Dar assessed him as openly. It was all a part of the eternal dance. After a moment he nodded. "I judge you an honest man, Dar—I think you would prefer an honest win."

Dar rubbed an idle thumb along his lower lip. "You judge quickly, Homanan. Too quickly, perhaps?"

"I think not. I have seen your kind before . . ." Hart grinned at narrowing brown eyes and tautening jaw. "Aye, I have, just as you have seen me before, in many men. Why bother to deny it? When it comes to it, Solindish, the *game* is more important than the man who plays it—*or* his loyalties."

The Solindishman laughed, eyes suddenly alight. For the moment, the quiet hostility was banished. "Aye, so it is. Perhaps we are more alike than we know, for all it paints me an unflattering color." He drew out his own belt-purse and opened it, pouring out the rich red gold of Solinde. The shape and weight as well as the color was different than Hart's Homanan wealth, and the value, coin for coin, was uncalculated, but it no longer mattered. They both knew the other for a man who wagered for the love of it, the *need* of it, not for the actual value of the winnings. "There you are, Homanan—red gold against your life."

It was red gold indeed, deeper, brighter, richer than Hart's yellow Homanan hoard. He ached to touch it, to feel its texture, its warmth, knowing what it represented. Not money. Not wealth. But victory over the game.

Dar grinned. With a single finger he flipped over first one coin and then another, so that they rang against one another. In the heavy silence of the common room, the siren song was eloquent.

Hart smiled. For the moment, they were *kinspirits*.

Dar turned and said something to the girl, who disappeared a moment and came back with a small wooden bowl. She set it down on the table; it was filled with flat, bone-colored oblong stones the size of a man's thumbnail.

Dar pulled several stones from the bowl and set them down on the table. Each bore a shape incised and colored, save for one blank one. "Bezat," he said. "A Solindish rune-game. Very simple; even a Homanan may learn."

"Did the others?" Hart asked. "The two who died?"

Dar's smile was faint. "They learned not to wager what they could not afford to lose."

"Show me," Hart said intently, thinking only of the game.

After a moment, Dar did. "You see the marks. Each rune represents a thing from Solindish folklore; I will not bore you with the stories, or we will be here all night and most of the next." He grinned. "Let it suffice you to know the runes have value within the context of the game: the moon, the sun, the plow, the scythe, famine, plague, war . . . and, of course, death." He touched the blank stone. "This supersedes the others. No matter what value the others give you, even the highest, this takes precedence." His expression was carefully noncommittal. "You do understand?"

"I understand death very well," Hart answered readily. "And I understand that in *this* game, for a Homanan, the death is literal."

After a moment Dar nodded. "We draw eight. The moon, sun, plow and scythe rank higher than famine, plague or war, but there are fewer of them. We match my stones against yours: the highest grouping wins."

"And the death-stone?"

"Stones," Dar said clearly, emphasizing the plural. "*Bezats*. Fewer yet, but hardly timid."

"How many times do we play?"

Dar shrugged. "As many as you like . . . ordinarily. In

this case, with these stakes, should you turn up a bezat—" he smiled, "no more games are possible."

Hart smiled back, unmoved by the possibilities. His luck would see through. "Once," he said, and a flutter of anticipation pinched his belly. "*Once.* To make it worth our while."

"Once," Dar agreed. "You will draw eight stones, I will draw eight stones—both of us drawing blind . . . and then we give them to one another."

Anticipation was smothered by shock. Hart went cold. "Are you saying you will draw *my* stones? The ones on which I wager?"

Dar laughed. "But of course! Therein lies the game. You wager that I will give you good stones, while I do the same with the ones you draw for me."

Hart no longer smiled. "Then my life—*literally*—is in your hands."

Dar shrugged casually. "It is the luck of the draw."

Hart grabbed the bowl and upended it, spilling stones across the table. One by one he turned them over, baring rune after rune. There were suns, moons, and other things—four stones were blank as death.

"Did you fear all of them were blank?" Dar smiled and nodded as Hart began to drop them back into the bowl. "Did you fear you *had* misjudged me?"

Hart was deliberate as he replaced the stones. One by one, they rattled into the bowl as he watched Dar's face. He knew very well he could refuse to play, but he would not. It was poor manners; worse, it marked him a coward and cheat, when he was neither. If anything, the stakes made him reckless.

A true test of a man's mettle, and certainly of his skill. If I beat this Solindish ku'reshtin, I can win back a measure of pride for the Homanans, who have been so readily insulted in this tavern. Moreover, I can win back respect for those who died.

But even more than that, much more, it was the challenge.

Hart flipped the last stone into the bowl. "It is a foolish man who wagers without knowing the stakes, *or* the contents of the game. And I am not a fool." No longer did he smile. "I have accepted your stakes; now I accept the game."

Dar looked at the wine-girl. "Stir them," he said, in clear Homanan. "Stir them well, Oma."

She put a slim hand in the bowl and stirred the contents, steadfastly keeping her eyes on Hart's face as if to emphasize her honesty. When she was done, she lifted the bowl in both hands and held it out over the table, so that neither of them could see in as they drew the stones.

"You may draw first," Dar said politely. "If it is a bezat—a death-stone—I lose at once, and the game is done."

And if he draws a bezat for me . . . Hart smiled. He reached in, drew a stone, placed it face up on the table in front of Dar. It bore the rune for famine.

"Not good," Dar said conversationally, tapping a finger against the tabletop. "Beaten, should I draw you a sun or moon, a plow or scythe."

"Draw," Hart said.

Dar did so, turning up the rune for scythe, representing a generous harvest. Through seven stones they went, one by one: suns, moons, famine and war . . . and then Dar drew the final stone for Hart.

He put it down in the center of the table, turning it from one side to the other, so that both were clearly visible to Hart and all the rest.

"Bezat!" the wine-girl cried.

"Bezat!" the others echoed.

Dar drew his knife and place it in the center of the table, next to the blank death-stone. "Bezat," he said quietly, and took his hand away.

Hart looked at the stone, at the knife, at the man. And then he began to laugh.

Three

Dar's eyes narrowed. "It is a fool who laughs in the face of death, or a very brave man. Which are you, Homanan?"

Still Hart laughed, though the initial burst of amusement faded, and then the laughter died away. He shook his head, grinning, and idly stirred his pile of Homanan gold and silver. "Neither, I think . . . or perhaps a little of both."

No one else spoke, though Hart was aware of the tension in the common room. The others stared hard at him, scowling, or looked to Dar in expectation. The knife blade gleamed a promise in the candlelight.

"Did you think I jested?" Dar inquired in an elegantly dangerous tone of voice. "Did you think, when I spoke of your death as the stakes of the game, I meant nothing of what I said?"

"Oh, I *know* you meant it," Hart answered, smiling. "I can smell the stink on all of you, this desire for my death." Again he stirred the coins, admiring their patina in the candlelight. Still he smiled a little, but mostly to himself; he preferred not to provoke the Solindishman further, and yet a part of him did not care. He met Dar's eyes and shrugged. "But I have learned that even a life may be purchased—or bought back—when the loser is wealthy enough." He paused. "Or has other means to force it."

Dar himself smiled. "There are three men behind you with knives in their hands. And more behind them."

Hart shrugged, shaking his head. "It makes no difference. The force I speak of has nothing to do with weapons."

"*Mine* does." Dar touched the hilt of his knife with a single eloquent finger.

Hart laughed. "Effective against a man, perhaps, but what about a hawk?"

"I think—" But Dar stopped short, interrupting himself. He looked at Hart in silence a long moment. And then, though his expression did not change, the tone of his voice altered perceptibly. "Cheysuli," he said flatly.

"Aye," Hart agreed.

Silence filled the room. And then was swallowed by murmurs of shock and muttered Solindish epithets.

Dar's nostrils were pinched, his mouth drawn flat and tight. For only a moment his fingers remained near the knife, and then he took his hand away. "Cheysuli," he repeated. "An accursed shapechanger in our midst."

"Now," Hart said, "shall we negotiate this loss?"

Dar smiled tightly. "It *was* a loss," he said, "and you knew the stakes. Your life against the stones. Cheysuli, Homanan, it does not matter. The wager stands."

Hart matched his tone. "I have only to summon my *lir*."

"Do it." Dar laughed as Hart frowned his incomprehension. "Do it, shapechanger—or should I say, *try*." His glance went past Hart to another man. "Even *I* know that a Cheysuli has no power before an Ihlini."

Hart swung on his stool and felt the knife blade against his throat. He sat very still, but he saw the man Dar's glance had indicated. "Ihlini?" he demanded.

The man inclined his head politely, though his smile was coolly derisive. "This *is* Solinde, is it not? Here, we go where we will go, just as you do in Homana."

For the first time since entering the tavern, Hart went into the *lir*-link to contact Rael. And instantly felt the blankness that signaled Ihlini presence and canceled out the link.

Oh, gods—oh, lir, what have I done now?

"Now," Dar said gently, "shall we speak again of the wager?"

Oh, gods, where is Brennan when I need him?

On his stool, Hart swung back around to face Dar, wary of the knife so near his throat. He forced a smile and tapped the pile of silver and gold. "Surely there is enough here to buy my life from you."

"No." Dar's tone did not waver.

"This is worth—"

"Worth*less*," Dar said distinctly. "This is Solinde, Homanan; do you think your coin has value here? I have seen how you look at our red Solindish gold; how you covet it with your eyes." His own narrowed. "Eyes *which*, I might add, are blue instead of yellow. Cheysuli? I think not. I think you are a liar who lives on the legends of other men."

That touched prickly Cheysuli pride. Hart went rigid on the stool, but dared not move with so many knives prepared to take his life. He scowled blackly at Dar. "And is every *Solindishman* the same color?"

Dar's mouth twitched. "But I have heard so much about the beast-eyes of the Cheysuli. . . ." He grinned, unable to suppress his amusement. "Glare at me all you wish, Homanan—blue eyes are less effective, I think, than yellow."

"*Ku'reshtin!*" Hart snapped. "Were there no Ihlini here— "

But there is," Dar said coolly, "and your claim has no validity."

Hart stripped black hair behind his left ear. "Oh no?"

The Solindishman shrugged negligently. "Many men wear similar adornment."

Hart gritted his teeth. "Then give me leave to show you *other* adornment."

Dar laughed. "If you wish. But if you mean to show us your *weapon*, Homanan, recall there are women present."

Even Oma laughed, eyeing Hart with derisive amusement. Heat coursed through his body and stung his armpits, but he rose slowly and unbuckled his belt with careful deliberation. He dropped it and the heavy knife on the table, then stripped out of the rich blue tunic. It left him aglitter in silver mail, and he saw a flash of irritation in Dar's eyes as well as envy in the eyes of others.

"I am laced," Hart said tightly.

Dar gestured. "Oma, unlace him. Tend him as benefits a *Solindish* lordling."

The girl's fingers were deft as she undid the laces of the mail shirt. When she was done Hart shrugged out of it, letting it slide to his stool where it lay in a shining pool of exquisite mesh. Ceremonial only, it was lighter than traditional Homanan ringmail, but was more than he cared to carry.

It left only the quilted linen shirt used to keep the links from his flesh. Quickly Hart divested himself of it and draped it casually over Oma's shoulder, though she immediately threw it to the floor. He smiled, knowing no man—or woman—in The White Swan would dare call him liar now.

Dar kept his face expressionless, but there was no hiding the grudging acknowledgment in his eyes as he looked at the massive *lir*-bands. There were mutters in the room, but he nodded. "Well enough, blue-eyed or not, you have the right to call yourself Cheysuli. But it does not change the wager."

Hart pointed. "There is my coin. If it is not enough, be assured I have the means to get more."

"I have already said Homanan gold and silver has no value here," Dar said patiently. His eyes were still on Hart's armbands. "*Cheysuli* gold, however—"

"No." The refusal was distinct.

"Then what?" Dar asked idly. "You say you have the means to buy your life from us, and yet you offer nothing."

No, I do have something, though undoubtedly Tarron will not like it. Hart drew in a deep breath. "Then I will buy it with something emminently *Solindish*." He pointed to the leather belt-purse. "There is something in there which should more than cover the worth of my life, Solindishman."

Lazily Dar reached out and took up the leather pouch,

upending it. He shook it; a ring fell out onto the table. It rattled, rolled, stopped. It was solid gold, red Solindish gold, and large enough to hide half of Hart's forefinger when he wore it. But he had never worn it.

And now I never will.

Oma bent close to look; Dar's rigid hand thrust her rudely away from the table. In the light from the fat wax candle, the heavy ring glowed.

"The Third Seal," he said in disbelief.

"Part of the Trey," Hart agreed. "Enough, do you think, to purchase the life of the Prince of Solinde?"

"There is no Prince of Solinde—has been none for eighty years or more, ever since Bellam's son Ellic was killed by Shaine the Mujhar." But Dar's tone was dulled by shock and comprehension. Slowly he reached out and took up the ring, turning it so the light fell fully on the incised pattern that formed the Third Seal of Solinde, and the key to almost limitless power. "No prince," he said distinctly, "until the Lady Ilsa weds and bears a son." He looked at Hart in dawning recognition. "There was a man, she said—a Cheysuli warrior, who carried the Third Seal . . . a man she nearly killed."

So, her name is Ilsa. Hart smiled crookedly and pulled hair aside, baring swollen brow and ugly scrape. "Nearly. But not, quite."

Dar tipped the ring into his palm and rolled it back and forth. "With this, a man could rule Solinde."

"No. Even *she* told me that much: without the other two, this one is not so important. And the other two are safely held by the regent and my father."

Dar looked at him thoughtfully. "Niall is your father."

"Aye. My *jehan*. Mujhar of Homana." He glanced at Oma and the others, marking how attentively they watched him. The hostility had altered significantly to shock and wonder. He found he preferred the latter. "I did not come of my own accord," he said, for their benefit as much as for Dar's, who held his life. "I was sent. I am to learn to rule Solinde . . . and I want it no more than you do."

Dar looked at him sharply. "You do *not*?"

Hart shrugged. "Not *now*. Later, aye—I have been bred and raised for it, and have no intention of turning my back on my *tahlmorra*—but as for now, my interest lies in other directions." He looked at the ring in Dar's hand. "Is it enough?"

"To buy back your life?" Dar's tone was incredulous. "This is worth much more than you can imagine, my Homanan-Cheysuli princeling. This is worth a woman."

Hart frowned as Dar began to laugh. "A woman?"

Still laughing, the Solindishman shook his head. "Ah, shapechanger, how you amuse me with your ignorance. Obviously you have no aptitude for ruling, else you would have steeped yourself in the politics of Solinde. And I refuse to be your tutor." He grinned. "Your life is duly bought. Take your borrowed clothing and your hawk and all your worthless Homanan coin and get yourself back to the palace."

He had never been dismissed so arrantly by anyone, even his father, who had more right. And yet he dared not vent his anger on Dar or any of the Solindish; in a way, he acknowledged their right to treat him as they did. He knew nothing of them at all, or their realm, and yet he came expecting to rule them, whether he wanted to or not.

In taut silence, Hart put on the linen shirt and gathered up mail, silken tunic, belt and belt-purse. Then he turned and walked out of the tavern.

In the morning Hart went to see the regent and briefly explained the circumstances of the evening before, glossing over the very real threat to his welfare and stressing instead the need to learn more about the woman called Ilsa, who could give Solinde a prince merely by wedding and bearing a son. He expected Tarron to express relief at his escape and compliment him on his resolution; instead, Hart was mildly startled to see the regent of Solinde gape unattractively, banishing his habitual dignity.

Tarron grasped the arms of his chair and thrust himself out of it stiffly. "You lost the *Third Seal?*"

"In return for *my life,* I allowed Dar to keep it," Hart

explained again. He shrugged. "One ring is as good as another. Have a duplicate made; it will serve as well."

"*Will* it?" Tarron's face was red, though the color slowly faded to white. He sat down again, but the motion lacked anything akin to grace. The regent stared blindly at Hart. "You have no conception of what you have done."

Hart sighed. He was restless, wanting little more than to go out of the palace and into the city again, leaving behind the responsibilities Tarron intended him to assume. Hands on hips, he faced the regent in Tarron's private council chamber. "What I have done? Aye, I think I do. I think—"

Tarron did not wait for him to finish. "*I* think you have placed all my work in jeopardy . . . possibly even the entire succession." He shook his head in disbelief. "The Mujhar warned me—he *said* you required watching until you learned the importance of your role. But I thought surely he exaggerated—" He shut his eyes. "By the *gods,* you have given over the Third Seal into the hands of those who would wrest this throne from your father . . . from those who would gladly see you dead so they can crown their *own* candidate Prince of Solinde. . . ."

"Tarron—"

"Be silent!" The regent sat upright in the chair and glared at Hart, who gazed back in astonishment. "Hold your tongue, *my lord,* while I try to think of a way to make certain you may keep the head that wags it!"

Hart scowled. "May I remind you—"

"May I remind *you?*" Tarron snapped. Then, more quietly, "Listen to me, my lord, and perhaps you will see that I am less concerned for your rank and personal pleasure than for your life."

After a moment, Hart nodded and sat down in the nearest chair. "I will listen."

Tarron sighed a little. "To put it as succinctly as possible: you understand, of course, that Solinde is an occupied land in vassalage to your father. All judgments concerning the welfare of this realm are made by him, and him alone, although he encourages and acts on advice from me as well as other Homanans he has placed to administer the governing of Solinde."

"Of course."

The regent nodded. "It is a necessary practice that documents requiring triple seals—the Trey of Solinde—must be sent to Mujhara for the Mujhar's acknowledgment. For all the days of his rule, Niall the Mujhar has held the First and Third Seals of Solinde, while I held the Second. Nothing in Solindish law can be done without the Trey, the *complete* Trey. No orders can be carried out, no armies paid, no judgments rendered to the petitioners who gather at court for such things. Without the Trey, the wheel stops turning." Tarron drew in a calming breath. "He gave you the Third Seal so that you could have an active role in governing the realm that one day you will rule absolutely, with no fealty paid to Homana."

Hart sat upright. "Do you mean he intends to give me *sole* responsibility? But—I thought I would rule in his name . . ." He frowned. "I thought things would continue mostly as they are."

The regent's smile was bleak. "How many times has he told you Solinde would one day be yours?"

Hart shrugged. "As long as I can remember, but—"

"But nothing," Tarron said flatly. "On the day of his death, you will become king in your own right. Solinde will be *yours*, my lord. Yours. To do with as you will."

Hart snorted inelegantly. "And if I choose to give it back to the Solindish?"

"So be it." To his credit, Tarron did not flinch. "Although you may have done that already."

Hart grunted skepticism. "How?"

"You gave over the ring, my lord. The seal. And into the hands of one of the men most likely to order your death."

Hart shook his head. "Dar had the chance last night. He let me live."

Because while the lady delays her decision, he has no power. Only promised power—whatever man she weds becomes Consort, and a son by him on Ilsa will be named Prince of Solinde. Power, my lord, is often gained through marriage. Or through children.''

Hart grunted. "That I know well enough. Of five children, my *jehan* betrothed two of us before we were ever born.''

"And you, my lord?"

Hart grinned. "A free man, Tarron, with no marital obligations.''

Tarron did not match his humor. "If the lady weds before you are fully accepted, she provides a threat to your security.''

"If she weds *Dar*.''

If she weds any man, although she will *not* wed 'any man.' She is too highly born. Too close to the old Solindish line of succession; her grandmother's mother was youngest sister to Bellam, the last king of Solinde." Tarron tapped his hand on the chair arm. "Dar is only one of several Solindish lords who desire to wed the lady, although it is said he has a better chance than most. He is young, handsome, wealthy—and dedicated to Solindish rule.''

Hart scowled at the regent. "I know the solution as well as you, Tarron. You intend to tell me that *I* should wed her, if only to keep her out of Solindish hands.''

"I intend to tell you no such thing," Tarron retorted. "For all I know, you may prefer a Cheysuli woman. So long as the lady weds no man, your path is safe. We watch her very closely, my lord—more closely than she likes. And she shows no signs of choosing any man.''

"But she *is* aware of what it could mean to Solinde?"

"Very aware," Tarron said grimly. "My lord, tread gently. I have seen the lady . . . I understand very well how a man could lose his head over her. But if you press her for anything, anything at all, she will bolt. And, most likely, she will bolt to the closest den.''

"Dar's." Hart nodded thoughtfully. "An interesting position, regent. If I pursue her, she bolts. If I *ignore* her, she may simply go to the same den more slowly." He smiled. "What would you propose?"

Tarron's voice was steady. "I would propose that you

get the ring back from Dar, my lord, before he puts it to use. With it, he stands a better chance of winning the lady. With it *and* Ilsa, your time in Solinde is done."

Hart swore beneath his breath. He was of no mind to wed, not even for the sake of a realm. Let Brennan make the sacrifice with Aileen of Erinn, and Keely with the girl's brother, Sean. His choice would be his own, and the timing of it.

The Third Seal— Abruptly he brightened. "There *is* a way I might be able to get it back, and without bloodshed. But it will require something from you."

Tarron did not hesitate. "Anything, my lord."

Hart smiled warmly. "Change my Homanan gold for Solindish."

Four

"My lord," the servant said, "the messenger will speak only to you, though he sends this with me."

Hart, more concerned with the dice he tossed across the table than the messenger's intentions, glanced only absently at the speaker. But his interest sharpened as he saw the palace servant carried the saddlepacks lost to Ilsa. He rose at once and took them from the man, relieved he could finally trade borrowed Solindish clothing for familiar Cheysuli leathers. "Have him come up at once."

The man bowed yet again. "My lord, he waits outside, in the bailey. He says he may not leave the gift intended for Hart of Homana, nor bring it into the palace."

Hart, digging leathers out of the packs, looked at the servant in distracted surprise. "A gift?"

"Aye, my lord."

He shrugged and resumed his search. "Well, then, I shall go down and tend to this gift. Tell the messenger I am coming."

"Aye, my lord." The servant departed at once.

Hart found the leathers he wanted and dumped the packs across the table, scattering dice. Quickly he stripped out of his borrowed finery and into leggings and jerkin, buckling on a wide leather belt tooled with runic glyphs. The buckle was heavy gold set with lapis; the knife he retrieved from the Solindish belt and slid it home in the Cheysuli sheath. Bare-armed at last, his race was plain to see.

No more doubts from Dar or his ilk, he thought in satisfaction. *Now, lir, shall we go?*

We go, Rael agreed, and lifted from the perch.

The gift was nothing at all a messenger might bring inside the palace, being a tall chestnut stallion with four white stockings and flaxen mane and tail, who eyed Hart with intense interest as he came into the bailey. At the stallion's head stood a man in blue-and-white livery, the royal colors of Solinde.

Though he was not the expert in horseflesh Brennan was, Hart nonetheless knew well enough the stallion was magnificent. The chestnut's height was impressive, as was his conditioning; a deep chest, long shoulders and strong legs bespoke his stamina. Fox-red ears tipped inward toward one another, and his brown eyes were large and intelligent. He stood quietly enough, but there was a quivering expectancy about him that told Hart he required a rider who was alert to equine tricks.

Another way to attempt my death? Hart smiled as Rael drifted down to perch upon the bailey wall. Quietly he approached the stallion and gently caught his head with both hands, cupping nose and jaw. The firm flesh quivered at once; the stallion lifted his upper lip to display awesome teeth as he tried to catch an unwary finger.

"*Shansu,*" Hart said quietly. "You and I will settle our differences another time; for now, you will leave my fingers intact." He nodded to the messenger. "I am Hart of Homana, now the Prince of Solinde."

The man's face was a polite mask, though his tone was civil enough. "My lord, I am given no title other than your name. It is my lady's contention that there is no other than your name. It is my lady's contention that there is no Prince of Solinde."

"The Lady Ilsa is stubborn." Hart laughed.

The man ignored that. "The Lady Ilsa sends to say this stallion cannot replace the one you lost, but will nonetheless provide a means of transportation. She acknowledges her part in the loss of your mount, and repays the debt freely." He held out the reins perfunctorily.

Hart accepted them, automatically stroking the firm layers of muscle lying beneath the flesh of the stallion's underjaw. "Tell the lady I am honored by her gift, if not by her refusal to acknowledge my Solindish title." He did not really care if she chose to ignore his status, but it was all a part of the game. "And tell the lady I will one day claim her forfeit."

"My lord, I will." Ilsa's messenger fell back as Hart swung up into the saddle. The gear was Solindish and unfamiliar, but he found it not uncomfortable. The stallion bunched massive hindquarters and essayed a single sidestep, then relaxed beneath Hart's quieting touch.

He grinned down at the messenger. "You may tell the lady I am pleased indeed."

"Aye, my lord."

Hart signaled and one of the stable lads came running. "Have word sent to the regent that I am about the business we discussed. I may return very late." And then he summoned Rael and rode out of the double gates.

Rael's dubiousness became patently clear as Hart reined in before The White Swan. *Are you certain?* the hawk inquired.

Quite, Hart answered. *If Dar is not here, I will look for him elsewhere. But he must be found, and the seal won back.*

There are other ways, lir.

And do you suggest I turn thief? Hart asked wryly. *Worse, yet, murderer?*

No. I suggest you think about what you intend to do.

Hart laughed and jumped off the stallion. *I intend to take you inside with me, and enter into a game. What other thinking need I do?*

Rael's tone was resigned. *More than that, I think.*

Hart tied off the stallion and waited for Rael to settle upon his forearm. The hawk was large, too large; it was not a comfortable position, but an impressive one—for the moment, precisely what he wanted. Once inside, Rael would find another perch.

The stallion snorted and shook his head, clattering brass appointments. The setting sun glinted off the metal, flashing in Hart's eyes. He turned away and thrust open the door.

He had not expected a welcome and did not receive one. Casual glances turned into frozen stares, and once again he heard the cacophony of the common room die into expectant silence. A single word through the link loosed Rael into the room, and the great hawk lifted to stir the air against staring faces. He flew to the roof-tree and perched himself upon it, shedding a single black-edged feather.

"Dar," Hart said only.

As one, the faces turned from him to stare at the man who walked out of the shadows into the candlelight. Standing, he was at least as tall as Hart, though his quilted Solindish doublet and padded trews hid much of such things as true weight, frame, strength. Hart's snug Cheysuli leathers did not.

Dar carried a silver goblet in one negligent hand. On his forefinger Hart saw the heavy ring he himself had lost but three nights before. Dar smiled faintly, and it was not without its share of honest amusement taken at no one's expense, least of all at Hart's.

"I thought you might be back." He waved a hand at the nearest table. The patrons deserted it at once.

Hart jerked his belt-purse loose and held it up in the light. "*Solindish* gold," he said pointedly. "Red Solindish gold."

Dar grinned. "Bezat, my lord? Or did you find the stakes too high?"

Hart crossed the room and hooked a stool free. "Bezat," he agreed calmly. "You had your chance at my life, and accepted payment in its place. This time we play for gold."

"Until I have won all of yours, and then you will wager something else." Dar sat down. "I know your kind, Cheysuli. You live for the wager, the *risk*—everything else is too tame." He slapped the flat of his hand down upon the table. "Oma! The bowl!"

She brought it at once and thumped it down on the table. Hart grinned at her and was rewarded, as he expected, with a muttered Solindish curse between small Solindish teeth.

Dar laughed, ordering a jug of wine and a cup for Hart. "She is all sting and no venom. Be assured, if you want her, you have only to win my gold. Oma goes with the man who has the most."

Hart busied himself with stirring the contents of the bowl. "My taste runs to fair-haired women."

Dar looked at him sharply, but Hart's face gave nothing away. He placed his own belt-purse on the table. "My taste runs to women, period. I have no preferences."

"None?" Hart smiled blandly. "But then, a man who aspires to wed the Lady Ilsa might not even see the others."

Dar did not smile. "You have learned well in three days, *my lord*."

"To survive in Solinde, I have to." Hart pushed the bowl in Dar's direction. "Stir them?—or shall I?"

Tight-mouthed, Dar stirred, and Hart drew the first stone for him.

They played the hours away, burning the candle down to a stub. Red Solindish gold changed hands many times, making one man a pauper, another wealthy, and then went the other way with the draw of a single rune-stone. Blank bezats held no threat for Hart, who had weathered the first high-stakes game and felt the others far too tame. But he would not risk himself again.

When at last he and Dar stared at one another across a pile of stones—red-eyed, dry-mouthed, stiff from hunched postures—no man could be called a victor. Each shared equally in the wealth.

Dar scraped his stool back. "Enough, shapechanger. The cock will crow within an hour, and my bed beckons me."

"One more time," Hart said intently. "Once more, Dar."

The Solindishman shook his head. "I have wasted enough time for now—"

"Then I will see to it there is no waste." Hart shoved

his pile of gold forward. "All of it, on but a single game."

Dar looked at the gold thoughtfully. Then he shrugged, dismissing it. "Not worth the effort."

"Wait—" Hart rose. "If we *made* it worth the effort?"

Brown eyes narrowed. "With what? You will not risk your Cheysuli gold; you have said so." He looked across the room at Rael, still perched on a limb of the roof-tree. "Unless you mean to put up your hawk."

Hart was incredulous that Dar could even think it. And then he laughed, realizing the man could not possibly know what the hawk was to him. "No," he said clearly, and thrust his left hand into the air. "Sooner this than my *lir*."

Dar shrugged. "Then again I must say, what have you to offer?"

Hart looked down at his right hand. On his finger glittered the heavy sapphire signet ring of his Homanan rank. Quickly he stripped it off and tossed it into the pile of coins. "This."

A light came up in Dar's brown eyes. It was not the ring so much, Hart knew, but the sudden desire for higher stakes, *high* stakes; they both of them lived to walk the edge of the blade.

"More," Dar said quietly.

Hart laughed. "You do not have nearly enough to match it. The wager would be no wager."

Dar's eyes narrowed. "Try me," he said. "I will match in worth whatever you have to wager."

Hart assessed him a moment. Then, smiling, he said, "A horse."

Dar shrugged. "I breed the finest horseflesh in Solinde. It would be difficult to offer me better than I have."

"Judge him for yourself. He is tied just outside."

The Solindishman's mouth twitched in amusement. "So prepared to lose . . . well enough, let us judge the worth of this horse."

Hart led the way outside. Once there, he was pleased to see the look of shock on Dar's face. "My horse, Solindishman. Worth enough, do you think?"

"That is *Ilsa's horse!* I myself bred him, raised him, trained him ... I *sold* him to her only because she refused to accept him as a gift." His face was white with anger. "How does he come to be with you?"

"A gift," Hart said lightly, "from the lady to me."

Dar's breath hissed. "You *lie!*"

"Send a messenger to ask her." Purposely, Hart kept his tone light. He had known all along divulging the source of the stallion would force Dar's hand, although he had not known the man himself had bred the stallion. It made the challenge all the sweeter. "If you will recall from the lady's story of our meeting in the wood, my own mount broke both forelegs and had to be destroyed. This horse was sent to replace him."

"*This* horse—" Dar was nearly incoherent as he swung to face Hart directly. "Name your wager, shapechanger. This horse is worth more than the gold I offer."

Blandly, Hart smiled. "The Third Seal of Solinde."

After a moment of taut silence, Dar said something succint in explicit—and idiomatic—Solindish. Hart's grasp of the language extended only to a few halting phrases; slang was beyond him. But the tone told him more than enough.

"Undoubtedly I am whatever you claimed I am," he said cheerfully. "Now, shall we go back inside and settle this?"

Dar looked at the stallion, who tugged at his reins and tried to reach out to the Solindishman. It set white dents of anger at the corners of Dar's mouth. His eyes were black as he stared at Hart. "You risked the Seal without knowing its worth," he said flatly. "I am not so foolish—I *know* its worth. Do you think I will risk it on a thing so inconsequential as a *game?*"

"Perhaps not," Hart said calmly. "But will you risk it for a woman?"

Dar spat at the ground, just missing Hart's boots. "*That* for your game!" he said tightly. "Inside, shape-changer, and we shall *see* who gains that woman."

In silence, they played a final game of Bezat. Hart did not look at the Solindish ring that sat atop the pile of red gold in front of Dar; he did not dare to. Nor did he look at his own pile, upon which waited the sapphire ring he risked as well as the horse. The stakes were not anything like the game in which he had risked his life, but he found it no less fascinating. If he won, it would prove there was a place in the world for his gaming.

If he won. If he *had* won.

But he did not.

Dar laughed aloud as he turned over the final rune-stone. No bezats, but the worth of his stones outweighed the worth of Hart's. And so the man who had risked more won more; Hart was left to stare at the gold that was now Dar's, knowing the sapphire and the horse were lost also.

The Solindishman raked red gold across the table amidst hearty congratulations. The Solindish ring he slipped onto his forefinger again; the sapphire he tossed to the wine-girl, Oma. "There!" he cried, in Homanan for Hart's benefit. "A token of my thanks, Oma, for good service throughout the years."

Hart found himself on his feet. "That ring is worthy of more respect, Solindish!"

"Is it?" Dar shrugged. "It is Homanan, is it not? And I say again, *this is Solinde.*" He poured his winnings into his belt-purse. "I will tell the lady how little you thought of her gift, shapechanger; so little you wagered it in a silly gambling game." His smile was eloquently derisive. "Ilsa does not entirely approve of such feckless pursuits, being so personally involved in something as important as the future of her realm."

"What of *you?*" Hart demanded. "Will you tell her how often *you* wager your wealth in silly gambling games?"

Dar laughed. "I thought I would leave it to the lady to reform me." He tied the now-bulging purse onto his belt. "I bid you good night and good morning, shapechanger . . . and my thanks for a worthwhile game."

Inwardly, Hart swore. Outwardly, he took his *lir* and left, hating the laughter that followed him.

*   *   *

In private chambers, the Homanan regent of Solinde perused parchments attentively. He read through one carefully, nodded thoughtfully, set it aside for further review. The next he scanned, then put it atop another pile. Briefly he glanced at the young man who waited impatiently near the table.

"You—lost?" Tarron nodded before Hart could answer. "Aye, I thought that was what you said. Well then, we must live with the fact the Third Seal is in the hands of the enemy, and we can no longer govern Solinde." His faint smile was wintry. "I have written to the Mujhar."

Hart swore, then scowled at Tarron. "There is still a chance I can get it back from him."

"In yet another game?" Tarron sat back in his chair. "My instructions from your father are quite clear, my lord. I am to give you no money other than the allowance he will provide."

"Payable how often?"

Tarron smiled. "Once a year."

"Once a year!" Hart nearly gaped. "How am I to make it last the entire twelve-month? Has he gone mad? Have *you* gone mad? How am I to live?"

"By learning not to wager it in foolish fortune-games." Tarron picked up another parchment. "My lord, if you will excuse me, there are things I must attend to."

"Then give it to me now."

After a moment, the regent glanced up from the parchment. "My lord?"

"My allowance. Give it to me now."

"I think not, my lord. It has not yet arrived from Homana."

Hart bit back another curse. "Then *loan* me the coin until it comes, and pay yourself back from that."

"I think not, my lord."

"Tarron!"

The regent set down the parchment. "Aye, my lord?"

Hart stepped very close to the table. "I can order you," he said quietly. "I am your liege lord."

Unexpectedly, Tarron laughed. "No," he said, "you

cannot. Because you *are* not. My liege lord is Niall of Homana."

Hart glared at him angrily. "Do you think I have no resources, regent? Do you think I *need* your coin? No. *No.* I have gold, good Cheysuli gold, and plenty of gemstones, in wristlets, buckles, rings—countless other baubles. Do you think denying me coin can keep me from the game?"

Tarron's face was austere, yet oddly compassionate. "My lord, you are welcome to strip your caskets of every piece of jewelry you possess; it changes nothing. You may *beggar* yourself, my lord, but it will not change my mind. I have my orders from the Mujhar."

Pushed too far, Hart bared his teeth at the regent. "And when I am king in his place?"

The answering tone was very calm. "The day that happens, my lord, I will excuse myself from your service."

Hart's anger evaporated instantly, replaced with cold shock. He stared at the man in dawning acknowledgment. "You hate me that much."

"What is there to hate, my lord?" Tarron asked. "No. I dislike you, aye, because you waste yourself. I know your father well; I know his good sense, his mettle, his generosity. I know the Prince of Homana; he is a responsible, mature adult who will do as well as his father when he assumes the throne. But what do I know of you?" He spread his hands. "I know you prefer taverns to council chambers, games to governing, personal gratification to responsibilities. Certainly there are many men who feel as you do. But none of them are Prince of Solinde."

Guilty, Hart chafed beneath the gentle reprimand. "Aye, aye, I know—and one day I *will* become the man you think I can be— "

"But not yet?" Tarron did not smile. "If you are not very careful, you will not live long enough to become that man."

Hart pressed both hands against the regent's table and leaned forward. "I can win the ring back, if you let me," he promised, working hard to charm the man. "I *know* I can. And I will. All I require—"

"No."

"Tarron—"

The regent was not charmed. "No."

"You *ku'reshtin*—"

But Tarron cut him off. "My lord, if you will forgive me, there is much I must attend to. Without the Seal, many things must be handled with delicacy and deliberation." He gestured toward the stacks of parchments. "Unless you care to aid me—?"

Hart merely laughed at him.

Tarron nodded. "Well enough, I shall deal with it. But if I may suggest it, my lord, you might wish to consider what you will wear to the feast."

Hart, heading toward the door, turned to look at him blankly. "The feast?"

"The feast to celebrate your arrival, my lord. In one week's time." Tarron waved a negligent hand. "All the Solindish nobility will be here, as well as all the Homanans in the city."

All the nobility?"

"Aye." Tarron's face was oddly expressionless. "Including the Lady Ilsa, and all the lords who wish to wed her."

"*Ku'reshtin*," Hart muttered. "I know what you mean to do."

"Do you?" Tarron's raised his brows. "I think perhaps not, my lord. What purpose would your marriage to Ilsa serve if you refuse to rule Solinde in the realm's best interests? What purpose if you died unexpectedly? She would still be Princess—or even Queen—and it would make it that much easier for the Solindish to throw us out of Solinde." He smiled thinly. "Such a wedding might well prove a disaster."

Hart jerked open the door. "I may be the wastrel second son, *regent*, but I am not stupid. And if you think I am blind to your backward attempt to push me *into* this marriage, you are the stupid one."

Tarron merely laughed. Swearing, Hart banged the door closed behind him.

Five

Hart walked quietly into the Great Hall of Lestra's palace with Rael perched upon his left forearm and saw the faces, one by one, turn to stare. Conversations eddied, trailed off, died out as the gathered Solindish nobility and the Homanans who governed them recognized the Cheysuli Prince of Solinde. And then the noise began again: whispers, murmurs, comments, in Homanan and Solindish, until Hart could no longer quite control the amusement that threatened to overtake his painstakingly practiced solemnity.

Those who know you, know better. Rael said pointedly.

Aye, but how many here know me? Tarron? No. He only believes he does. Dar? He knows me only as a mark. As for the lady . . . inwardly, Hart sighed, *by now surely the lady knows me only as a fool who risks her realm in silly games.*

The chamberlain mounted the white marble dais and formally announced the Prince of Solinde. Hart, unaccustomed to such pageantry arranged solely for his benefit, winced visibly, then recovered himself almost instantly. His years in Homana-Mujhar had taught him that kings conducted themselves with decorum at such formal festivities even when they did not feel it. He was not a king yet, but he needed the practice. Besides, the Solindish would expect it.

Now? Rael asked.

Now, Hart agreed. *The better to impress them.*

Accordingly, Rael lifted from Hart's arm and circled

233

the huge hall, banking toward the high-backed chair set upon the dais. Women cried out at his passage and men set hands to knives; Rael swept relentlessly to the throne and settled himself upon the carved back. He spread his wings and shrieked aloud his dominance, then settled, folding his wings away, and surveyed all down the sharp hook of his deadly beak.

Hart moved toward the dais, mounting the steps even as the throng fell back. He was aware of the whispers and hissed questions, as well as the subtle hostility on the part of the Solindish. From the Homanans he sensed only a quiet, abiding pride; if they did not relish the thought of having Homana held by shapechangers in place of Homanans, they at least were willing enough to put the Solindish in their place by using the reputation of the Cheysuli.

He turned, trying to still the flutter of nervousness in his belly. Never before had he faced so many people as a ruler. Even in Homana he was only the second son, the prince who would trade his home for foreign lands. He was not Brennan, whose duties included nearly as many rituals and formalities as his father, the Mujhar. In Homana, he was simply Hart; *Prince* Hart, perhaps, by dint of his birth, but he had been easily overlooked. Now, he found he *could not* be overlooked, even if he preferred it.

How they stare, all the eyes.

He drew himself up, though his posture did not require it. And then he smiled. "I am Hart," he said quietly, pitching his voice low; he had learned from his father the art of making men listen by underplaying the moment. "Hart of Homana, second-born son of Niall the Mujhar, and styled Prince of Solinde." He saw narrowing eyes and tightening faces among the Solindish; how glibly he stole their title. "I am sent to learn kingship in the land I will rule; to learn how to govern a people in vassalage to Homana." Solindish mouths drew taut and flat, though some of the faces were conspicuously blank so as not to give anything away. "It is my wish that Solinde know peace, not war; that the hostilities of the past be buried along with those who have died." He drew in a steadying breath. "It is my personal desire that the overweening ambitions of the Ihlini be laid bare for all to see, so that there need be no discord in a land that deserves far better."

That, as he expected, sparked shocked murmurs and curses of disbelief among the Solindish; the Homanans merely watched him curiously.

"It is known to Cheysuli and Homanan alike that the Ihlini call Solinde their homeland," Hart continued quietly. "It is not my intention to banish them from it, because not all serve Asar-Suti. But it *is* my intention to halt the hostility that they foment, and let Solinde remain *Solindish*—instead of a servant of the Ihlini."

All the eyes stared back, divulging nothing and everything; Hart realized, somewhat belatedly, that he had learned more from his father than he had thought.

He smiled, spreading his hands. "Enough of such talk; I am more in mind of a celebration than a declaration of war. Let the dancing begin." And abruptly he stepped down from the dais into the gathered throng.

It did not take long for Tarron to make his way through the couples who danced, or those who stood in groups and discussed politics. The regent, clad in habitual black, stepped to Hart's right side and said, quietly, "My lord, perhaps it would have been better if you had worn Solindish garb. Perhaps you should have left your hawk in your chambers—"

"—and perhaps it would have been better had I not attended at all." Hart smiled coolly at Tarron. "Would you say so to the Mujhar, regent? Would you bid him dress Homanan when he is a Cheysuli warrior?"

The brown eyes reflected shock. "My lord—"

"I am not my *jehan*," Hart said quietly. "I do not mean to be. But I am, first and foremost, *Cheysuli*. If I choose to wear leathers instead of velvets, I shall. If I choose to take Rael even into my bridal chamber, I shall. *I shall,* regent, do precisely as I please when it comes to my personal conduct." He caught up a cup of wine from a passing servant. "The Solindish will have to accept me as I am, Tarron. So will you."

"So much *gold,* my lord." Tarron's distaste was plain. "They will say you are a barbarian."

Hart grinned. "At least a wealthy one." He sipped wine, watching the regent over the rim of his cup. He was not surprised Tarron found his garb displeasing, for he was a man who abhorred ornamentation. The regent's black clothing, though of good cut and quality, was very plain. Hart's soft leathers, equally black, were also equally plain—except he had put on rune-scribed wristlets, torque, plated belt, sheath and knife, all of heavy gold.

Tarron's mouth was flat. "And how long will you keep it?" he asked grimly. "You will lose it all in a fortune-game."

Hart grinned. "Here it is called Bezat."

The regent's jaw bunched as he gritted teeth. "My lord, if you will excuse me—"

"No." Hart smiled blandly. "It is time you made the introductions, regent, as you are the one who knows all the Solindish nobility. May I suggest you begin with those lords who desire to wed the Lady Ilsa?"

Tarron stared back. "*Now,* my lord? *All* of them?"

"Those who desire to wed the lady," Hart said evenly. "Those whom you think may well have a chance."

Tarron's expression gave away nothing. "Aye, my lord. Of course."

Over the next two hours Hart met more men than he cared to acknowledge, and yet he had to. In execrable Homanan they greeted their newly-arrived prince and bid him courteous, insincere welcome, politely offering whatever assistance or companionship he might require. And as he opened his mouth to answer the first of them, he realized he dared give him only Homanan, or he would never be understood.

Jehan—and Brennan—always said I should pay more attention to my language lessons . . . that one day my ignorance would catch me up. . . .

Hart looked at the gathered Solindish aristocracy. Uncomfortably, he realized that the vanquished always were required to give up more than land or status. They gave up language and culture as well, replacing both with the preferences of the victor.

How was it during Shaine's qu'mahlin? he wondered idly. *How was it for the clans that had to flee Homana to live in foreign lands?*

"My lord." Tarron again. "My lord, may I present Dar of High Crags, born of one of the oldest lines in Solinde."

Hart came out of his brief reverie to find Dar standing before him in silence. The Solindishman's smile was blandly polite, offering nothing more than the courtesy demanded of his rank, but Hart saw the glint in his brown eyes and the twitch of amusement at the corner of his mouth.

"Dar of High Crags," Hart repeated. "How old a line is it?"

"Very old, my lord," Dar answered politely. "At least as old as the Lady Ilsa's; my kin has served hers for more than seven centuries."

"And in all of that time has none of you ever wed into the royal house?"

The barb went home. Dar's eyelids flickered, but he managed a benign smile. "History changes from one night to the next, my lord . . . surely you know that better than most. Is it not true that the Cheysuli ruled Homana for a thousand years, then gave it over to the Homanans?" He paused for the benefit of Homanan ears. "And *now* you take it back?"

"In accordance with the wishes of the gods," Hart said smoothly. "Have you not heard of our prophecy? Surely you have, Dar . . . surely the Ihlini in service to the Seker have made certain you know *of* it, if not the truth." He sipped wine. "The Wheel of Life is a thing no man may fully know, except that the gods have a purpose when they set it into motion."

"*Tahlmorra.*" Dar nodded. "Aye, I have heard of the fatalism that rules your race. And I have heard how blindly you serve it."

Tarron cleared his throat. "My lord of High Crags—my lord prince—"

"I think you may leave the lord of High Crags with me," Hart interrupted, without taking his eyes from Dar's. "Are there not things you must attend to?"

"Aye, my lord." In obvious relief, Tarron bowed quickly and departed.

"Neatly done." Dar scooped a cup of wine from a passing servant.

Hart was not ready to change the subject. "There is a purpose in all things," he said quietly. "All things, Dar . . . even the handing over of a Solindish throne to a Cheysuli warrior."

The woman's voice was cool. "And was there a purpose in risking my horse in a *game?*" she asked. "And the Third Seal, *my lord*—what purpose in losing that?"

Hart inclined his head to acknowledge Ilsa's arrival. "He was my horse, lady—freely given. As for the Seal, well—" He shrugged, grinning ruefully "—had I known it was the price that bought your willingness to marry, surely I would never have risked something so valuable."

She gazed at him wide-eyed in unfeigned astonishment. "My willingness to *marry?*"

Dar interrupted smoothly. "Lady, he seeks only to turn the subject. That he should be so thoughtless as to risk your horse on the very day the gift was received, or to risk him *at all*—"

Hart looked only at Ilsa. "You might ask him," he suggested. "You might ask him how he considers the ring as a way of securing you for a *cheysula*."

She frowned. "A what?"

"Wife," he amended. "Do you intend to marry him?"

Dar's hand was on Ilsa's arm. "That is none of your concern, shapechanger."

She slipped free easily, obviously well accustomed to avoiding the possessiveness of men, and turned to face Dar squarely. "But it is *my* concern." Delicate color deepened in her face to compete with the frost in her eyes. "Is it true, Dar? Do you think I will wed you because you hold the Seal, when it should be mine regardless?"

Brown eyes narrowed minutely, weighing the need for

frankness against the requirements of diplomacy; Dar discarded his elegant courtier's manner instantly. "I think you will wed the man best able to help Solinde," he said flatly. "You *must* wed such a man—a strong, loyal, dedicated Solindishman, who wants only the best for his land . . . a man who can forge the warring factions into one united front—"

"And take Solinde back from Homana?" Hart interposed. As they stared, he shook his head. "You reckon without the Cheysuli, who *require* this land—or at least the bloodlines from it."

"And do you require *me?*" Ilsa demanded icily. "The last of Bellam's line, born of the oldest House of Solinde . . . how could you overlook *me?*"

"How could I?" Hart grinned. "Not easily, Lady Ilsa—no more easily than Dar."

She looked from him, to Dar, back again. And then she laughed, surprising both of them. "And do you think I would wed either of *you?*"

"Ilsa—" Dar began.

Still she smiled, though her eyes remained cool. "No," she said, "I would not. I want no man who values games over the welfare of Solinde."

"Then I will stop," Dar said flatly. "I will stop altogether, here and now, no more to waste my time and wealth in foolish games of chance."

Ilsa turned to Hart. "What of you?" she asked. "Will you make me the same promise?"

Without hesitating, Hart shook his head. "No, lady, I will not."

Her mouth twisted, briefly ironic. "Honesty from *you*, at least, displeasing though it may be." She looked at Dar. "You are all you have described—strong, loyal, dedicated, and capable of uniting Solinde. I will indeed require a man with the same abilities, *but I will choose him myself.*" Coolly, she smiled. "I find it shameful that Solinde demands a *man* to rule when a woman could do as well—and I am deserving of it." She put out a slender hand. "Give me the ring, Dar. You know it is rightfully mine."

He spread eloquent, empty hands. "Alas, I have left it home."

Her tone was very grim. "Dar—"

"*Ilsa.*" He cut her off. "We are old, old friends, and older adversaries in this game of men and women. You ask for honesty? I give you honesty . . . *I give you a truth you may not like.*" He glanced at Hart as if regretting his presence, but continued regardless of it. "The Third Seal is mine, won fairly from a man who did not know what he risked. He lost. He lost it *all,* including his only chance to marry the woman he needs to marry, in order to hold this realm. But I won. *I won.* And I keep what I win, regardless of who else might want it . . . *unless they are willing to pay the price.*"

She was awash in candleglow. In crimson and gold she set the hall ablaze; rubies glittered in braided hair. But they could not compete with the determination in her eyes, or her pride. That and her dignity were palpable. "I am Ilsa of Solinde," she said evenly. "I can rule without the ring."

"But not without a Consort." Dar sipped wine; his eyes were alight with inner amusement. "The lords of Solinde will require a male heir as soon as is humanly possible, lady, to insure the succession. It seems to me you have need of me as much as I of you."

"But I can take another man," she reminded him gently, patently unaffected by his challenge. "Where will that leave you?"

"Without," Hart said succinctly.

Dar shook his head. "She will do what is required. Ilsa has pride, integrity, honor . . . and an incredible sense of duty." He bowed his head in a courteous salute. "In the end, rather than leaving it to others, she will make the decision herself."

"Then leave me to it!" Ilsa said sharply. "Leave me altogether!"

Dar bowed. "Aye, my lady. At once."

As the Solindishman left, Hart looked at Ilsa in mild surprise. "A sharp tongue, lady."

"With him, I need one." Ilsa took the cup of wine out

of Hart's hand and drank down what remained, eyes
aglitter over the rim. Abruptly she pressed the cup back
into his hands. "Dar always makes me angry, which
makes me all the angrier."

Hart skillfully eased her through the throng, guiding
her slowly toward a quiet corner. "Are you enemies, or
bedmates?"

Ilsa looked at him sharply. "Not bedmates," she said
dryly. "Nor enemies, to tell the truth." She sighed and
sat down on the padded bench against the wall, deftly
spreading crimson skirts to decorously cover gem-crusted
leather slippers. "Since we were young, there was talk of
uniting our houses. It was believed that Dar could provide Solinde with the strong leadership she requires."
She slanted him a glance from eloquent eyes. "You know,
of course, that we prefer self-rule. We want no foreign
overlord."

"I know. And were there no prophecy, I might be
disposed to grant it, once in the position to do so." Hart
shrugged as he sat down beside her. "But I am not, and I
am a dutiful Cheysuli. I serve the prophecy."

"Why?" she asked bluntly. "If it does not please you,
turn your back on it."

"Because I aspire to the afterworld." Hart grinned and
leaned back against the wall, stretching out long legs.
"Out of character, she is thinking. A man who wagers
the Third Seal of Solinde could not possibly concern
himself with what happens after death." Then, more
solemnly, "But I do. Every Cheysuli does. The gods
have given us a place here in the world, and promise a
better one when we are dead." He smiled wryly. "We
need only be faithful children."

"Faithful to a daydream dreamed too many years ago."
But Ilsa's smile removed the sting of the words. "So, you
serve your prophecy in hopes of reward after death. It
seems such a futile thing . . . and perhaps a little childish."

"I am not a child."

Ilsa looked at him a long moment. "No. I think you
are not."

He gazed out at the people: at those who danced; who

clustered to mutter of politics; who advocated rebellion and the taking of his life. "We are an old race," he said finally. "Thousands and thousands of years. We are children of the gods: it is what *Cheysuli* means." Still he stared, though his vision blurred and he saw only colors and candlelight. "The Homanans tried to slay us all, to annihilate us entirely, in a purge that lasted decades . . . the Ihlini have done it again and again, through sorcery, plague, intrigue. So many centuries of hatred, prejudice, fear . . . so many years of being the hunted, not knowing if we would survive." He blinked and turned his head to look at Ilsa. "We survived because of the gods. Because of the afterworld. *Because of the prophecy*." Silently he turned a spread-fingered hand palm-up. "All of it shapes our lives. Without it, we would perish."

She said nothing for a long moment, seemingly unable. And then she shook her head. Rubies glistened in her hair. "How is it a man—a Cheysuli—who is so dedicated to this prophecy can risk himself in a *game?*"

Hart laughed; it was a single burst of sound. "Because I cannot help it."

Ilsa frowned. "Cannot?" She shrugged. "I say, simply *stop*."

" 'Simply stop,' " he echoed, and grinned to himself.

"If you pride yourself on the discipline of the Cheysuli—"

"I pride myself on nothing." Abruptly he rose to tower over her. "Lady, we speak of private things. Let us dance instead."

Ilsa rose also, but disdained to take his outstretched hand. "No," she said coolly. "I think I would rather not." She turned to go, took four steps, turned back so abruptly rich skirts swung against the floor. Golden girdle chimed. "Dar has the right of it," she warned with infinite distinctness. "In the end, regardless of how I feel, I will do what is best for the realm."

Hart watched her rigid back as she slipped into the crowd and was lost. He was more than a little stunned by her sudden retreat—no, it was not a retreat. She had simply *left* him; he was not a man much accustomed to women leaving him.

Not accustomed to it at all. Morosely, he searched for her in the throng. Had she gone to Dar? Possibly. He thought it entirely possible—until Dar himself approached.

He carried two silver cups in his hands and offered one to Hart. "I swear, there is no poison. It would cheat me of my wager."

Hart, still stinging from Ilsa's rebuke, slanted her foremost suitor a black scowl. "No doubt the bet is against me."

Dar grinned. "Not entirely, though it does involve you." He tipped his head in the direction of the departed Ilsa. "Shall we drink to the lady, my lord, and to her unerring tongue?"

Reluctantly, Hart smiled. And then he laughed ruefully. "Aye, she has that. And uses it on us both."

They clanged cups and drank; the wine was dry, hearty, powerful. Hart liked it very much.

"The lady has used it on *me* for many years," Dar remarked. "It is time she had a new target, though not a permanent one." His smile offered a challenge. "Are you interested in my wager?"

"And if I said I was not?"

"You would be a liar, and I think you are not that." Dar smoothed a lock of sandy hair away from his eyes. "For all we are Cheysuli and Solindish—and rivals to one another—I think we are much alike," he said lightly. "Once, had a man suggested that, I would have slain him outright; Cheysuli and Solindish? But I am a man for realities if nothing else; you are here, you intend to *stay* here, and—short of having you slain—there is little to do about it."

Hart grunted. "You might still try."

"To slay you?" Dar shook his head. "I think not. I think it would result in too much trouble, for me and for Solinde. No. No killing. Perhaps a wager will do as well."

Hart sighed. "What wager?"

"One worth our time, my lord. One worthy of *both* of

us." Dar paused. "I propose we place a wager on the lady . . . and on ourselves."

"Dar—"

The Solindishman gestured expansively. "Deny it all you wish, but I have seen that expression before when a man looks at Ilsa. It has been on my *own* face often enough." He shrugged and smiled ruefully. "You want her, *I* want her, every man in *Solinde* wants her. But only half a dozen stand a chance, and only one will get her."

"You," Hart said dryly.

Dar grinned. "I am willing to wager on that."

Hart smothered a laugh as he lifted the cup to his mouth. He drank, thinking it over, and watched the anticipation light Dar's eyes. *He is as bad as I. . . .* After a moment, he sighed. "What is the wager, then?"

Dar's face was very intent. "For all she says she will marry who and when she pleases, Ilsa knows full well it cannot wait much longer. Perhaps a month at the most; the lords already request a decision from her." His eyes shrewdly assessed Hart's carefully arranged noncommittal expression. "She need only wed a Solindishman—myself, or another of equal wealth and station—in order to unite the warring factions of this realm. We cannot hope to win Solinde from Homana until we are as one, and there is only one way of uniting us: under a single man."

"You," Hart said, tasting ashes in his mouth.

"Or my son." Dar's tone was steady. "Under our laws, the man who weds Ilsa does not become King of Solinde, he becomes Ilsa's Consort—a position lacking the magnificence of a proper royal title, perhaps, but none of the power accorded his place beside Ilsa. Nor will she be Queen; Solindish law requires a male sovereign. But a son born of the lady and her Consort *does* become king upon his majority." He smiled. "Until he reaches that majority, his father acts as regent."

"And if she weds me?"

To his credit, Dar's expression did not alter. "If Ilsa weds you, it would alter the traditional lines of succession. No doubt you would claim yourself King . . . since

Solinde is a vassal to Homana, it seems likely that title would not be contested." He shrugged. "We have been soundly beaten repeatedly by your ancestors. I doubt there would be any rebellion."

Hart shook his head. "There is no wager, Dar. Ilsa would never allow Solinde to be ruled by a Homanan."

"Would she not?" Dar stared grimly into his wine. "Do not discount yourself, shapechanger. There are those in Solinde who do not want another war, preferring peace even to self-rule. They are very persuasive. And Ilsa—" He broke off, scowling blackly, then continued. "Ilsa is guarded by those who desire peace."

Hart recalled the man who had accompanied her the day they had met. A Solindishman whose task it was to guard her, and who allowed her so little freedom in order to protect her welfare.

He looked hard at Dar, assessing the man's intentions. He knew Dar wanted Ilsa, wanted Solinde, wanted self-rule. He knew also that Dar enjoyed the challenge of a wager as much as he did, which was substantially indeed; he could not live without it. But he did not know how far Dar was prepared to go.

Idly, Hart drank wine. "What are the stakes?" he asked.

"The highest," Dar answered. "I wager with my life."

Hart looked at him sharply. "Your life," he echoed, disbelieving the man.

"Aye," Dar agreed curtly. "Let it stand so: if Ilsa chooses you, I will give up my life and give back the Third Seal of Solinde."

"I do not want your life."

Dar's eyes did not waver. "If you do not take it, my lord, be assured I will do what I can to throw you down from the throne of Solinde."

Hart knew the Solindishman meant it. "I do not want you for an enemy."

"If you win, you will have one."

Hart sighed. "Aye, aye, well enough—if I win the lady, you forfeit the Seal and your life. But what of me? What if *you* win the wager?"

Dar smiled. "You go home to Homana."

Hart stared. "Go *home*—"

"Alive. Unharmed. Quite well . . . very much as you came." Dar, still smiling, shrugged. "But you will forfeit your claim on Solinde."

"And if she chooses neither?"

"Then we will find another game."

Hart chewed at his bottom lip, hearing the siren song of the challenge. *If I lose Solinde, my jehan will forfeit me*—

But he found himself clasping Dar's forearm; the wager was made and accepted.

Six

Hart awoke with the haunted feeling of something gone wrong. He snapped out of sleep and into daylight so abruptly it left him disoriented, and then he realized the disorientation had less to do with the sudden awakening than from late hours and excess drink; he and Dar and three other Solindish lordlings had wasted most of the night closeted in a private chamber, gambling and drinking, while the rest of the guests disported themselves in the Great Hall.

A pang of guilt pinched his belly; such behavior in Homana-Mujhar would be considered unconscionably rude, particularly as the celebration had been in his honor, and he sincerely doubted he would have been allowed to slip away. But here no one dared attempt to dissuade him or otherwise remark on his behavior.

Hart sighed grimly. *Save for Tarron.*

But Tarron had said nothing, because Hart had taken care to slip away unnoticed, too hungry for a game to consider the consequences.

Consequences. The haunted feeling came back. Hart, tangled in tumbled bedclothes, frowned up at the draperied canopy of the tester bed and tried to name what caused his discontent.

Abruptly, he remembered.

His eyes popped open. *The wager . . . the wager with Dar, on Ilsa.* Swearing, he rolled over onto his belly and buried his face in feather-stuffed bolsters, half hoping he could smother himself and forget all about Dar and his

247

infamous wager. *Oh, gods, lir . . . I have wagered away my freedom!*

Rael stirred on his perch. *Have you?*

Hart groaned aloud and clenched fingers in the silk of his bedclothes. *The wager with Dar, on Ilsa—on who will win her hand—* He groaned again, feelingly. *How could I have been so foolish?*

The last is easy to answer. Rael's tone lacked sympathy. *When the craving is on you, you are no man, no warrior, no prince—you are nothing more than a hound smelling a bitch in season . . . save the bitch is no dog at all, but the wager itself.*

After a moment Hart lifted his face out of the bolsters and turned his head to stare at the hawk through the gauzy draperies. "How eloquent," he said grimly; there was no humor in his tone.

How do you know you have lost your freedom? Rael asked. *In order to lose it you must win the woman, and there is nothing that leads me to believe you will.*

Unexpectedly, the dry summation hurt. Hart frowned. "Nothing?"

Nothing. Rael's pattern within the *lir*-link was infinitely assured; for once he did not offer the crutch of meaningless reassurance to his irresponsible *lir*, though the habit was hard to break.

Hart sat up and tried to drag the hangings aside, swearing as fabric tangled and obscured his vision of Rael entirely. Finally he ripped them apart and climbed out of the huge bed, naked save for *lir*-gold.

"Nothing?" he repeated, elaborately distinct.

Rael heard the subtle challenge in Hart's tone. He stirred on his perch and fixed his *lir* with a bright eye. *Tell me what you offer the woman, then.*

"A title. Improved status. Greater respect in the realm." Hart shrugged, spreading his hands. "Power as well, though not as much as I hold."

What power do you hold?

He smiled, victorious. "I am the Prince of Solinde."

Who spends his time wagering on improbable outcomes such as who the last of Bellam's line will wed. Rael couched his words in brutal candor. *Say again what you offer the woman, lir—and then realize that she can have precisely the same if you are sent home to Homana . . . or if you are dead.*

It banished the smile entirely. Hart felt as if one of Brennan's horses had kicked him in the belly—no, not a horse, and not the belly. It was one of Rael's talons, and he stabbed lower than the belly, aiming for something very different, something personal, something eminently more vital.

"Rael—"

Think, lir. For once. See yourself as others see you. Rael paused. *No. See yourself as the lady herself must. And tell me again you have wagered away your freedom.*

It curdled the wine in his belly. Hart turned from the hawk and went back to the bed, clutching one of the testers for support. It was never pleasant listening to others decry his habits, but he had always had the enviable capacity to cheerfully dismiss the comments, the fraternal and paternal lectures, knowing no one stayed angry at him for very long. He was not a man for moods and high temper, as Corin was; neither was he willing to shoulder all the burdens of his rank and future, as Brennan had always been. What he offered was friendly camaraderie, cheerful companionship, generosity of spirit. He was not a bad man. He was not a bad brother, bad son, bad friend, or bad warrior.

"But I *am* a bad prince."

Rael did not answer. Hart shut his eyes and set his forehead against the wooden tester, regretting the wine he had drunk. More than that, he regretted his willingness to overlook so many things in pursuit of personal pleasure.

After a retrospective moment Hart turned back to the hawk. "She will not have me."

No.

"And if she takes Dar in my stead, as is likely, the wager is lost . . . and I will be sent out of Solinde in disgrace."

Much as you were sent out of Homana.

Again the talons stabbed into him.

"If I go home, having lost Solinde—" Abruptly Hart sat down on the bed, realizing the enormity of his situation. "Gods, Rael, if I lose Solinde because of something so infinitely trivial as a *wager*—"

If you lose Solinde for any reason, lir, you alter the prophecy.

It snapped Hart's head up. "No," he said firmly. "*No.* I will not allow you to give that guilt to me."

And if it is the truth?

"How?" Hart challenged. "I am a second son, the *middle* son, obligated to no betrothal. It does not matter who I wed, how many children I sire—or who *they* wed. Let Brennan know that burden, *lir* . . . I need not."

The wine has replaced your wits. Rael's tone lacked the bite of earlier comments, sliding instead toward customary patience and wry acknowledgment of Hart's shortcomings. But it did not make his words less telling. *Whether you wed a Solindish woman does not matter—it does not matter if you wed at all—but it* does *matter if you hold Solinde. The prophecy involves four realms, not three. If you lose Solinde now, it will be lost forever . . . and the Ihlini victorious.*

Hart swore feelingly, knowing guilt as well as consternation. "If only there were no wager . . . then there would be no risk."

Is that not the point of the wager?

He raked tousled hair with rigid fingers, trying to make sense of the circumstances; knowing it unlikely. "Aye, aye, always before it was the risk, the *chance* I might lose, and the pleasure in knowing I had won—or *would* win, next time. But now—" Hart shook his head. "This is different. The game is different. The stakes are too high—" Trapped, desperate, despairing, he swore again. "Gods, Rael, it is the *ultimate* wager . . . and now I cannot enjoy it."

Which do you mourn? Rael asked gently. *The loss of that enjoyment, the loss of your freedom . . . or the loss of a realm?*

Hart did not answer at once. He stared blankly into

the room, lost inside his head, knowing only that his need of the game had accounted for more than his current predicament. For the first time he fully acknowledged that he alone was responsible for the fire, for the loss of life in the Midden. Regardless of the *kind* of people they were, they had not deserved to die because of his selfish irresponsibility.

"Thirty-two people," he said hollowly, and his mind fashioned a vision: Brennan, standing before the stained-glass casements in the Great Hall of Homana-Mujhar, visibly stunned by the loss of life; Brennan, shouting at Corin that it did not matter if he felt inconvenienced about having to go to Atvia when people were dead; Brennan, feeling more keenly the deaths of the people in the Midden because he was a *responsible* man.

Oh, rujho, I wish you were here to tell me what to do.

But Brennan was not. And so Hart did his own *responsible* decision-making for the first time in his life. He put on his clothing and went to see the subject of the wager.

Hart was admitted at once into the city home in which Ilsa dwelled and was shown to a small walled garden. At first he did not see her, wondering if he was meant to wait for hours while his impatience grew; then he *did* see her, and his fine intentions went out of his head. He could think of no way to speak plainly with her, to tell her of the wager that reduced her to chattel instead of independent woman, knowing how she would feel. And knowing what she would say.

And so, lamely, he smiled, and drew for strength upon the abundant charm he had used unthinkingly so often in the past.

Only the night before he had seen her clad in brilliant crimson, ablaze with gold and rubies. She had been elegant, incandescent, incredibly beautiful. He found her no less so now, though the fine gown, gold and gems were gone, replaced by nubby wool skirts of a cream and russet weave and an amber-colored tunic belted with supple leather. She wore scuffed boots in place of soft slippers, and there was mud on one cheek. The glorious white-blond hair was bound back in a single tight-plaited braid, tied off with brown leather. Around her face the shorter hairs came loose, straggling, curling, tangling, serving only to make him want to smooth them back.

Looped over one arm was a basket full of flowers. A profusion of delicate, black-eyed moss roses, ruffled like crumpled parchment, all of bright golds, rich yellows, pastel apricots. In her right hand she carried small silver scissors connected to her belt by a fine-linked silver chain. She rose, intently tucking flowers into the basket, and then turned toward him only to stop short.

"Come out with me," he said. "Come ride with me, Ilsa."

Winged brows rose. "Ride with you? On what, my lord? You wagered your horse away."

He crossed the garden walk and put out his hand to take the basket from her, bending to set it down beside the path. Her wrist was slender in his larger hand, almost to the point of fragility. She seemed delicate as a lily, and yet her spirit and pride burned brightly as his own.

"Aye," he agreed, "I did. Foolishly, selfishly, I sought to goad Dar into a wager that would win back the Third Seal, knowing he could not turn his back on the knowledge you had given the horse to me. And the gambit was successful."

"Except you lost the horse."

"Losing is always a risk, Ilsa. Even now." He did not release her wrist. "The palace is rich in horses, though none so fine as the one you gifted me. I have another." He smiled. "Come with me, lady. Come out of the city and know a little freedom once again."

"We have nothing to say to one another."

"Oh, lady, we do." His thumb rubbed the top of her forearm, glorying in the delicate texture of her skin. "Come with me, Ilsa. Please."

Coolly she pulled free of his hand and its intimacy, bending to scoop up the basket. She hooked both arms through calmly, as if to put up a barrier between them.

"I will order a horse saddled for me. You may wait, my lord."

And he did, somewhat impatiently, wondering why women took so long to ready themselves for a ride when the wind would only muss them almost instantly. But Ilsa did not, and when she appeared he discovered she had not changed at all, save to clean the mud from her face and to put on a fitted leather doublet with silver-rimmed horn buttons. Engaged in working hands into snug gloves, she hardly looked at him as she walked past him toward the front entrance.

Hart exited with her. "You need take no guard. My *lir* and I are enough, I think, to ward you against most dangers."

She slanted him a cool glance over one shoulder as she turned toward the white mare she had ridden at their first meeting. "Are you? I think a man need only offer you a wager, and you would name *me* as the stakes."

He stopped short, staring at her in shock. *She knows . . . oh, gods, she already knows, and this is nothing more than a travesty.*

But Ilsa gave no sign, no hint she knew anything of the wager between Hart and Dar. She merely waited for him to hand her up into the saddle, and when he did not move to do it at once she led the mare to a mounting block and did it on her own. Belatedly, Hart hastened to lend her a hand, though now she did not require it.

The white mare nosed him, pressing muzzle against neck and blowing even as he tried to turn her head away. He looked up at Ilsa, backlighted by the sun, and opened his mouth to speak. Then abruptly turned away.

Hart swung up into his saddle and waited for Ilsa to fall in beside him. It was midmorning and cool; the air chilled his bare arms and lent an icy sheen to his *lir*-bands. He had brought nothing out of Homana save Cheysuli leathers. Solindish clothing would be warmer, but he preferred familiar garb.

How can I tell her? How can I explain?

Rael offered no answer. In silence, Hart escorted Ilsa out of Lestra and into the countryside beyond.

He found it no easier when they were free of the city. He *did* find it easier to forget about the wager altogether, losing himself in the pleasure of the moment. And so he did.

Ilsa was an accomplished rider, as her flight through the wood had proved. He did not hold back now; together they galloped across the turf and lost themselves, for the moment, in the sheer joy of good horseflesh. Running on, *running on,* he could forget all about wagers and risks and titles, thinking only of how the stallion should move beneath him; how fast, how smooth, how willing. For an unblessed human, it was the closest thing to *lir*-shape.

The moment was spent too quickly. Hart eased his mount from a gallop to a canter, then to a walk, even as Ilsa did. In companionable silence they listened to the horses blow, jangling bits and shanks and ornamentation. He could smell the acrid tang of his stallion's sweat, the scent of flowers in the turf, the promise of summer coming. It was a good time to be alive. Better yet, it was a good time to share it with a woman.

"Is that your hawk?" she asked, pointing.

He glanced up and saw the shape against the sky; the outspread wings and lazy spiral. "Aye. Rael. He keeps his distance today, knowing this is a thing between man and woman, requiring no *lir*."

She looked at him sharply. "He *knows* such things?"

Hart laughed. "Did you think him mute? A pet, or a tame bird like those kept mewed up at the palace?" Grinning, he shook his head. "No, lady. A *lir* is far more than anything you might imagine. Rael is an extension of myself, though his conscience is his own. We are bonded. He speaks to me, I to him, though it is all done silently."

"And does he value games as much as you?"

He heard the dry tone in her voice. So close to the edge of contempt; it hurt. "No," Hart said quietly. "Rael does not. Rael *does*, however, suggest I turn to things more important, such as learning how to rule."

"Then indeed, he is wiser than you."

"The *lir* always are." He felt safer discussing Rael than his irresponsibility. "Do you know nothing of them?"

She shrugged. "I know only the things I have heard: that they are magical animals with awesome arts, allowing the Cheysuli to assume shapes other than their own." Her glance betrayed no distaste, but quiet curiosity. "You can really become a hawk? With wings and feathers and talons?"

The laughter was gone. "Aye."

"Does it hurt?"

Hart frowned. It had been so long since he had thought of *lir*-shape in terms other than an automatic exchange of human form for raptor that the words were harder to find than ever. In Homana, the Cheysuli were no longer the enemy, but part and parcel of the present. No one required explanations.

"There is no *pain*," he said thoughtfully. "Not as you know pain. But there is an oddness, an alienness, when I put off my human shape for another." He shrugged a little. "Knowing what I will become, it does not frighten me. I will come through it; I always do, and back again. But the first time, not knowing, is frightening and exhilarating all at once." He looked at her intent face, wishing he could share *lir*-shape so he need not struggle for words that were inadequate no matter how glib his explanation. "From birth we are told that to be whole we require a *lir*. And although we have no reason to anticipate being left without one, the hidden fear is always there . . . the fear that somehow the gods have forgotten to prepare the animal that is to become your *lir*." He shrugged. "The first time you assume *lir*-shape, you are so eager the fear recedes and you think only of the need, not the fear of what you do."

Ilsa looked into the sky to watch Rael's soaring flight. "And when you are a hawk, what do you feel then?"

The answer was instant. "Freedom." As she looked at him, he smiled. "*Freedom.* No more am I earthbound; no more do I require legs, feet, horse, or other means of transportation. I have only myself, *requiring* only myself . . . and I become the freest thing alive."

"But you are still a man."

"Mostly. I keep my human thoughts and feelings, although I experience things as a hawk. Human instincts are augmented, not overcome. I know I am a man in the form of a hawk. I am still Hart."

She turned from Rael to him. "Is there danger in it?"

He shrugged. "There is a question of balance. A Cheysuli in *lir*-shape is both and neither; it *is* possible for him to lose himself to the animal form, but it only rarely happens. It is something we are carefully taught, this balance." He saw the comprehension in her eyes, and the realization of the dangers. "I will not lie to you, Ilsa. If a warrior in *lir*-shape should grow too angry, relying too much on animal instinct instead of both, he can tip over the edge and lose humanness altogether."

"And remain an animal."

"Or something made of both." He plaited the mane of his bay stallion, thinking through the best way to explain to her what he had learned quite young. "It is one reason the shapechange is more difficult in extremity. In pain, a man might lose himself. In anger also, and sheer exhilaration. The shapechange requires concentration, and responsibility. There is always the risk that a warrior in *lir*-shape may become something other than himself."

"And risk is something you understand very well." Ilsa smoothed hair back. "I have known Dar nearly since birth; his family has served mine for centuries. I have seen how it is with him, this need to risk his wealth in wagers. The coin means little to him, other than representing victory over the odds." Briefly, her mouth twisted ironically. "I see much the same in you, although you are worse. Dar enjoys a good wager, but I think you *need* it."

"For as long as I can remember." He did not smile, not try to avoid the topic. "I do not lose myself in *lir*-shape, perhaps, understanding the need for self-control . . . but a wager is different. I *do* lose myself."

"And so the balance is broken, and you tip over the edge." Ilsa looked at him squarely. "Last night you told me you take pride in nothing. I think you lied, albeit unknowing. If nothing else, you take pride in being Cheysuli; in the ability to become a hawk and know the freedom of the skies."

He did not look away. "Aye."

"Then I offer you a challenge, my lord. I offer you risk." Ilsa smiled a little. "Put it aside, Hart. Set aside this need of the game, and look instead to becoming a prince in fact. Solinde is in the palm of your hand. Grasp it, my lord, or surely you will lose it."

"It is *out* of my hand," he said. "Blame me, blame Dar, blame us both, but we have undertaken a wager that will end this controversy over Solinde. One of us will be the victor, the other the vanquished . . . with you and Solinde in the middle."

Ilsa went rigid in her saddle. "What have you done?" Her face was taut and pale. "*What have you done?*"

Hart drew in a deep breath. "I came to see you intending to tell you the truth at once. I delayed it because it was easier, as always, to avoid speaking of it at all, and because I wanted to spend time with you. And so now the time for truth is on me once again, I find I have no more desire to spoil what is between us than I did before."

"Hart—"

"You must wed," he said clearly, overriding the beginnings of her protest. "And wed soon, for the sake of Solinde. For all I avoid responsibility whenever possible, I am no stranger to political intrigues and marriages. Three choices face you, Ilsa: wed me, wed Dar, or wed another powerful Solindishman with the ability to help you hold Solinde."

She said nothing.

Hart did not look away. "If you delay, my own hold on Solinde increases; are they not advocating you wed within a month?" Grimly he nodded, though she remained locked in rigid silence. "If you wed Dar, Solinde will one day revolt; he has as much as promised it. If you wed another Solindishman, there will always be those who advocate rebellion. If you wed *me*—"

Ilsa cut him off. "Why?" she asked flatly. "Why would I wed you? You offer me nothing, my lord wagerer . . .

you offer nothing to Solinde save irreverence and irresponsibility."

"The wager is this," he said quietly. "If you wed me,
Dar gives over the Third Seal—and his life. If you wed
Dar, I am sent home to Homana . . . and Solinde re-
mains Solindish."

"Under a Homanan regent!" Color spilled into her
face, then out again. "Dar put up his *life?*"

"Aye, lady—at his own behest. I do not want it."

"But you accepted the wager!"

"I am on the edge of the blade," he said clearly. "If I
go home to my *jehan*, having lost Solinde, I will have lost
him as well. Worse, I will have destroyed the prophecy."
Hart nodded slowly. "Aye, Ilsa, I accepted the wager.
Dar gave me no other choice."

"What choice did you give *him?*" He saw tears in her
eyes. "If he loses this wager, he loses his *life!* I think that
is more important than a Cheysuli prophecy—"

"One life is little when balanced against a race," Hart
told her quietly. "Hear me, Ilsa, when I tell you that
above all, I serve the prophecy. Wastrel that I have
been, I am fully committed to this. Aye, you spoke of
pride—and I *do* take pride in something. I take pride in
the prophecy."

"So you leave the choice to me," she said bitterly.
"Yet again you turn your back on responsibility and
reduce the future of Solinde to a wager and a woman's
choice of husband." She said something more, equally
bitterly, but the words were Solindish, and he did not
know them. He knew only that he had angered her far
more than even he had anticipated.

"Ilsa—"

"Did Dar put you up to this?" she asked abruptly.

He considered lying, knowing the truth made him appear vindictive. But he nodded. "It was his suggestion."

Ilsa shook her head, pushing hair out of her face in
irritation. "You are a fool, my lord prince of wagerers.
Dar knows me too well, and he has learned you also. As
he expected, all my pride screams at me to wed Dar if for
no other reason than to *force* your loss, and your subse-

quent loss of Solinde. And I would . . . if my better judgment would allow it." She looked at him squarely. "If only to pay him back, I should refuse him. But it would cost him his life, and that I cannot bear."

"There is an alternative," Hart said quietly. "Wed another man entirely."

"*What* other man?" Ilsa asked bitterly. "There is no other man in Solinde who can do what Dar can to rally the Solindish to war again. We are too weary of such things. Niall and those before him have defeated us soundly too many times. Without the right leader, what good would it do us now?" She shrugged. "But Dar could do what is necessary, and would. If I wanted this war, I would be a fool to wed a Solindishman other than Dar." He saw the turmoil reflected in her eyes, in her features. "But if I wed you to save my land from war, it costs me Dar. And that price I will not pay."

"Then wed no one."

Ilsa's sharp laugh was little more than a sound of despair. "If I do not choose *someone*, I will be forced to it. The situation warrants it; they have not done it only because they respect me personally, and my heritage. But for Solinde, to thwart Homana, they will. They will have no other choice."

"Ilsa—"

She gathered her reins and turned the mare toward Lestra. "Forgive me, my lord, but I desire solitude. I have no taste for your company."

He knew better than to allow her to depart under such circumstances. But he knew also that to stop her was to destroy all hope of winning her. And so he let her go.

Seven

Tarron's move to assemble more parchments was arrested in mid-motion. "I must have misheard you. You want *what*, my lord?"

Helpfully, Hart gathered the parchments from the table and placed them on the stack in Tarron's arms. "I want you to teach me how to rule. It *is* what I came for."

"No," Tarron said plainly, "you came because you were *sent*."

Hart scowled at him. "Aye, aye, all right—I came because I was sent. But I am done with shirking my responsibilities. Teach me how to rule."

"Have you seen the Mujhar do none of it?"

Oh, aye, he had, in bits and pieces. But he had steadfastly refused to attend council sessions, petition hearings and other assorted requirements of kingship, perfectly willing to let Brennan do it all instead. He had a rudimentary knowledge of what constituted governing—the ruler had to sit in judgment on citizens who had disputes, settle treaties between other realms, levy taxes, tribute, and so on, plus innumerable other duties— but when it came down to it, he had not the faintest idea what was expected of him. Particularly in a foreign realm.

"Teach me," he said only, hoping it was enough.

Apparently it was, although Tarron eyed him doubtfully. "Well enough, my lord; follow me. I am bound for a hearing regarding a petty dispute between two northern Solindish lordlings. They are feuding over a boundary formed by a river; the river has changed its course, and now they dispute ownership of the land it has laid bare.''

Dutifully Hart followed Tarron out of the chamber into a corridor, though his heart was not in it. He opened his mouth to beg off, then shut it sharply. It was time he learned to accept tedium as gracefully as his father and brother.

"Without the Third Seal, what can you do?" he asked.

Parchment crackled. "Delay," the regent said succinctly. "No real business can be conducted without it, but until I hear from the Mujhar I cannot let slip the news the Seal is lost. We must hope the Solindish do not grow restless over countless delays and obfuscation . . . I think they will not understand why it is you lost it in a *game*."

Hart ignored the latter. "And if Dar has already let it be known?"

"It would certainly serve his own interests." Tarron nodded as guardsmen in Homanan livery swung open the heavy wooden doors of the audience chamber. "But perhaps this will serve yours, my lord; if you are the one to make the decision, it will let the Solindish know you are indeed planning to rule." He nodded greetings toward the men waiting in the chamber and made his way to a table on a dais.

"Me?" Following, Hart kept his voice low. "I have no experience in such things."

"I suggest you get it, my lord, as any man does: by listening, and by determining which party deserves the judgment rendered in his favor." Tarron put the stack of parchments on the table and stepped away, motioning Hart to accept the only chair. "And now, my lord, I leave you to it."

Astonished, Hart watched the regent turn and walk away. He wanted to shout after him, to *order* him back, but he would not, not before the Solindish lordlings who waited to present their case.

Oh, gods. Lamely, he smiled at the lords. They stared back grimly, hard old men, prepared to humor no one. *Oh, gods.* But he summoned what he could of his courage and sat down, intending to do whatever it was a ruler did to the best of his ability.

Even if he had none.

After dark, Hart ordered a horse and rode to The White Swan. He felt after a day spent listening to two old Solindish lordlings arguing who had more right to the new parcel of land—mostly in incomprehensible Solindish no matter how many times he requested Homanan—he deserved an evening's entertainment. But he made up his mind not to wager, only to while away the hours in a hospitable tavern.

Or even an *in*hospitable tavern.

By now most of the regular patrons were accustomed to his presence. He still was not precisely welcomed, but neither was he greeted with hostile stares and crude comments. Now most of them shrugged and turned back to their games, leaving him to his own devices.

Unless Dar was present. But this time, for the first part of the evening, he was not, so Hart sat by himself at a table and drank ale, forgoing wine entirely.

The wine-girl, Oma, made a particular point of flashing the Homanan signet ring in his face whenever she could. Eventually he called her over and offered to buy it back, but she merely grinned and shook him off. She was too shrewd to give in so easily, and too pleased by the grim frustration she caused him. And so in the end he gave it up entirely, turning back to his ale, and lost himself in contemplation.

Until Dar came.

The Solindishman glittered with silver and sapphires at collar, cuffs, wrists, fingers and belt, ice against indigo velvet. The royal colors, Hart knew, and wondered if Dar had dressed for him in the spirit of the wager. But then he spoke, and Hart knew he had dressed for no man at all.

"I have been with Ilsa," he said calmly, sitting down at the table without bothering to wait for an invitation. "A most sumptuous meal, and served by the lady herself." A raised finger brought Oma with a cup and his favorite wine. "She told me an interesting tale."

"Did she?" Hart drank ale.

Dar waited for Oma to pour his cup full, then waved her away. Over the rim of the cup he assessed Hart. He sipped thoughtfully, then thumped the cup down onto the table. "So, you thought to win her through frankness."

"I thought to be frank with her for the sake of honesty and honor, not because of the wager," Hart said quietly. "Let us end it, Dar. It is a travesty. It is unfair to Ilsa *and* Solinde."

Dar did not smile. "Then declare it a forfeit. Go home to Homana in the morning, and do not come back again."

Hart matched him stare for stare. "You know I cannot."

"I know you *should* . . . and, one day soon, you will. When I have won."

"You are so certain of her, then?"

Dar smiled. "What choice is there, shapechanger? She wants me to live—she told me so herself—so she will not choose you. She would prefer Solinde remain Solindish; again, so she will not choose you. She would prefer a man she knows as Consort, so she will not choose one of the other lords." He drank again, then leaned forward intently. "She will name *my* name, shapechanger. Be certain of it."

Hart smiled. "Then why are you so *un*certain?" His smile widened as Dar's lids flickered. "No matter what she may have said to you tonight, you still are not sure. You still have doubts. You know there is a good chance she may choose me after all."

"Ilsa will do what is right for Solinde."

"She will do what is best for all concerned." Hart poured more ale into his cup. "It is how such decisions are made; one weighs all issues, and then one decides which best serves all involved." It was what he had done with the old lords and their river dispute, though he could offer nothing until the Seal was recovered.

Dar said nothing for a long moment, then shouted for Oma to bring the Bezat bowl. But Hart shook his head as the stones were offered.

"No?" Dar's sandy brows lifted. "*You* say no?"

"I say no." Hart drank ale. "The game begins to pall, Dar . . . I will pass."

Dar slapped his belt-purse down on the table. Red gold chimed.

Hart smiled. "No."

Dar stripped his fingers and wrists of gem-studded silver.

Still Hart smiled. "No."

"What do you want?" the Solindishman asked. "The Seal is already wagered." He smiled suddenly. "The stallion. You want to win back the stallion Ilsa gave you."

Slowly Hart shook his head.

Dar's brown eyes narrowed. "Then *what?*"

"To watch you squirm," Hart said softly, "and now I have seen it without wagering even a silver penny." He pushed his stool back, scraping it against hardwood, and rang down a red coin on the table to pay for his ale. "You *will* lose, Dar. Ilsa. Solinde. Your life. Because I have learned when to stop, and you have not even begun."

Dar rose abruptly. "Shapechanger—"

"Cheysuli," Hart said gently, and walked quietly out of the tavern.

He was in a private room adjoining his bedchamber, slumped in a chair and lost in thought, when a servant knocked at his door. He considered ignoring the knock, then gave it up and went to the door.

"My lord." Not a servant at all, but Tarron. "My lord, a message has come from the Lady Ilsa. She requests your presence at once." He paused. "I know the messenger; the summons is genuine."

"Now?" It struck him as odd she would send a message at night, though it was not late.

"Aye, my lord." Although perfectly polite, the tone in Tarron's voice told Hart the regent thought it just as unusual. "The message is that a decision has been made, and she would have you and Dar of High Crags know it at once so the travesty may be ended." Tarron frowned. "My lord—"

Hart raised a silencing hand. "Do not ask, regent. When I return, you will have your answer. It may please you—or it may not." He chewed his bottom lip a moment, thinking deeply. "Tell her messenger I will come at once."

"Aye, my lord." But still Tarron lingered. "If there is anything you wish to confide in me, be certain I will hold it in strictest confidence."

Hart smiled. "I trust you, Tarron. But this is between a man and a woman—no, between *men* and a woman— and until I know the lady's answer, there is no sense in confiding anything. When I can, I shall."

The regent inclined his head. "Aye, my lord. Of course." And he was gone.

Hart shut the door and turned to look at Rael, perched on his now-empty chair. "Well? Do I dress to celebrate, or to exile myself from yet another realm?"

If you delay to change your clothing, she may change her mind.

Hart grinned. "Aye. And if she has chosen in my favor, I would do well not to give her that chance." He nodded thoughtfully and opened the door again. "We go, *lir* . . . to gain a *cheysula*, or lose a realm."

He thought of Brennan as he ordered a horse saddled and brought. No doubt his *rujho* would compliment him on his decision to take a *cheysula*, even if it was not his decision at all. Brennan would tell him he was finally growing up, maturing, becoming the man he was meant to be.

He sent a wry glance heavenward. *Brennan would no doubt tell me I am only answering my tahlmorra.*

And perhaps you are. Rael, sounding insufferably smug, circled over the bailey as the horse was brought.

Hart sighed and swung up, gathering reins hastily as the bay stallion stomped and snorted his displeasure at having his evening meal interrupted. Hart took a deeper seat and reined him in, calling his thanks to the groom, and went out of the bailey at a long-trot.

Iron rang on stone as Hart guided the bay through the winding streets of Lestra. Ilsa's dwelling was not far from the palace, but the journey took too long nonetheless; his belly was so twisted up he was afraid he might never be able to eat again. He could not begin to predict Ilsa's decision, though he had been foolish enough to wager on it. And, the gods knew, wagered more than he could afford to lose.

Much more, he thought hollowly as the shadows and torchlight played tag along the walls. *Fool that I am, I should have known better. It is no wonder jehan banished me for a year; I have been gone but three months, and already I have risked a realm, myself . . . the prophecy.* He gritted his teeth. *Rael, what do I tell him if the wager is lost?*

The truth. Rael responded. *No matter what the punishment, the loss of Solinde is worth it.*

It was not the comfort Hart sought. Disgruntled, he withdrew from the link altogether.

One of Ilsa's servants waited outside as Hart drew the stallion to a halt. He dismounted slowly, delaying the moment of truth, and handed over the reins. Rael perched himself upon the roof. No light showed from the house, for all the windows were shuttered against the night air. Hart drew in a breath so deep it made him light-headed, and then he knocked on the door.

He was shown to a private receiving chamber warmed by a blazing fire and was offered wine, ale or *usca*. He declined all, too nervous to drink, and asked when the lady would present herself.

"As soon as my lord of High Crags arrives, my lord," the servant answered, and bowed himself out.

"Except the lord of High Crags is already present." Dar stepped out of a curtained antechamber. With him were six men, all in Solindish livery.

Oddly, Hart felt relieved. At last the man had shown his true colors. "Where is Ilsa?"

"Ilsa has gone to bed," Dar said quietly as one of his men moved to lock the door from the inside. "Ilsa has done her part of this night's work by summoning you here; the rest is left to me."

Hart nodded. "And what are your plans, Dar? To pack me off to Homana before the wager is settled?"

Dar grinned and waved a casual forefinger. His men moved closer to Hart. "Which wager, shapechanger? The one between you and me—or the one I struck with Strahan?"

That, Hart had not expected. He was unsurprised by the six men who clearly meant him no good, but he had not considered that Ihlini would enter into it. "What has Strahan to do with this?" he asked curtly, trying to ignore the tightening of his belly. "*You* are not Ihlini; Rael would have known it."

"No, I am not Ihlini," Dar agreed. "But I *am* an ambitious man, as well as one desirous of winning favor with those in power, and Strahan offered me something I could not pass by. Of course, he couched it as a wager; he said he did not believe I could do it. So now I have done it, and he will pay me my price." Dar grinned. "One way or another, the lady will be mine."

Hart felt strangely relaxed. There were no Ihlini in the room, and Rael was on the roof. Although the windows were shuttered against his entry, his closeness still lent Hart all the power he needed to assume *lir*-shape. Dar had badly underestimated his enemy.

"Dar—"

But he was given no chance to finish his sentence. Six men laid hands on him, and none were gentle.

"Bring him here." Dar indicated the ironwood table.

Hart resisted, but six to one were not good odds. "Dar, it is easy enough to trap a man, but not so easy to trap a hawk—"

"Draw your sword." Dar ignored Hart altogether, speaking to one of the men. The Solindishman did so, waiting attentively.

Rael— Triggering the link, Hart drew on the magic in his blood.

"Hold him," Dar said. "Stretch out his left arm so the flat of his hand is on the wood. *Quickly!*"

Hart tapped the power.

Smoothly, Dar drew his knife and stabbed it through the splayed hand, pinning it to the table. "There," he said. "Shapechange *now*, shapechanger."

Pain burst in his hand and set the world afire. Too shocked to do anything more than gape, Hart knew the shapechange was banished. As he had so clearly told Ilsa, a man in extremity lacked the required concentration.

Dar's eyes were dilated black. "Once you told me you would sooner wager your left hand than your *lir*, shapechanger. Well, you have lost the wager. And now you have lost the hand." He signaled the man with the sword. "Hack it off. *Now*."

The blow was swift and very clean, slicing through flesh and bone to stop short in the ironwood. And painless, so stunned was Hart. Standing only by dint of the men who held him up, he stared at the arm that now ended at his wrist.

Rael—Rael—RAEL—

Dar made a moue of distaste. "So much blood," he said. And then he himself fetched the iron from the fire and slapped white-hot tip against stump.

Hart meant to scream. But it died aborning as he collapsed into the arms of Dar's men.

Interlude

Lillith looked down on her brother. Strahan knelt on one knee at the rim of the vent, at the edge of the Gate itself. One hand was outthrust, palm down, as if he intended to summon Asar-Suti himself. As perhaps he did; white flame licked up, touched, curled around the fingers, gloved his hand entirely, then deepened to lilac, to lavender, to deepest lurid purple. In its reflection, Strahan smiled his beautiful, deadly smile.

She saw a tendril of flame slip beneath the cuff of his doublet, beneath the white edge of his linen shirt. Where it went she could not follow, for it cloaked itself in his clothing; then, abruptly, it blossomed at his collar, caressed the flesh of his neck, touched a gentle fingertip to the sharp-edged line of his jaw.

Still Strahan smiled. Even *she* no longer smiled, but he was lost to her utterly, caught up in eerie intercourse with the god of the netherworld, who made and dwells in darkness. Still he knelt, smiling, as the flame flowed out of the Gate to his hand, then upward to his neck, and began to lap at his face.

Strahan's lips parted. A thin, tensile wire of flame touched, withdrew, touched again, then flowed up to shape his mouth into something more than flesh. Emboldened, more tendrils appeared, and within a matter of moments Strahan's face was alive with a webwork of fragile purple lace. It overlay his features, shaping them into those of another man—or into the god himself.

"*Strahan*—" But Lillith stopped herself. It was not her

place to remonstrate with her brother, who was the god's own chosen. It was her place only to serve, accepting all that was asked, offering whatever she could.

Strahan laughed. He was ablaze with delicate fire, and yet fabric and flesh was untouched. Kneeling, he was an incongruous torch; laughing, he was far more than merely human, even by sorcerous standards.

And then, abruptly, the webwork came undone. Tendrils withdrew, untying knots; untied, the knots fell into disarray. Within moments Strahan was merely Strahan, and the god was gone from him.

He shut his eyes and released a shuddering breath of deep satisfaction, as if he had lain with a woman. Head bowed, he made his obeisance to the god, and then he rose to face his sister across the glowing Gate.

"Done," he said. "Dar has won his wager."

"One you are pleased to lose." Lillith sighed herself; he seemed perfectly normal again. "And the woman? Will you pay his price?"

Strahan smiled. "Dar is an overly ambitious man with overweening pride. One day he and his pride will stumble over those ambitions, and he will fall."

It was not precisely the answer she wanted; perhaps he was still caught in the thrall of the god, speaking of things she could not know. "How will you break this one?"

Strahan shrugged. "I think it is already done, or very nearly so. The Cheysuli can be a hard, seemingly heartless race, even with their own; the clans require *whole* men as warriors, unmaimed—whole in flesh as well as spirit—in order to maintain the viability of the race. Much like animals, they cull the pack of the weakest in order to protect the rest." Again he shrugged. "Perhaps they have the right of it; *I* have no use for the weak."

Lillith, smiling secretly, thought it an understatement. "And how will you 'mend' this one?"

Strahan laughed. "By offering him a reason to live again. Service to me can make him whole, though not in the way he might wish. But by *then* it will not matter—he will be too firmly bound."

Deftly she smoothed the velvet of her skirts. "Only one—the youngest—remains. It is time I went to Atvia."

Strahan looked at her, but she knew he did not see her. "Safe journey," he said only, then knelt again at the edge of the Gate.

PART IV

CORIN

One

Faster. Faster. *Faster—*

He bent low in the saddle, *low,* so that the pommel ground into his belly and his cheek was pressed against the stallion's dampening neck. Whipping gray mane stung Corin's eyes until they teared; he found release in it, knowing he need not be ashamed of tears shed because of irritation to the eyes themselves, and not anguish of the heart.

Faster—

The world was a collage of green and blue, brown and gray, all blurred together by tears. He clutched leather reins and pushed them forward against the stallion's neck, giving him his head. On and on the blue roan ran, doing his rider's bidding.

Beneath clamped legs fluid muscles bunched, rolled, stretched, tautened, fed by the pumping of the stallion's great heart. Corin tasted dirt and horsehair; smelled the acrid tang of sweat and wet blankets. In his ears was the song of a winded horse; the rhythmic pounding beat of iron-shod hooves against hard-packed road. In his heart was anguish.

Oh, gods—forbidden my home for a year— And he squeezed the stallion yet again with legging-clad legs, urging him faster yet.

You will kill the horse.

For a moment Corin did not recognize Kiri's tone. He was so caught up in the sound and rhythm of the horse and the weight of his own pain that he had neglected to think of the vixen.

He turned his head against damp horsehair and peered over his shoulder. Far behind, in the sienna-colored dust of his passing, he saw the rich red flash of his *lir*.

If not the horse, you will kill me.

That stopped him as nothing else could. Corin sat upright in the saddle, gathering reins, and eased the stallion down. Slowly, carefully; for all he was angry and hurt and frightened, he had no wish to ruin the roan.

If he had not already.

Slowly. Slowly. From gallop to canter, canter to trot, trot to winded walk, head dropped, nostrils sucking and blowing great gulps of air as the stallion tried to answer the demand of his heaving lungs. Guiltily Corin freed his right foot from the stirrup and swung it over the roan's damp, blue-washed rump, letting his weight linger briefly in the left stirrup and against his thigh. He did not halt the stallion but let him walk on, knowing the roan needed careful tending if he was to recover completely.

Corin dropped off and kept moving, dragging reins free of the dangling head to lead the horse onward. Sweat ran down the roan's face. Lather flecked chest and flanks. He stumbled over hooves but newly-shod.

Still walking, Corin half-turned and looked over a shoulder for Kiri. No longer did she run, trotting instead; he could see the brush of her black-tipped tail swinging behind her hocks. Closer now, he could see the glint of eyes in her mask, and the lolling of her tongue.

Remorse surged up at once. *Oh, lir, I am sorry. I should know better than to punish you.*

Save your apologies for the horse. I have a choice; he does not.

Corin looked again at the roan stallion. He had served well and faithfully for three years, and was rewarded with thoughtless, cruel behavior. Walking on, not daring to stop until the stallion was cooler, Corin ran a soothing palm down the proud nose and promised him better treatment.

Guilt clenched the wall of his belly yet again. *It is no*

wonder jehan *feels it necessary to punish me . . . I give him reason enough.*

Then stop, the vixen suggested.

"How?" Corin asked aloud, clearly frustrated. "There are times I grow so angry I cannot control myself, knowing only that I have been wronged. And when I try to explain, *jehan* will not listen."

What is there to explain when your behavior has accounted for the lives of twenty-eight people—perhaps even more?

The guilt rose higher in his belly, reaching out cruel fingers to grasp, twist, pinch. "That was Hart." He had meant it to defend and accuse all at once, but his tone was subdued instead, full of acknowledgment. Aye, twenty-eight people dead, probably more, all because he and Hart had insisted on going to the Midden, which was a place none of them frequented for a very good reason.

Well, it *had* been Hart's idea.

And yet he had contributed.

"To save my life," he said aloud. "They would have slain us all."

Kiri caught up and trotted next to his left leg. Briefly she pressed a shoulder against him, then dropped aside again. *Courage, lir—the Mujhar disputes your self-defense less than the reasons for your presence in the tavern. All of you disobeyed orders—that is the bone of contention. Had you not, no one would be dead.* She paused thoughtfully. *Or at least they would be dead by their own murdering hands, and not by careless fire.*

"No one *meant* it to happen," he murmured unhappily. "And yet *jehan* refuses to listen to that, hearing only that his sons were involved in yet another tavern brawl." Corin shrugged a little, rolling shoulder blades uncomfortably in an attempt to assuage his guilt, or to push it away. "Had he given us the chance, we might have been able to help. He might only have stripped us of our allowances, giving them to the survivors, rather than of our freedom."

Lives cannot be bought. Kiri's tone lacked even a trace of sympathy. *As for freedom, you would not know it if it bit your nose from your face. A man can only know true freedom when he understands or experiences its loss, so the value becomes greater.*

Corin slanted her a resentful glance beneath half-shut lids. "Are you finished?" he asked grimly.

Are you?

Corin sighed heavily, expelling acknowledgment along with breath. "Aye," he said unevenly, "I am. One way or another, I will have to learn to depend only on myself. And right now, that does not please me. Another man would not depend on me—how can I? I know what I am as much as anyone else." He kicked a stone out of his path and watched it skitter across the road into the turf of the meadowlands. The stallion was so winded he did not even notice. "I am, betimes, sullen and resentful, selfish and moody, unresponsive and angry. Or so my *jehan* has said, and Deirdre, and Ian, over the scope of years. No doubt others have said more, and worse." He sighed. "I like it no more than they, but I cannot help myself."

You are already helping yourself.

Corin drew in a breath that filled his belly with doubt. "And you? What of you, Kiri? Do you stay with me only out of duty to the gods, and not through loyalty to me? Do you dislike me for my temper?"

I dislike your temper, not you, the fox said quietly. *As for staying with you, what choice have I? I was chosen for you and you for me . . . there is a purpose in all things the gods do. As for personal loyalty, why question it? I would not leave you even if you beat me.*

"I would never beat you!"

Yet you beat the horse in the name of your fear and anger.

Corin looked at the stallion. The roan breathed more easily and was no longer wringing wet, although he was hardly fully restored. Corin stroked the blue-white nose again, scratching the heavy jaw, and promised he would never ride him so hard again.

Lir.

Corin glanced around. Kiri had stopped, standing in

the center of the road, and stared upward into the sky. Corin did likewise, holding the stallion back, and lifted a hand to shield his eyes against the sun.

"Hawk—" he said. His pulse quickened; was it Hart sent to fetch him back? Corin had left a day early. Had his *jehan* repented of his sentence?

But he knew better. Niall had made it a royal decree as well as a parental one; the banishment would hold for the precise number of days it took to fulfill twelve months.

The hawk spiraled, drifted, floated down, and Corin nodded as the blur of the shapechange swallowed the raptor. His senses, as always, reeled momentarily, then settled; the disorientation faded quickly as the hawk exchanged bird-form for human.

Keely grinned. "Did you think I would let you go out of Homana alone?"

He stared at her. "You cannot mean to come *with* me!"

"Why not?" She spread her hands. "There are no duties incumbent upon me except to give my *rujho* whatever aid and support he requires."

Corin looked at her. She was slim and wiry in snug Cheysuli leathers, dressed like a warrior though there was no doubting she was a woman; the brass-buckled belt hid nothing of slender waist or the smooth swelling of breasts and hips. Gone were the days she could stuff her hair beneath a huntsman's cap and swagger like a man with impunity. Now she did neither, for her tawny hair hung free in a plaited braid, and she made no attempt to swagger. She had no need of it; as much as any of them, Keely claimed inbred pride and confidence of carriage.

He smiled, and the smile spread slowly into a grin. Trust Keely. . . . "You should not come," he told her, though it lacked true conviction. "The banishment is my punishment, not yours. In this we need not share."

"We share in everything, *rujho*." Her blue eyes were very steady. "*Everything*—except, perhaps, your taste for bedding women." Her mouth hooked ironically. "That I leave to you."

"*Your* taste runs to bedding men?"

The humor slipped perceptibly. "My taste runs to belonging only to myself," Keely said grimly. "If that means I keep myself apart from men, so be it. I am willing."

He grunted. "Sean of Erinn may have something to say about that."

"Sean of Erinn will have nothing at all to say." Keely was very calm, *too* calm. "Sean of Erinn will take what he gets—or look to wedding another woman entirely."

Corin laughed. "If he *does* get you, Keely, be certain he will take you." He used the word in the crudest sense, knowing it might be the only way she would hear what he had to say. "Aside from needing an heir for Erinn, he might wish to enjoy his *cheysula*."

" 'Enjoy,' " Keely said grimly. "Indeed, 'enjoy.' I hope he will *enjoy* a foot of steel in his belly if he presses me when I have no desire for it."

He shouted aloud with laughter. "Since I think you will be naked in your marriage bed, Keely, it might be difficult to hide a knife." Corin raised a hand as she started to protest. "Have you come to discuss your personal dislike for the betrothal, or my own banishment? You will forgive me, I trust, if at the moment I am less inclined to sympathize with *your* plight when I have my own."

Abruptly she was contrite. "Oh, Corin, I know. It is so unfair! *Jehan* had no right to do it, no right at all . . . how *can* he do it? How can he send two of his sons out of Homana into things they cannot know?"

There were times he wished he shared more of Keely's temperament in addition to coloring. She was outspoken and high-spirited, and equally subject—as he was—to outbursts of hot temper, but she was more charitable, more generous in her feelings. She thought less of herself than of others, and always supported him without thought for what such support might mean to her father's opinion of her.

"He can do it," he said, "because he is our *jehan*, and because he is the Mujhar."

"Rank excuses nothing," she flung back instantly.

"Aye," Corin agreed wryly, "and *jehan* would say it certainly does not excuse the behavior of his sons."

Trapped, she glared at him. "Do you *want* to go?"

"No," he said succinctly. "Do you?"

Keely opened her mouth, then snapped it shut. After a moment she shook her head a little. "Defy him. What could he do to you? You are his son. Moreover, you are a part of the prophecy."

"A dutiful son does as his father commands. A part of the prophecy knows better than to defy him."

"But *you* have never been dutiful," Keely retorted, "and who is to know what your *tahlmorra* is but you " She shrugged. "Come back to Homana-Mujhar and face him down, Corin. Defy him. Refuse to go. He cannot have you tied up and hauled bodily to Atvia. It would soil his own honor as much as yours." Keely grinned. "If we *both* faced him—"

"If we both faced him, it would only underscore the need for discipline," Corin said grimly, "and all the while Brennan would be standing there like the dutiful son—nodding, agreeing, supporting our *jehan*—because that is what he does best. *Jehan* need only look at his heir to see the sort of son he desires, and then he *would* order me tied up and hauled bodily to Atvia."

Exasperated, she glared at him with rigid hands clamped on hips. "Then what *do* you intend to do?"

"Go to Atvia." He sighed and rubbed the roan's muzzle. "With a stop in Erinn, as *jehan* has ordered."

Keely's eyes narrowed. "You would do well to listen to yourself sometime, *rujho*. On one hand you blow and bluster and threaten to do this or that . . . on the other you meekly give in and do what you have been asked—or told—to do. If you *intend* to do as told, why make so much noise in the first place?"

For an answer, Corin turned sharply and walked on, taking the stallion with him. And then he stopped short, swinging to face her again. "Listen to *yourself*," he suggested curtly. "It is no wonder Deirdre despairs of ever making a woman out of you."

"Oh?" Her tone was infinitely deadly.

Corin indicated her clothing. "Do you ask why? You are in leggings every time I see you, disdaining skirts or gowns . . . you talk our *su'fali* into teaching you the knife and sword and bow when the Homanan arms-master will not . . . you absent yourself from Homana-Mujhar to run wild in the wood . . . you spend no time with Deirdre's women, learning how to behave as the Lady of Erinn must. . . ." He shook his head. "You drink *usca*, Keely, and dice nearly as much as Hart—"

"—and nearly as well." She smiled grimly. "Go on, Corin. Do not stop now."

He signed. "And you persist in denying a willingness to wed a man who will one day be king of Erinn and, through you, a part of the prophecy. You deny your own *tahlmorra*, and then tell me to do the same with mine."

"It is hardly a denial of willingness when I do not *wish* to wed him," she said coolly. "As to the others, I will not deny that I would be as soon forswear womanly things altogether. Given a choice, I would be warrior in place of wife."

"And man in place of woman?"

Keely laughed in genuine amusement. "No, you fool— even *you* seek the easy answer! I have no desire to be a *man* . . . what I want is to be myself. I want the freedom to choose what I will do instead of fulfilling expectations of my behavior." She shrugged. "I would do better in the clan than at Homana-Mujhar, but even there I would not know the freedom I crave. There are no women warriors . . . and I am the daughter of the Lion. They see that before all else." She sighed and tugged pensively at her braid. "Shall we go, *rujho*? I ache to see Hondarth. I have never been *anywhere* but Clankeep or Mujhara."

Corin considered ordering her home; discarded it at once. He considered *suggesting* she go home; he knew better. For all she prated of having no freedom, she claimed more than most. It took a stronger man than he to enforce his preferences when Keely's determination was so firmly entrenched.

I will leave it to Sean. Corin surrendered, nodding. "I am walking, for the moment. The roan needs rest."

"So I see." Keely shook her head. "Better you shout at me, next time, than burden your horse with your anger. At least I know when to defy you."

"Defiance," he muttered. "Is that all you know?"

"Better to ask the same of yourself." Sweetly, she smiled at him. "Shall we go? Hondarth beckons."

He raised his brows and pursed lips thoughtfully. "Hondarth will never recover."

But he said nothing more as he started walking and Keely fell in beside him. His *lir* trotted ahead, head dipping as she sniffed grass and dirt. The day was warm, the sun bright, the sky infinitely blue. Moreover, he was *Cheysuli*; it made him a man truly blessed.

Abruptly, unexpectedly, Corin was content. If he had to go to Atvia, at least he had the best company he could think of.

They sold the stallion in Hondarth, much as Corin hated to part with him. There would be no room on the ship for a mount, and he could get another in Atvia. He would have sent the roan home with Keely, except she refused to go back. And so with their purses considerably plumper, they stopped before a tavern.

Keely gestured. "As good as another, *rujho*."

He looked askance at her. "A waterfront tavern? I think not. We would do better to go farther from the docks."

She stood with booted feet planted. "I want wine, and I am hungry. If you fear trouble because I am a woman, remember I have a knife."

"See how I shiver from fear?" Corin asked dryly. "I think the men who frequent taverns of this sort will hardly be deterred by a knife in a woman's hand."

She shrugged. "Then I will resort to *lir*-shape, if they force me. Corin—let us go *in*—" She caught his jerkin and dragged him toward the door, even as he craned his head to look for Kiri.

Inside, Keely had the good sense to release his jerkin, which he absently pulled back into shape. He thought briefly, in case of trouble, he would claim her his woman;

a glance at Keely's face made him think better of it. In sleeveless jerkin, leggings and boots much like his own, with identical coloring and similar features, no one would believe it. Their kinship was too evident.

Keely sniffed. "Fish."

"Hondarth *is* a seaport." Corin glanced around the tavern. He had seen better; he had certainly seen worse. The light was dim, but not nonexistent. Nothing led him to believe they courted trouble. There were no covert glances hiding ill will, no rude comments on Keely's apparel, no private jests about the vixen who flanked one side. The patrons looked at the newcomers curiously, as anyone would, then turned back to private business without excess incivility.

"A table." Already Keely was striding toward it, boot heels thumping against hardwood floor. Men watched her, elbowed partners, made comments, but they watched with an appreciation significantly lacking in rudeness or raillery.

Corin let out a breath, surprised to discover he had been holding it. All his life he had done what he could to keep his headstrong sister free from trouble, and sometimes he succeeded. But the task was more difficult when she seemed purposely to flout convention. He did not entirely blame her—he himself would go mad as a woman, confined to women's work—but neither did he fully understand her dedication to defiance. She *was* a woman—should she not behave as one?

She is also a Cheysuli, and gifted more than most, Kiri reminded him. *She has the Old Blood in abundance. Do you expect her to behave as a dutiful Homanan woman?*

The thought of Keely portraying herself as a meek, docile woman thinking only of her man's pleasure made Corin grin. But he was doing an injustice to the female portion of Homana's population; they were not *all* meek and docile. Certainly enough of Deirdre's Homanan ladies were spirited, in bed or out of it.

Women. Following his sister, he cast an assessive glance around the tavern. If there was a likely wine-girl present, he might pass the night pleasurably indeed.

And then he recalled Keely. Glumly, he reflected he could hardly tell his sister to hunt up a private room for herself while he disported himself with the wine-girl. It would only invite trouble. He sighed. With Hart or Brennan things were much less complicated; although Brennan tended to keep himself to court ladies, neither he nor Hart were averse to spending time with wine-girls, and they certainly made no protest when Corin did. But Keely might.

He reached the table. She was already seated, hunched forward on a stool, and looking about with interest. Corin could not remember a time he had taken her into a tavern, even in Mujhara; away from the palace, away from Clankeep, they generally frequented inns or road-houses, where the clientele was different.

Corin hooked out a stool and sat down slowly, one hand touching Kiri's heavy ruff. Her presence, he saw, had been noted, remarked on, accepted. If there were mutters of beasts and shapechangers, he heard none of them. And yet he recalled the stories of how his grandsire, Donal, had met only hatred and prejudice when he had come to Hondarth.

A step sounded behind him. He thought nothing of it until he saw Keely's hand slip to her knife, and then he half-turned. He was stopped by a big hand on his shoulder.

"Be ye Cheysuli?" asked the man with the paw of a bear, or so it seemed to Corin. "Or a Homanan masquerading as such?"

Corin tried to shake off the paw. Keely, he saw, was leaning forward as if to rise; beside him, Kiri's lips peeled back to show sharp white teeth. "Why?" he asked coldly. "And why should it matter which?"

"Because if ye be Cheysuli, I'll be buying you a drink, you and the lass. If ye only *play* at it, lad, I've no business with either of ye."

The accent was familiar, though far thicker than Deirdre's fading lilt. Corin grinned, and even Keely began to relax. "Erinnish?" he asked.

"Aye, lad, name o 'Boyne. But ye have yet to answer *my* question."

Boyne was a huge, bearlike man, black of hair and beard, though gray generously salted both. His nose was bent from some accident—or fight—in the far past, and he lacked two teeth to boot. But the smile was genuine, lighting dark eyes as Corin nodded.

"Aye, Cheysuli, both of us." He gestured. "Will you join us?"

Keely's jaw was tightly set; he saw the reprimand in her eyes. But it was too late. Boyne had plopped his bulk down on a bench and was shouting for fresh wine.

He grinned at them both, eyes alight as he looked at Keely. "*Captain* Boyne," he said, "sailing home to Erinn on the morning tide. But when I saw the fox and all your gold, I knew ye must be Cheysuli, and I said to myself I must buy ye a dram before I sail."

"Why?" Keely's tone was cool.

He raised black brows. "Because o' the ties between our countries, lass, why else? Erinn's own fair Aileen will wed into the House o' Homana, and Prince Sean will take the Mujhar's Cheysuli lass for his bride. 'Tis good manners to drink to such happiness, lass!" He reared back as a wine-girl thumped down a jug and three cups. He poured generous measures, then handed them out. "To Aileen and her Cheysuli prince; to Sean and his sweet lass!"

Following his lead, Corin raised his cup. Keely's motion was considerably slower, but Boyne seemed not to notice as he clacked his cup against theirs.

" 'Sweet lass,' " Keely said sourly, and tossed back a gulp of wine as if to wash away the taste of unpleasant words.

Boyne leaned forward. "Aye," he said, "sweet lass. Would Sean be having any other?" He grinned, guffawed, slapped the flat of one huge hand down upon the table. "Hot for her he is, too, our lusty lord . . . 'twill only be a matter of weeks before he sends for her. He's a man now, our Sean, and of no mind to wait longer for his bride. 'Tis time he started a son!"

She lifted one tawny brow in an eloquent arch. "Is that how he values a woman, then—by the children she can bear?"

" 'Tis her only value, lass . . . what *else* can she do?" Boyne gulped wine, then set his cup down so hard the remaining contents slopped over the rim. "Mind ye, I can hardly be speaking for my lord, but I *can* say he's no wilted flower. He'll be wedding her, bedding her, getting a son upon her . . . within a year, I'm saying." He slopped more wine into his cup, then thrust it upward again. "To all the fine wee bairns!"

Keely set down her cup and refused to drink. Corin, knowing Boyne meant well and that to refuse was rude as well as unnecessary, sipped his own and tried to ignore the look on his sister's face.

"We too are sailing for Erinn in the morning," Corin began, intending to ask passage of the flamboyant captain. But Keely interrupted.

"No," she said coolly, "*we* are not. Only my brother sails."

Astonished, he nearly gaped.

Keely's smile was excessively insincere. "I am needed at home."

"Have you gone mad?" It did not bother him that Boyne was an interested onlooker. "You said you were coming *with* me!"

Keely sipped her wine thoughtfully. "I have changed my mind," she said after a moment. "Is it not what a woman does? Certainly the sort of woman Boyne's beloved prince might prefer."

He scowled at her. "You might have changed it *before* I sold the roan."

Keely shrugged. "I will buy him back."

"And if he is sold already?"

"Then I will *steal* him back." Keely grinned at Boyne to remove the sting from her words; the big man's answering smile was fatuous.

For all she protests womanly behavior, she knows how to use it when it suits her, Corin reflected irritably. "Keely—"

"We will speak of it later," she said calmly. "As for now, I want some food."

Boyne nearly overset the table as he rose to shout for service.

Later, when they were alone in the small room Corin had rented, Keely faced him squarely. Never did she avoid a confrontation or deserved punishment; nor did she now.

"Why?" he asked.

She watched in silence as he sat down on the edge of his cot and drew off his boots, one by one. The belt with its long-knife was next; the remaining leathers he would sleep in.

"You heard him," she said finally, working at the lacing that bound her braid. "You heard that big-mouthed fool of a man, bellowing about how his lusty prince was hot for his Cheysuli bride." She stopped fussing with the knots and crossed her arms instead, all her unexpected vulnerability suddenly evident. "*You* heard how he will wed her, bed her, and get a son upon her—all in the space of a year!"

"Aye, well, I think Boyne exaggerates out of habit." Corin scooted back on the cot and leaned against the wall as Kiri jumped up and settled herself next to him. "He enjoys the sound of his own voice, Keely, little more. There is no malice in him. Only goodwill."

She sat down on the edge of the other cot, no more than four feet from his own. "I cannot go, Corin. I *cannot*."

"You are afraid."

She did not demur. "Aye."

"Of what? From what Boyne said, Sean is a good man . . . kind to dogs, horses, children—" He grinned. "In all likelihood he will be as kind to his woman."

But he had erred in thinking humor might soothe her. All it did was drive her farther from him, knees drawn up to shield most of her face as she hunched against the wall. "I want none of it," she said. "No wedding, no bedding, no children . . . I want *none* of it, Corin! All I want is to be myself, and if I go with you to Erinn, I will lose myself that much sooner. At least this way I may wait until Liam of Erinn and *jehan* decide it is time."

"Sean himself may have a say in it. And if he does—"

"If he does, let him do it the way it is always done," she said bitterly. "He will have to tell his *jehan*, who will in turn send to ours . . . it will buy me a little time. If I go with you, that time is halved." She sat up straight and stared at him. "I cannot afford to lose it, *rujho* . . . not even a single day."

"But there *will* come a day—"

"I know." She cut him off. "I know. But that day is not tomorrow." Keely bent forward and jerked her boots off, dropping them to the floor. "I am sorry, Corin—but in the morning I go back."

He nodded as she blew out the single candle. In the darkness he heard the crack of the leather webbing that bound her mattress to the frame. In the darkness he heard the sound of her uneven breathing, and knew she was more frightened than he.

And he swore to himself that when he arrived in Erinn with his words of Aileen's betrothal, he would also speak of his sister's.

Two

Boyne stood next to him at the taffrail as sea-spray broke over the prow of the ship and splattered them both liberally. "There, lad—d'ye see it? 'Tis called the Dragon's Tail. 'Tis what divides Erinn from Atvia—a league or two of ocean, and centuries of war."

Corin clutched the rail. The Dragon's Tail was a narrow channel winding its way between two islands. Winds lashed the water into heavy chop, turning much of the shoreline of both islands into jagged teeth instead of smooth beaches. But lest the fisherfolk lament such harshness, there were also two natural harbors, sheltered and less treacherous.

"I did not know Kilore and Rondule were so close," Corin remarked in surprise. Next to him, Kiri pressed against his leg.

"Aye." Boyne, beside him, leaned on the rail, wind whipping graying hair into dark eyes. "Legends are saying once the islands were joined into a single kingdom ruled by a fair man. But that fair man's younger brother was desiring a kingdom of his own, and so they fought." Boyne grinned and spat over the taffrail into the slate-gray ocean. "They battled day in and day out, day in day and day out, till each realized if they kept it up, there would be no men left to lead. And so they agreed to fight no more."

When Boyne did not continue, Corin glanced at him. "But that does not explain how two islands were made out of one."

The big man tapped his badly bent nose. "I'm but warming to the tale, lad . . . ye never rush a good story, now, or ye'll be ruining the ending."

"Forgive me." Corin smiled in amusement. "I will leave the telling to you."

Boyne nodded. Thoughtfully, he stared toward the Dragon's Tail. "'Twas the younger brother's doing. Not satisfied with the truce, because it gave him nothing he didn't have already, he sought the power to overcome his brother, the king. He begged the aid of a powerful sorcerer, bargaining with his soul. And when he had slain his brother and won the war, he was king by conquest." Boyne grinned. "The only thing was, now the sorcerer wanted his soul. Since no man, newly crowned, is wanting to give up his soul, he said no."

Corin nodded. "And so the sorcerer took his due."

"Oh, aye. He split the kingdom in twain and took the soul of the king."

"Leaving two kingdoms in place of one, and no men to rule either of them."

Boyne grinned. "Each brother had a son. Each cousin took a throne. And to this day their descendants are fighting over a single title."

"Lord of the Idrian Isles." Corin nodded. "That much I *do* know." He wiped spray out of his eyes and tasted salt. "What happened to the sorcerer?"

Boyne frowned dramatically, black brows knitted. "Well, 'tis said he got the soul he was promised. But 'tis also said he soon grew tired of such pettiness and turned his back on it all. Some say he died; others are saying he went belowdecks and became king of the world down there." An eloquent gesture accompanied the final sentence.

Corin looked at him sharply. "Do you mean Asar-Suti?"

Boyne shrugged and turned to call out an order to one of his sailors. When he turned back, he was frowning. "I'm not knowing the name, lad. All I know is the story. Whether there's truth in it, I'll not be saying one way or another."

"Asar-Suti, the Seker, who made and dwells in darkness," Corin mused thoughtfully. He glanced at Boyne, knowing what he said would sound like a tale to rival the captain's. "The Solindish Ihlini worship him as the god of the netherworld. In his name, they try to take Homana to make it part of his earthly kingdom."

Boyne shrugged. "I'm not knowing so much of Ihlini, either, being Erinnish-born. But they could be one and the same: sorcerer and god."

It was a new concept to Corin, who was accustomed to viewing sorcerers as men—or women—with magical power, but no godhood. If indeed the sorcerer had become Asar-Suti, then what was to prevent other sorcerers from doing much the same?"

Strahan made a god? Corin felt a chill at the base of his spine. He looked at Kiri. *What becomes of our gods if the Ihlini make their own?*

The vixen's thick, bright pelt ruffled in the wind. *It is a question I cannot answer.*

He looked at her more sharply. *Cannot, or will not?*

Bright eyes glinted as she turned away. *One and the same, lir. I have no answer for you.*

Again Corin thought of Strahan. He had been raised on stories of the man who led the Solindish sorcerers, those who served Asar-Suti. The Mujhar had said more than once that not all Ihlini did, and that only those sworn to the Seker were men to be wary of. But Strahan was different. Strahan was more than merely sorcerer, being blessed with an uncanny charm that beguiled good and bad alike. He was already extremely powerful because of his dedication to the Seker. If his reward for such service and dedication was godhood, then he offered more than idle threat to the Cheysuli and the prophecy.

"Kilore," Boyne said. "And now, lad, I must tend my ship."

Distracted by his thoughts, Corin watched the Erinnish giant go. It had been a long time since he had thought much about Strahan or the Ihlini, or even the prophecy. That he was a link in it was old news. Except for Maeve, all of Niall's children were; it was why Strahan had tried to kidnap them as infants with Gisella's participation. But Boyne's fanciful tale had reawakened old memories and questions.

Twenty years ago my jehana tried to give her children to the Ihlini. No doubt he had a use for us then. But what of now? What would he do with us now?

And then, as abruptly, he forgot about Strahan and his half Atvian mother because the ship was docking.

Corin clutched the rail and stared. Kilore the city spilled along the waterfront like a tangle of seaweed, streets and wynds interlocking to form a webwork he did not think he could ever decipher. And above the city, thrusting up in a jagged line of palisades, were the white chalk cliffs his father had mentioned so often. Kilore was a place of mist and magic, Niall had said, and Corin saw at least half of it was true. Shrouded in dampness, the cliffs formed a bright white curtain wall against the darker world.

And atop it, almost ominous in its bulk, stood the fortress from which the city took its name: Kilore itself, Aerie of the Eagles.

"Kilore!" Boyne called, and then added considerably more in Erinnish, which Corin understood well enough, thanks to years spent with Deirdre.

I wish I were arriving home, like Boyne, instead of here. Corin looked up at the castle and tried to suppress his nerves. *I wish I were doing anything but playing messenger for my jehan, and proxy suitor for my rujholli.*

The ship was secured handily, the ramps lowered, the unloading commenced. Corin, having nothing more than a set of shoulderpacks, proceeded down one ramp with Kiri trotting behind.

Fish, she said fastidiously.

Corin smiled crookedly. Aye, fish indeed. Deirdre had told him much of Erinn's economy depended on fish, and the stench made it more than evident. He smelled fish, old and new; sea salt and seaweed; the effluvia of ships toiling for months on the Idrian and beyond. There was nothing romantic about voyaging, Corin thought, when one looked at realities.

He and Kiri picked their way around nets and coils of rope, conscious of the shrieking of the gulls and the chatter of fisherfolk going about their work. It was late afternoon; the tide was in and so were the fishing boats. He and Kiri, wandering along the quayside, were distinctly in the way.

"Hai, Cheysuli!" Boyne called, and Corin turned back as the captain strode across the docks in his rolling sailor's gait. "Will ye be looking for someone in particular, or biding your time for a spell?"

Corin, who had told the Brinnishman no more than his name and destination, shrugged beneath the shoulderpacks. "My business is with the castle."

Boyne's black brows rose. He was a garrulous man but not a stupid one; he knew better than to ask questions that were none of his concern, and had not during the voyage. But it did not stop his thoughts, and he chewed idly on a tattered thumbnail. "Aye, well, I'll not be keeping ye from it, then. I thought to buy ye a wee dram o' ale or wine in the grogshop before I saw to my own business."

Corin looked up at the Aerie. No, not yet. He smiled at Boyne. "No, captain, it is my turn to buy for *you*. Shall we go?"

Boyne looked down at Kiri. "What of the vixen, then? Will ye leave her on my ship?"

"Kiri goes with me."

The Erinnishman shrugged. "Aye, aye, and welcome to her. Come along, then, lad. Let us be wasting no more time flapping our mouths when we could be swilling ale." He clapped Corin a buffet on the shoulder that nearly knocked him down and strode off toward a row of buildings not far from the quay.

Boyne was engaged in another of his lengthy, colorful tales when a woman's angry voice distracted both of them. For a fleeting instant Corin thought she was protesting Boyne's loquaciousness, then realized there was more to it than that. It stopped Boyne dead in his tracks.

"Here!" he called, looking toward a narrow wynd that twisted down toward the sea. "Hai, lass, *here*—"

The woman's protest was silenced at once, and forcibly. Boyne slapped Corin on the shoulder and took off at a run, filling the wynd with his bulk and voice. After only a moment's hesitation, Corin followed.

Three men, Corin saw as he turned a corner—and a woman bundled in blankets. Near the end of the wynd, close to the quay. One of the men turned to face Boyne; the other two lifted the women off her feet and effectively controlled her struggles.

After a brief exchange between Boyne and the spokesman for the others, Corin realized civilities had been abandoned.

Boyne shouted with mocking laughter. "Oh, aye, and my mother was a queen!" He turned to Corin. "Yon man is saying the woman is drunk, and they're taking her home to her husband. But *I* know better than that—she shouted for help, and there was no drunkenness about it. And if these men are Erinnish, I'll be giving them my ship! Atvian, more like, trying to spirit away an Erinnish lass for evil purposes." He advanced a step. "Come, lad, 'tis a lass in need of us."

Kiri, Corin said within the link, and the vixen darted past Boyne's opponent to the others. Even as Boyne engaged, slapping away the knife that appeared in the Atvian's hand, Kiri was nipping at ankles amidst kicks and curses.

Corin grinned and waded into the fray himself. As Boyne settled his score, reducing their number to two, Kiri forced the men to neglect their prisoner. It was easy enough for the girl to tear herself away even as Corin and Boyne converged on the remaining opposition.

Boyne's fight did not last long. Corin's took longer, since he lacked the other's sheer bulk and strength. But as Kiri continued to nip at ankles, Corin smashed the Atvian's nose and sent him reeling off balance. A second blow snapped his head back and took his senses from him. He collapsed on the cobbles.

"Aye, *aye,* lad, 'tis the way of it!" Boyne clapped him on the shoulder. "We've saved the lass from the scum!"

Boyne's "lass" still sat on the ground where she had

landed, half wrapped in dark blankets. Slowly she levered herself up on elbows, feet flat, knees drawn up,
skirts tangled around her boots. She stared up at them
both, then put out a hand to yank heavy skirts decorously into place.

Corin reached down an open hand. "Lady, will you
come up?" He caught her, pulled her, steadied her as she
rose, clasping one arm around her, pulled her, steadied
her as she rose, clasping one arm around her slender
waist.

She was pale and a trifle shaky, but apparently unharmed; slight, but decidedly not fragile. Another woman
might have cried or fainted or both; this one did neither.
She eyed him closely a moment with incredibly bright
green eyes, shrewdly assessing intentions, then pushed
tangled hair—very *red* hair—away from an oval face. She
blew out an explosive sigh of relief that also melted the
tension out of face and limbs.

Guardedly, she smiled; the mouth was eloquent in its
mobility, wide and willful beneath a straight, bold nose.
She was not a beauty, not as Corin reckoned women—
her coloring was far too flamboyant—but she was a striking girl, the kind of girl whose vibrant liveliness of spirit
made beauty unimportant. Almost without thinking, he
found himself responding.

"*You're* not Erinnish." She glanced at Boyne. "*You*
are, captain, but the lad's not."

"No, lass, he's Homanan. Cheysuli, more properly."
The big Erinnishman grinned at her expression of surprise, then replaced it with concern. "D'ye fare all right,
lass? Did they have time to harm ye?"

She withdrew her hand from Corin's and deftly smoothed
clothing into place, tightening snug belt, twitching the
folds of her skirts, resetting the fit of tunic and under-
blouse. She wore the plain garb of a fisher woman, and
yet Corin had felt the softness of her hand, which did not
at all coincide. No more than her carriage or her manner; he had seen the like in Keely.

And, by Keely, he knew her. Inwardly, he smiled.
Highborn, if not the highest.

"They were meaning no harm," she said grimly. "They wanted me for Alaric, I'd lay a wager, and not for their own."

"Atvian scum!" Boyne turned his head and spat. "Come, lass, we'll be taking ye to your husband or your father; one or the other'll be wanting to know of this."

She tried to untangle the mass of hair and could not; the task required a brush. Distractedly she combed it back with her fingers, grimacing as she found additional tangles. The curling ends shifted against her belt. "I have no husband. My father's not in Kilore, nor is my brother or mother—which made it all the easier for the *skilfins*." She cast a scowl at the unconscious men. "But 'tis my fault as much as anything else; I should not have come down alone. I know better, as my father is one for telling me. And now he can tell me again." She shrugged and smiled a rueful smile. "For all I hate to say it, he may have the right of it. All Alaric *needs* is leverage, and I nearly gave it to him." And then she stopped short, as if she had said too much to men who could not understand, and cast a bright glance at Corin. "Why does a Cheysuli come to Erinn?"

"Business with her lord."

Straight red brows jerked upward. She was not subtle in her thoughts, but he found it rather engaging. "With Liam, then? Well, 'twill have to wait. He's on the other side of the island tending to disputes." She jerked her head upward to indicate the fortress. "Will you come up, then? 'Tis where I'm bound." She looked at Boyne and grinned. "You as well, captain. 'Tis grateful I am for your service, and you're both due reward. What would you say to a meal in the Aerie, and a purse of gold apiece?"

"In the *castle*?" Boyne stared. "Lass, lass, ye shouldn't be promising things ye can't deliver."

"But I can," she said calmly. She glanced at Corin briefly, saw his expression, and her bright eyes twinkled. "But then I'm thinking *you* might understand."

He grinned. "Aye, lady, I do. And I think Boyne will, also, although you will steal his tongue. I have heard him

speak of you; I think he worships someone other than
the gods."

She grimaced wryly and indicated her mussed appearance. "Not for much longer, I fear." One of the Atvians
groaned and shifted on the cobbles. She scowled. "Let us
tarry no longer. We'll be leaving the rats in the gutter
. . . they'll crawl home to their master and suffer for
their failure."

"Lass—" Boyne stopped her as she swung away, ready
to march out of the narrow wynd. "Lass—the *castle?*"

"The castle," she agreed. "D'ye think you're not fit
for it?" And as he nodded, she laughed and took his
arm, turning him toward the cliffs. "Not fit to face the
eagle when you've saved one of his fledglings?" She
paused. "Except the eagle is not in the Aerie, nor any of
the others. *I* shall have to do."

"Boyne." Corin fell into step as Kiri trotted beside
him. "Have you not told me what the Princess Aileen
looks like?"

The captain grinned as he slackened his pace to the
girl's. "Aye, lad, many times. 'Tis only from a distance
I've seen her, mind you, but 'twas enough." He grinned
and tucked her slender arm into his elbow. "Red-haired
she is, like this lass here, and I've heard her eyes are
green as Erinn's turf."

"Turf," the girl echoed morosely, twisting her mobile
mouth into something akin to an offended wince, although the laughter in her eyes belied the truth of it. "Ye
might at least compare them to *emeralds,* man, not *turf.*"

"*Your* eyes are the emeralds, lass," Boyne said gallantly.

At that she burst out laughing and stopped him in his
tracks. "Ye great-hearted, blathering fool, can ye not
hear what this Cheysuli is trying to say? *I* am Aileen,
man . . . *I* am the Princess of Erinn . . . turf-green eyes
and all."

Boyne gaped. "You're *not.*"

"I am," she said solemnly, but her bright eyes were
alight with humor. "And when I invite you to take sup-
per with me and accept a purse of gold, you *will* do as I
say."

"Oh, *lass*—I mean, *lady*—"

"Fie on that blather," she said cheerfully. "Come up with me, captain, and let me thank you for your courage."

Grinning at Boyne's discomfort, Corin possessed himself of silence. But he wondered what Brennan would say when he met his Erinnish bride.

Three

Although Aileen struck Corin as an unaffected, uninhibited girl, she was also a princess and well understood the responsibilities of rank. Once within the towering walls of Liam's fortress, Corin and Boyne were shown to guest chambers to refresh themselves before the meal. It took neither of them long—Corin bathed and put on fresh leathers, Boyne bathed and put on his well-worn flamboyant silks because he had nothing else—and then they were escorted into a private hall made ready for the evening meal.

Corin was impressed. Both his father and Deirdre had said Liam was not a man much concerned with show, preferring simplicity over elaboration, and Kilore itself reflected the tastes of simple men. But in a short amount of time Aileen had ordered her guests treated with the utmost respect and hospitality, the meal and hall prepared, and her servants had quickly complied.

A figured white cloth covered the wide table. Iron gimbles filled with candles hung from massive roof timbers, providing a wash of illumination that glittered off glass and silver. Covered platters looked like silver turtles steaming. Servants neatly attired in Liam's green livery waited quietly, indicating that Corin and Boyne were to be seated. And then Aileen came in.

Gone was the fisher girl in homespun wool and knee boots, with unruly red hair an unbound mass of tangles. In her place was the Princess of Erinn, gowned and garbed appropriately. And yet she maintained a simplicity in dress and manner, for there were no jewels or haughty ways, merely a simple green gown, a slender fillet of gold threaded through shining hair now free of snarls, and a wide, impish smile.

Corin rose with alacrity, although Boyne's matching response was so abrupt it overset his chair. One of the servants hastened to right it as Boyne, unheeding, gaped at Aileen.

"Lass," he rumbled, "oh, *lass*—"

Aileen's brows rose expectantly as he stumbled to a stop; when he appeared incapable of continuing, she laughed and bade them both be seated.

Good manners, Kiri approved.

Corin put a hand down as he sat and passed it through the vixen's ruff. As always, the touch soothed him. *Do you judge her in Brennan's place?*

I merely comment. Kiri settled her rump on the floor next to Corin's chair and curled tail fastidiously around black paws.

"We'll be dining first," Aileen told them, "and then I'll be asking all the things I want to know."

The meal was superb, particularly after weeks of ship's stores, which were intended for longevity and ease of storing rather than for flavor. Corin's table manners reasserted themselves after the long voyage, but Boyne suffered from inexperience. He quaffed wine freely, consumed incredible amounts of rare beef, partridge, eel, oysters, and a variety of fish. Corin and Aileen, with more refined appetites, finished long before the captain, and exchanged amused grins as Boyne continued his culinary attack.

At last he shoved his platter away and belched contentedly. "Aye, lass—*lady*—'twas a meal fit for a lord. My belly is in the way of being grateful."

" 'Twas only the beginning of showing you my own gratitude." Aileen motioned the servants to begin clearing as she rose. "If you'll come with me now, I'll be showing you the rest."

She led them to an antechamber well-warmed by a huge brick fireplace. Plush pelts covered the stone floor and tapestries cut the chill from thick walls. There were chairs, small tables, two wooden cabinets carved in Erinnish knotwork patterns. Altogether the chamber formed a homey, comfortable place, reminding Corin of Deirdre's solar.

Aileen motioned them to sit, then withdrew something from one of the cabinets. As she turned, Corin saw two leather pouches in her hands. Her expression was solemn as she faced them, but her green eyes were alight. "I know neither of you did me the service out of greed or ambition," she said, "and you weren't hoping for reward, either—not from a fisher girl all wrapped in dirty blankets—but I'll be giving you a token of my gratitude regardless. And I'll not be hearing modest refusals from you, either—would ye say them to my father?" She looked each of them in the eye, forbidding them to answer, and handed out the pouches. "You'll be staying the night as my guests."

Boyne stared down at the pouch, dwarfed in the palm of his huge hand. He chewed at his lip, scowling blackly, then sighed and tucked the pouch away with the air of resignation. Aileen, watching his struggle, smiled and went to him.

"And as a measure of more personal thanks, a kiss." On tiptoe she still had to urge him to bend, and kissed him squarely on the cheek when he acquiesced. Boyne turned scarlet.

Aileen laughed and stepped away. "Off with ye, captain, I'm no blind fool; you've been at sea a long time, and no doubt you'd rather be spending the night with a lady. Well, 'tis a host's responsibility to provide hospitality, woman or no; I think you'll be pleased with the girl."

Boyne's color deepened. "*Lass*—"

"In my father's place, I am host," Aileen said cheerfully. "I know my duties, captain."

In the face of her matter-of-fact announcement, Boyne was clearly unable to answer. And so he backed toward the door, bowed awkwardly, and went out at once, bagged coin clinking against one massive thigh.

Aileen laughed, eyes blazing amusement, and turned to Corin.

"Did you really send him a woman?" he asked, wondering what she intended for him.

Her laughter was arrested. "Aye," she said in surprise. "D'ye think I am a liar?"

"No, no, but—" Suddenly uncomfortable, he shrugged. "It—seems odd to think of a woman sending a man a girl to share his bed."

" 'Tis not a habit of mine," she answered cheerfully. "But I spoke the truth: there are customs of hospitality, regardless of sex, and that is one. I *could* send him back to the waterfront, but I thought a night in the Aerie might be worth a drink or two in the taverns." She shrugged disarmingly. "My father is a lusty, plain-speaking man, and so is my brother. I know a man's needs, and so I tend to Boyne's." Her mobile mouth moved into a crooked smile. "Besides, 'twas Moira's *desire* to bed him. She told me so as I bathed."

Corin laughed aloud. "Then what of *me*, lady? Do you tend my needs also?"

She eyed him thoughtfully, then flung a gesture toward a chair. "Sit, sit; Boyne was easy to predict, but you are harder to know. And I have never met a Cheysuli."

She poured wine as he sat down, handed him a heavy goblet and settled herself in a chair opposite his own. The fire- and candlelight was kind to her coloring and features, enriching the former and enhancing the latter; Deirdre also wore Erinnish green frequently, but now that he saw the color on Aileen, Corin felt Deirdre's choice less suitable.

He set the pouch of gold on the table and made a gesture indicating polite refusal. "Your words were well-spoken and I admire their intent, but I cannot accept your reward."

She arched a single eyebrow. "Too proud, then? Or is it that Erinnish gold means less to you than those bracelets on your arms?"

Absently Corin touched one of the heavy *lir*-bands. "No, nor am I too proud, though you may think otherwise." He shrugged slightly. "Let us say it is—unnecessary."

"Why?" she asked bluntly.

Corin smiled. "Your father and brother are not the only plainspoken eagles in the Aerie."

Aileen laughed and swung a foot. "No, no, I have my share of a forthright tongue as well. 'Twas the price of living with my father." Her eyes did not waver from his. "Why is it unnecessary?"

"Because for a kinsman to do less is unconscionable. For him to do it for reward is unspeakable."

The foot stopped swinging. "*Kinsman.*"

"Corin," he said, "as I have told you. "But it is Corin *of Homana* . . . I am the Mujhar's son."

"*Niall's* son!"

"Aye."

She pursed her lips thoughtfully. And then shook her head. "But we're *not* kin. Through my aunt we would be, but Niall and Deirdre are not wed." Her expression was cool. "He holds to Gisella, does he not?"

"He holds to the laws of Homana," Corin told her calmly. "You honor the customs of hospitality, Aileen . . . *he* honors the laws of the land he rules."

She sipped wine, then shrugged and thumped the goblet down on the table. "So, you've come to see my father. Official business? Or personal?"

Her eyes were watchful, no matter how casual her tone. He opened his mouth to tell her the business concerned her betrothal to Brennan—and found he could not. "It is for me to speak with your father."

Aileen's smile was slow, but no less eloquent. "I *am* his daughter."

"I have been charged with this message—for the Lord of Erinn—by the Mujhar himself." He thought the evasion was answer enough, and not so far from the truth.

She considered it, tilting her head slightly. Candlelight blazed off the gold fillet and the glory of her hair. And then she shrugged slightly, dismissing the topic entirely. "Well, 'twill have to wait regardless. My father is, as I have said, on the other side of the island. He could be home tomorrow; he might come home in a month."

Corin thought of Keely. "Sean is not here?"

Aileen shook her had. "Sean has a new ship, the *Princess of Homana*." She sighed and swung her foot again. "Men and ships—who can say how long he will be gone? 'Tis her maiden voyage . . . but he should be back by spring." Her eyes were steady. "In time to have Liam write the Mujhar about the betrothal between son and daughter."

Corin drank hastily to cover the rigid expression on his face. He could not very well tell Aileen *his* sister wanted no part of *her* brother; it would be rude as well as an insult. Plainspeaking she might be, and Liam, but in negotiations between the royal houses such bluntness was deemed unwise.

"She is lovely, your fox," Aileen said, looking at Kiri curled on the bear pelt beneath Corin's feet. "And so quiet; I'd be thinking she'd prefer the out of doors to castles."

He smiled. "She does. So do most Cheysuli; it is the *lir*-shape in us. But a warrior adapts, and so does a *lir*."

Aileen bent forward to take a closer look. "We know of Cheysuli, of course, but little of your animals. My father says Niall had none when he was a guest here so long ago."

"Guest?" Corin grinned. "You bend the truth, Aileen. My father was held hostage against Alaric of Atvia."

She laughed ruefully. "Aye, aye, *hostage* then, but will you be telling me he lost by it? In the end he got his Atvian wife, but he got my aunt as well. *And* a bastard daughter."

He inclined his head to indicate concession. "Maeve and Deirdre thrive. Bastard or no, she is his favorite child."

Aileen's brows rose. "*You* are not?"

"Hardly." Corin felt the familiar bitterness rising. "Maeve is Deirdre come again; my father adores his Erinnish *meijha*, and the daughter as well. As for *me*, I come last in his regard."

"Why?" Aileen frowned. "Why do you rank your brothers and sisters? Does he not love you all equally?"

"There is little to love in me." Corin blocked out her face with the goblet, drinking deeply. "Equally? No." He shrugged. "There is Brennan, who is the heir to Homana and therefore the most important of us all." Though he tried, for her sake, to mask the resentment in his tone when he spoke of Brennan, he heard its echo regardless. Quickly, he went on. "There is Maeve, dutiful daughter of his beloved *meijha*. And Hart, who is as good-natured as he is irresponsible, and impossible to dislike." He smiled. "And Keely, impetuous, passionate Keely, who tests his patience with her wild ways, and yet pleases him with her spirit. As for me," Corin shrugged, "I am, perhaps, my own worst enemy . . . but I cannot help it." He looked at her over the rim of his goblet, seeing himself through her eyes, and found he did not like it. But he did not look away. "There are times I hate myself, and therefore I make it easy for *others* to hate me."

Aileen looked straight back at him. "Then 'tis up to you to change it."

He waited for the upsurge of anger or resentment. It was a solution others had suggested many times, and each time it had made him blacker of temper than ever. But before Aileen, he found himself regretting his contrary moodiness for the first time. And sincerely desiring to change it.

He smiled ruefully. "I have said more to you than anyone save Keely, and half the time she *supports* me instead of suggesting I change my behavior."

"It does a person no good to abet his insecurities," Aileen said flatly. "My brother is the proudest, most honorable man you could ever meet, and yet he's hot-tempered and hasty as well, and equally plainspoken. If I stood by him when he is wrong, nodding and 'ayeing' and buttressing his flank, I'd be doing him a greater injustice than Sean his victim." Her tone was one of understanding courtesy, and yet there was also an inflexible note of determination. "I'd make of him a tyrant,

believing in only himself without granting others the right
to disagreement or other forms of self-expression . . .
and 'tis a poor man *that* makes.''

Corin laughed sourly. "My father has said as much,
and Brennan as well . . . but it makes more sense coming
from you."

" 'Tis usually the way of it." Aileen shrugged. " 'Tis
why 'tis important to listen to your kin. Let *them* show
you what you are and what you do, so you give others no
opportunity." She paused a moment, watching him. "And
then you won't be having to sit there across from me,
wishing there was a hole you might crawl into."

He grinned and rubbed at an eye. "Gods, but you are
good for me. Brennan is fortunate—" And he broke off,
realizing that yet again his brother would take precedence over him. And this time, this time *particularly*, he
resented it badly. More than ever before.

*But you have known all along she was intended for
your rujholli,* Kiri told him. *For all the days of your life.*

Rigidly, he stared at Aileen. And then he set the
goblet down unsteadily and rose. "If you will excuse me
. . . it was a long voyage, and I would like to retire."

Aileen stood quickly and awkwardly, bewildered by
his sudden withdrawal. "Oh, aye—of course." She
frowned. "Corin—"

"I am weary, Aileen," he said curtly, and saw the
color blaze in her face.

Her eyes glittered with an acknowledgment of his rudeness. "Then go," she said coolly. "The servants will show
you to your chambers."

With Kiri, Corin left.

*He was a child again, in his dream, overlooked be-
cause of his age. Around him the women gossiped, cluck-
ing over the latest of Hart's habitual pranks or Keely's
willfulness; praising Maeve's sweet temper and Brennan's
maturity. But they said nothing of him, nothing of Corin at
all.*

*In his dream he heard their praises, and Brennan—
Brennan—Brennan.*

Corin awoke. He touched Kiri sleeping at his side. And then fell into darkness again.

Older now, but no less overlooked unless he made them look. And he did, whenever he could, using wits and willfulness, forcing the women to look, to see, to hear, even if the result was punishment, because then its name was Corin . . . then they spoke his name. Even if cursing it.

Asleep, he reached for Kiri, who heard him whenever he spoke. And even when he did not.

In the dream, he was himself, no longer a child but the Corin he saw every day when he looked in the polished plate. And suddenly he was the polished plate; he saw himself, as if he were someone else entirely, outside looking in, and the Corin he saw was a stranger.

But not a stranger at all. Corin stood in the Great Hall, before the Lion Throne, facing the Mujhar of Homana, the man who had sired him. Alone, he faced him . . . and then he was not alone, for with him was a woman, a slim, red-haired woman with eyes clear and green as emeralds— green as Erinnish turf—and the woman's hand was in his hand, and she faced the Mujhar, as he did, and together they recited the private Cheysuli vows that bound a warrior and his woman.

Bound . . . bound . . . bound—

—Until Brennan stepped out of the shadows and tore Aileen's hand out of his.

"No!" Corin cried. "No—not *again!*"

And he was awake, and knew it, and knew what he had dreamed.

Four

The dream haunted Corin for days. He did his best to
ignore it, to push it away into the recesses of his subcon-
scious, but its aftertaste remained, like the sour flavor of
sweet wine turned to vinegar. When he looked at Aileen,
he saw the woman who had recited the Cheysuli vows
with him before the Lion of Homana, defying Niall himself. And defying her betrothed as much as Corin did
himself.

Theirs was an uneasy companionship at best. Aileen
hosted him with as much hospitality as she could muster
in the name of her absent father, but the uninhibited
generosity was gone. She eyed him warily at times, like a
dog with an unkind master; other times she relegated
him to obscurity, too busy to pay him mind. But occasionally he saw an odd sort of compassion in her eyes, as
if she began to understand him and what made him the
man he was.

At last the dream lost its immediacy, freeing him to
relax, and Aileen responded at once, as if she had been
waiting.

The relationship changed. The companionship deepened. They shared the things good friends shared, things
kin shared, things he shared only with Keely. But he
sensed a bond between them that superseded mere kinship, much as the one with Keely. With Aileen he was
another man, freed of resentments and irritability; freed
of the insecurity of being the third-born son. Here there

was only Corin. No Brennan. No Hart. No ranking according to birth. Here there was merely *Corin*—

Corin and *Aileen*, who saw what he was and cherished it. As much as he cherished her.

Four weeks after his arrival—to celebrate, she said—Aileen took him out to ride along the headlands overlooking the Dragon's Tail. Kilore fell away from them, dropping below the horizon as they moved ever westward. The massive stone fortress gained invisibility; with it fled the last vestige of moodiness. He laughed again, unencumbered by doubts or recriminations, when Aileen told him a tale about her brother, and gloried in the banishment of the dream that had so plagued him. Free of it, he was also free of Brennan.

Until Aileen said his name and conjured him between them.

Such a simple question: "Is Brennan much like you?"

They had run their horses, tearing across the headlands, laughing into the wind and calling out challenges. Now they walked them, afoot, reins looped through their hands. Ahead of them, Kiri trotted; between them hovered Brennan.

"No," Corin said curtly.

She waited for more. When he gave her nothing, she looked at him directly. "D'ye hate him so much, then?"

He opened his mouth to refute the question at once. But nothing came out. Nothing at all; the denial died aborning. He had never thought of it as hatred; even now he felt the word incorrect. But he would lie to her no more than to himself.

"He is my brother." Purposely, he used Homanan in place of Cheysuli.

Aileen's mouth twisted. "Kinship has little to do with like and dislike, when it comes to a man's heart."

Corin sighed. The wind came up from the ocean below and curled over the rim of the cliff to buffet them both. He smelled sea and salt and fish.

"I asked for *me*." Aileen said quietly, "thinking of myself. But now I ask for Corin."

He looked at her sharply. And then at once away; he could not bear to see the compassion in her eyes.

"No," he said finally. "No, I do not hate him. I dislike him, but I dislike myself more for giving in to it."

Wind threatened to tear her hair free of its braid. Shorter strands teased her eyes. She stripped them back automatically, one hand still leading the horse. "Why?" she asked quietly.

Corin fought his own losing battle with wind and hair. "Because . . . because he is *Brennan*."

Aileen laughed. "Such a black scowl, Corin! Is he truly so bad?"

"No. He is truly so *good*." He shook his head, feeling a vague sense of guilt. Only Keely really knew how he felt, because of their birth-link, and because she shared a measure of his resentment. She and Brennan were no closer than *he* and Brennan, although she was less bothered by troublesome resentments. Corin thought it was because Keely, being a woman, knew there was no chance she might inherit the Lion; in Corin's case, he was prevented only by the order of his birth. "I should say nothing more, Aileen . . . he is your betrothed, and it does no good to color your opinions of him when you should form them fairly."

She laughed. "D'ye see? You don't dislike him as much as you think . . . if you did, you'd not be defending him to me."

He sighed again, deeply, giving up the final vestiges of decorum. This was a subject he had avoided from the beginning, unable to raise it with the woman Brennan would wed. But if Aileen wanted frankness, he would give it to her.

"Since I can remember, it was always Brennan *this*, Brennan *that* . . . Brennan, the Mujhar's son; Brennan, the Prince of Homana; *Brennan*, heir to the Lion. Part of the past and of the future: Cheysuli and Homanan." He slanted her a glance, fearful he might offend her, but saw only that she listened without judging. "All my life he has been held up as an example of what a man can and should be—what *I* could be if I tried!—and I am so weary of it. If he had earned it, I would not care so much, but it is because of his birth . . . because he was born *first*—" He broke off, stripping tawny hair out of stinging eyes. "It might have been Hart. *Hart* might have come first, and then *he* would be heir to Homana"

"Or you." She said it calmly. "Is that what you're resenting so much? That you were not born in place of Brennan?"

Corin stopped dead. The horse nearly walked over him, but he did not care. "Aye." He did not avoid her eyes. "*Aye*, Aileen, it is. I have always wanted the Lion."

She turned to face him. The wind ripped hair from her face and bared it for him to see. "But you'll be having *that*."

He followed the line of her lifted arm. Beyond her hand he saw the island across the Dragon's Tail. "Atvia," he said sourly, "is poor proxy for Homana."

Slowly she lowered her arm. "D'ye want it because you *want* it? Or because your brother will have it?"

He stared at her. He had never considered that view of his desire. He knew only that for as long as he could remember, he had wanted Brennan's place.

He looked at Kiri. *Oh, lir, is that it? Do I want what Brennan has only because he has it?"*

The fox did not answer. Corin shivered, discovering something within himself he did not like at all; acknowledging it for the very first time, and liking it no better.

If I had what Brennan has, would I be content? Or would I search for new unhappiness and ways of expressing it?

Corin looked at Atvia across the choppy gray water. Slowly he sat down, giving the horse his head, and stared out into the skies. "I want power," he said. "I want freedom. I want contentment. But—mostly I want the chance to be myself without being weighed against my *rujholli*."

Aileen released her horse and sat down beside him, deftly settling her skirts. "Not so much," she said. "You're not in the way of being a greedy man."

The island across the channel was awash in spray and sunlight, tinted with myriad colors. "Atvia is a land of strangers," he told her. "A land of old hatreds and resentments, of wars and vassalage . . . I will not be welcome there."

"No," she agreed. "But for a man who wants power, you might look on it as a challenge. You can go *in* a foreign prince, and come out a beloved king."

"Beloved." He smiled. "What king is beloved?"

"My father," she answered quietly.

Corin sighed. "And, I think, mine."

Aileen stared into the distances, seemingly lost in thought. Her voice, when she spoke, was quiet, but he heard the subtleties in her tone as loudly as if she shouted. "If Brennan is anything like you, perhaps I can be content."

"Anything like *me?*" He stared at her in shock. "Aileen—*no* . . . Brennan is *nothing* like me, and you should be grateful for it!"

"Why?" Now she looked at him. "Should I be grateful because he lacks your complexities? Because he lacks your depth of emotions? Lacks your *passion?*" Her eyes did not waver. "Should I be grateful because there is no need for him to say what is in his heart?"

"And if the heart is *black*—"

"Not black," she said quietly. "Only bruised by childhood resentments, and I'm thinking those can be easily banished."

Corin shook his head. "Brennan is more suited to the Lion. He thinks before he speaks, speaks before he acts, then acts responsibly. He understands what makes a man feel the way he does, and respects that man for his feelings. He *listens*—" Abruptly, Corin broke off. And then he began to laugh. "Oh, gods, *woman*—do you see what you have done? From telling you why I dislike my *rujholli* I am become his champion!"

"I'm thinking he needs none," Aileen told him. "And—I'm thinking too that Atvia's gain is surely Homana's loss."

Corin thought not. Corin thought something else entirely, and found he must express it. Slowly he drew in a breath. "And *I* am thinking that my loss is Brennan's gain—" He broke off a moment, then went on bitterly. "Except you cannot lose what you never had."

They stared at one another for a long moment, unable to look away, knowing only that he had said what was better left *un*said, between *them*; between the woman meant for his brother and the man who wanted her for himself, even as he had wanted so many things Brennan had. But this time, *this* time, he wanted less to win her *away* than simply to win her, period.

Slowly, she put out her hand and touched his, gently; he felt the trembling in her fingers. "For that, I am sorry."

Corin pulled his hand from hers and made a gesture: an upturned hand, palm bared, fingers spread. "*Tahlmorra lujhalla mei wiccan, cheysu,*" he said grimly, "and I can change the fate the gods have given us no more than I can change the order of my birth."

He stood before the Lion Throne and faced the man within it. Not his father; Niall was gone. In his place was Brennan.

Corin inclined his head. "My lord," he said politely, "I wish to steal your queen."

He sat up with a muffled shout. All around him was darkness and the swathing of the bed. And once again, as always, he reached out for Kiri.

Lir, oh, lir, I think I am going mad.

No, the vixen said, *you are only losing sleep.*

He was. Each night. He slept, dreamed, wakened, then repeated the cycle. He was ashamed of some of the dreams. He had thought, fleetingly, of bedding one of the serving girls, if only to banish the dreams, but the thought died nearly the instant it was born.

What he wanted was Aileen herself, not one of Aileen's women.

Corin rolled over onto his belly. *If I went to Atvia now—* But he knew he would never go. While Liam was from the palace, he had every right to wait. No one could suspect him of remaining for anything else.

Not even Aileen could.

He slept. He dreamed. He awakened.

"My lord," he said politely, "I wish to steal your queen." In his hand there was a sword—

Aileen touched his shoulder and the vision fled at once. "Where are you, Corin? I see the look in your eyes."

He blinked, knowing himself back in Kilore. No more Lion, no more Brennan. Only Brennan's betrothed.

"Nowhere," he said curtly, rising from the stool.

They had shared a meal, exchanged favorite stories of mishaps suffered by their kin, told tales on one another, recalled childhood games. Now they sat before one of the giant fireplaces within a private chamber, and he knew they tempted fate.

"Corin—"

"Will Liam never come home?"

Aileen, still seated, stared up at him as he turned to pace away. Back and forth he moved, restless and angry, swallowed by desperation. She saw it in him, and grieved.

"I can send for him," she said at last. "I didn't do it before only because you said there was no need for urgency."

"No. No need for urgency." He stopped pacing and swung back. "What I *need* I cannot have."

Clearly she understood him. She did not look away. "Who is saying you cannot have it?"

"*Brennan*—"

"Brennan is not here."

Corin watched her rise. No more than three paces separated them; he knew he dared not take them. Yet hoped *she* would, so he could live with the guilt. And knew it was unfair.

"Aileen—"

"You came unknowing," she said, "intending nothing. I received you in place of my father, offering nothing more than courtesy. And, eventually, compassion and understanding. From that grows the vine that tangles us in its thorns."

"Then I will cut us free."

Aileen's smile was bittersweet. "Will you, now? But how?"

"By telling you the message I have for Liam is that the betrothal is to end." He saw the whitening of her face. "A wedding is desired; Brennan requires an heir."

Aileen said nothing for a long moment. And then she clenched her hands in the folds of her heavy skirts. " 'Tis a sharp knife, Corin . . . sharper than the thorns."

"Brennan will bind the wound."

"And who will be binding *yours?*"

"Oh, gods—*Aileen*—"

But she took the paces and closed the space between them, closing his mouth as well with cold, slim fingers. "No," she said, "no. I'm wanting no cruelty from one another, nor *for* one another. Ah, Corin—will ye *hold* me? I've been wanting it so long—"

He held her, as she asked, thinking he might fool himself into believing he did it *only* because she asked, but he knew better. He knew. He was lost, and so was she.

And so was their innocence.

Lir, Kiri said, and someone threw open the door.

They broke, but not quickly enough. And then the dogs were begging for Aileen's attention, so many dogs, all wolfhounds, pushing them apart, and he knew Liam was home at last.

"Lass," her father said mildly, and then he looked at Corin.

Oh—gods—

Liam grinned and strode into the chamber, parting the sea of dogs. He was a big man, a strong man, with Deirdre's brass-bright hair and Aileen's green eyes; wind-chafed, weather-burned, hardened from years of warfare. He was fifty, Corin knew, but the years did not weigh him down.

"Niall's lad," the lord of Erinn said in a vast and abiding satisfaction. " 'Tis in your face and your color, though you lack the height and weight." He caught Corin in a brief, bearish hug, then set him back for perusal. Green eyes glinted; beyond him, white-faced, Aileen stared. "I see none of Gisella in you."

Corin drew in a deep breath. "My lord—"

"So, have you come to woo my lass?" Liam strode to a table and poured wine. "Or is she already won?" He grinned and raised his cup. "To Brennan and Aileen, future king and queen of Homana."

For one insane moment Corin wondered if it were possible to keep Liam in ignorance. Hart, he knew, might try it, merely to win a wager.

But this was not a wager; Aileen was worth far more.

"No," he said hollowly.

One thick blond brow rose. "No?" Liam echoed. "Will you not let me drink to your happiness?"

"You may drink to the happiness of *Brennan and Aileen*," Corin said with as much control as he could muster. "But I am not part of it."

Liam lowered the cup. "Are ye daft, lad? D'ye insult my daughter so soon after you kiss her?"

"My lord." Corin moved to face Liam squarely, no longer able to see Aileen. "My lord, you saw what you saw. But I am not Brennan."

"Not—" Liam broke off. He set down the cup with a thump; wine slopped over the rim. "Then who *are* you, ye *skilfin*, and why were you kissing my daughter?"

"I *am* Niall's son, my lord . . . he has three, if you will recall. I am the youngest of them."

Liam's levity and high spirits were banished, replaced with a frowning intensity. The sheer power in the man's gaze made Corin want to squirm. But he held his ground, unmoving.

"Corin," Liam said finally. "That much I know from Niall's letters." He flicked a glance past Corin to Aileen and his mouth tautened. "Well, lad, have you come to tell me Brennan and Hart are dead, and *you* are heir to the Lion?" His tone was harsh. "I'll accept no other explanation for why you would take the liberty of kissing Brennan's betrothed."

"Will you take this one?" Aileen spoke for the first time since Liam had entered the room. She moved forward to stand by Corin, facing her father even as he did, but with less courtesy. "Will you accept it when I say I'll be taking Corin in place of Brennan?"

Corin snapped his head around to stare at her in shock.

Liam's brows rose. "*Will* you?" he asked mildly. "D'ye think it so easy, then?"

Corin had expected more than that from him. But when he looked back at Liam, he saw the light tone did not entirely dispell the intentness of his manner. He put Corin in mind of a mountain cat feigning indolence until it was time to leap.

But who is prey? he wondered uneasily. *Aileen, or myself?*

"Not easy," Aileen said, "but right. I know it was a political thing, the betrothal . . . I have no quarrel with that. But I'm saying we need only wed me to Corin in place of Brennan."

Liam turned idly and walked around the table to the immense fireplace. He stared into the flames, putting his back to them. He wore black hunting leathers and golden spurs; blond hair was tumbled against his shoulders, combed by the wind of his ride. Around him, wolfhounds gathered.

"Corin is pledged to Atvia."

It was all Liam said, and to the flames. Corin and Aileen exchanged puzzled glances; she shrugged a little, indicating ignorance of the reason for Liam's odd manner.

"Aye, to Atvia," she said finally, when it became apparent her father intended to say no more. "But 'twould be a good alliance, my lord . . . 'twould help to forge peace between the realms."

" 'Twill be for others to do, when Alaric and I are dead." Liam turned, warming his back, and Corin saw the Lord of Erinn was not as indifferent as he sounded.

Not indifferent at all . . . he merely waits for the proper time.

"What would it alter?" Aileen asked. "Brennan and I have never met, nor even exchanged letters. He won't be

missing what he never had, nor made any *effort* to have."
She gestured. "There is Ellas, Falia, Caledon . . . let him
have one of *their* princesses instead of Erinn's only one."

Liam's eyes flicked to Corin. "D'ye want her, lad?"

He raised his head. "Aye, my lord, *I do*."

Liam looked down at his dogs. "I could write Niall,"
he said absently. "I could write him . . . could be telling
him the very things you've told me . . . perhaps it *could*
be arranged—" he looked up from his dogs, "—but then
'twould be the end of the prophecy . . . the end of the
Cheysuli."

In shock, Corin stared back at him. In despair, he saw
the truth in Liam's compassionate eyes. *He* knew, did
Liam; he understood very well. Better than Aileen, who
heard only the denial; better even than Corin, who knew
a great shame in overlooking the obvious. In nearly
betraying his blood.

"Are ye daft?" Aileen asked. "How could it be the
end of anything? And what does a prophecy have to do
with *us?*"

"Aileen." Corin wanted to touch her, but did not dare
it. "Aileen, I have told you of the prophecy . . . how it
governs Cheysuli lives."

"Aye, *aye*," she said impatiently, "you've told me all
about it. 'Tis a fine, shining thing, Corin, and worthy of
dedication, but what has it to do with *us?*"

"With *you*," he said clearly. "The first son you bear
Brennan will be another link in the chain, taking us one
step closer to fulfillment."

Aileen shrugged. "And if I bore *your* son, would it not
please the gods as well?"

Corin slowly shook his head.

"Why *not?*" she cried. " 'Tis a son they want, is it not?
Then I'll *give* them that son!"

"Aileen." Corin drew in a breath. "It comes down to
Brennan. It comes down to you. I do not figure in it."

"And why not?"

"Because—" he gestured emptily. "Because it has to
do with how the blood is mixed. Brennan is Cheysuli,

Homanan, Solindish and Atvian. You are Erinnish." He sighed. "The prophecy requires—"

"But *you* have all those bloodlines, Corin!"

"But I am not the Prince of Homana!"

They stared at one another, transfixed by pride, by anger, by anguish. And then Aileen made a gesture of defiance and determination. "Does it matter *so much* that I wed the Prince of Homana?"

"Aye," he said wearily. "It all begins with Homana . . . one day it will end with Homana."

"Aileen." It was Liam, very quiet. "Aileen, has he taught you nothing of the Cheysuli? D'ye see nothing of his pride, his honor, the strength of will that rules his life?" He looked older now, and saddened by what he said. "Niall spent a twelve-month here, and in that time I learned a little of the Cheysuli—enough to respect them *and* their determination."

"D'ye not respect *me?*" she asked. "D'ye not think me capable of judging a man? Why *else* d'ye think I want him?"

"Then ask him," Liam said gently. "Look at him and ask him."

After a moment, Aileen turned to Corin. "D'ye say you're not wanting me?"

She would never be beautiful, but he was blinded by her pride; by the brilliance of her spirit. "You showed me what it was to look out of myself to others," he told her gently. "You showed me how to be myself, not judging myself against others, or what others wanted *of* me. You taught me to be free in spirit if not in body, bowing to necessity, and to accept the latter with grace." He smiled a little. "Lastly, you taught me to love my brother, and for that I am very grateful. *Leijhana tu'sai, meijhana* . . . but I cannot steal his queen."

Aileen's face was a white blotch against red hair. Her eyes swam with tears. But she said nothing, nothing at all; she merely turned and walked from the room.

After a moment, Liam put a large hand on Corin's shoulder and gripped it briefly, then released him. "Until this moment I never regretted what Niall and I did,

promising sons and daughters to one another. 'Tis the
way of royal houses; the requirements of rank." He
picked up Corin's forgotten cup of wine and put it into
his hands. "But it seems we dealt too lightly with unborn
souls."

Corin stared into the lukewarm wine. "I came here to
tell you my *jehan* desires the wedding to go forth." He
looked at Liam. "Aileen is to make ready for the voyage."

There was pain in Liam's green eyes, and more than a
share of regret. Slowly he reached out and took the cup
away. "Go to her, lad. She's a spirited lass, saying what
she thinks, and likely she'll have harsh words for you . . .
but *go*. I'll not be making the mistake my father did
when Niall was sent from Deirdre. Go to Aileen and say
your good-byes. It won't be enough, but at least 'tis
something."

All Corin could do was nod. And then he left the
chamber.

At last he found her on the battlements of the fortress.
If she cried he could not tell; the wind scrubbed her face
clean of everything save the starkness she turned on him.

Her fingers clutched the brick. The line of her spine
was rigid. "Go, Corin. I'm wanting to be alone."

"That is a lie," he told her plainly. "What you want is
for me to say I was wrong . . . to say I'll take you
regardless of consequences . . . to say I want you badly
enough to steal my *rujholli's* betrothed."

The mobile mouth was tightly drawn. "But you won't.
You *don't*."

He stood next to her, turning to stare out at the sea
that pounded Erinn's shores. "I want you," he said simply, knowing no other way, no *better* way, to put it. "If it
is not enough that I say it without qualifications, then I
am sorry for you. But I know you better, Aileen . . . I
know you better than anyone save Keely, if in an entirely
different sense."

"Do you?" They were close enough to touch, but
neither moved to do it.

"Aye." The wind carried most of it away. "I know that

if I turned my back on my kin, my race, my *tahlmorra,*
eventually you would hate me. Perhaps even tomorrow."
He turned to her, scraping leather knife sheath against
the wind-scoured stone. "There are women in the world
who would be pleased to have such sacrifice made in
their names, but you are not one of them."

Her hair was a banner in the wind, whipping back
from her face. "No," she said, "I am not . . . but I
almost wish I could be."

A laugh rose from deep inside of Corin, a single gust
of sound. "If you were," he told her, "if you were, I
could never love you the way I do."

Aileen swore bitterly and banged the wall with her fist.
"Why is it," she cried, "why *is* it I meddle where I
should not? Why is it I took it into my head to ease a
man's pain, to show him what it is to know contentment
within oneself?" Slowly she shook her head. "If I'd left
you alone, never trying to understand you, never trying
to ease that pain, we'd not be in this coil!"

"Why is it you took it into your head to show me that
underneath all my childish resentment, I really care for
Brennan?" Corin sighed and rubbed aching eyes with
rigid fingers. "Well, we have fashioned me into someone
I can live with, and now I must live without you."

"Brennan," she said bitterly. "Each time I look on
him, I will think of you. Even in *bed*—"

It was a vision he had purposely pushed aside, and
now she brought it back in all its intensity. He could not
bear it. "Aileen, *stop.*" He caught her wrists. "Stop. You
punish *me* as well as yourself."

All the anguish was in her face, but so was her pride.
"And when I call him by your name?"

Corin shook his head. "Aileen, I swear, when you
meet Brennan you will understand. You will never mistake him for me. We are so different, so very different
. . . temperament, coloring, preferences . . . so many
other things." He swallowed tightly. "I promise you,
Aileen, it will not be an empty marriage."

She jerked her wrists away. "I might prefer it that
way."

All the pain rose up. "Do you think I want that?" he cried. "Do you think I want to spend my life knowing you hate every moment with my *rujholli*, when there is nothing for me to do? *No,* Aileen. I would sooner believe you content enough than living your life in sorrow, lost in some futile hope that someday I might come. It would twist *you,* twist *me* . . . it would destroy any hope of happiness for either one of us."

"So," she said, "you tell me to go to Homana and wed your brother . . . to be his wife and bear his children . . . to be everything to him that I want to be to you."

"Aye," he said harshly. "That is what I tell you."

She drew in a deep, unsteady breath. "You are a hard man," she said, "and I wish I could soften you. But in doing it, I would destroy the thing I love."

"Aileen—"

She thrust up a silencing hand. "No more," she said. "No more from you, I say. And now I must go . . . 'tis time I began to pack."

He watched her go. And when she was gone, when he stood alone on the battlements, he slid slowly down the stone to sit with legs drawn up, staring blindly at his knees.

Later, Liam came to him in his chambers. "Come out with me, lad. Now."

"*Out* with you—?"

But Liam did not answer. He motioned Corin to follow him out of the chamber and immediately left it, dogs trailing in his wake, and after a moment Corin went as well.

They left Kilore entirely, riding across the headlands with an escort of giant dogs, and also Kiri, a blotch of rust and black against emerald turf. Liam said nothing at all of his intentions, nor what he expected of Corin; he merely rode, wrapping himself in silence, and Corin rode with him.

At last Liam halted. Before them was a grassy tor, swelling out of the turf, and Corin saw a crude stone altar on its crest. He thought they might dismount and go

up to it, but Liam remained in the saddle. In his eyes was
the opacity of memories recalled.

" 'Tis of the *cileann*, this place," he said finally. "The
oldfolk of Erinn, born of ages past. The tor is sacred,
blessed with ancient magic . . . can ye not feel it, lad?"

"Aye, my lord. I do."

Liam looked at the tor. " 'Twas where I took Niall
when he went out of Erinn to Atvia . . . leaving my sister
behind."

Pain rose; he would leave Liam's *daughter* behind.
Thinking: *You forget, my lord. Niall left her, but Deirdre
came to him later. I cannot hope for the same.*

"I was angry, lad . . . angry with Niall, with Deirdre—
angry with myself." Liam grimaced. "I thought it a waste,
that a man such as your father had to bow to the dictates
of his *fate* and trade Deirdre for Gisella. I saw what was
between them as clearly as I see the thing between you
and Aileen. And I cursed it, and them, and myself,
because I knew I would have to end it." He fell silent a
moment, and the wind teased his hair. "Lad, 'twas no
easier for me then than it is now. And I understand it no
better. But I know it must be done. Niall taught me that
much, and you have reminded me."

The horse stomped under Corin, who soothed it absently. "I am nothing like my *jehan*. I wish I might be,
that I could offer her better; or that I was firstborn, so I
would be more like Brennan—" He broke off. "But even
then, I could offer her nothing."

"And you're a blind man, lad." Liam turned his horse.
"Come, then. One day you will be king in Alaric's place;
we must speak now of trade and treaties, while we have
the time."

Silently Corin followed, while the wind blew down the
tor.

Five

She was, he thought, the most beautiful woman he had ever seen. The power of her allure touched him as it touched all men, nearly engulfing his wits. But he knew better. He knew *her*: Lillith of the Ihlini, sister to Strahan himself.

Corin drew in a steadying breath as he dismounted in front of the palace steps. A boy took his horse. Alone, afoot, afraid, he faced the sorceress.

She stood at the very top of the steps. She watched him. And she smiled. "You are well come to Rondule."

"Am I?" He made himself mount the first step.

"But of course. Are you not the Crown Prince of Atvia?"

A second step. "That is for Alaric to say."

"But of course." Still Lillith smiled. "If Alaric *can.*"

Corin paused, then forced himself to climb. "An odd thing to say."

"Not when you have seen him." She wore blue, deep, rich blue, girdled with silver and pearls. Large, irregular pearls, some creamy, some gray, some black, with a tinge of silver-blue. More threaded the weave of her braid.

Closer, ever closer, until he could see the silver tips of her nails; the kohl-smudged lids. The eerie youthfulness of features and form.

This woman seduced my su'fali.

Corin looked at her as he climbed. He began to understand how. *Lirless,* Ian had stood no chance. Her power was manifest.

Lillith smiled. "I see you have brought your *lir.*"

Someone, some*thing,* touched an icy fingertip to his spine. He did not like the way Lillith looked at Kiri. To change the subject, he said, "My *jehan* sent word I was coming."

"No," Lillith said. "I already knew."

He stopped short. He was but three steps below her. She was young, he saw, genuinely *young.* Not older. Not age, masquerading as youth. He had only to compare her to Aileen to know that the sorcery was powerful indeed. It did more than lend her the *illusion* of youth and beauty, it gave her both in full measure. The Seker was an unstinting god.

Oddly, he recalled Boyne's story. The tale of a sorcerer become god. The memory made him shiver.

Lillith smiled. Calmly she stood at the top of the steps, giving nothing away of her power, but showing it all the same. "There is no doubt who sired you."

He had heard it before. He and Keely had both inherited Niall's coloring—blue eyes, tawny hair, fair skin— and a resemblance in facial structure, but neither claimed his frame. Keely was tall for a woman, but nothing more; he himself was considered short for his Cheysuli heritage, being less than six feet. Brennan and Hart both topped him by a handspan.

"And no doubt who sired *you.*"

Lillith laughed. "And did you know Tynstar well?"

"Only by reputation."

"With *him,* that is all that is needed."

Her tone was a trifle cooler, her black eyes more assessive; Corin disliked intensely the sensation of being judged. It was bad enough when his father did it; worse when done by an Ihlini. "Lillith—"

"Come in," she said abruptly. "There are matters to discuss, and better places to discuss them."

He wanted to refuse her, to leave her and go somewhere she could not touch him, even with her eyes. But an innate sense of self-preservation and a desire to play

the game very carefully kept him from blurting it out.
This was Atvia, not Homana. Lillith had been Alaric's
light woman for a very long time, and was Ihlini to boot;
her influence would be well established by now. Until he
knew better how things stood, it was not his place to
quibble.

At least until reason is plainly given. He followed
Lillith in silence.

She took him to a private chamber within the heart of
the palace. The servants they passed bowed quickly to
Lillith, but watched him with curious eyes. He wondered
how Lillith had known he was coming; he wondered if
she had not, and simply said she had. Mostly, he wondered how he would manage to last the year.

"Here." Lillith indicated a carved, high-backed chair.
The room was shadowed, lacking windows, illuminated
only by candleracks. Most were unlit, like the fireplace.
It dulled the colors of the tapestries and robbed the room
of welcome.

He sat down. Kiri took her place by his feet, sitting
rigidly in front of his legs. She watched the woman intently as Lillith poured wine.

Corin shook his head as the cup was offered. Lillith
did not withdraw it. "A fool will often go thirsty."

"But at least the fool will live."

Briefly she looked at Kiri. She smiled. "You *are* a
fool, Corin. Why should I stoop to poison when I have
other means? And why, for that matter, should I desire
to take your life? You are more useful to me alive."

"Useful?" Lillith still held out the cup; he stared at her
over the rim.

She did not answer at once. Instead, she gazed thoughtfully at the cup she held, as if troubled by his refusal. She
lifted it to her own lips, sipped distinctly so he could see
she did indeed drink the wine. And then, idly—as if it
were no more than an afterthought—she tipped the cup
over and poured out the wine.

Corin jerked back into the depths of the chair, trying
to avoid the torrent. Even Kiri dodged aside. But there

was no need. In midair, as the wine spilled out of the cup, it turned into coils of lavender smoke.

"One need not concern oneself with unwanted residue," Lillith said obscurely, and threw the cup to Corin.

He caught it, as she meant him to, and then cursed himself for following her lead. He leaned over the side of the chair to put the cup down on the floor; as he did, stretching out his arm, the cup began to change.

Aghast, he jerked his hand away. But the cup followed. In his hand the silver melted, reformed, braceleted his flesh. Cursing, he tried to fling the silver away, but it had formed a rigid cuff around his wrist. A seamless, shining shackle.

"I will be very plain," Lillith said quietly. "If I wanted you, I would take you. There is nothing you could do."

His hand trembled, then spasmed. "Take it *off*—"

Lillith shook her head. "For now, I will leave it. It will be a reminder, so you do not forget who holds the power here." She turned from him and moved to the nearest chair, spreading blue skirts as she settled into black cushions. She did not seem to notice that he was transfixed by the silver cuff, unable to look at her. "I want you to understand very clearly how things are in Atvia."

"Lady, I *do*." He fisted his hand and thrust it into the air, displaying the shining shackle.

"Good." Lillith smiled. "I have no intention of robbing you of your birthright."

He frowned before he could hide it.

"No," she said, "why should I? You are Alaric's grandson, kin to Osric and Thorne and Keough, and all the lords before them. I would be a fool if I stripped Atvia of her rightful blood."

"Then why are you *here*?"

"Because it pleases me to be here." Lillith's tone was bland.

"As it pleased you to seduce a *lirless* Cheysuli?"

Black eyes glinted. "Does Ian dream of me?"

"No more than I will, Ihlini." He tried to ignore the silver on his wrist. But it was cold, so *cold*. "What is your purpose? Why do you stay with Alaric? If you speak the truth about my inheritance, you must know I will not want you here."

"By the time you inherit this realm, there will be no *need* for me here."

"Lillith—"

"We must speak of the future, Corin," she said quietly, overriding him easily. "Alaric is an old man. His wits fail. Atvia suffers from the lack of a strong hand at the helm. If something is not done, Atvia will fall to those who wish to conquer her and take her for their own."

He frowned. "Who would benefit from conquering Atvia? The realm owes fealty to Homana."

"Liam would take the island in a moment if he knew of Alaric's weakness. It has nothing to do with Homana; Atvia and Erinn have battled for years."

That he knew well enough. But he shook his head. "No, I think Liam—"

"*No,*" she said plainly, "you do *not* think. You know nothing of Liam at all, having met him only yesterday."

"My *jehan*—"

"Your father has not seen Liam in twenty-two years," Lillith said flatly. "And even then, he knew him as Prince of Erinn, not the lord himself. Power changes men. Power will change you." She spoke coolly, without excess emotion, expressing things the way his father might. He found he did not like it; Lillith was enemy. "I will not waste my time trying to convince you Liam means Atvia harm," she continued. "You would never believe me. But I will say this: unless a strong man assumes the throne, Atvia will fall. If not to Liam, to someone else." She paused, and her tone was subdued. "There are other realms in the world besides those we know."

It was an odd statement. To Corin, the world was made up of a handful of realms: Homana, Solinde, Erinn, Atvia, Ellas, Falia, Caledon, and the Steppes. In childhood, he had learned a little of them all. There had been no others named.

"And you want *me* to assume the throne. Now. Ahead of time."

Lillith's shrug was eloquent. "Alaric's time grows short."

"Then why precipitate it?"

"For the reasons I have given."

"No," he said flatly, "there must be something more." He grasped the ensorcelled silver with his left hand, sensing a disorienting ambience in addition to the icy touch, and tried to twist it off. But the silver was solid, inflexible, hugging his wrist as firmly as the *lir*-bands hugged his arms.

"It would serve you," she said. "Take the throne now, establish your claim . . . make certain Atvia understands *you* are the lord. Give the people no chance to be swayed by foreigners."

Foreigners. Again she spoke of external threats. And yet, to his knowledge, there *were* no foreigners; the world was made of eight realms, those he had already named. Four of them were part of the prophecy.

But this was Lillith. "You are lying," he said curtly. "You are Ihlini, and you are lying, and I want no part of your plots."

"But Atvia is your responsibility, Corin."

She was so cool, so calm, so *certain* of her influence. "Not yet," he answered firmly. "Alaric is lord until the day he dies, and I go home in seven months."

"Alaric will be dead within seven *weeks*," Lillith said gently. "Unless, of course, I should prefer it be seven days—or perhaps seven *hours*."

Corin swore, pushing himself from the chair. The silver was heavy on his wrist, heavy and cold, unneeded ballast for his spirit. "So help me, Ihlini, I will have you sent from Atvia *now*—"

Lillith also rose. They faced each other across a space no wider than five paces, knowing centuries of contention.

Corin frowned as he stared at her. He badly wanted to ask Kiri's advice, but their link was blocked by Lillith's nearness. "What do you want?" he asked. "What is it you want, Ihlini? My cooperation?—you know I will never give it. My departure?—on Alaric's death the realm is mine, regardless of where I am. But you stand here and tell me to reach out my hand and take the throne;

you hint you will put Alaric out of my way. Collusion? No. I will never condone his death. And yet I wonder . . . I wonder *if* I refuse it, *if* I go, does it serve some unknown Ihlini purpose? Do you tell me to stay, to take the throne, only because you know the asking will make me go?"

Lillith laughed. "Have I confused you, Corin? Do I show you the two-sided mirror?"

"You show me the perversity of your race," he retorted. "Do you think I will listen to you?"

"If I choose to speak, you will." Lillith gestured and the door flew open to slam against the wall. "Simple tricks," she told him derisively. "The old gods saw to it the Ihlini could not level most sorceries against their brother race, but some small powers remain."

"And Asar-Suti?" he asked. "Does he promise godhood in exchange for servitude?"

For a moment, a moment only, Lillith's color changed. And then she smiled, smoothing her skirts, and gestured for him to go. "A servant will show you to your chambers."

There was little for the servant to do with Corin's shoulderpacks other than remove the contents and put them away in trunks and casks. Corin, watching in silence, realized there was little about him that denoted his rank. He had come away from Mujhara with few belongings; under the circumstances, he had not wanted to ride with a baggage train. Now he was dependent upon Alaric for such things as extra clothing, and he did not like it.

Had I thought about it, I might have planned more carefully, he told Kiri, and then flinched away from the interference in the link. Lillith's presence was everywhere in the castle, imbuing even the walls with the stink of sorcery. Outside, at greater distance, he had no doubt the link would be re-established, but within the walls of the castle he was cut off from his *lir* in everything save physical contact.

The servant bowed himself out. Corin, hardly noticing, went instantly to Kiri. He sat down on the bear pelt by the bed and gathered the vixen into his arms. She was warm, alive, affectionate, but he badly missed their interior dialogue, the link that gave him the ability to change his shape. He felt stripped of half his identity. "Gods, Kiri . . . I am so *alone*."

As he bent down, she pressed her muzzle against his neck. He felt cold nose, warm breath; smelled her familiar musky scent. Bright amber eyes seemed to tell him all was well, but it served only to make him even more restless and ill at ease. Suddenly Kiri seemed no more than a tame fox, little more than a pet. It made him angry, resentful, uneasy; it robbed him of his sense of *self*, so important to the Cheysuli.

Is this what it was like for my jehan? Lirless all those years, despairing of ever knowing the magic of our race . . . Corin shivered once. *Gods, I could not bear it . . . this is bad enough, and I know it is temporary.*

Against her fur the silver wristlet gleamed. He felt his fingers curl, tighten, *fist,* until he wanted to smash it into the nearest wall. It did not matter that he would shatter delicate bones; he wanted only to rid himself of the shackle Lillith had put on him.

"No chain," he said aloud. "No *chain*, but this is more than enough."

He turned his hand over, baring the underside of his arm. The silver was seamless, displaying no joints; a solid ring of metal. Corin pulled his knife, slid the tip of the blade beneath the cuff and tentatively pried. The shackle was very snug, leaving no room for the blade. Steel scraped on silver; a subtle stinging told him he sliced hair instead of metal.

The door swung open.

Corin, seated on the floor with Kiri in his lap and the knife in his hand, prepared to send the servant away. But when he looked up, scowling, he saw plainly the woman was not a servant at all.

Cheysuli was the first word that came to his mind. And then another: *jehana.*

Corin said it aloud. And then, awkwardly, he sheathed the knife and rose, turning Kiri out of his lap.

He had, he thought, prepared himself for the meeting.

On the voyage from Hondarth he had, every night in his bunk, carefully considered what he would say and do when he saw Gisella. But now, seeing her, he could do nothing at all.

"Which one are you?" she asked. "Which son does he send?"

For a moment his tongue was locked in silence. Having heard of Gisella's madness from his father, his uncle and others, he had reconciled himself to incoherence, wandering wits, perhaps even tantrums. But not such clarity. Never such conciseness.

"Corin," he said hoarsely. "Third-born of his children."

"Mine, too," Gisella said. "*Mine, too, Corin.*"

He drew in an unsteady breath. He was accustomed to his father's disfigured face, even beneath the patch; to the wear derived from worry and the experiences of his past. And somehow Corin had unknowingly transferred much of it to Gisella, expecting to see identical signs in her flesh. But there were none.

At thirty-nine she did not share the same uncanny youthfulness as Lillith, but she was not what Corin expected. She was, plainly, Cheysuli; the Atvian was unseen. Black hair was pulled back from her face, displaying the widow's peak that lent her features an odd elegance. There was no hint of silver, no trace of age in her coiled braids. Her flesh was taut and dark, unlined except for a delicate tracery at the edges of yellow eyes. Most striking of all, having borne two sets of twins, she retained the slenderness inherent in Cheysuli women. And she certainly claimed the posture.

Corin and Keely were Niall; now he saw Brennan and Hart.

"*Jehana*," he said again, and wished that he had not.

"*Jehana*," she mimicked, shutting the door behind her. "Aye, I am your *jehana*. Gisella of Atvia; Gisella, *Queen of Homana*."

"Aye," he said carefully, wary of her mood.

"I have ordered the packing begun."

He blinked. "Packing?" He felt a fool, cursing himself for his inability to say more than a single word.

Gisella smiled. "It is time I was a wife to my husband again."

"Wife—" He stopped himself, drew in a deep breath, tried to keep his tone uninflected. "There is no place for you in Homana."

"Then I will make one." Yellow eyes glittered a moment; he was reminded of Brennan and Ian. Of a predator stalking its prey. Gisella, watching him, laughed. "They told you I was mad."

Corin was foundering quickly. "Aye," he said plainly at last, giving up on diplomacy.

"Do *you* think I am mad?"

She waited expectantly, clearly unoffended by the possibility he might say he believed she was. He wondered what *he* would say if it were given out that *he* was mad. "All I know," he said slowly, "is that you tried to give all of us to Strahan."

"Is that proof of *madness?*" Gisella asked. "It was not what Niall wanted, nor any of the Cheysuli, but it hardly makes me mad. It makes me an *enemy.*"

"Are you?" He stared at her. "*Are* you an enemy?"

"Would I give you to Strahan now?" She laughed. "Oh, no, *no.* That time is passed. I would rather keep you."

That pleased Corin no better; he pictured himself a lapdog on her leash. *Or a dogfox in a cage.* He looked at Kiri uneasily, wishing they could converse.

Gisella moved into the room almost idly, playing with the girdle that clasped slender hips and spilled down the front of her skirts. She wore red, deep, rich red, and rubies set in silver. "That time is passed," she repeated. "The time now is for me to stand at Niall's side . . . to share my husband's bed." She turned abruptly, catching him off-guard. "To send that whore from my place."

Anger rose instantly. "Deirdre is my *jehana.* You will not call her a whore."

He had never, to anyone, claimed Deirdre was his mother. From childhood it had been made plain that Deirdre was mother in blood only to Maeve; that she was not *cheysula*, but *meijha*; not queen, but beloved of the

Mujhar. The lines of descent were too important for dissembling or convenience, even among the Cheysuli; all of Niall's children knew Gisella was their mother. But he would not claim her now.

"*Meijha*," Gisella said sweetly. "*Meijha*, then, if you like. It changes nothing. *I* am Queen of Homana. *I* am Niall's wife. I am mother to his children, and I intend to assume my place."

"He will never have you." He was adamant in his certainty.

"Homanan law will *make* him." Gisella's eyes were on Kiri. "I will go before the Homanan Council and I will plead my case." Her voice was quiet and even. "I am the forgotten wife, the forgotten *Queen*, conveniently pushed aside in the name of Niall's lust. I bore him four healthy children—three of which are *sons*—and I have borne exile meekly, with no thought to disagree." Her eyes were eerily feral. "But now I weary of such treatment. I desire better. I desire the place to which I am entitled, the privileges of my rank, the respect and honor of my husband." Her lids half-shuttered her eyes, but he saw the yellow glint. "I desire to know the love of all my children."

"Get out." He was shaking. "Get out of my room. Go. I want nothing to do with you—"

"But you do." Gisella stood before him. "You do, Corin. You want to love me. You want to have me love you in return. You want a mother, a *jehana*. You want a *cheysula* for your *jehan*. You want things to be right in your world, so you can feel good again. You want to know that all those years were not wasted; that indeed, your mother loves you. And *would* have loved you better, had your father allowed it. Had he not sent me away for the sake of an Erinnish princess."

"*You would have given me to Strahan—*"

"What other choice did I have?" Her shout stopped him cold. "What choice, Corin? Lillith raised me. Lillith shaped me. Lillith *told* me to."

"Lillith is Ihlini," he said tightly. "What did you expect?"

"I expected—and received—*love*," Gisella told him.

"It was what she gave me. It was what my father gave me. In the name of that love, I did what I was told."

"To *Strahan*—"

Gisella looked away. "I was confused," she said softly. "Confused, afraid—so *afraid*." She crumpled the silver girdle so that the links bit into her flesh. "I did what I was told."

Corin stared at her for a long, stricken moment. And then he backed away. Hugging himself, he backed away. Knowing himself as confused.

And perhaps equally afraid.

"Go." He stared at the floor. "Just—go."

She went. He heard the chime of silver links, the rattle of clashing rubies, the swish of heavy skirts. He heard the door thud closed. And then he was alone.

Alone with the wondering.

Six

Alaric of Atvia was indeed an old man, though Corin could not venture how old. A few years more than sixty, he knew, and yet he seemed much older. His hair was white. His frame was wracked with palsy. When Corin compared him to Liam, but fourteen years Alaric's junior, the contrast was astonishing.

And somehow *frightening*.

He had been called to attend his grandsire in one of the massive halls. He had gone immediately, in deference to the courtesy Deirdre and Niall had taught him, but he did not like it. And now, facing the man, he liked it even less.

The old man, the old *king*, was a pile of bones in an oversized chair. Rich cloth adorned the bones, but it did not hide the fragility of his flesh or the brittleness of his spirit. The loss of many teeth altered the line of mouth and jaw. The flesh over the nose had thinned so that it was little more than a blade-thin beak jutting out of a hollowed face. His brown eyes were rheumy, nearly swallowed by drooping lids, and he stank of insidious decay.

One hand stabbed out peremptorily, indicating a place before the throne. *"Here!"*

Uneasily, Corin approached. Even with Kiri warding one leg, he wanted to take his leave.

"Here!"

Corin stopped before the throne. The hand with its rigid finger was little more than thinning hide stretched over bone. He could see dark, mottled blemishes and knotted sinews beneath the flesh.

"Here." The hand was lowered at last.

Corin waited. He could think of nothing to say, of nothing to *do*, other than to force himself not to stare. And so he looked at Alaric's feet, wishing himself anywhere but where he was.

"Gisella says you are my grandson."

"Aye."

"*Look* at me, boy! Tell me what you see!"

Startled by the thready shout, Corin looked at the man. "My lord?"

" 'My lord,' " Alaric mimicked. " '*My lord*' indeed! *Tell me what you see!*"

Corin's short-lived courtesy vanished; he did not like this man. "I see death," he snapped. "Death, decay. disillusionment, and the destruction of a man."

"Tell me what you *see!*"

"An *old man!*" Corin cried. "The man who killed his *cheysula* . . . the man who destroyed his daughter . . . the man who lay with an Ihlini witch in exchange for petty power!"

"*What* power?" Alaric demanded. "What power do I hold? Atvia? No. Sorcery? No. The control of my wits and body?—*no!* Lillith has stolen them all."

Corin frowned. This was not what he had expected. Alaric had always worked *with* Lillith, trying to shape the downfall of Homana. "You reap what you sow," he said shortly.

Alaric laughed, although the sound was unlike any Corin had ever heard. And the tears ran out of his eyes. "The seed of my destruction was sown so many years ago," he said. "More than forty, when Lillith first came to Atvia."

"You should have sent her away."

"At the time, she served a purpose." Alaric's fallen mouth moved into a travesty of a smile. "I gave her freedom. I gave her power. I gave her everything she wanted, and willingly. There was no coercion. She used no sorcery on me. We worked toward similar goals." He bent forward, coughed; spittle flew out of his mouth. "I even gave her my daughter."

"And now she wants your throne." Corin tried to keep the distaste from his expression.

"Lillith *has* the throne in everything but name." The old man thrust himself more deeply into the huge chair, thin hands gripping armrests. "She is done ruling through me. Now she wants *you.*"

Cold radiated outward from the silver on his wrist and encompassed his entire body. "No," Corin said. "Do you think I would give in to her? I am not as you."

"But I am *in* you." Alaric smiled again. "Will you tell me there is no ambition in you? No desire for power? No need to rule other men?"

"Grandsire—"

"Will you tell me you do not want it?" Alaric's acid tone, though diluted by age, retained enough of its arrogance and spite to stop Corin's protest dead. "Will you stand there, blood of my blood, and tell *me* you do not dream of holding the Lion Throne?"

Appalled, Corin stared.

"Aye," Alaric said. "*Aye* . . . I know what you feel. Because *I* felt it . . . *I* desired it . . . I even dreamed of it. We know better, you and I. There is more to this world, much more, than petty island kingdoms. There are places such as Homana."

"You are disgusting," Corin said. "A disgusting old man awash in the stink of his death. Atvia will be mine on your death because I am your grandson, not because I *need* it—"

"But you do. You *do.*" With great effort Alaric grasped the armrests and pulled himself out of the chair. He was stooped, twisted, wracked. But the flame of his hatred blazed. "She drains me . . . *drains* me to feed Gisella . . . to replace her addled wits. Once it is done, I am dead. And then she will turn to you."

"Grandsire—"

"She means to send Gisella to Homana," Alaric said steadily, "where they will see that she is *not* mad, not mad at all, merely the victim of Niall's lust for Deirdre of

Erinn. And because there are Homanan laws governing
the rights of husbands and wives, the lives of kings and
queens, they will make him take her back . . . they will
make her Queen again, not knowing what she is." Tears
ran down his face. "My beautiful, addled daughter. . . ."

"Grandsire." This time, Corin overrode Alaric. "Do I
understand you? Lillith is using *you* to restore Gisella's
wits?"

Alaric tapped his head. "It grows emptier by the day—"

Lillith laughed. "So it does, old man. I think your time
grows short."

Corin spun even as Alaric sagged and fell back into the
chair. Lillith stood in the open doorway, one hand on the
door, and then she swung it shut.

Kiri's upper lip lifted. Hackles rose. Corin could not
touch her through the link, but there was no need; what
both of them felt was obvious, requiring no conversation.

"Old man," she said, "are you unhappy with your lot?"

Alaric mumbled something.

"Old man," she said, "you knew it would come to
this."

The old man stirred uneasily in his chair. Between
them the tension was palpable; Corin wanted to back
away, to leave the hall entirely, wanting no part of this.

"Old man," she said, "it was what you wanted. To see
your daughter made whole."

"Gisella," Alaric whispered, and the tears ran down
his face.

Lillith looked at Corin. "He asked it," she said. "He
begged it of me: to make his daughter whole. To restore
her wits so he could see the woman she might have been,
had he not destroyed her mother."

"I know the story," Corin said hoarsely. "Alaric shot
her out of the sky. Bronwyn was in *lir*-shape, a raven,
and he shot her out of the sky."

"Not knowing it was her," Lillith said quietly. Her
hands were folded in dark green skirts, hiding the silver-
tipped nails. "Not knowing the fall would steal the wits
from his unborn daughter, whose birth was so rudely

precipitated." Her eyes were on Alaric, huddled form-
lessness in the throne. "He begged it of me, Corin: to
make his daughter whole."

Corin swallowed back the bile that tickled his throat.
"For how long?" he asked. "How long will it last?"

Lillith shrugged. "Once Alaric dies, the wits die. The
power is not unlimited. Gisella will become what she has
been from the moment of her birth."

"Mad," Corin said.

"We are all a little mad." Lillith approached the throne.
She put her hands on Alaric's head. "Oh, my lord, I
promise the pain will end. In a day, two, three, you will
not know its name anymore. You will only know senselessness."

"*Knowing* she will go mad, you send her to Homana."

Lillith barely glanced at Corin. "It will be sweet to
trouble Niall."

Beneath her hand, Alaric stirred. And Corin, looking
into the face of approaching madness, found he could no
longer. He turned and walked rapidly from the hall with
Kiri close beside him.

Lillith's laughter followed him. "Welcome to Rondule."

With Kiri, he left the castle. He ignored the servants
who asked how they could serve him; ignored the soldiers stationed at the gates who offered to fetch him a
horse. He ignored them all, too intent on escaping the
castle, and said nothing at all to them. He went out of
gates, out of the walls, out of Rondule entirely, climbing
to the headlands. To the top of the dragon's skull.

He shut his eyes and reached for the earth magic with
all of his strength. And as it came tumbling forth, surging
up to fill his bones with power, he summoned his other
self.

Now— His eyes snapped open.

It hurt. It *hurt*. Perhaps it was Lillith's proximity that
twisted the power, perhaps it was something else. But
the shapechange was slow and sluggish, wracking his
bones with pain.

He gasped. He fell, kneeling on the turf, and tried to

thwart the pain. But it came at him in waves, as if intending to keep the earth magic from reaching him.

Kiri—Kiri—Kiri—

He gagged, then retched, as his belly twisted. He felt the shapechange start, then stop, then waver, then withdraw, only to try again. What he was he could not say, knowing only that if it continued he would no longer be Corin at all, but someone else. Some*thing* else; beast instead of man. Or something even worse.

He cried out, hearing the echoes of an eerie yapping howl. Sweat blinded him, distorting his vision. Kneeling on the turf with arms outstretched, fingers clawing at the dirt, he saw the silver on his wrist. Lillith's seamless shackle.

Muscles knotted. Cramped. Spasmed. Altered shape, then altered again.

This time, Corin screamed.

Kiri.
Here.
Kiri.
Here. Her nose pressed against his neck.
Lir—
I am here.

He was stiff. He ached. Flesh, muscle, bone, all ached with unremitting pain. Not blinding, screaming pain, but the deep-seated ache of a body abused within and without. Corin felt as though someone had stretched all his muscles out of shape, binding them tightly around the bones of an ancient man, to form a new one entirely.

Or was he a new *thing?*

He stirred. *"Lir—"*

Here, she said. *Here.*

He opened his eyes. The world was the world again, though he could not speak for himself. He lay curled on his side, arms and legs tucked up, and stared in shock at the woman.

Girl, more like. She sat not so very far away, clad in gray wool skirt and blouse, leather tabard, boots. And she bared a knife in her hand.

Corin blinked. She did not vanish into the air. She remained seated and silent, watching him warily.

He tried to move and found it incredibly painful. Gritting his teeth, he forced arms and legs to straighten. It drew a hiss of discomfort from him. The girl, he saw, frowned. The knife glinted in her hand.

He swallowed. His throat was dry. Even his teeth hurt. He tongued them, relieved to find human instead of vulpine. He *felt* fully human. But he knew he could not be sure.

"Am I a man?" he asked, and heard the croak that issued forth. It stirred him into a movement his body was yet unready for; he fell back, gasping, and wished he had not tried. "Am I a man?" he repeated; this time the words made sense.

"With two arms, two legs, a head," the girl agreed. "Did you think you might not be?"

He sighed. "Aye . . . aye, there was a chance." Slowly he sat up, locking his jaw against the stiffness, and felt a little of it fading. Perhaps once he was up and moving, things would return to normal. He looked at nails, fingers, hands. Then he touched his face.

"Man," she told him firmly. "What else might you be?"

Corin touched Kiri, who sat so close beside him. "Fox," he told her. "Like this one, though dog instead of vixen."

Her eyes narrowed. She was brown-haired, brown-eyed. Not pretty, not plain, though her features had a familiar cast as well as an uncanny, arresting power. Oddly, she reminded him of Aileen. "Are you Cheysuli, then?"

He nodded. "Aye. Kiri is my *lir*."

After a moment of consideration, she slid the knife home in the sheath attached to her belt. "I heard you shouting," she said. "I heard you *screaming*. So I came to see what caused it, and found you there, on the ground, all bound up like a newborn babe." One hand splayed briefly across her abdomen; the gesture was eloquent, divulging much to Corin. "But when I found you,

I saw nothing that caused such pain. Nothing except the fox, and *she* wanted only to protect you."

Corin rolled shoulders, head; flexed hands. Everything responded, though a residual ache remained. "I tried to assume *lir*-shape," he said. "Something prevented me. Something twisted the magic." He looked more closely at her, seeing a look in her eye that hinted at wariness, and something close to fear. "I promise, I mean no harm."

"Something might mean *you* harm," she said flatly, pointing to his wrist. "That is the witch's handiwork."

Corin smiled. "You do not appreciate Lillith?"

The girl shivered. "I would sooner live without her." She pressed herself up from the ground, shaking out gray skirts. "There is a tower not far from here . . . an old watchtower, built to warn us of Erinnish invaders. But it is mine, now; will you come? I think you could use the rest."

Corin got up slowly, hearing joints and tendons snap. He could not recall ever feeling so stiff and sore, not even after lengthy arms practice with Hart or Brennan, or even against his uncle.

She took him to the tower on a cliff overlooking the Dragon's Tail. The edge of the world, it was; jagged, craggy, promising death to the man who fell over it. He could see Erinn from here, and the palisades, showing their chalk-white faces. It made him think of Aileen.

The interior was clean, washed white with lime. The tower was round, supporting only a second story. A wooden stair was tucked behind the studded door, winding to the upper floor and beyond, up to the watchtower roof. There was a table, benches, chests, and baskets of wildflowers. Also the dome of a tiny fireplace where she undoubtedly cooked her food. It was a cozy, airy home unlike any he had ever known.

She served him bread, cheese, ale. Her name was Sidra, she told him; she owned a goat, some chickens, grew vegetables, made cloth out of wool on her loom. In town she traded for the other things she might need.

He looked at her in surprise. "You are *alone?*"

"Aye," she said; her chin rose a little.

"Why? Have you no husband "

"No husband."

"And no man to protect you?"

"I protect myself."

"With what, that knife?"

"I have also a sword," she said clearly, looking toward one of the trunks.

Corin thought of Keely, so proud of her weapons-skill; of her independence. But Keely, he thought, had sound reason for both. She *was* skilled with sword and bow and knife, because her brothers and uncle had taught her. As well as her father's arms-master before Niall had stopped it.

"Sidra," he said quietly, "what are you hiding from me?"

She sighed, staring down at the table as she turned her cup in restless circles. "No man will harm me," she said quietly. "No man who knows who I am, and my father takes care to make it known."

"Why?"

She lifted her head to look at him. "I am Alaric's bastard daughter."

Seven

"*Alaric's* bastard?" Corin stared at her in surprise. And then he began to laugh.

Sidra was unamused. Color stained her cheeks and set her ale-brown eyes to glittering; she moved to rise, but he reached across and caught her hand.

"No," he said, "no. Forgive me. I do not laugh at *you*, but at the situation." He suppressed another laugh, though the sound threatened his throat. "How old are you, Sidra? Eighteen? Nineteen?"

"Nineteen." She removed her hand from his. "Why do you ask?"

"Because you are my *su'fala*." He smiled at her frown of incomprehension. "Aunt," he told her plainly. "Gisella, who is your half-sister, is also my mother."

This time there was no quick color in Sidra's cheeks, but a draining of it entirely. "Gisella's—" She broke off, staring at him blankly, and then she thrust her stool away to rise and move from the table. "Cheysuli . . . aye, now I see it. Gisella's son—*one* of them . . . would your name be Corin?"

He affirmed it with a nod.

Sidra sighed, combing brown hair absently. She did not braid it like so many other woman, but wore it tied back with a strip of leather. Mostly free, it curled to her hips. "Corin," she murmured, "Crown Prince of Atvia . . . if the witch lets you have it." She turned back sharply. "You do understand what she does, do you not? The witch? My father's Ihlini whore?"

Corin recalled very well what Alaric looked and sounded like. He wondered how much Sidra knew. "I have seen him only today."

"Then you *do* know." Abruptly she sat down again, leaning forward against the table. "He was not like this, Corin—not always. Oh, aye, I have heard all the stories— you have little reason to love Atvia *or* my father—but I swear, he was not always as you see him. That took *her*."

"Sidra—"

"I saw it," she interrupted. "I saw what she did to him, and what it meant, and I told him. I *told* him to send her away, to make her *stop* it, so she would not destroy him. But I should have known. I should have reckoned with her power over him." She shrugged a little, pulling slender shoulders forward; the gesture was eloquent as a sign of her helplessness. "Lillith had me sent from the castle."

"Against Alaric's wishes?"

Sidra sighed heavily, staring blindly at her cup of ale. "By then he had no more wishes—no more power to demand them of her. But she is not a fool; she used no sorcery against me, nor tried to have me slain. No. She simply sent me *here* . . . where I am away from my father."

Corin could not reconcile the Alaric of his father's stories and the Alaric of the girl's. "Forgive me, Sidra— but I do not see him as you do."

"No." She scraped a nail against the wood and drew an idle pattern. "No, you would not." She fell silent again, then flicked him a glance from under heavy-lashed lids. "It was after Gisella went to Homana to marry the Mujhar. The Lord of Atvia, being lonely without his daughter, turned to other women. My mother was one of them. And on her he sired a daughter, whom he named Sidra." Her mouth hooked down briefly. "My mother died. He took me in. There was no secret of my birth, but he did not care. He loved me, and made it known."

"What happens when he is dead?"

The question was cruel, but she did not avoid it. "What more than *this*?" she asked. "I have no place in the succession. My mother was a simple Atvian girl whose beauty, briefly, caught the eye of Atvia's lord. She was nothing to him. Once, *I* might have been, but Lillith ended that." Sidra shook her head. "I have nothing to offer Atvia."

"Except the child you carry."

Again he saw the telltale hand splaying itself across her belly. "How do *you*—"

"You give it away yourself." He mimicked her gesture distinctly. "I have seen it before."

Sidra looked away from him. "It was one of my father's guardsmen. He is gone, now—sent away by the witch . . . but at least she leaves me the child."

"For now." Corin shook his head. "I have grown up in the midst of political intrigue, Sidra. Bastard you may be, *and* the child, but it bears royal blood. If it is a son, what is to keep the people of Atvia from deciding to follow him instead of a stranger who shifts his shape?"

She stared. "Do you think it will threaten *you*?"

"You yourself said Lillith allowed you to keep the child—at least for now. But once it is born, and if it is a son, what is to say she will not take it for herself? Surely a child would be easier for her to control than a Cheysuli immune to her power."

"Immune," Sidra echoed. "Is that why you wear her wristlet?"

He had forgotten. Now, reminded of it, he felt the weight on his wrist. Cold. It was so *cold*. Bleakly, he shook his head.

Unexpectedly, Sidra smiled. "Aunt," she said in amusement, "to a man who is older than I."

He might have smiled back, but he was thinking of Aileen.

"What is it?" Sidra asked. "What troubles you, my lord?"

It was the first time she had used his rank. It was customary, and something to which he had grown accustomed since childhood, but it was odd coming from her. "Corin," he said. "I was thinking of a woman."

"Ah." She nodded, sighing. "Even as I think of a man."

His hand was lost in Kiri's pelt as she sat by his stool. "Did he know there was a child?"

"No." Sidra poured more ale and drank. "No, he left before I could tell him. Before I knew for certain."

"And if you sent word to him now?"

Her eyes filled with tears. "I could not begin to say where he is. The witch would never tell me."

"And Alaric?"

Sidra brushed the tears away quickly, as if disdaining them. "I doubt he knows. I doubt it was his doing."

"I might ask him for you."

Hope colored cheeks and glistened in widened eyes. "*Would* you?"

"I promise nothing," he told her gently. "I will ask. But I doubt Lillith would tell me anything more than she has told you."

Sidra nodded, staring down at the hands she twined in her lap. "Anything is welcome."

Corin rose. "I should go back. I left somewhat abruptly." He was still stiff, still sore, but the rest had done him good. "I will see what I can find out, and bring you word as soon as I can."

"Oh, my lord, thank you!"

Corin shrugged as he turned toward the tower door. "It is the least I can do after what you did for me." Kiri trotted past him out into the afternoon. It grew late, and dark; the sun slipped low in the sky and was hidden behind a wall of heavy clouds. The wind had an icy bite.

Sidra, framed in the doorway, watched Corin go. "Be wary of the witch."

"Here, I am wary of everything." He lifted his hand in a farewell wave and turned away from her. And then, abruptly, he stopped. "Why not come *with* me, Sidra? Ask Alaric yourself."

"*With* you!" She gaped inelegantly. "I told you how I was turned out of the castle!"

"This time you come at my invitation. If Lillith desires to turn you out again, she will have to contend with me." He put out a beckoning hand. "Come with me, Sidra. We will approach Alaric together."

She did not hesitate. She slammed the door shut behind her and ran down the path to join him.

Lillith's black eyes glittered. "You are a fool," she said coldly.

They faced her in one of the private receiving chambers. Corin had meant to take Sidra immediately to Alaric and had very nearly succeeded, but Lillith ruled the castle. Guardsmen had halted them at the Lord of Atvia's door. In short order, at Lillith's command, they had been forcibly escorted to the chamber.

Corin did not flinch beneath her stare. He was too angry. "What I *am*, Lillith, is Alaric's grandson and heir to Atvia's throne. If you think to keep *me* from him, you had better reacquaint yourself with the succession."

"He is dying," she said plainly. "He has the night to live, or perhaps tomorrow. I can think of better ways for you to spend your time than bringing bastards here."

"I will bring whomever I choose," he retorted. "She has more right here than you."

"She was sent from this castle at her father's behest—"

"*Your* behest," Sidra said sharply. "Why not let me see my father? Let *him* say if he wants me here or not."

Lillith looked at Corin, ignoring Sidra altogether. "She has no place here. There is no provision for bastards in this castle."

"*I* will make provision."

"How?" Lillith asked. "Who are you to do so? A stranger. A foreigner. A *shapechanger* sent from the Mujhar, who sucks Atvia dry of wealth. Do you expect a welcome? Do you expect to be loved? Do you expect to *rule*?"

"By the gods, Ihlini—"

"By *my* god!" Her voice rang out to fill the chamber. "You are a long way from Homana, Corin. You are a long way from your gods." Before he could speak, Lillith crossed the room to him. She put her hand on his wrist and the silver blazed to life. "You have no power here. But do you feel mine?"

The pain was intolerable. He felt it run through his

body like fire, eating at every joint. Yet somehow, dredging up what remained of his waning strength, he managed to pull away. And in doing so, he retaliated. Before Lillith could avoid it he struck her full across the face.

She staggered and nearly fell. He saw the mark of his hand upon her; saw the fury in her eyes. Never had he witnessed such hatred. Never had he seen such control.

"What can you do?" he taunted. "I am a *Cheysuli,* witch."

Lillith threw fallen hair back from her face. Corin's handprint was vivid red against the pallor of her skin. "What can I do?" she asked. And then, oddly, she laughed. "I can *watch,* Cheysuli. That will be more than enough."

It chilled his bones. "Watch *what?*"

But she was gone, leaving them alone in the chamber.

"Gods," Sidra said weakly, "I thought she meant to kill you."

"Come," he told her grimly, "it is time we saw your father."

He took her to see Alaric. But her father was already dead.

"No," Sidra said, as they stood outside the chamber door.

"Aye," the guardsman told them. "Only a moment ago."

"Was Lillith here?" Corin asked curtly.

"My lord, she was. She was with him when he died."

"Convenient," he said flatly, and moved to go inside.

The guardsman dropped his halberd across the door. "No, my lord, I beg you—let them prepare him first."

"Or let them hide the signs of Lillith's touch." Corin put a hand on the halberd. "Guardsman, move aside."

"My lord—" But the door was opened, and Gisella came out of Alaric's chamber.

Corin fell back a step. "*Jehana—*" And cursed himself instantly.

She stared at him blankly. There was nothing in her eyes save grief, and an odd opacity. Corin recalled what Lillith had said about Gisella's borrowed wits. Now that

Alaric was dead, his mother would revert to madness, to
the woman who had so willingly agreed to give up her
children.

"Dead," Gisella said. "Dead—dead—dead—" But she
broke off the refrain. She looked at Corin expectantly.
And then she began to smile. "Have you come to take
me home? Has he sent you to take me home?"

Corin suppressed a shudder. "*Jehana*—no. Not to
Homana. Your place is here—"

She stopped him. She put out a hand and touched the
tawny hair that reached his shoulders. "My beautiful
boy," she said. "My strong, beautiful boy . . ."

He wanted to move away, to avoid her entirely, disliking the look of her eyes, but she had backed him against
the wall. And even as he tried to pull away her hand, she
locked fingers in his hair.

"*Jehana*—"

"Stay here," she said, "stay with me. No Homana.
Atvia. Atvia is my home. Stay. *Stay*. Niall has all the
others . . . *you* will stay with me—"

He nearly gagged as he jerked her fingers from his
hair. "*Jehana*—let me *be*—"

"*Corin will stay with me*—"

He caught her wrists and thrust her away, sacrificing
some hair. But he was free of her at last. And before she
could reach out again, before she could trap him again,
he turned and lurched away. He could not bear to face her.

"My lord." Sidra caught him halfway down the corridor. "Corin, wait—"

He pulled free of her hand as well, wanting no one at
all to touch him. "Gods," he said. "*Gods*—" And he fell
against the wall, turning his face from her.

"I know," she said, and he saw the tearstains on her
face. "*I know*. Come with me, Corin."

She took him away. She took him out of the castle.
She took him to the tower, and gave him bitter ale. She
herself took two sips, then pushed her cup away. There
was grief in her eyes, and weariness; a stark, bleak look.
But after a time it faded, and it was his turn to deal with
it.

He sat on the floor and gathered Kiri into his arms. "He was nothing to me," he said blankly. "Less to me than to you."

"I know," she said gently. "To me he was always kind, but I know what he has done."

He cradled the vixen against his chest, needing Kiri's strength. "I never wanted Atvia. I have known for as long as I can remember that one day it would be mine, but I never wanted it. I wanted Homana instead."

"It is your home," Sidra said.

"More." He stroked Kiri gently, lost in reverie. "More. It was not just that I longed to stay in a familiar place . . . it was that I wanted it for *mine*. To hold. To rule. To love. I wanted to be Prince of Homana instead of Prince of Atvia." He tilted his head and rubbed his cheek against Kiri's fur. "I wanted Brennan's title. I wanted Brennan's birthright. And now I want his woman."

Sidra sat very still.

"I went to Erinn to tell her it was time she wed my *rujholli*, and fell in love with her myself. Knowing she was Brennan's. Wishing she might be mine." He stared blindly into the gloom of Sidra's tower. "But she must wed the Prince of Homana."

"Oh, my lord . . . I am so sorry for you."

Corin sighed and shut his eyes. "*He* will have Aileen. *He* will have the Lion. *He* will have Homana."

Night had come down fully. It had begun to rain. Sidra rose and lit a second candle, shielding it with her hand. She turned and looked at him over the flame. "We needed to know," she said. "We needed to have the key." And then she opened the door to Lillith.

The storm was in the room. "Strahan wants you," she told him. Behind her were Atvian soldiers.

Corin looked at Sidra.

"*Strahan's* child," she said.

He did not waste time thinking. Almost at once he was up and running, with Kiri darting ahead. Together they scrambled up the stairs to the second story, then higher still, heading for the roof. He unlocked and threw back the trap-door at the top of the ladder, boosted Kiri through, lurched through himself. Slammed the door down, knowing they would break through.

Slashing wind and rain stripped his eyes of vision. He was soaked through in an instant. Cursing, Corin made his way to the low wall and peered out into the storm.

Everything was blackness. No stars, no moon, no torches. He could not see the edge of the cliffs. He could see nothing at all.

Behind him, the door was thrown open.

"Kiri—" he said aloud. "Let me go first, *lir*—let me break your fall."

He caught the edge of the wall. Climbed over, clinging to the rocks. Boot toes grabbed for footholds. The stone was wet, slick, unforgiving. In a moment he would fall.

He heard the shouting of the soldiers. And let go.

He fell, scraping bare arms. And then he landed, toppled, fell—pushed himself up again, wet, muddy, aching. He stared up at the wall, fighting the rain, trying to see the vixen. Now she could jump. Now he could catch her. Without him, the fall would kill her.

"The fox is taken." Cutting the darkness he saw a lurid glare of purple light and Lillith's silhouette.

"*Kiri*—"

"Give yourself up," she called. "He has no plans to kill *you* any more than to kill your brothers. Strahan has need of you."

He knew better than to surrender. If Strahan wanted him whole, the Ihlini would never harm Kiri. Corin knew it would be difficult, but there was a chance he might free his *lir*.

Provided I free myself.

Accordingly, Corin turned and ran.

Through the rain and the wind and the darkness—
—and fell off the edge of the world.

There was no time for even a scream.

Interlude

The glare from the Gate backlighted Strahan, making him little more than a shape before her eyes. She could not see his face. She could not see his expression. But she heard the satisfaction in his tone.

"One, two, three." He paused. "Though I might have wished the youngest was less damaged."

"He will heal," Lillith told him. "It was—unexpected. There was no one who could stop him. I think he was as surprised as any of us when he fell from the top of the cliff."

Strahan considered it. "I think it will have its uses . . . if, for nothing else, to help me sway the others." Light was a nimbus around him. "I think it is time to begin."

Lillith smiled. "Who will be the first?"

Flame licked out of the Gate, fell back in a shower of sparks. It illuminated Strahan's face. "First I must test them, one by one, to learn who is the weakest link. None of them will be easy. It will be a task of discovery . . . I must be very gentle. Nothing will be done in haste." He knelt. His back was to her. She saw him bend over the rim of the Gate, extend a hand, then he rose to face her again. In his hands was a silver cup. It was filled with viscid liquid and a pungent purple smoke. "I think the first-born shall be the first."

Lillith drew in a breath. "He will be the hardest of all."

The cup glowed silver-purple. "What I have to offer Brennan may not be enough . . . it is possible he has overcome his fear. But I can use his brothers . . . I can use his twin. The bond between them is nearly as strong as that between warrior and *lir*."

"And do you think Hart will break?"

"He may be the easiest. What I offer *him* is continuity as a Cheysuli. They are an immensely proud race, as we have reason to know, and more intractable than they should be." Strahan smiled and rubbed thoughtfully at his bottom lip. "But now he lacks a hand. Now he is *mained*. Lacking a hand, he lacks a race . . . I think it should be enough."

"And if *Hart* does not break?"

Over the cup he looked at her. Smoke wreathed his face, but the eyes were still paramount. "Then all will be left to Corin. With one, I can break them all." Strahan slowly nodded. "He is an ambitious man, and jealous of the eldest. It is a formidable weapon. It should not be difficult."

Lillith frowned. "Do not misjudge them, Strahan. None of them is weak."

"But all of them have *weaknesses*. And I intend to exploit them."

It did not erase her frown. She was older than her brother by nearly two hundred years. She knew the Cheysuli better. She knew them very well.

Lillith looked at her brother. Strahan drank from the cup.

PART V

One

The door was opened. Light spilled into the cell. Brennan, hunched against the wall, shut his eyes at once.

"Come out," the voice said.

The syllables were strange. Brennan did not at first know them, hearing only sound. And then he pieced them together, understood them, stared through the crack he made in the shield of his fingers.

"Come out," the voice repeated.

He pressed himself against the wall and tried to climb inside it.

"Bring him out," the voice said, and hands were laid upon him.

They got him as far as the door. Light fell full upon him. To a man who had lived too long in darkness, the flame was intolerable.

But no more so than the fear.

He was poised on the threshold, blinded by the light. He turned his head aside, shutting his eyes, trying to avoid it; a torch was held nearer yet.

"*Behold* the Prince of Homana."

The voice was Rhiannon's voice. Brennan opened his eyes.

Alone in the darkness, he had lost track of time. He knew it had been weeks; he had not expected months. But she was big with the weight of his child.

"Behold the *Prince of Homana*." Her tone mocked him. Then she gestured to those who held him. "Take him at once to Strahan."

Slowly it penetrated. He was out of the cell—*free* of
the cell—they had taken him out of the cell. The stink of
it clung to him, but the scent of hope replaced it.

They took him up endless spirals of winding stairs. He
was weak from inactivity, cramped from the tiny cell,
bound up by the burden of fear. He knew he was not
mad; he knew also he was not quite sane.

More stairs. And then at last a door. They opened it,
thrust him through, shut the door behind him.

Brennan spun, staggering, and tried to claw open the
door. They had shut him up *again*.

His nails broke on the wood. The latch did not give
beneath his desperate fingers. The door was securely
locked. It was no less than he should have expected. He
closed his eyes and pressed his face against the wood,
trying to calm himself, but the fear was ever-present.

It was all he had known for months.

Finally he turned. Expecting anything, he set his back
against the door. But the room was empty of men or
women. No one inhabited it. Brennan drew in an unsteady breath.

The chamber was small, but large to him, after captivity in his cell. The walls were black—Valgaard's domi-
nant color—but soft rugs carpeted the floors even as
tapestries brightened the walls. Fire blazed in the fireplace. There were chairs and tables and candleracks, all
ablaze with light. It made him squint; he was yet unaccustomed to light.

And then he smelled the food.

His belly cramped instantly. They had not starved him,
preferring instead to keep him alive, but the food had
been much less than he was accustomed to, and the diet
very plain. His body cried out for better, and now it was
offered to him.

Brennan stared at the silver platters. Hot meat: beef,
venison, pork and poultry. Fresh bread: brown, white,
hard and soft, redolent of fresh baking. Wheels of cheese:
creamy ivory, pale yellow, ocher-gold. Baskets of fruit:
apples, grapes, pears, peaches, plums and countless others. Beakers of wine and ale and *usca*. ·

Quickly he crossed to the table, reaching out to scoop up the food. He grabbed a goblet of wine. Tore off a chunk of beef. And then, even as his belly cried out, he ate and drank none of it.

His hands trembled. Wine slopped over the rim of his goblet, dripping on his boots. The aromas were overwhelming.

He dropped the beef onto the platter. Set the goblet down. It overturned in the unsteadiness of his hand, ringing against the wood of the tabletop. All the wine spilled out in a river of blood-colored liquid.

Brennan backed away. And then, still shaking, he sought a chair and fell into it, leaning forward to press his face against his hands.

The flesh was slack and lifeless. His nails were rimmed in black. He smelled the stink of himself. He was awash in the filth of his cell. The Brennan he knew was gone.

And his belly cried out for food.

"You insult me," Strahan said.

Brennan started. He had heard nothing, nothing at all, and yet the door was open. And then Strahan closed it and came to greet his guest.

"I offer you food." He indicated the table. "I offer you wine, ale, bread. Yet you touch none of it."

Brennan had spoken to no man for weeks, for no one had spoken to him. All he could do was stare.

Strahan's eyes narrowed slightly. And then he smiled, and sat down across from his kinsman.

Brennan had not, until now, ever seen the Ihlini. He had been raised on stories of the man, on tales of his sorcery, but never had he seen him. And now that he did, now that he sat but four paces from him, he realized the stories paled beside the man. Strahan was power incarnate.

The eyes, Brennan thought. *Gods, what evil eyes.*

One blue, one brown, set slightly oblique in a face built of flawless bones. His beauty did not in any way make him effeminate, but the features were as arresting as those of a beautiful woman. Straight, narrow nose, winged black brows; the fall of raven hair, held back by a silver circlet.

He was a man who ruled through beguilement, and Brennan felt its touch.

Strahan looked at him. Looked at him and smiled. "You should see yourself."

Brennan did not need to. He knew what Strahan saw; what he had ordered shaped to precise specifications.

The Ihlini's skin was fairer than Brennan's. Slender white hands were ablaze with brilliant gemstones: ruby, sapphire, emerald. A diamond and a bloodstone. His nails were clean and buffed. Idly, he leaned his chin into one hand and tapped at his upper lip.

Brennan did not know at which eye to look, and so he looked at neither.

Strahan sighed a little. His leathers, soft and gray, were far cleaner than Brennan's soiled brown ones. He smelled of scented unguents more fragrant than Brennan's stink.

"It is unfortunate," Strahan said quietly, "that you have come to this state. A prince should never be brought so low, nor a Cheysuli warrior."

Brennan locked himself up in silence.

Strahan gazed at curiously. "Was it the Womb of the Earth that did it? I have been there, you know. I have seen the marble *lir*, the bottomless oubliette, the rune-carved walls of the narrow passageway." He nodded. "I myself have never been afraid of small places, but it must be a difficult thing to bear. Particularly for a Cheysuli." He paused. "Particularly for *you*."

Brennan was no longer in the room. He was back in the Womb, seeing the marble *lir*. Seeing the oubliette. Learning the meaning of fear.

"It must be terrifying to know yourself locked in, unable to leave . . . to know yourself trapped and helpless, alone in a tiny place. Knowing no one can hear your screams. No one can soothe your fear. No one can bear it for you."

Brennan's breathing quickened. Rigid fingers made knots of his hands.

"And so filthy, too," Strahan said sympathetically. "Such humiliation, on top of all the fear. Having to relieve yourself in a corner like an animal instead of like a man . . . contending with dungeon vermin . . . smelling the stink of one's own body." He shifted in his chair; gemstones glittered on his fingers. Glittered to mirror his eyes. "Hearing things . . . seeing things . . . and too afraid to sleep."

Brennan shut his eyes.

"And knowing all the time such a simple thing will free you."

Brennan opened his eyes.

Strahan leaned forward and took up a cup of wine. "Will you serve me, Brennan?"

Brennan's scalp itched. Lice infested him. All he could do was stare.

Strahan drank wine.

Brennan drew an unsteady breath. The room was warm, dry, brightly lighted, filled with the beguiling aromas of food and drink. His body cried out for kindness again. His battered spirit demanded it.

Strahan put down the wine. "I have a smaller cell."

Brennan flinched, and hated himself.

"More suitable to your condition."

Brennan wet cracked lips. "No," he croaked, prepared to argue it.

Strahan rose. "You will excuse me, I am sure; there are things I must attend to. My servants will escort you back."

He turned away. A casual flick of one finger caused the door to swing open. Men waited there.

"The prince prefers his cell." Strahan's tone was one of complete indifference.

Men surrounded him. They lifted him out of the chair and put him on his feet. Before he could speak a word, before he could begin to struggle, they had taken him from the chamber. Back down the winding stairways into the depths of Valgaard's bowels.

At the cell door, he rebelled. But they were too strong

for him. The door was opened. They flung him through. They locked it on his outcry.

Brennan stared blindly into the darkness and knew Strahan was not finished. And then he began to shake.

A second door was unlocked. A second man brought out. Him also, they took to Strahan.

The sorcerer turned from the casement as Brennan's brother was ushered in. He looked at Hart's gaunt face, looked at the leather-wrapped stump, looked back at the haunted eyes. "I apologize," he said kindly. "Dar was overly enthusiastic."

Hart was plunged back instantly into the room at Ilsa's dwelling. To when they had pinned his hand to the table. To when the blade had fallen. To the moment he realized he no longer had a left hand. And the memory of the pain.

Rage boiled up inside. But he said nothing at all; he would not give Strahan the satisfaction.

"It makes you angry," Strahan said. "Do you think I cannot see it?"

As was becoming habitual, Hart cradled the stump in his remaining hand, pressing it gently against his chest in an unconsciously vulnerable gesture of retreat and self-protection.

Strahan indicated food and wine. "Will you eat? Will you drink? I should hate to see it go to waste." And then he paused, as if arrested in mid-motion. "But of course, I had forgotten . . . someone will have to cut it for you.

Humiliation tied Hart's belly into knots and briefly, too briefly, colored his face a deeper bronze. It took all his strength to keep the anguish from his tone. "What do you want me for?"

"Sit down, my lord of Solinde . . . I see an alarming pallor in your face."

Hart fully intended to ignore the suggestion. But the pallor was unfeigned; shock coupled with fever had served to sap his strength. Slowly he seated himself, preferring the chair to falling down. He found the motion uncomfortable; he was accustomed to using two hands.

"Does it hurt?" Strahan asked. "Is the loss of a hand anything like the loss of an ear?"

Hart looked at him in shock. He had forgotten that Strahan had only one ear. The other had been cut off in a fight with one of Hart's own kinsmen long ago on the Crystal Isle.

Strahan hooked long hair back and bared the side of his head. "We all suffer losses, some of us more dramatically than others." He moved the hair back into place. "It was my misfortune the ear was lost entirely. Had I found it, the Seker might have made me whole . . . but I was somewhat pressed for time."

Hart stirred. "If he is as powerful as you claim, why did he not simply make you a new one?"

"Flesh born of flesh," Strahan said. "The original was required."

Hart looked down at the stump of his wrist. He *felt* the hand there, and yet when he looked he saw nothing at all. When he moved it, nothing grasped. But the reflexive pain was undiminished.

"I know, of course, the loss of a hand precludes you from returning to your clan." Strahan's mouth shaped the words with a deep and abiding compassion. "We Ihlini are not so harsh. A man's mind may be useful even if the body is not."

Hart gazed blindly at the hand that no longer existed.

"But it would be so difficult for a maimed warrior to contribute to his clan," Strahan remarked. "How can you use a bow? How can you mount a defense? How can you ward your woman and children against the enemy?"

Hart did his best to ignore him, but the gentle probing found its mark.

"And, of course, as part of the prophecy . . . well . . . what is left to you?" Strahan poured wine. "What is there for you to do? How can a warrior serve when he is no longer recognized as a warrior?"

Hart stirred at last. "My *jehan* lost an eye."

Strahan made a dismissive gesture. "Oh, aye, he did . . . but then he had another."

"I have another hand."

"A hand is not an eye." Strahan paused. "What will they do?" he asked. "Will they strip you of your gold? Blot out your rune in the birthlines? From the path of the prophecy?"

Breath caught in Hart's tight throat. He felt the slow churning of his belly.

"Will they tear down your pavilion? Take *cheysula* or *meijha* from you?" Strahan paused. "Or will no Cheysuli woman be allowed to speak your name?"

"Stop," Hart whispered.

"Will they strip you of your *lir*? Or will the *lir* go regardless?"

"*Stop.*" Hart said.

"There is no place for you, Hart. You are now a clanless warrior, unable to serve your race."

Hart stood up so fast he overset the chair. "*Ku'reshtin!*" But before he could move to strike him, Strahan caught hold of his wrist.

"No," the sorcerer said, and closed his fingers on the leather that warded the healing stump.

The pain was excruciating. Hart wavered on his feet.

"No," Strahan said, "I can offer you better."

Sweat ran down Hart's face to mix with tears of pain. "You offer me loss of honor . . . the loss of who I *am*—"

"Service to me will replace it."

Hart tore his wrist free, then hugged it against his chest. Pain robbed him of the words. All he could do was shake his head.

Strahan sighed. "You Cheysuli are so stubborn. Nearly as stubborn as I." And before Hart could answer, he summoned men to take him away.

The hand was cool on Corin's brow. It took the heat away. For so long there had been heat. Heat and unbearable pain. And now Strahan took it away.

"You are a fortunate man," the sorcerer told him gently. "You very nearly died."

The eyes transfixed him utterly.

"But you are better now. The bones begin to heal. I think you will walk again, though possibly with a limp." Strahan paused. "Do you recall what happened to you?"

Vividly, Corin did. "I fell." The voice echoed the weakness in his body. "I fell off the dragon's skull." He gazed clear-eyed up at Strahan. "She said it was *your* child."

Strahan's winged brows lifted to touch his circlet. And then he smiled. "May the Seker grant it perfect health."

Corin itched. He ached. He wanted badly to get up, but knew he could not. "Kiri?" he said plainly.

"Mine. She is well, I promise you." Strahan made a sign and a stool was instantly brought. He sat down close to Corin's bedside. "You understand, I am sure, why I wanted you."

"You want Atvia."

"But only for my lord. I am not a greedy man." Strahan smoothed the covers. "Is there much pain, Corin? I can drain it from you."

Corin recalled how Lillith had drained Alaric of wits and life. He said no distinctly.

Strahan smiled, and then he laughed. "Why do you think the worst of me? If I wanted you dead, I would have left you at the bottom of the cliff, to wash out into the sea. Perhaps to wash up on Erinn's shores, where Aileen could grieve over you."

Corin shut his eyes. "I will not give you Atvia."

"Atvia, for the moment, is quite within my grasp." Strahan's palm touched his brow again. "I was thinking of Homana."

Corin's eyes snapped open.

"Aye, I thought that might get your attention." The fingers dripped with ice; the fever began to fade. "Sidra tells me you want your brother's bride. That you want your brother's title. That you want your brother's throne."

Corin bit his lip. "Take your hand from me."

After a moment, Strahan did. The pain renewed itself. "The Seker is a generous god. What a man wants, he often bestows."

"Then why does he not simply *give* you the realms you want?" The level of pain was rising. He was transfixed by Strahan's stare. "Why does he not simply *take* them?"

"Through men like me, he will." Strahan tore back the

covers to bare splints and linen wrappings. "Both legs, Corin. And ribs I cannot count. You are fortunate the bones of your head were left intact, else I could offer you nothing."

"You offer me nothing I will accept." Corin threaded bruised fingers through his hair and stripped it back from his face, pulling hard purposely to deflect the pain from his mending bones. "I will heal. The pain will die. You offer me nothing at all."

"You will heal. The pain will die. But I can offer you much more. I can offer you what you want."

Corin grunted his irony. "Homana is not mine to give."

"And if it were?" Strahan asked softly. "If I offered to share it with you?"

"Share *what?*" Corin demanded. "You will make me a minion regardless, and then I will need no throne."

Strahan carefully covered him up again. "A minion has its uses, but so does a living man. I would prefer to use the latter."

Corin turned his head away.

"I can turn your legs to jelly," Strahan said softly. "*You* have the power to heal, but I can undo it all. With only the touch of my hand." Jewels glittered on his fingers.

"You have my *lir*," Corin said hoarsely. "How can I hope to refuse you? What pleasure is there in it for a man like you?"

"You should hope instead to aid me." Strahan touched Corin's head. "I will be here if you need me. Dream awhile, my lord. Dream of your red-headed princess . . . dream of your brother's throne."

Corin slipped into darkness. He dreamed of his brother's bride.

Two

Light spilled into the cell. Strahan stood in the doorway. "A gift for my stubborn kinsman."

Brennan turned his back.

"Surcease from your fear."

The voice was endlessly tender. Brennan shut his eyes.

"Behold," Strahan said. "I show you the life of a warrior."

Brennan stood facing the wall. Spread fingers touched fetid slime; nails dug into slick stone in an effort to beat off beguilement. He hated the cell. Hated what it did to him. Hated himself because of it. He had grown used to the stench, but not inured to the distaste. It made him want to vomit.

And then the wall moved. Stone melted away. Brennan opened his eyes.

The world unfolded before him.

Homana. The grassy plains outside of Mujhara, stretching east toward Clankeep. He was free of Valgaard at last—free of the tiny cell—free of consuming fear. All around him lay the world, a bright and shining world, made of earth and sky and sun and moon and the warmth of a summer day.

Brennan's breath hissed out of his mouth. Filth sloughed off him. Fresh leathers adorned his body. He was young and strong and full of life, bursting to run free.

Then come. Sleeta said. *What keeps you from it, lir?*

And he ran, he *ran*, trading human flesh for feline, knowing the endless freedom of *lir*-shape. Running on, through meadowlands, woodlands, forests, shedding the weight of fear. All he knew was freedom and the promise of the day.

Gods, he exulted, *this is the best of all—*

And then all was snatched away. All was torn apart. All was swallowed whole by the darkness of the cell.

Beneath his hands was slime. Banished was his freedom, traded for degradation.

"Sleeta," he said only.

"Come out with me," Strahan said. "There is something you should see."

Brennan was too dazed to mark his way. He knew only that Strahan's servants took him up stairs, then down them, then through narrow passageways. Eerie *godfire* glowed, negating the need for candles. Beneath his booted feet fell away stair after stair, shallow, hollowed, smooth, worn down after decades of use. Or was it centuries?

Down, down, down. Briefly, he thought of the Womb of the Earth. But this was far deeper. Blacker. It stank of the netherworld.

One man before him, one behind. Fleetingly, he considered an attempt at escape. But it fled the moment he thought it; he was in no condition to try such folly. Captivity had worn him to the bone just as time had worn the steps. Even a child could knock him down; Strahan's men were not children.

Down, down, *down.*

Something gibbered in the wall.

Brennan's breath was an audible rasp. He tried to silence himself, but the months had stripped him of control. He was frightened, and it showed. Strahan knew his man; knew how to diminish his pride.

Down.

And then the servants stepped aside.

On the threshhold, Brennan halted. He thought to turn and run, but a door closed quietly behind him. Through the columns, an echo ran.

"Behold," Strahan said, "the Presence Chamber of the god."

Brennan looked down the columned corridor, stunned

by the vastness of the cavern. It unfolded before him into a multitude of vaulted glasswork ceilings, arch upon arch, each reaching higher then the last. Much like the rune-carved hammer-beamed timbers in the roof of Homana-Mujhar, the cavern displayed a filigree of fretwork. A lattice of delicate glass, set aglow from the glare of the Gate.

Something hummed through whorled columns. *Godfire* rose, then died.

"Come forth," Strahan said, *"and behold the Gate of the god."*

Steadily, Brennan walked. Behind him, humming followed.

Beyond the Gate, Strahan waited. He wore black leathers and a velvet doublet of deepest, blood-red purple. *Godfire* glowed in the creases. On his brow, the circlet blazed. Raven hair cloaked shoulders.

Brennan walked steadily on, transfixed by the maw in the earth. Around its lips flames danced, licked, beckoned; the spittle of the god was foul.

"There," Strahan said. In his hands was a rectangular black-lacquered box alive with writhing crimson runes.

Brennan halted. He was but two steps from the rim of the Gate, but he did not look. Strahan faced him across it. Between them lay the glowing sphincter of the Seker's netherworld. The realm of Asar-Suti.

He was *afraid*. But in that moment, anger swallowed fear. "One might think." Brennan said, "the Seker would *smell* better."

Strahan's smile vanished.

"One might *realize*," Brennan said, "that a Cheysuli cannot be broken." He paused. "Not by his brother race."

The runes ran in frenzied circles around the edge of the box until there were no runes at all, only a blur of lurid light red as blood. Strahan's expression was unreadable.

"Lock me up," Brennan said. "Lock me up forever. But I will never serve you. Not in madness *or* sanity."

Strahan's winged brows rose slightly, touched the curve

of the gleaming circlet. It was of gnarled, twisted shapes, wracked in blood-born silver. "I am suitably impressed by your confidence." One eloquent finger tapped the lid of the wooden box; the runes fell back into place. "I admire your strength of will. But I make no idle boast: I can break a Cheysuli. And I intend to do it."

"How?" Brennan asked. "You hold my *lir*; so be it. I can do nothing to free her. You may slay her if you choose; doing so frees me forever, and you will lose me entirely."

"There will be no death-ritual," Strahan told him. "No escape from the madness *lirlessness* will bring. Do you sentence yourself to that?"

Madness was anathema to the Cheysuli. The loss of control in *lir*-shape or out of it was considered inexcusable, in addition to being potentially deadly. A Cheysuli warrior made *lirless* was, in time, little better than a beast; death was preferable. And so the ritual had been born. But in order to make the ritual have meaning, suicide was taboo. A paradox. And clearly, Strahan knew it.

Brennan had been raised to respect the customs of his race. At his Ceremony of Honors, following the bonding with Sleeta, he had accepted the responsibilities of a warrior knowing full well that even the Mujhar of Homana owed his life to the will of the gods. The ritual bound Niall's heir as well as others, and he had accepted it.

And now, his commitment was tested.

"You have spent the better part of several months attempting to drive me mad," Brennan said. "*Lirlessness* will succeed where imprisonment could not, but of what use am I then? What good is a mad Mujhar?"

Strahan's smile was sweet. "More malleable than one who is sane. Look at Shaine." A tendril of living flame licked up from the Gate, touched his boot, tapped, as if to remind him; fell back as Strahan nodded. "Look at Shaine, your distant kinsman, who once gave *us* Homana-Mujhar because he preferred Ihlini to Cheysuli."

"But Carillon took it back . . . it *and* Solinde. Your homeland, Strahan . . . and now a vassal to the Cheysuli."

Brennan shrugged. "Do your worst, Ihlini. I can hardly gainsay you, but idiocy may thwart you."

"And if I chose to kill the cat with an excess of— incivility? What would you say then?"

"That I will suffer," Brennan answered. "No doubt I will beg you to stop. But when you *have* stopped, and I have my wits about me, the cycle will start again."

Strahan shook his head. "You do not understand. I do not *need* you sane . . . I can control a hollow man easier than one stuffed full with Cheysuli pride."

"Then why this mummery?"

Strahan sighed. "An amusing divertissement. But now, shall we to the bargain? You may find it interests you."

Brennan merely shrugged.

"I want Homana," Strahan said. "Through you I can have it."

Brennan shook his head.

"In good time, *you* shall have it; I will not take Niall's life. Let him live out his years . . . I have as many as I need." Strahan's eyes narrowed. "The bargain, Brennan: serve me, and I will spare your father's life. I will spare the life of your *lir*. I will give you the years of your life and beyond, through the benificence of the Seker."

"I have no desire to live forever." Brennan folded his dirt-crusted arms. The *lir*-gold was dulled by grime, but it did not dull his determination. "I will not accept your bargain."

"Not even to save your kin?"

He dared give Strahan no advantage. Brennan set his teeth. "You can only kill them once. *Then* where is your power?"

"I can destroy the prophecy."

"You have tried so many times."

Strahan sighed. "This, I see, leads nowhere."

"No." Brennan smiled. "What have you left, Ihlini?"

"*This*," Strahan said, and opened the wooden box.

Through the smoke, Brennan looked. And then he stared in disgust at Strahan, his distaste as plain as his bafflement.

"Do you not recognize it?" Strahan asked.

"A human hand," Brennan said flatly. "Ensorcelled, no doubt; else it would have decayed by now."

"More than a human hand. It is a *Cheysuli* hand."

As he was meant to, Brennan looked again. His belly knotted itself.

Strahan closed the box. "I should be very careful. Hart may want it back."

When he could, Brennan breathed again and swallowed back the bile. "There was no ring," he said tightly.

"He wagered it away." Strahan looked past Brennan. "Why not ask him yourself?"

Brennan swung around. Through the columns came his brother. At his left wrist there was no hand.

"I have the power." Strahan spoke with infinite kindness. "Serve me, Brennan, and I will make him whole."

"*Rujho!*" It was Hart, whose voice echoed shock throughout the cavern. "Gods, Brennan—not *you!* I thought he had only me!"

Strahan smiled warmly. "Welcome to the Gate."

Hart barely spared a glance for the Ihlini. He ran forward toward Brennan. "*Rujho—*" But he slowed as he reached the Gate. The light was odd on his face, limning gauntness and despair. "Brennan, are you whole?"

Brennan swallowed tightly. "More so than you," he said. "Oh, gods, *rujho—*" Abruptly he turned away.

"Brennan!" Hart halted raggedly. Shock made him awkward. "Do you already cast me out?"

"*Ask* him!" Brennan spun and thrust out an arm toward Strahan. "Ask *him,* Hart!"

Hart turned toward the Ihlini. Shock at seeing Brennan had overtaken the immediacy of his disability, but now it was obvious that Brennan had been told. He had *expected* it. And it obviously made a difference.

Emptiness overwhelmed him. Despair was overpowering.

"I offer your brother a choice," Strahan said, "now I will give it to you."

Hart sighed wearily, too weary to protest as he stripped fallen hair out of his gaunt face. Cheysuli were characteristically angular, formed of remarkably striking bones, but captivity, illness and strain had fined Hart down too far. If the dark skin were any tauter, the cheekbones would cut through flesh. "You asked him for Homana. Now you ask me for Solinde."

"But your bargain is different." Strahan's fingers splayed across the lid of the box, tapping idly. "He says there is no inducement to make him accept my service. But you are a different man. What would *you* have of me?"

Hart's laughter had the edge of madness in it. "My freedom," he said promptly. "The freedom of my *rujholli*. No further dealings with you."

"Unacceptable." Strahan smiled. "Serve me, Hart. Accept the Seker as your lord."

"And destroy the prophecy." Hart shook his head. For all he meant to sound fierce and adamant, unimpressed by Strahan's words, he knew he sounded precisely what he *was:* badly frightened, nearly worn through, on the brink of breaking down from the loss of hand and clan. It took all he had to speak steadily, betraying nothing of what he felt inside the dwindling shell. "You have taken my hand, Ihlini . . . you have stolen my heritage from me. I am, as you have said, clanless and unwhole. There is no place for me among the Cheysuli." He spread his arms and displayed hand and stump. "What have I left to lose?"

"Your *lir*."

Hart laughed at him, though it had a ragged sound. "Rael is *free* . . . Dar never caught him. Try again, Ihlini."

"He may be free," Strahan conceded after a moment, "but you are separated. Eventually, the *lir*-bond shall grow thin, *too* thin . . . grow brittle, *so* brittle . . . until it cannot survive, and *breaks*."

Hart drew in a deep breath. "So be it, Ihlini. Madness—and eventual death—is preferable to serving you and your noxious god."

Strahan tilted his head toward Brennan. "The life of your twin-born brother."

Hart looked at Brennan. He saw the rigidity of the

body, the bleakness in yellow eyes. He looked for some suggestion, some hint of what Brennan desired him to say. But there was none. Brennan looked soundly defeated, cocooned in futility.

That shook Hart more than anything else. He drew in another deep breath. "An idle promise, Ihlini. Brennan would sooner be dead than have me become your minion merely to save his life."

Brennan's smile was bittersweet.

Strahan considered it. He stroked the wooden box. "I will give you the girl."

Anger flared anew. "Is she not what you promised *Dar?*"

"Dar is expendable." Strahan brightened. "Would his life be enough for you?"

Hart drew in his left arm and hugged it against his chest. "You will kill whomever you choose, regardless of what I want. I would be a fool to accept such terms."

"Give in." Strahan suggested. "The service will not harm you. You will still be Prince of Solinde. Still have the white-haired woman. Still have your games of chance. What more could you want?"

Hart's hard-won demeanor began to slip. In his eyes was emptiness. "What I want you cannot give."

Brennan, clearly afraid, took a step toward him.

"No." Strahan's tone was a whiplash of sound that hissed in the glassy cavern. "This is *his* choice, now."

"No!" Brennan shouted. A tendril of flame flowed out of the Gate and slapped him to the ground.

A second gout deftly blocked Hart's move to reach his brother. It beat him back until he cursed aloud.

"Now," Strahan said, "tell me what you want."

Hart hugged his arm, swaying on his feet. "I want my clan!" he shouted. "I want the regard and honor of my race, not the ouster I am due." He thrust his left arm into the air and displayed the emptiness at the end of his leather-cuffed wrist. His arm shook with the tension of his rigid body. "With one blow of a sword, Dar had me stripped of my heritage. Maimed warrior, *worthless* warrior . . . not fit to be part of the clan. And so I am *kin-wrecked*—" He shut his eyes a moment, then drew in an unsteady breath and went on. "Where does it leave me, Ihlini? Why should I serve *you?*" Hart stood on the edge of the Gate, oblivious to its flame as the tears ran down his face. "You cannot give back my hand—no more than grow back your ear!"

Strahan opened the box.

In noisy silence, Hart stared at the hand in its bed of silk. There was no blood. The cut had been clean, leaving no gore at all. Oddly dispassionate, coldly assessive, he studied the severed hand. He marked scars won in childhood and arms-practice. The enlargement of one knuckle. The sinews beneath brown flesh. There was no mistaking the hand. He knew it was his own.

Instinctively he made an impossible fist. As the tremor spread through his stump, the hand in the box closed its fingers.

Hart cried out. He wavered on the brink. Flame licked up and drove him back, staggering, until he fell to his knees. He cradled his arm and rocked.

To and fro.

To and fro.

Oblivious to his brother.

Strahan's tone was gentle. "You have only to say you will serve me."

Hart hugged his arm and rocked.

Strahan looked at Brennan. "*You* have a choice as well."

Brennan knelt on the glassy floor. All he could do was stare at Hart, sharing a measure of his anguish.

"I will let you consider it." A flick of his hand built an encircling fence of flame to keep them near the Gate. Then Strahan walked away. As he moved, smoke followed. The columns sang their atonal song.

Corin leaned back on his elbows, gritting his teeth in response to the discomfort of ribs and legs. He was indeed fortunate, as Strahan had pointed out, to have survived the fall from the cliff. To survive the fever that followed. But he had, and now he healed; with healing came renewed and abiding anger: he was prisoner to the Ihlini.

And yet he was not in a cell. His room was small, but hardly bereft of luxuries. The bed was comfortable. The hangings were richly patterned, if in runic glyphs he did not know and feared to learn. The door was clearly unlocked. If he could walk, he might go free. But his legs were not quite healed.

He had tried, time and again, to contact Kiri through the link. But Valgaard was the font of Strahan's power; even Old Blood was neutralized. It would take wits instead of magic to win free of his captor's grip.

The door swung open. Corin tensed as Strahan entered. He saw rich dark clothing, rune-wrought circlet, the compelling mismatched eyes. And he knew the time had come at last to meet absolute power in human form.

The room lay in darkness in deference to his rest. But now Strahan bent over a gilded candle, blew, set the wick ablaze. The flame was purest purple.

Another. Another. Until the room ran with lurid *godfire*, the excrescence of the god.

Strahan stood over him. "The time is come," he said gently. "You must make your choice."

Corin slowly leaned back against piled bolsters and uncrooked his elbows, hearing the pop of weakened joints; feeling the fatigue of battered flesh. He tried consciously to ease the tension from his rigid body, knowing he would fail.

"I have something for you." Strahan put it into his hand.

Corin stared at it. A ring. A circlet of heavy gold, incised with careful runes, and a brilliant blood-red ruby held firm by taloned prongs. The ring of the Prince of Homana.

Chilled, Corin looked at Strahan. "You have my *rujholli*."

"Brennan. Hart. *You*." In the eerie light, Strahan's

face was etched in fretwork shadows. "In addition to your *lir*."

Corin's eyes went back the ring. It was too large for him, he knew, because he had tried it on once. Brennan was taller, heavier, more strongly made than Corin; Hart was very like him. Their fingers were longer, stronger, browner. More Cheysuli than his.

Corin looked at his own signet. The emerald still glittered against his flesh. The gold shone brightly as ever, if perverted by the *godfire*. Strahan had not touched it.

"Trade," Strahan suggested.

His hand spasmed closed, trapping the ring in his palm. "This is *Brennan's* ring."

"Put it on, and it is yours," Strahan smiled. "And all it represents."

Corin swallowed tightly. "Is he dead? Have you killed him? Is that why you taunt me with it?"

"He is quite unharmed, and I do not taunt. I *offer*." Strahan paused. "If you want it, it is yours. You need only put it on."

"I am Crown Prince of *Atvia*."

"You are prisoner to me," Strahan moved a trifle closer. "There is no need for dissembling, Corin. I understand very well what it is to desire something very badly. I understand passion and ambition and the *need* for a thing fulfilled. Do you think I do this for pleasure?" His eerie eyes were black in the purple glare. "Brennan is unfit for his inheritance. Homana lacks a proper prince. There is a *need* for you."

"Unfit—" Corin clenched the ring in his hand. "What have you done to him?"

Strahan's gemstones glittered. "Shown him what he is: a man unfit to rule."

"Brennan is more fit to rule than *any* man I have seen!"

"More fit than you?" Strahan smiled coolly. "I think you discount yourself needlessly . . . and I think you misjudge *him*." He turned away briefly, paced three steps, turned back. And halted. "If a man is unfit to rule, should he not be replaced?"

"My *rujholli*—"

But the angry protest was overridden. "If a man is incapable of holding the Lion, should he be its master?"

"And if Brennan *were* unfit, Hart is next in line!"

"Hart will have Solinde."

Corin spoke distinctly. "My *jehan* was most particular in parceling out the realms. Mine is Atvia."

"*Your* realm, Corin, has been mine for several months, because of Lillith's power over its lord. But now Alaric is dead. His heir has disappeared. Into the confusion, I have moved to quell the fear." Strahan smiled. "There is no need for you there."

Corin sighed. "They would still turn to Hart. He is second-born. *I* would end up with Solinde."

"Hart will never be accepted in Homana . . . at least by the Cheysuli."

A chill touched Corin's neck. "What have you done to Hart?" Foreboding knotted his belly. "*Why* would they not accept him?"

"Becaused a maimed warrior has no place in the clans." Strahan shrugged. "Through great misfortune—he lost an important wager—Hart now lacks a hand. The Cheysuli will no longer honor him as a warrior. He is, as he himself says, *kin-wrecked.*"

"Maimed—" Corin mouthed it. The ring bit into the flesh of his palm. "Oh—*rujho* . . . no—"

"Aye," Strahan said, "and none of *my* doing. So—you see?—Homana is in dire need of a prince. A healthy, whole prince, willing to hold the Lion—"

Bitterly, Corin finished it, "—in the name of Asar-Suti."

The Ihlini lifted a single eloquent shoulder. "A minor price to pay. Look what you will get—Homana, the Lion . . . *Aileen.*"

Corin's head snapped up; he stared at the sorcerer.

Strahan smiled warmly. "Need I remind you? She is to wed the *Prince of Homana.*"

Gilded candles guttered. Flame danced and smoked.

Corin clutched the ring. "Show me," he said hollowly. "Show me my *rujholli*."

Strahan bowed his assent.

Three

The Gate emitted a deep gurgling belch, like a man suppressing laughter, as Strahan left the cavern. *Godfire* continued to play around the rim. Tendrils of it licked out of the hole, probed the air, withdrew in a splash of smoke. Caught in tiers of glassy arches, the echoed hiss was amplified.

Brennan rose, pressing himself to his feet with one thrust of a splayed hand. He went immediately to his brother.

Hart still knelt on the uneven floor, left arm hugged against his chest. The rocking had ceased, but not the rigidity of his body or the emptiness of his eyes. His face showed the strain of his captivity: pronounced hollows beneath high cheekbones, dark circles beneath blue eyes; a stark bleakness of expression that had nothing to do with captivity and everything to do with the choice Strahan had given him.

Gently, Brennan touched the crown of Hart's bowed head. "*Rujho*, I am sorry."

The sound of Hart's swallow was loud in the circle of flame. "The worst," he said, "the *worst* is knowing I can never fly again."

Brennan drew in a very deep breath, knowing there was nothing he could say to assuage his brother's anguish.

Hart turned his face up to stare at Brennan. "All of those other things I think I could learn to live with, given time—even being *kin-wrecked* . . . but to know I am earthbound *forever*—"

"I know." Brennan's fingers touched Hart's head. "I know."

"You do *not* know." Awkwardly, Hart got to his feet. "No warrior whose *lir* lacks wings can understand the freedom there is in the air, the manifest miracle of *flight*—" He broke off a moment, realizing he walked too close to the edge of control. "I do not discount Sleeta or your own *lir*-shape, Brennan, but it is not the same as mine."

"No," Brennan said. His eyes were on the leather-wrapped stump. "Hart, what happened?"

"Foolishness," Hart said bitterly. "Idiocy, and worse. I put myself in the hands of the enemy for the price of a stupid game."

"You wagered your *hand?*"

"No. Worse. I wagered Solinde." Hart drew in a deep breath, than blew it out. "It is complicated, *rujho*, and I am not proud of it. You can see the result plainly." Frowning, he looked more closely at his brother. "What has he done to you?"

"To me? To *me?* Nothing." Brennan turned away, paced a few steps, swung back. "Nothing that shows, *rujho* . . . he is too clever for that."

"Sleeta?"

"He has her. Somewhere here. Somewhere hidden." He shook his head. "Close enough to keep me from the edge of *lirlessness* and madness."

"But only just," Hart said flatly. "Do you think I cannot see it? I can see it in your *eyes*—"

Brennan waved it off. "Aye, aye," he said shortly, "but what of Strahan? I know why he wants us—to use as puppet-kings—but why this protracted mummery? Why not simply *force* us to do his will? He can. Easily. This is Valgaard, the Gate of the netherworld—his power is manifest. It should be a simple task—"

"Should be," Hart echoed, "but is it? Could there be a limit to his power? Does he require *willing* victims?"

Brennan's expression was a scowl of consideration. "He has other minions, but none of them are Cheysuli . . . none of them have the Old Blood—"

"But this is *Valgaard*. Why should it matter here?"

"Supposedly, it should not." Brennan shrugged. "Wishful thinking, *rujho*—but could it be that he needs more power to make a Cheysuli his? That one who fights his influence could drain him of his strength?"

"Strahan's strength seems boundless."

Brennan rubbed a hand through dirty hair. "Aye. But what other explanation? Why does he try to induce us when force should be enough?"

Hart stared toward the Gate. "Perhaps it is nothing more than a facet of his perversity. Which would please him more, *rujho*—a Cheysuli who was forced, or one who accepted service willingly?

"Even Gisella was not forced."

Hart shivered once. "No. What need? Lillith twisted her so badly—"

"—at least, what was left from the unfortunate circumstance of her birth." Brennan's expression was unsettled; only rarely did he give over any time to thinking of his mother. "But this is different, *rujho*—"

"Aye," Hart said harshly. "He *knows* what inducements to use."

Brennan looked at him sharply, suddenly afraid. The note in Hart's voice, the expression in his eyes . . . foreboding was iron in Brennan's belly. "Hart, I can hardly *begin* to comprehend what you have lost—"

"Aye," Hart said curtly. "Look to yourself, *rujho*. My choice is my own to make."

And abruptly, the fence of fire died away.

Smoke boiled up from the Gate and carpeted the floor. It touched their knees, no higher; spread out to engulf cavern and corridor, wreathing glassy columns. Through the smoke came Strahan, holding the rune-worked box.

Hart's breath was harsh in his throat. Brennan looked away.

"*Tahlmorra lujhala mei wiccan, cheysu*," Strahan said as he walked. Echoes thrummed in the Seker's harp. "Such an all-encompassing statement, this thing of gods and fate. Have you never thought to question it? To free yourselves of such blind and binding service?"

Slowly, Brennan shook his head. "No more than you have questioned your own service to the Seker."

"Ah, but I have my reasons." Strahan paused between them, near the lip of the Gate. And then circled it calmly to stand on the other side. He smiled and made a gesture. "A full complement of Niall's sons."

As he meant them to, Hart and Brennan turned to look. And stared, rigidly, as Corin was brought into the cavern. That he could not walk was plain; both legs were tightly bound in wooden splints and linen wrappings. Ihlini carried him on a litter. He reclined against piled bolsters, but gripped the litter with both hands.

"You may blame me as you like," Strahan said, as Hart and Brennan turned back to him with anger in their faces, "but it is not my doing." He shrugged. "Broken legs mend. He will be whole soon."

"Provided he accepts the bargain you offer him," Brennan turned his head and spat. "You are *abomination*—"

"Am I?" Strahan smiled. He watched as his servitors brought the litter to a halt near the Gate and set it down. "I was thinking I might prefer to be known as *deliverance*."

Hart went to Corin. "*Rujho*—"

"I am well enough," Corin said. "For all I hate to admit it, Strahan does not lie. I am nearly healed." His eyes were on Hart's left wrist. "He told me—he *told* me—"

Hart's mouth twisted. "Strahan does not lie." He sighed. "You know what he wants from us."

Corin averted his gaze. "Aye. He has made it very plain."

Brennan came to the litter and knelt. "Corin—"

"Enough," Strahan said. "The reunion may come later. I want you to listen to *me*."

After a moment, Brennan rose. Hart turned to face the Ihlini squarely. On his litter, Corin watched.

"I am no more abomination than *you*," Strahan told Brennan. "What I do, I do for my god, my race, myself. I *believe* in what I do, because what I do is just."

"The destruction of the Cheysuli? The fall of Homana?" Brennan shook his head. "I think—"

"You do *not* think!" Strahan shocked them all with the abruptness and intensity of his passion. The sound reverberated in the cavern, threading its way among the columns of the Seker's monstrous harp. "*If* you thought, you would realize that what I do is no different from what you do, if for a different reason." Now his tone was cold as he looked at each of them individually. "When I was a boy, and very young, I learned what hatred was, and I learned that it had no place in what I was meant to do. *And so I do not hate you.*" He drew in a breath, strung so tightly the others thought—prayed—he might snap. "I learned what it was to prepare myself to serve my father's god with absolute loyalty, knowing the way of the Seker was the only way for me. And when Carillon slew Tynstar and Electra, stripping me of my parents, I learned what it was to know of the desire for revenge— and how to *detach* myself from it so it did not affect my judgment, my needs, my loyalty to my God and to *his* needs."

"No doubt." Brennan said coolly. "We see the design quite clearly."

"Do you? I think not. I think you see only *yourself* caught within a trap, when the trap involves much more than a single man." Strahan shook his head. "You give yourself too much value, too much weight in the fabric of life . . . you are but a slub within the cloth, subject to rejection."

Brennan's brows rose. "If that were true—"

"—I would not want you?" Again, Strahan shook his head. "You are an ingredient, but hardly the dish itself."

"What is this nonsense?" Hart asked harshly. "What is this senseless talk of hatred, revenge, *cloth*—?"

Strahan's odd eyes were incredibly compelling. "I am no different from any of you. I serve my god as you serve the pantheon of your own, as dedicated to destroying the prophecy as you are to fulfilling it. Why? Because fulfillment destroys the Ihlini." He spread one hand; the other held the rune-scribed box. "You see? A *simple* answer for you: I believe in what I do every bit as strongly as you do in your prophecy. Does it make me a monster?

Does it make me abomination? Does it make me different from you?"

"We do not kill people arbitrarily," Corin said curtly. "We—"

But Strahan's laughter overrode his retort. "Oh, *no?*" the Ihlini asked. "Then what of the thirty-two innocent souls who burned to death in the Midden? Was *that* done with purpose?"

For a long moment all any of them could do was stare, stricken. And then Hart stirred, knowing himself most guilty.

"But we do not set about destroying an entire race," he answered flatly. "What of the plague, Strahan? Twenty years ago it nearly killed us all. What of the *wars*, Strahan? How many hundreds of years has Homana fought Solinde merely to stave off the Ihlini? What of all the trap-links and other sorcerous things designed to bring us down?"

"War requires harsh measures," Strahan said, "and this *is* war. A battle for survival that you would fight as hard, if you were not so blind."

"What are we blind *to?*" Corin demanded in frustration.

"Yourselves," Strahan told him, looking from Corin to Hart to Brennan. "Once the Firstborn have come, we will be redundant. Ihlini *and* Cheysuli; the need for us is gone."

Brennan's disgust was plain. "I have heard that before." He thought of Tiernan and other similar sentiments. "It is idiocy, Strahan—why would the gods sentence us to death on the birth of other children?"

"It is the way of things." Strahan said. "When you breed a stallion and mare to improve exisiting bloodlines, you desire offspring combining the best of both. And then you breed get to get to *fix* the characteristics. It is the same with dogs, with sheep, with cattle . . . and one day, when you have the characteristics you want, you realize there is no need for the progenitors; they are obsolete. The new breed is much better." The light was odd on his face. *"It is the same with people."*

Corin laughed once. "You reduce the House of Homana to a collection of studs and mares."

"Look at your prophecy," Strahan snapped impatiently. "Are you blind to its commands?" Glibly contemptuous, he quoted. " *'One day a man of all blood shall unite, in peace, four warring realms and two magical races.'* " He stared at them angrily. "Marry here, wed there, get the blood for the prophecy . . . look to no other kingdom because we need *this* one, to fulfill the prophecy." He shook his head in disgust. "A collection of studs and mares . . . what *else* do you think you are?"

None of them could answer.

Strahan nodded slightly. "You are all of you one of the final links in the prophecy. You combine the blood of three realms: Homana, Solinde, Atvia. You lack only Erinn, but children born of Brennan and Aileen will fulfill that portion, as well as children of Keely and Sean. And that leaves only the blood of the Ihlini." Black brows touched the circlet in an expression of delicate amusement. "The hardest feat of all, getting Cheysuli to lie with Ihlini."

Brennan's flesh went suddenly hot on his bones.

"Of course," Strahan continued, "the precedent *has* been set. By Ian. The unspeakable was accomplished once—and then again." He looked at Brennan. "And yet an impediment exists. The child will not quite be a Firstborn, lacking some of the blood . . . it will not *quite* be the human equivalent to fulfillment of the merging of power and bloodlines—but it *will* have a complement of powers greater than most of ours. And I will put it to good use in breeding it for my own."

"Then Sidra's child *is* yours," Corin blurted.

"Of course." Strahan smiled. "The Cheysuli have done well breeding so close to the prophecy, so I will adopt a successful strategy and use it for my own. Rhiannon's child shall marry mine, once the genders are in balance." His glance at Brennan was amused. "I doubt Brennan will freely participate again, but Sidra is young and I am potent. In time, I shall have the pair I require."

"Then let us go," Hart suggested. "Of what use are we to you?"

"To *me,* not so much. But to the Seker, aye. He wants

the realms, and I will do what I can to win them from those who would keep them from him."

"*Why* does he want them?" Hart demanded. "Why all this greed, this overweening ambition? He *has* the netherworld—why must he want the rest?"

Strahan, for the first time, looked truly perplexed. "Why? Because he does." He shrugged. "It is not *my* place to question the ambitions of a god."

Corin nodded. "And when *you* are become a god?"

Strahan's motion was arrested. He looked at Corin blankly.

"Aye," Corin said, "I begin to put it together." He struggled to sit more upright on the litter. "A faithful servant, Strahan, working for the god—but when the task is done? When you have succeeded? Does he give you what *you* want?"

"What *I* want is immaterial—"

"A godhood of your own?"

"Godhood!" Brennan stared. "Is *that* what—"

"*I serve Asar-Suti!*" Strahan's shout reverberated in the cavern. "He is my god, my lord, *the Seker,* the font of all my strength—"

"And you want parity." Corin smiled. "I understand an ambitious man. But I wonder . . . does Asar-Suti?"

Strahan's eyes narrowed slightly, but his smile remained unblemished. "And does Brennan know how much you want Aileen?"

Corin's arms collapsed beneath him. He slumped back into the pillows.

"Aileen?" Brennan said blankly. Then he looked at Corin. "*You* want—"

"He said you were unfit." Corin's tone was curt and characteristically defensive.

"Unfit! I? And you believed him?"

"Are you not?" Strahan asked.

Brennan nearly gaped. "I have spent nearly twenty-two years of my life learning *how* to rule—I doubt I am unfit!"

"Are you not?" Strahan repeated. "Think back, my lord of Homana . . . think back to your fear."

Brennan's color faded.

"Aye," Strahan said. "Your fear of small, dark places—the terror of close confinement . . . the diminishment of the *man* who becomes nothing more than a beast." He smiled. "Do you think I have not seen it? Rhiannon told me of it, and I have watched you in your cell."

"Enough!" Hart shouted, seeing Brennan's eyes.

Strahan looked only at Brennan. "I ask you to serve me willingly, as I have done before. Accept, and I will free you forever of this fear."

Brennan swallowed tightly. "No."

"Then live in it again . . . show Corin how *fit* you are to rule." Strahan raised his hand and Brennan's world was changed.

He was small, so small, so *tiny* in the abyss of the world. He knelt on the ground and hugged himself, wrapping himself in his arms, trying to withstand the pain and fear of knowing himself alone.

The vastness amazed him. It made him insignificant, reduced him to obsolescence. Alone in the world he knelt on a vast stone plain, watching the world around him, and saw it begin to move.

—how it *moved*—

Like a sphincter squeezing closed, it began to move upon him. Fold upon fold, swallowed by itself. The world grew smaller and smaller and smaller, until he could put out his hands and touch it, and then it grew smaller still.

All around him the world trembled. And then it touched him, even as he withdrew. It drew closer, *closer,* until he could not breathe without feeling its caress; without smelling the stink of its fetid breath and the slime of its glass-black skin. Awash in the power of helplessness, he felt the world draw closer.

—so small—

—he could not straighten legs—could not sit up—could not stretch out his arms—

All around him the world squeezed.

—so dark—

He was entombed within the world, and it was deaf to his cries.

Brennan fell backward, rolling from one hip onto his spine. Cramped thighs spasmed and trembled, jerking twisted tendons. His skull banged against the floor, released from the rigidity of his neck. He lay on the stone and shook, wet from the sweat of his fear.

Dimly he heard movement. But no one came to aid him.

"What kind of king," Strahan said, "fears confinement more than death? Fears it *so* much that it robs him of control?" He pointed slowly to Brennan's trembling body on the floor. "Do you, Corin, truly believe him fit to rule? Fit to hold the Lion? *To sire children on Aileen?*"

"Stop!" Corin shouted.

Strahan ripped open the box. "Accept service with me, and I will make your brother whole!"

Sickened, Corin stared. "Oh—gods—*stop*—"

"You see what Brennan is—*I can free him of that!*"

"No more!" Corin cried.

"Take the Lion for me. Hold Homana for me. *Take the woman for yourself!*"

Corin clapped both his hands to his head. "Make him *stop*—"

Hart tried. Even as Strahan shouted something more, he lurched forward and threw himself across the expanse of the Gate.

Flame licked up. It bathed Hart briefly as he leaped. He cried out, came down, landed hard on the other side, too near, *too near* the Gate—

Brennan, still weakened from his ordeal, struggled to hands and knees. "Hart—*no!*"

Strahan stood his ground. "*Corin*—"

"No—" Hart scraped his knees and boots against the rim of the Gate, grimacing in pain.

"*I will give your brothers their lir*—"

"Corin—*no*—" Hart gasped.

Brennan rose unsteadily. "Hart—get back—*Hart*—"

Abruptly, Strahan knelt on one knee before Hart. His hands held out the box. "Do you want it? *Do you want it?* You have only to say the word—"

"*No*—" Brennan shouted.

Strahan's smile was unearthly. "To be a whole Cheysuli, honored by all the clan—"

"Leave him alone!" Corin cried.

"*—to be able to fly again—*"

Brennan stumbled forward. "Hart—*get back*—"

Flame exploded from the Gate and blinded all save Strahan.

"*—to know the freedom of the skies—*"

Hart wavered on his knees. "*Ku'reshtin*—"

"Take *me!*" Corin shouted. "*I* will accept the service—"

"Corin—Corin, *no*—" Brennan tried to round the Gate. Flame licked out, slapped him down, smashed him against the floor.

"Take *me!*" Corin cried.

Hart threw himself at the Ihlini. Strahan fell heavily, landing on hip and elbow. A shower of sparks exploded from the Gate.

"He is forsworn!" Strahan shouted. "You heard what he said—"

Hart dragged himself forward, bodily preventing the sorcerer from rising. Steadfastly he ignored the rope of Ihlini *godfire* that caught an ankle and tugged, trying to jerk him into the Gate.

"He is *forsworn!*" Strahan shouted.

Hart's hand was on the box. Runes blazed up and writhed, then circled the rectangular box in a blur of uncanny script. Faster, *faster*, until the blur ran off the wood and leaped onto Hart's remaining hand. He cried out in pain, but did not release the box.

Brennan, badly disoriented, tried to stand up and failed. Nearly senseless, he crawled slowly toward his brother.

Hart jerked the box from Strahan's grasp. Twisting, he turned back toward the Gate. "*—my* choice—" he gasped, and hurled it into the flames.

The loss was new again. He felt the sword blade come down, divide flesh, muscles, vessels, shear easily through bone. He saw the blood. Saw the severed hand. Saw Dar laughing at him.

Pain.

Hart screamed.

One Ihlini servitor caught Brennan. A second dragged Hart off Strahan and pushed him back around the Gate. Strahan sat at the rim and laughed, one foot wreathed in icy Ihlini *godfire*. And then it crept up slowly, so *slowly*, to touch his knee, his thigh, his hip; caressed his genitals. And exploded in ecstacy as it swallowed the rest of him.

The fire died quickly before their astonished eyes. In its place was a delicate webwork of lavender lace, a lattice of living light that cloaked exposed flesh. Hands. Throat. Face. It even pooled in his mouth; licked out of nostrils as he breathed. Through it all, Strahan laughed.

He rose. He went directly to Corin; inclined his glowing head. And then knelt to catch the wrist that still bore the silver shackle.

"No more need for *this*." It caught fire, flowed off Corin's hand, pooled in Strahan's webworked palm. And then shaped itself into a silver goblet. "There." Strahan rose, turned, knelt again at the rim of the Gate. Dipped the cup. Came up with dripping *godfire*. His smile was for Corin alone. "I give you the baptismal cup . . . and good welcome to the world."

Corin's face was awash in the glow of he cup. His eyes were blue, all blue, with only a speck of pupil.

"Corin!" Brennan shouted.

Corin's gaze was transfixed by Strahan's altered appearance. The Ihlini offered the cup. Fingernails glowed. "Drink of Asar-Suti."

Hart struggled impotently against the man who held him. "Corin, *no*—I threw it away—*I threw it away*—no need for this sacrifice—"

"Drink," Strahan said, and helped Corin hold the cup.

"*Ku'reshtin!*" Brennan shouted. "Did you do this for Aileen?"

"No." Corin said, "I do this for myself."

And drank of Asar-Suti.

Four

In Strahan's luxurious tower chamber, they faced the sorcerer. They did not sit, though he did, preferring instead to stand. Hart cradled his arm; Brennan waited rigidly.

The Ihlini stretched out elegantly booted legs. The unearthly living lace had died from his flesh, but there remained an aura of power. Subtle, but intoxicating; both Cheysuli felt it. Neither succumbed to it.

In his chair, Strahan smiled. "The game is somewhat altered."

"Is that what this is?" Brennan asked harshly. "An afternoon's entertainment?"

"It *is* entertaining." Strahan, chin in hand, slouched casually against the chair arm and braced his elbow on it. "Entertaining as well as enlightening . . . but no, not a game. For none of us, now; certainly not for Corin."

Hart took a single step forward. "What have you done to him?"

"I?" One winged black brow rose. "*I* have done nothing at all."

"That *bile* you made him drink—"

"The blood of Asar-Suti," Strahan corrected calmly. "And I made him drink nothing; did you see him turn away? Did you see him choke? Did you see him spit it out?" The Ihlini shook his head with its fall of raven hair. "No. He did none of those things. He drank it willingly, and was filled with the spirit of the Seker. *You* saw his eyes."

Brennan's temper flared. "He had no choice—"

"He had *every* choice." Strahan leaned forward in the chair. "He accepted my offer of his own free will. He *drank* of his own free will. I used nothing at all on him save persuasion, and *that,* my Cheysuli kinsman, is power no different from your own." He sat back again. The elaborate courtesy and negligent humor were gone, replaced by a sharp intensity. "Now. I have Corin; that is finished. What do I do with you?"

"Finished," Hart echoed. "*Finished?* If you think we will let it rest—"

Strahan's eyes blazed. "*I think you will do exactly as I tell you.*"

It stopped both of them cold.

The Ihlini uncoiled and pressed himself out of the chair. He stepped very close to Hart, though he did not touch him, and held him in place with an unwavering stare. "It is your misfortune," he said clearly, "that you chose to destroy your own flesh. Now you are truly cut off from your people, and through your own doing. Blame *yourself* for that; I will have none of it!"

Hart wanted to fall back, but forced himself to stand still. This close to the Ihlini he could feel Strahan's power as if it leaked out of the pores of his skin.

"Your determination is commendable." Strahan continued, "and its seeming boundlessness is a trait I do admire. I *want* steadfast, loyal men, willing to sacrifice that which they prize most. But I think you misjudge my willingness to mold such men into the shapes that serve me best."

"Willingness." Brennan was elaborately distinct. "A familiar refrain, Ihlini . . . but why is it so important? If you have so much power, why not *force* Hart and me to do your bidding? Why *not* mold us into the shapes that serve you best?" He spread his hands. "Here we stand, sorcerer—why not shape the clay?"

Something flickered in Strahan's mismatched eyes. Briefly, so briefly, but Hart had seen it, and so had Brennan.

Hart's eyes narrowed. "You have us," he said intently.

"What can we do to gainsay you? *Make* us the minions you want."

Strahan flicked a finger and the door slammed open. "You are dismissed."

Hart held his ground. Brennan moved to stand beside him.

Strahan's fair skin burned darker in slanted cheekbones. "You are *dismissed*."

"All those threats," Hart said quietly. "All those promises . . . empty, all of them?"

"Is it that we *must* be willing?" Brennan asked. "Why else do you waste so much time on trying to break us physically, hoping to *persuade* us? Is it that an unwilling minion lacks something you need in us? Something peculiar to *us*?"

"So peculiar that without it, your efforts would be in vain?" Hart smiled. "I think we have beaten you, Strahan. I think we have won at last."

Strahan said nothing at all.

Brennan began to smile. "And what are we? Princes. More than Cheysuli, but *princes,* meant to inherit realms. Homana. Solinde." He nodded. "You cannot rule on your own, so you hope to rule through us. But there is no puppet-king if the king is *too much* a puppet—"

"You need us sane," Hart said intently. "You need us complete in wits. And if you *force* us to your service, we will lack the thing you require—"

"—and the people will throw us down." Slowly, Brennan spread his hands. "Kill our bodies, kill our wits . . . and you are left with nothing."

"So," Hart said, "where is the leverage now? If you kill Sleeta, Brennan will go mad. No minion in Homana; the people will not have it. Rael you do not have, so what is there for me?" He lifted his left arm. "I threw it away, Strahan—you cannot use my hand."

"Leverage?" Strahan nodded, turned away, swung back. "Aye, there is a need. And I do have it."

"What is there left?" Brennan asked.

"Corin," Strahan said, and their triumph poured away.

*   *   *

The youngest of Niall's sons stared at the man who faced him. For a long moment he did not know him, barely knowing himself, and then a name came into his head. *Strahan*. Strahan, called the Ihlini.

Strahan's outline was blurred. His face was a blaze of white, marred only by the holes for eyes, nose, mouth. And then the blaze became more distinct, and the holes dissolved themselves into things identifiable, and Corin knew whom he faced.

He shuddered once, like a man awakening from a deep, dreamless sleep. He was, he realized, ensconced within a massive chair, supported by tall back, tall sides, cushioned seat. It cradled his lax body like a woman a sleeping child.

Sleeping. Aye, he had been. Or something close to it.

Strahan stood before him, holding a cup in his hands. A black glass goblet, unlike the silver one that had held the blood of the god. This one smelled of wine.

"Drink." Strahan held it out. "It will help restore you."

Slowly Corin took it. The world was dulled to him, wrapped in swaddling clothes. He felt heavy, ponderous, movements slowed accordingly. His fingers closed on the cup, felt the warmth of the glass, carried it to his mouth. He drank deeply, sighed, felt his head thump against the chair.

Strahan took the cup away. "It takes time," he said, "to accustom yourself to it. You will know discomfort, but it will pass. I promise."

Corin looked at the sorcerer. He saw the fine planes of jaw, cheekbones, brow; the oblique angles of mismatched eyes. Such fine, delicate features, yet there was no mistaking his sex.

Strahan smiled and sat down in a chair opposite. "I thought it might be Hart," he said calmly. "I underestimated him, believing his need for his race would outweigh his dedication. But you will do well enough."

Corin swallowed heavily. His voice seemed very distant, as if another man spoke. "Hart is often misjudged.

People see only his fecklessness, his desire for amusement. They look no farther than that."

Strahan considered it. "What will sway him, then? I
cannot replace his hand."

"The loss of his place in the clan." Corin frowned a
little. "You have cut away his anchor . . . he will founder
on the rocks one day, no matter what he says. Offer him
succor. In time he will repay it."

The Ihlini stroked one eyebrow. "And Brennan?"

"Him you may never win." Corin shifted in the chair.
His bones tingled. He *itched*. "I know of no way to
convince him. Brennan's particular strength lies in his
unequaled loyalty to kin, clan and prophecy." He
shrugged. "It will make him a predictable Mujhar, but
also a very good one."

"Then perhaps he should not *be* Mujhar." Strahan
nodded thoughtfully. "I made you promises, and I intend
to keep them. Brennan will undoubtedly become expendable . . . Homana will need a new king. You I can
put in his place."   ⟍

Corin rubbed at his tingling scalp. "Aileen . . ." He
shivered. "What of *Aileen?*"

Strahan waved a hand. "With Homana and Solinde
under my control, it no longer matters whom she mar-
ries. The prophecy will not be completed no matter what
child is born." He shrugged. "I no longer need her.
Alaric failed to spirit her to Atvia, and there was no time
for a second try. Now there is no need. You may have
her, Corin. It was a part of our bargain."

Corin blinked repeatedly. The chamber was bright, too
bright; he squinted against the light.

"It will be difficult," Strahan said softly. "I will not
discount the steadfast determination of your race . . . the
arrogance of your convictions. But I need your brothers,
Corin. May I count on you?"

Corin frowned. "There may be a way," he said. "Will
you trust me to do it?"

Strahan showed even teeth in a silent laugh. "Trust?
There is no need for *trust*. If I tell you to do a thing, you
will do it without question. That is the way of the service."

Something flickered deep inside Corin. Mute denial. But it was snuffed out so quickly by apathy he hardly recognized it.

"There may be a way," he said again. "What they want most is freedom. Their need of it may overshadow their caution and distrust."

"Aye." Strahan nodded. "We shall devise a scenario, and then give them what they want."

Corin shut his eyes. The world was too bright to bear, his flesh too heavy to carry. "I can deliver them."

"Good," Strahan said. He poured himself more wine.

The cell was new to Brennan, though not so to Hart; larger, brighter, more comfortable than the tiny one Brennan had known for months. Two fat candles burned in corners opposite one another. A narrow cot lined one wall, which was, like the others, cool but dry, lacking fetid slime. The occupant, unlike his brother, had also been provided with a bucket in which to relieve himself.

Hart sat down on the cot and hunched against the wall, cradling his left arm. He stared into invisible distances.

Brennan saw the withdrawal at once. "Hart—"

"Gone," he said. *"Gone."* He looked at the emptiness where once his hand had been. "And I did it to myself."

Slowly Brennan sat down on the edge of the cot. He felt a vague sense of relief that *he* still had both hands, and guilt because he did. "If you had accepted Strahan's bargain—"

"I *know!*" Hart cried. "*I know, Brennan*—I do not require reminding!"

Inwardly Brennan recoiled, though his body did not move.

"I know," Hart repeated. "I know what I did was right. I *know* it was for the best—to remove the possibility I might succumb to the temptation—but knowing it makes it no better. Corin *did* succumb . . . what I did was for naught."

Brennan drew in a steadying breath. "Not for naught," he said quietly. "That bargain was offered me as well, before you were brought into the cavern. And once I saw your face, how the knowledge ravaged your spirit, I knew there was a very good chance Strahan had judged me too well."

"He promised you *my hand?*"

"To make you whole again, just as he promised you." Brennan scratched viciously as a louse ran against his scalp.

"What else?"

Brennan sighed. "The lives of all my kin." He looked at Hart. "*And* release from the fear."

Hart massaged his forearm above the cuff. He frowned a little, clearly reluctant to speak. "You never told me," he said finally, obviously hurt. "You never told me about your fear. You told me *everything*—"

"Everything but that." Brennan stared at the floor. "I was ashamed."

"To tell *me?*"

"To tell anyone." He flickered a glance at Hart. "You most of all; you are afraid of nothing."

Hart's face tightened; his mouth hooked down briefly in mute argument. "So you locked it away inside of you, until Strahan discovered the secret." He sighed heavily. "Oh, *rujho*, I am sorry . . . I might have helped you with it."

"For me to do." Brennan shrugged. "But now—" He stopped. "Oh, gods, Hart—what are we to do? How do we deal with Corin?"

"As we have dealt with Strahan."

"He is our *rujholli!*"

"And he has turned his back on his race to serve Asar-Suti."

"Has he?" Brennan asked. "*Has* he?"

"You saw his eyes. You saw how his legs were healed." Hart leaned his head against the wall. "You saw how he rose and walked; how he knelt down at the rim of the Gate."

"To make his obeisance to the Seker." Twitching in distaste, Brennan shut his eyes. "What will Strahan *do* with him?"

"Use him," Hart said flatly. "What else is leverage for?"

Brennan turned his head and looked at his brother. Before, overwhelmed by what the loss of Hart's hand represented, he had looked at nothing else, *seeing* nothing else. But now he looked, now he *saw,* and was shocked by the tension in the body so like his own; equally stunned by the pronounced lack of conditioning. Hart had lost weight, muscle tone, the hard fitness characteristic of a Cheysuli.

Worse, and indicative of something far graver than physical discomforts, Brennan saw Hart had also lost the high-spirited good humor that marked him different from any of Niall's other children.

It frightened him for some obscure reason. He did not expect Hart to be *amused* by the circumstances, nor particularly cheerful, but Brennan was accustomed to his brother's uncanny ability to find the good in the bad. He realized, in that moment, that for all he had longed for Hart to shed some immaturity, he treasured his brother's relentless search for diverting entertainment. And now that propensity was lacking.

Brennan forced a smile. "If we had us a fortune-game—"

Something flared in Hart's eyes. First shock, then recollection, then a deep and abiding anger that stunned Brennan with its virulence.

"*No* game!" Hart said viciously.

"Hart—"

"*No game—*" And he was up, thrusting himself one-armed from the cot, to pace the cell like an animal.

Brennan stared in shock. "Hart—what *happened* in Solinde?"

"This!" Hart thrust out his left arm. "*This*—and my stupidity . . . my incredible gullibility."

"Hart—*everyone* is gullible at one time or another."

"Not like this." Hart stopped pacing and fell back against the wall, pressing shoulders into stone. "Oh, Brennan, I was such a fool. They laid a trap most carefully, baiting it so well, and I gobbled it whole, not even bothering to *sniff*." He sighed. "But I thought she was a pawn as much as I."

"Ah." Brennan sighed. "She."

"*Never* have I been such a blind, witless fool."

"You are not the first."

"But I should have *known* . . . I should have *seen* it." Hart closed his eyes. "All a wager, the *ultimate* wager, and I primed to be the loser, regardless if I won."

It was too obscure for Brennan, who was more concerned with Hart's well-being than his reference. "Aye, well, take consolation in the fact you did not give Strahan the *child* he wanted." He pushed himself back until he leaned against the wall. "The girl from The Rampant Lion—do you recall?"

Hart frowned. "The Lion? No. What girl? And what *child*?"

"The girl I rescued from Reynald of Caledon, Einar's illustrious cousin."

"Oh, aye, I recall." Hart frowned. "What has *she* to do with this?"

"*She* set a trap for *me*. A most intricate trap indeed." He hooked one arm across his face. "I made her my *meijha*, Hart. I sired a child on her."

"It does happen. But why—"

"She is Ihlini. Daughter to Lillith and Ian." He removed the arm. "The child who will lie with *Strahan's* child to give him the power he needs."

Stunned, Hart stared. "Oh, *Brennan*—"

"But I did not lose a hand." Brennan rose and went to Hart, hooking an arm around his neck to pull him close. "Gods, *rujho*—I am so very sorry—"

The door swung open. Corin came into the cell.

He was whole, lacking splints or bandages. He had shaved, bathed, was clean again, smelling of scented oil instead of the stink of Valgaard's bowels. His hair was washed, cut, shining, indisputably free of lice. His clothing was immaculate, and of a decided Ihlini cut.

At his side was Kiri. Behind him two Ihlini.

"I wanted my *lir*," he said, "and Strahan gave her to me."

Brennan unwound his arm from Hart.

Corin lifted his right hand and displayed the ruby signet ring that once had hugged Brennan's forefinger. "I wanted Homana," he said, "and Strahan promised me it." His eyes were odd, more iris than pupil, with an eerie, unfocused cast. "I wanted your title, I wanted your throne, I said I wanted your woman. And Strahan will give her to me."

"This is for *Aileen?*"

"Aileen and all the rest."

Brennan's belly rolled. "By all the gods of Homana—"

But Corin shook his head. "By the god of the netherworld."

"No—" Hart cried, but missed as Brennan leaped.

Corin was slammed back against the wall. Brennan's fingers dug deeply into the flesh of his throat. "I swear, I will save the Seker the trouble of freeing your soul of its shell."

"Brennan, *no.*" Hart grasped at Brennan's arm and caught only cloth. "Brennan—"

The two Ihlini plucked Brennan from Corin and threw him across the cell. He tripped, fell, stayed down, legs asprawl as he hitched himself up on both elbows and stared unblinkingly at Corin, who gestured the two away. They went as far as the corridor.

"Your treatment is up to you." Corin told his brothers. "Certainly this sort of accommodation is not *required.*"

"Provided we do what Strahan wants," Hart said sourly.

"There is that." Corin looked at the cot, the slops pail, the two dim candles. Then he looked at Brennan. "You have never been a fool. Not in all the years I have known you. Why be one now?"

Brennan turned his head and spat deliberately.

"Corin—" Hart moved forward, saw the Ihlini tense, stopped and held his ground. "Corin, you *know* what he has done to you—what he made you do—"

"I did it of my own choosing." His eyes should have been dilated black in the shadows, but his pupils were nonexistent. "There are things in this world I have always wanted, and this is how I get them."

"By stealing them." Brennan's tone was deadly as he slowly sat up. "My title, my throne, my *bride*—"

"Aye!" Corin hissed. "Why should *you* want her? You never even bothered to *write*."

Brennan stood and tried to pull his crusted jerkin into something resembling a proper fit. "Obviously you did more than that while in Erinn."

A thin white line banded Corin's mouth. "I did not come to speak of Aileen. I came to speak to *you*, to suggest the course you should take."

"To tell us, no doubt, that we should do as Strahan suggests," Hart said in dry disgust.

"It *is* best," Corin told him quietly. "You have the right of it, both of you." He flicked a glance at the silent Ihlini. "He does require men *willing* to become minions. Without that willingness, the Seker exerts force . . . the results are—unattractive." His strange eyes focused a moment, than resumed their eerie cast. "Strahan prefers to rule through men with minds, as you have said. But he *is* willing to do it another way." He brushed back a lock of hair, frowned, then continued. "If it becomes necessary, he will force you to accede, and use what is left of you."

"He can hardly rule through idiots," Brennan said. "The people will never accept us."

"For a while they would. You would not go mad right away." Corin shrugged. "It would take time, during which Strahan could firm his grasp on the thrones of Solinde and Homana. Eventually, of course, no wits would be left in your heads, and you would be locked away. But by then, the damage would be done." He looked from one to the other. "Why persist in refusal? It does no good, none at all . . . he will break you, and eventually you will die. *Lirless*, friendless, alone." He stopped short, frowned again, then sighed. "Consider this: accept him and rule with dignity, with integrity, or deny him and lose anything even slightly resembling freedom of mind and soul."

Brennan drew in a deep, deep breath. "There was a time, Corin, and not so many years ago, that you swore an oath before kin and clan. Your Ceremony of Honors, where you named as *shu'maii* our *jehan*. Where you put on the *lir*-gold and accepted the responsibilities of a warrior, and all the loyalties it entails." His voice was very steady. "Do you stand here before me now and say you willingly *break that oath?*"

Corin did not blink. "I have sworn another."

Hart sat down awkwardly on the cot, as if his hamstrings had been cut. "No—no—*no*—"

"Oh, aye, he has," Brennan said coldly, "and I renounce him as my *rujholli*."

Nothing moved in Corin's eyes. "You may renounce *yourself* for all I care, Brennan . . . it has been a long, long time that I have watched you play your part as Prince of Homana, coveting it myself. And now, in the end, it *is* mine—"

"How?" Brennan shouted. "If I *do* accept this service, Homana will still be mine!"

Corin smiled. "No," he said, "no. In the end, it will be mine. Your fitness to rule will be questioned. After all, is your *jehana* not known as mad Gisella?"

"She also bore *you*."

"But I am not afraid of small, dark places. There is no doubting *my* sanity." He turned toward the Ihlini waiting in the corridor. "Do not wait. They will agree to nothing in front of you. Go to Strahan. I will bring them immediately I have an answer."

The Ihlini turned and melted away into the shadows.

Brennan slowly shook his head. "If you think I will agree to anything you suggest, or step one foot outside this cell with *you*—"

"I think you will." Corin briefly massaged his throat. "You give yourself away. You are so willing to believe the worst of me. If I were Hart, you would not be so quick." He sighed, bent to touch Kiri, then straightened again. He smiled a little, though it had an ironic hook. "Aye, you *did* believe it . . . well, so did Strahan. At least I know last night was worth it."

Hart sat slowly upright on the cot. All Brennan could do was stare.

Corin sighed. "I spent all of last night with fingers down my throat, trying to rid myself of that foul, malodorous bile Strahan calls the blood of the god. But if you tarry any longer, I will have to drink it again . . . two cups remain before I am truly his." He gestured toward the door. "I *would* suggest we go."

Speechlessly, they went.

Five

Corin led them down a twisting corridor illuminated by torches set in infrequent iron brackets. The flame was pure and yellow, not lurid Ihlini purple, but Hart, accustomed to little light, and Brennan, accustomed to none, found discomfort in the illumination. They squinted, avoiding the pools of light; Corin's nearly pupilless eyes remained wide and strangely unfocused.

Brennan's walk slowed. At last Corin turned. "If we tarry—"

"What if we do?" Curtly, Brennan overrode him. "I go nowhere without Sleeta."

Corin smiled a little, glancing down at Kiri. "I know. I do not expect you to. Sleeta is in the cavern."

"The cavern?" Hart stopped short. "You are taking us *there?*"

"Would you suggest we depart through the front entrance?" Corin's tone was dryly disgusted. "Valgaard is a maze of tunnels and corridors, as well as secret exits. But I only know of one; I am newly come to the god, and Strahan does not tell me everything as yet." He looked at them more closely and saw doubt in grimy faces. "Oh, aye, I know—now you are uncertain. Well, the choice is yours. Come with me, or stay." Corin turned and went on as Kiri trotted beside him.

Hart swore. Brennan sighed and shook his head. And then he shrugged and pushed off the wall, muttering resigned imprecations.

"Kiri is with him," Hart pointed out. "If he meant to trick us, would she accompany him?"

"The *lir*-link is obliterated here," Brennan said over his shoulder. "She knows as much of his intentions as we do."

"But would he lead *her* astray?"

"He is not the Corin we knew. Who can say what he will do?"

They turned a corner and came up on him as he waited in the shadows. *Lir*-gold gleamed in tawny hair; armbands were hidden beneath sleeves of a dark gray doublet.

"What I will do," Corin said distinctly, "is take you out of here."

"Then do it," Brennan told him.

He led them into yet another corridor. It was short, too short, showing a dead end. But Corin halted, touched a stone, and a piece of the wall slid aside. Cool air rushed out of the tunnel. The nearest torch was snuffed out.

Brennan's breath rasped in his throat as darkness settled around them. Behind him, Hart stepped closer and touched his shoulder briefly in a gesture of support.

"Almost there," Corin told them, and went into the shadowed tunnel.

"The gods forgive me if I do our *rujholli* an injustice—" But Brennan did not finish. He merely followed Corin.

The tunnel soon gave way into an alcove cut into polished basalt. And the alcove gave into the stairway leading down to the massive cavern. *Godfire* dripped from seams of rock, splattering on the stairs. Corin went on without pausing, steadily descending.

In the distance, harp strings thrummed. Something gibbered in the wall.

He took them out of the passageway into the archivolted cavern and led them to the Gate. He paused at the glowing rim and pointed into the glare.

"Down *there?*" Hart demanded.

"I am with you," Corin said. He gazed at them both with an eerie, unfocused stare. "*I* can show you the way."

As one, his brothers backed away from the lip of the Gate.

Corin stepped closer. "It is your only chance."

"Ours—*all* of us?" Brennan's eyes narrowed. "Or only Hart and me?"

Corin frowned. "I am coming with you. Do you think I would dare remain?"

Hart chewed on a lip as he stared at the opening. "Through the Gate itself?" His tone was dubious.

Brennan's was distrustful. "Into the lap of the god."

Corin bent down. One hand reached into the gate and scooped up livid *godfire*. "Cold," he said, "*cold*. You will shiver, but never burn."

"No," Brennan said. "I will forgo that exit."

"Then why not try *this* one?"

As one, they spun in place. Strahan stepped out of basalt.

Godfire edged his robe of deepest black. The silver on his brow glowed lilac-white in the glare of the Gate. Behind him was only shadow; no exit could be seen.

He gestured, indicating stone. "In there, Sleeta awaits. Why not go and see her?"

"Trap," said Brennan succinctly, unimpressed by Strahan's avowal.

"Is it?" Strahan moved closer to them, between the Gate and the glass of the cavern wall. Corin, at the rim, dropped down to his knees instantly in perfect homage. He bowed his head.

"*Ku'reshtin*," Brennan said bitterly, as Hart closed his eyes.

The Ihlini nodded slowly and put an approving hand on the tawny hair. "Well done, Corin. You have done as you said you would."

Corin turned his face up to Strahan. "And you have done as I *hoped*—" He lunged upward, off his knees, locking both arms around Strahan and pinning the sorcerer's arms. Even as Strahan twisted, Corin thrust out a foot to trip Strahan and tumble him into the Gate.

Flame gushed up. Strahan screamed something, and then the voice was silenced.

"*Now!*" Corin ran for the glassy wall.

"But nothing is *there!*" Brennan cried.

Corin and Kiri disappeared.

"*I* am not waiting." Hart ran for the darkness as well.

Brennan took a step after him, then stopped. He recalled too clearly the power that had reduced him to obsolescence. He recalled too clearly the fear that had engulfed him.

He shivered. Sweat broke out on his flesh.

And then the Gate disgorged the Ihlini, blazing like a pyre, and Brennan did not look back.

There was a seam, he saw at once. A fault in the stone, or else something cut by god or man. The naked eye could not see it, but the hand felt its gap. He slipped through and departed the cavern even as Strahan shouted.

He ran. The passageway engulfed him, scraping against bare arms. He heard the chime of *lir*-gold on basalt. It was a narrow, low conduit, alive with the stink of the netherworld. *Godfire* glimmered in crevices. For once, he was thankful; he would be blind without it.

He ran on, ignoring the knot in his belly. Small, dark place . . . and the only available exit.

"Hurry!" Hart called. The echo carried back, reverberating, and then Brennan saw them all. Hart. Kiri. Corin. And Sleeta just beyond, eyes aglow in purple *godfire*.

"*Lir*—" He tripped and nearly fell.

"No time," Corin said breathlessly. "The bailey is just beyond."

Brennan caught his balance. "Strahan is *alive*."

Corin's face was stark. Fear turned blue eyes black. "Then he can still *gainsay* me." He turned abruptly and thrust the hidden door open.

Cheysuli and *lir* spilled out of basalt into the bailey, footsteps echoing on cobbles. All around them was darkness and the breath of Asar-Suti. Stars were but a dim glow through the veil of malodorous smoke.

"I have forgotten what daylight is like." Hart remarked, half laughing. "Will we ever see the sun?"

"Not if we tarry here." At a run, Corin headed toward

the gates with Kiri streaking behind. Hart caught Brennan's arm. With Sleeta, they followed their brother.

Stone shifted beneath their feet. It burst from under boots and threw them to the ground. Once, twice, thrice; each time they lost more distance. Some stone melted, clinging to their boots. Other cobbles exploded around them and rained down as smoking missiles.

Hart fell. Pain set his stump ablaze. The missing hand spasmed and tried to clutch at stone.

"Up—up—" Brennan dragged him from the ground.

Corin was at the gates. Frenziedly he threw the bar out of its brackets.

"No guards," Hart gasped. "Why does he post no guards?"

"Does an Ihlini require any?" Brennan dodged as a cobble exploded beneath his right boot, sending fragments of smoking stone slicing through the air. Splinters cut one cheek.

"Now—*now*—" Corin's shout was mostly swallowed by the shrieks and whistles of flying cobbles.

Massive gates tore loose of hinges and slowly began to topple. Corin scooped Kiri up and ran through as they crashed down. The sound of thunder filled the bailey; if Strahan did not already know precisely where they were, the noise would surely tell him.

Brennan gaped in astonishment as he and Hart ran on, pounding over the fallen wood. "By the gods—Strahan is using Valgaard *itself* to stop us!"

"Trying—" Hart rasped. "Oh—gods—I had forgotten *this!*"

They were through. The walls of Valgaard fell behind them; the field of fire lay before, stretching into the night. Fold upon fold of stone, all piled on one another; ripple here, curl there; a treacherous carpet of ensorcelled stone. The god had a sense of humor.

They ran. Staggered. Tripped. Got up and ran again, cursing the pockets of shadow that reached out to catch their boots. Cauldrons gurgled, fumaroles splattered, smoke issued forth from vents. It coated flesh, clogged throats, filled eyes with irritation. Coughing, wheezing, gagging, they stumbled through crumbling crusts and tripped over the spine of the earth itself, wrenched free of flesh and muscle. The viscera was foul.

Shadows loomed. Darkness incarnate, stretching across the ground. And then the rules were changed.

Unexpectedly, there was movement in addition to their own. They snatched hurried glances out of the corners of reddening eyes, and then the eyes abruptly widened. The field was a grotesque boardgame made by the god himself, and the pieces were alive.

"The stone—*moving*—" Brennan croaked.

Shadows altered. Darkness shifted. The pattern of fear mutated. Strahan's stone menagerie came to life in the sulfurous murk.

Hart recalled his father telling stories of how he had voluntarily come into Valgaard, alone, leaving behind even his *lir*, to make a bargain with Strahan. He recalled very clearly Niall's descriptions of the canyon of the god, cut so sharply from black basalt. As a child he had smelled the sulfur and squinted against the fumes, imagining Strahan's lair. Now he was in it himself, experiencing the same doubts and fears that Niall himself had known.

"Watch out for the stones," Corin rasped. "Remember how *jehan* told us they can move—?"

Brennan fell over a coiled protuberance. He landed hard, jarring his senses; a vent cracked open beneath him. Cursing, he tried to rise before the Seker's spittle burst forth.

Hart snatched one arm, Corin the other as steam gushed out of the vent. Together they dragged him free, scraping boot toes against rock, and forced him back into a stumbling run. Dodging paws and teeth and slashing tails, all formed of sinuous stone, they fled toward the defile that would give them exit from Strahan's domain.

"Not so far—" Hart panted. "Almost there—" Stone parted beneath his boots even as he spoke. He leaped, stumbled, staggered on, ignoring the angry gurgle.

Through the shadows Sleeta flowed like watered silk on velvet. Brennan longed to go into the link, to reestablish the communication he wanted so desperately, but such an attempt was futile so close to the Gate. Here the Ihlini was paramount, so long as he worshiped the god.

Corin swore as a wave of steam coated face and hands. He slowed, halted, rubbed hastily at stinging eyes. Tears rendered him incapable of seeing, and he dared not run blind.

Kiri yapped, then nipped at his ankles. And then he sensed the *presence*—"

"Corin—*run!*" Brennan cried.

He cleared his vision in time to see a monstrous gryphon bearing down on him, stone beak agape. Beneath the hiss of steam was the grate of stone on stone, and the yapping of his *lir*.

Corin twisted away, feeling the touch of ensorcelled stone as a wing cruelly caressed his scalp. He saw his brothers waiting, both poised to flee again. But their unwillingness to leave him renewed his fading strength.

"—coming—" he gasped, and ran.

And then, abruptly, could not.

He fell hard. Tried to rise. And then knew what Strahan had done.

"My legs!" he cried. "*My legs—*"

Jelly, Strahan had threatened. As Corin lay sprawled on hot stone, trying in vain to rise, he knew the healing had been recalled. There was no tremendous uprush of pain, no snapping of brittle bones, merely a return to what they had been before he had committed himself to the god. Nearly healed, but not completely; it left his bones fragile and his muscles weakened by confinement in splints and linens.

Kiri licked at his face. A cool nose nudged his neck and urged him desperately to rise. And then Hart and Brennan were lifting him, *dragging* him, as the world caught fire around them.

"—not so far—" Hart gasped, wrenching one-handed Corin's left arm across his shoulders.

"We will steal you from him yet." Brennan told Corin firmly.

And even though they dragged his feet, Corin shut his mouth on complaints.

Slowed by their burden, Hart and Brennan had more difficulty avoiding the Seker's grotesque mimicry of *lir*. None was especially mobile, being rock instead of flesh, but the advantage lay in being impervious to fumes and heat and flame. As Hart and Brennan slowed to negotiate the safest way with Corin, the monstrous creatures advanced.

Corin shivered. "Cold," he said. "—*cold*—"

Brennan's laugh was hoarse. "If only winter were this 'cold'—"

"Almost, *rujho*—" Brennan gasped, "—nearly through the defile—"

"Look!" Hart exclaimed. "Look above the opening!"

Brennan looked, saw the pristine line of white wings against the darkness, and laughed hoarsely. "Did you think Rael would *leave*?"

"—so long—" Hart croaked.

"*Put me down*—" Corin said. "Down—down—*down*—"

"Almost there—" Brennan's throat burned. "Nearly through—"

"*Down!*" Corin cried.

They carried him through the narrow defile choked with steam and into a different world. This one too had suffered the presence of Ihlini, but here the damage was less extensive. Instead of stone there was soil, if thin and discolored in places. The trees were wracked by wind and whim, roots bared to the elements, but they were wood instead of stone, foliage in place of steam.

In Strahan's lair, it had been summer. Here it was winter, and frost lay upon the ground.

"That tree," Brennan rasped, and as they reached it carefully put Corin on the ground.

Almost immediately he tried to crawl away from them, heading unerringly for the defile.

"Corin—*wait*—" Hart caught an arm and was shocked at the rigidity of sinew beneath the flesh. "Corin—"

"—go back—" Corin gasped. "—go back—the Seker—"

More roughly than they intended, his brothers dragged him back and forced him into place.

"Look at his eyes," Brennan said.

Hart shook his head as he saw the shrunken pupils. "The poison is not wholly banished."

Corin tried to draw up his legs, but weakness and stiffness forbade it. "Gods—" he said, "—oh—*gods*—"

"At least he calls on *ours*," Brennan said dryly. "Hold him down, Hart."

"The farther from the Gate, the safer he will be."

"No doubt. But we need to wrap his legs—"

"We need to *heal* him," Hart said sharply. "But this close to Valgaard, I doubt we can summon the magic."

Corin shuddered beneath their hands. "—burning—" he muttered. "—*burning*—"

Above them, Rael shrieked in agitation.

"Whole legs or broken, we go," Brennan said firmly; together they hoisted Corin up again.

Distance closed the defile. With each step they left behind the field of smoke and stone, the brooding, glassy fortress and the Gate of the netherworld. Stars shone more brightly. The moon was freed from smoke and steam and painted a pathway for them.

"—*down*—" Corin begged.

"Not yet," Brennan told him through gritted teeth. "Not until we put more distance between you and Valgaard."

"The Seker—*the Seker*—" Corin shuddered in their grasp.

"Beat him off," Hart ordered succinctly. "Somewhere in that Homanan-fleshed body is the Old Blood, Corin . . . as much as in Brennan or me. Call on it. *Use it*—" He tripped, cursed, bit his lip against the pain in the stump of his arm.

And then, abruptly, the *lir*-links came blazing back into life, and all of them cried out.

"Down—" Brennan gasped, and they put Corin down as gently as they could. At once, Kiri pressed her muzzle into his throat. As Brennan opened his arms to Sleeta, he saw comprehension creep back into Corin's eyes.

Even as his twin knelt to grasp Sleeta against his chest, Hart rose. He moved away from his brothers, clearing the tangle of arms and legs and *lir*, and thrust both arms into the air. From out of the darkness came the white hawk he called Rael.

*Lir—lir—oh, gods. Rael—*Hart discovered an uncommon incoherence, even within the link. *Rael—Rael—Rael—*

Shansu, the hawk soothed. *Shansu, my lir . . . my proud, brave warrior—*

Do you see? Do you see? Hart appealed. *The Ihlini has ruined me—*

Rael soared closer yet. *I see strength and pride and an unrelenting determination to withstand the arts of Asar-Suti.*

Ruined, lir—

Shansu, the hawk soothed. *Oh, lir, it has been so long—*And he settled briefly, with infinite gentleness, on the handless, outthrust arm. He touched his hooked beak to Hart's shoulder, eyes alight, then lifted from flesh to seek the air again, saying nothing about Hart's tears.

On the ground, Brennan's arms were filled with cat. Bare flesh felt the dry texture of her pelt, fingers touched protuding ribs beneath taut flesh, eyes sought the truth in her own.

Sleeta, he began, intending to question her, and then put away words to lose himself in the renewal of the link. There was no need to ask her anything, all was present for him to discern through the thing that bound them. He knew fear and pain, anguish and anger, the pride that made her so strong.

All is well, she said. *All is well, lir.*

She was heavy, so heavy, though lacking her normal weight. Gently, she set her teeth against cheek and jaw and nibbled, more catlike than was common. One huge paw patted a thigh, the other kneaded a hip.

"*Leijhana tu'sai*" Brennan whispered. And could not say if he intended the thanks for Sleeta or the gods.

On the ground, Corin writhed. His bones were alive with fire.

Lir, Kiri said, *try harder to overcome it.*

He thrashed, and his legs spasmed. *The Seker*—he said. *The Gate*—

Think of me instead.

—burning— In the link, he felt her strength. *Gods, Kiri—it burns*—He hitched himself up on one arm, meaning to reach for her. Without warning, he vomited.

Abruptly, Brennan and Hart discontinued greetings to *lir* and turned to their brother again.

"We are too close," Hart said anxiously.

"Then send Rael to seek out safety, some place we can settle him until this crisis passes." Brennan's tone was sharp. "There is no opportunity for us to heal him until we have found proper refuge."

Instantly Hart went into the link. *We need a place of safety,* he said. *Some place Strahan has no power to find us.*

Done. Rael said, and soared eastward toward the Molon Pass.

"*Shansu,*" Brennan told Corin. "I promise, *rujho,* Strahan will not win."

Hart felt Corin's brow. "Nor his malodorous god."

Corin's breathing was labored. "I thought if I made myself vomit the blood . . . I could win . . . could overcome the power—" He grimaced from unseen pain, baring teeth shut tightly. "Strahan wanted you so badly . . . I thought if I *acted* like he had won, if I tricked him, I could find a means to escape—" His head thrashed against the earth until Brennan trapped it and held it still. "I knew if I drank again, I would be truly lost—" Teeth bit into bottom lip. "I needed to know a way out . . . I let him think he had won, so he would show me—show me a hidden exit—" He spasmed. *"Oh, gods, it hurts!"*

"Hold your silence," Brennan told him gently. "There will be time for this later."

Corin's eyes were transfixed on Brennan's face. "But— you have to know . . . I *do* love Aileen!" His mouth warped into a rigid rictus of pain. "I *do* want her, Brennan . . . Strahan found my weakness."

"And uncovered your strength." Brennan's face was stark, though his tone reflected none of it. "There are things all of us want, Corin, even against our wills. Much of Strahan's power is that which we give him . . . he lets us make our own guilt, instead of forcing it on us."

"And I *did* want the Lion . . . long as I can remember—"

"Corin." Brennan bent close. "I swear, it does not matter. Do you think I could hate you for it after what you have done for us?"

"I could." Corin tried to smile. "In your place, I could. But now—*now*, I think . . . I think there will be no place for me—"

Hart caught his rigid hand. "Do not give in *now*."

"So *tired*," Corin murmured.

Lir, Sleeta said sharply. *The man.*

Brennan looked up quickly. And then gaped in astonishment. "*Jehan*—?"

Hart twisted to look. Like Brennan's, his face reflected shock. And then he expelled a breath, laughing a little. "Not *jehan*, Brennan . . . Carillon's bastard son. The deaf-mute."

"Carollan," Brennan breathed. "By the gods, I had forgotten he lived in Solinde."

Carollan approached at a jog. He was, like their father, a big man, tall and strongly built, though now age stole flexibility and fluidity of movement. His hair was gray, bound back into a clubbed braid. Unlike Niall, he still had two eyes of unwavering blue. Both were fixed on Corin.

He knelt as Hart and Brennan moved aside. His hands were infinitely gentle as he examined eyes, mouth, ears, wiping away the trickles of discolored blood.

"*Jehan*—?" Corin's head rolled weakly from side to side, until Carollan stilled it. "*Jehan* . . . has Strahan given you back your eye?"

The large hands were soothing. Carefully Carollan scooped Corin up, settled him against a broad chest and started back the way he had come.

Hart and Brennan did not hesitate, but fell in to flank him on either side. With them went the *lir*.

Six

He was white-haired, but oddly youthful. There was no age in his face, none at all, though the expression in sky-blue eyes told of things seen in ages past as well as anticipating all the days of the future. He tended Corin with endless patience and gentleness, though he required Carollan's aid because of his ruined hands. Quietly courteous, he turned aside anxious queries from Brennan and Hart and gave all his attention to the youngest of Niall's sons. And at last, Hart and Brennan subsided into a forced, rigid patience.

Taliesin. They knew him well enough, though neither had met the man. More than man, at that: Ihlini, once servant of the Seker, harper to Tynstar himself, Strahan's father, and later to the son. Taliesin of the Ihlini, who lived apart from everyone save Carillon's bastard son.

Hart looked at the harper's hands. Such wracked, twisted things, incapable of functioning normally. There were some small things Taliesin could do, but more intricate chores called for straight, flexible fingers and hands with unknotted bones. Once he had made music for Solindish kings and queens and sorcerers; now he saved a Homanan king's Cheysuli son from death.

He looked at the stump of his wrist. How he hated the absence of his hand, the lack of fingers, thumb, palm; knowing the lack sentenced him to a life apart from his people. Slowly he sat back in the chair and scratched absently at his scalp, taking solace in Rael's presence upon the chair back, and yet knowing the *lir*-link was forever tarnished by his inability to fly. The lack of a hand, translated out of human mass into raptor's, meant the lack of too much wing; short hops, perhaps, would be possible, but to resemble chicken instead of hawk—

Hart shut his eyes. He was so weary, so *diminished* by reaction . . . he needed rest badly, and solid food, and an escape from worry and fear.

A hand touched his arm. His eyes snapped open and he looked up at Brennan, who tried to smile encouragement and failed. By Brennan's face he knew his own; too pale, too gaunt, too dirty. And the eyes, though yellow instead of blue, were full of memories and more than a trace of confusion.

Strahan has touched us all— Hart sat more upright, then leaned forward as Brennan moved back to the pallet on which Corin lay. Taliesin had made it clear he required none of their help—Caro was enough, he said— but still they could not keep themselves from returning time and again to the pallet. To stare down helplessly at the one who had done most to thwart the Seker and the Ihlini, and all the while they had believed him traitor to their race.

Taliesin sighed, brushed back a strand of fine white hair, and turned to look at them both. Caro still knelt at Corin's side, unable to hear what was said; unable to speak of it if he could. "He will recover," the harper told them. "He started it himself, by forcing himself to vomit . . . the draught I have administered will ease the burning in his blood until it passes normally. It is a side-effect of drinking the Seker's blood; I experienced it myself. He is lucky he drank only one goblet, or we would be hard-pressed to win him away from Strahan." He sighed. "As for the legs, well, time will heal them of its own accord, but time is not a luxury any of you may lay claim to." He rose and slipped ruined hands inside the wide sleeves of his blue robe. "If I thought you would go without him, I would send you on to Homana-Mujhar."

"Why?" Brennan asked sharply. "Is something wrong in Mujhara?"

The harper sought and found a seat on a stool, settling

himself with a calmness that belied the intent of his words. "Nothing that your return cannot help put to rights, although it will not settle things entirely. Your cousin has done too much harm in your absence. There is unrest in the clans."

"Cousin?" Hart frowned. "Teirnan? Why? What has Teir done?"

With feeling, Brennan swore. "He meant it, then, the fool."

"Meant *what?*" Hart scowled at his brother. "Enlighten me, *rujho*."

Brennan made an impatient gesture. "He swore to renounce the prophecy because he refuses to acknowledge that some day Cheysuli and Ihlini must coexist, cohabit, in order to merge the bloodlines."

"Aye, well, I am not so fond of that idea, either. But—to *renounce* the prophecy?" Hart shook his head. "Teir is too quick to act sometimes, but to turn his back on what gives our lives meaning? I think not."

"I think *aye*," Taliesin said gently. "He has done it, Hart. I hear little enough here in Solinde, and rumor is often blown out of proportion, but some truth leaks through. And you must recall that in *Solinde*, the people are willing enough to hear words of Homanan trouble."

"Which are?" Brennan prodded.

"That Teirnan has withdrawn from his clan," Taliesin answered. "He has struck his pavilion and formally petitioned the *shar tahl* to remove his rune-sign from the birthlines." So calmly he spoke of things Cheysuli. "He has gathered other malcontents and together they have gone from clan to clan, all across Homana, to win warriors to the cause of the *a'saii*."

"Idiocy!" Hart's startled disbelief was manifest. "What does he think to do?"

"What he *hopes* to do is fracture the Cheysuli into separate factions, those dedicated to the prophecy and those who are newly turned against it." Taliesin shrugged. "Niall has done as I expected, once I had told him the truth of things. No longer could he—and Ian—believe implicitly in Ihlini *evil*, when only a portion of us worship

Asar-Suti. They have acknowledged that we are not so bad after all, most of us, and that perhaps it would not be impossible to believe a Cheysuli could lie down with an Ihlini and bear children with all the required blood." In his eyes was serenity, though his words were heresy. "Some of you already have begotten children on Ihlini."

"But not Firstborn." Brennan's tone was taut. "And not willingly."

"You lay with Rhiannon willingly enough," Taliesin retorted gently, "though, admittedly, you were unaware of her heritage."

"And so are we to believe the Firstborn will result from *trickery?*" Brennan shook his head. "I am not Teir, harper, but I find it impossible to believe the day will come when Cheysuli and Ihlini can live in peace."

"Or lie down with one another?" Smiling, Taliesin shrugged. "The gods are not fools, Brennan . . . they arrange things deftly and with surpassing subterfuge, when it is required. I give you a prophecy of my own." His eyes were very distant. "There will come a day when a prince of the House of Homana takes to wife an Ihlini woman, born of Asar-Suti—"

"No." In unison.

"—and from that willing union will come the child known as the Firstborn, the boy who will one day rule."

"And this is what Teirnan fights," Hart said grimly. "I begin to understand."

"And will you join with him?" the harper asked. "Or take up your part in the prophecy?"

Hart shook his head. "I have no part. I am the middle son, unpromised to House or princess." Briefly, he glanced at Brennan. "Once I was Prince of Solinde. Once I was a warrior." He displayed the stump of his wrist. "Now I am a man without a clan."

"And Solinde a realm without a king." Taliesin's smile was inexpressibly gentle. "Whatever you may think of me because I am Ihlini, I hope you will also realize that I am a man who loves his country. The House of Solinde is in descent. It is time for a *new* House, built on strong, proud rootstock. Yours would do, I think."

"I am Cheysuli—" But Hart stopped short.

"You are many things," Taliesin told him gently, "and all of them of incalculable value."

Brennan saw mute, bitter protest rising in Hart's eyes and moved to make the explanation himself, knowing it was too painful for his brother. "Taliesin—I think you misunderstand. We were taught, in childhood, all Cheysuli traditions. All the customs, rituals, beliefs." He scrubbed wearily at his forehead. "One custom, cruel as it may sound, is that a warrior stripped by physical dismemberment or permanent handicap of his ability to perform a warrior's duties voluntarily leaves his clan. He is—"

"—kin-wrecked." Hart's clipped interruption stopped Brennan dead. "It is not so heavy a sentence as the death-ritual, perhaps, requiring no forfeiture of life—" his tone was bitterly ironic, "—but what he *does* forfeit is his clan. His kin, unless they choose to accompany him." Hart shrugged one shoulder in eloquent acknowledgment of his plight. "I can hardly expect the Mujhar and everyone else of the House of Homana to follow me into self-exile."

Taliesin's blue eyes were oddly complacent. "A harsh custom, indeed."

"Born of necessity." Again, Hart shrugged, as if trying to dismiss the ramifications of the custom that made him clanless. "The law of survival."

Thoughtfully, the Ihlini harper nodded. "I understand: the weak can pull down the strong."

Brennan's tone was subdued. "In the days of our ancestors, when the world was very young, the weak were left to die so the strong could continue." He did not look at his twin, whom he judged strong enough despite the loss of a hand; knowing the old custom, in its day, made sense even in its cruel practicality. "A man dying of disease in a time of famine eats food better given to another, and perhaps causes two deaths in place of one."

Taliesin did not smile, but his tone was strangely sanguine. "I will not argue that, perhaps once, the times warranted such harsh customs. Certainly we Ihlini have made difficult adjustments in order to survive. But the time you speak of has passed. Hart is more than merely a warrior, but also a Prince of Solinde." He shrugged, forestalling incipient protests. "Besides, I think you should recall—loyal fatalists that you are—there may be a *reason* for this."

Hart's face was stark.

"*Tahlmorra*," Brennan said hollowly. "A word more eloquent than 'reason.' "

"Then, my lord, you might argue that the need for such rigid adherence to an outdated custom has declined," the harper suggested. "You might go before Clan Council, as the *Cheysuli* Prince of Homana, and tell them the need is no longer valid. Now is the time for a new custom, where a man maimed can be valued for things other than physical abilities."

Hart looked at Brennan sharply, abruptly cognizant of what such change could mean to him as well as to others. Brennan was clearly stunned by the magnitude of the idea, but Hart knew it would not gainsay him. Yet he also knew better than to hope too hard for something that might not occur. Clan Council and the *shar tahls*, whose job it was to insure the continuance of tradition, were incredibly protective of Cheysuli customs; it was what made the race so difficult to destroy, from inside as well as without.

"The need *is* no longer valid," Brennan said thoughtfully. "Hart is as good a warrior as any Cheysuli I know, and there is no reason to believe the lack of a hand will gainsay him from his responsibilities." He nodded. "If I *were* to go before Clan Council—"

Hart shrugged. "Peacetime, *rujho*. If war were to return—"

"There will be no war again, ever. With Corin in Atvia and Keely wed to Sean of Erinn, who is left to fight us? Solinde?" Brennan spread his hands. "Would you levy war against your *rujholli*?"

Hart sighed and sat back in his chair, gazing up at Rael perched on the back. "No more than against my *lir*."

"And so the prophecy nears completion." Taliesin smiled and rose. "You are so close, you cannot see it. But you have, just now, completed a major requirement for fulfillment: four warring realms united in peace."

"Which leaves the two magical races." Brennan said grimly. "I think even the gods underestimated the strength of hatred between Cheysuli and Ihlini."

"I think the gods knew very well how strong that hatred would be," the harper countered. "A parent is not blind to resentments among his children." He looked from one to the other, starting with Brennan and ending with Corin. "There comes a time, however, when the children must outgrow them. And so it will be with Cheysuli and Ihlini." The harper moved toward the door. "It is for you to call on the earth magic to complete the healing of Corin's legs. You cannot wait for them to heal normally. And so I will go from here for awhile, so my presence does not hinder the magic."

The door was shut. "Gods," Hart said, "I am so weary, I doubt I can summon *anything*."

"For Corin, we will have to," Brennan knelt briefly and locked his hands into the pelt behind Sleeta's ears, drawing strength from the contact. *Lir, oh, lir, we are all so weary, so cursed weak, and yet we must all be strong.*

She shifted forward and pressed her head against his jaw. *You will be as strong as is required.*

Hart moved to the pallet and touched Carollan's shoulder briefly. "*Leijhana tu'sai*," he said, knowing Caro could not hear; knowing also it did not matter, nor tarnish the gratitude. "*Leijhana tu'sai*, kinsman, but this is for us to do."

Carollan moved aside with alacrity, though there was nothing of subservience in it. He merely gave them the room they required, retiring to Taliesin's stool, and watched out of their father's eyes.

Brennan joined Hart at Corin's side. Kiri lay curled at his hip, pointed nose tucked beneath his slack hand. Her bright eyes watched the movements they made in preparing to summon the magic. Sleeta sat beside Brennan, pressing one haunch against his doubled leg. Rael did not depart the chairback, but his link with Hart was not weakened by such a brief distance.

"I have never done this," Hart said nervously.

"Nor have I." Brennan pushed a lock of fallen hair out of his face. "Come with me, *rujho*. Now—"

He slipped into the void quickly, *too* quickly; he knew fear and an overwhelming sense of helplessness. What if his ignorance cost Corin his life?

Lir. Lir. Sleeta was in the link with him, lending him a measure of strength and courage, though her own was stretched dangerously thin.

Hart! he cried in the void. *I need you, rujho—*

And Hart, abruptly, was there, tumbling through the emptiness like a cork caught in a millrace. Brennan sensed his fear was equal to his own. And inwardly he laughed; two frightened warriors meant to heal their unconcious brother, summoning a power neither had fully tapped.

We need a shar tahl, he told Sleeta.

You need to heal your rujholli. Delicate dictatorship.

Brennan sighed. Linked, he and Hart dissolved the contact with their bodies and sank beneath the level they knew as the world.

Down.

Down, until they touched layers of sentience they had not known existed. Such boundless power as they had never imagined.

Come with us, Brennan said.

We need you, Hart explained.

Sluggishly, Power stirred.

There is a man who requires your aid. Brennan told It. *A warrior, Cheysuli, born of the Old Blood, descendant of the Firstborn, ancestor of those to come again.*

In need, Hart echoed. *Touched by Asar-Suti, who would destroy the gods as we know them so he may hold dominion.*

Power raised Its head.

Come with us, Brennan invited. *Show the Seker that his power is nothing compared to yours.*

He needs you, Hart explained.

Power rose up and set them ablaze with a single touch. And then, too quickly, It hurled them upward, through all the layers and strata and broke them free of the world, where they saw a man on his bed of pain, and took it from him easily. Bones knit themselves into wholeness. Stiffened sinews grew flexible. Vessels pulsed with blood set free of the Seker's fire.

And then, as quickly, the Power was gone, and they were men again; exhausted, dirty, sick of the stink of themselves. And knowing they must go on.

Conscious, Corin gazed up at them both. "*Leijhana tu'sai*," he said drowsily. Even as Brennan protested, he worked the ruby signet from his finger and pressed it into his oldest brother's palm. "Yours," he said as firmly as he could, and fell asleep with a hand locked in Kiri's ruff.

Hart lay back on the wooden floor, not caring that his sprawl was more than a trifle undecorous, nor that the floor was hard. He shut his eyes, sighed deeply, gave himself over to the luxury of complete relief for the first time in months.

"In the morning, we go," Brennan said hoarsely. "We cannot waste a moment."

"In the morning," Hart agreed wearily, and fell asleep himself.

Brennan laughed raggedly, stroking Sleeta's pelt. *If our jehan could see us now—*

He would cry, Sleeta answered. *But they would be tears of joy.*

Taliesin did not have the means to offer Brennan and Hart the sort of baths they needed, having no half-cask or carefully crafted oak tub, so they did the best they could. Water was heated in a cauldron over the fire and they scrubbed themselves down with harsh soap and harsher cloth, scraping away layers of filth. Taliesin gave them an herbal soap for their hair, to rid themselves of lice, but they forbore cutting it. It could wait; there were things more important than the length of their hair.

Teirnan. Brennan told his brothers what he could of their cousin's treachery, and his treasonous intent. Then, turn by turn, each confessed how he had been taken by Strahan, betrayed by love, lust, greed, ambition. They raised old resentments, hidden emotions, true feelings, and dealt with them as best they could. By the time, morning dawned and it was time to leave, each had come to terms with himself in relation to his brothers; each believed he was a better man for it.

And each knew more than ever how binding was a *tahlmorra*.

Taliesin examined the stump of Hart's wrist, pronounced it healed, did not avoid the acknowledgment of persistent pain.

"And it *will* persist," he said gently. "The loss of a limb is something the mind does not fully understand. It will take some time before you stop reaching for things with your nonexistent hand, expecting to close your fingers upon it. It will take time for the sensations of a hand to abate. One moment you will swear it is still attached . . . the next you will know better." His own twisted left hand was gentle on the wrist. "I am sorry, Hart, but there is nothing to be done. Even the gods cannot give back that which was so decidedly destroyed."

"Asar-Suti would have," Hart said grimly. "Or so Strahan promised. It was his price."

"But not *yours*." Taliesin's blue eyes were kind in his ageless, unseamed face. "Do not curse yourself for being an honorable man. You did what was required."

"Required." Hart sighed and replaced the snug leather cuff that warded the stump against injury. "Aye, required— *and* my own decision."

"And I tell you again to recall that—should Brennan fail to sway the Cheysuli in altering tradition—customs are different in Solinde. We do not throw men away." Taliesin turned away to look at Brennan and Corin. "You cannot afford to waste more daylight. Caro has food and water for you outside. Best go now."

Brennan's face was cleaner than it had been in weeks, but tension had etched permanent lines into the flesh. He frowned. "You are certain Strahan will not punish you for this?"

The harper nodded. "He has no idea where I am, and I use simple magic to keep it so. Strahan is too arrogant to recall the ward-spells I have used; he thinks in terms of conquest, not simple protection." He smiled. "He will not search far. He will be more concerned with placating the Seker, who grows impatient with men who fail him. He will spend his time in Valgaard, not seeking you." The eyes sharpened. "But I warn you, be wary of him still—he *will* seek another way. One day, he will try again to thwart you."

"Best go," Corin said.

Thanks were not enough, but it was all they had. And they offered it in abundance as Taliesin stood in the door and watched them go out into the frosted world. Three battered but gods-touched men, and their *lir*; cat, fox, hawk: the children of the gods.

Seven

In Deirdre's solar, Niall bent over her shoulder and placed a finger on the lion patterned in the tapestry. "Who is this?"

"Shaine," she told him, batting his finger away. "This one is Shaine, that one Carillon, *that* one—"

"Where am *I?*"

"Here." She pointed out the proper lion. "But 'twill be some time before I get to you. All those other lions, and the histories of each—" Deirdre grinned. " 'Twill be *years.*"

Niall sighed and straightened. "Aye," he agreed grimly. "And years before I know what has befallen my sons."

She looked up quickly, saw his face, set aside her massive tapestry. "Niall—"

"Months!" he exclaimed. "And how many of those were wasted? How many of those months did I believe Hart and Corin merely in their respective realms, learning how to rule, while I believed Teirnan and the *a'saii* responsible for Brennan's disappearance?" He cursed and strode angrily to the nearest casement, glaring out on the inner bailey. There was a commotion within the walls, but he was too distracted to wonder at its cause. "By the gods, I should have known. *Strahan* yet again, and eternal Ihlini meddling."

She stood behind him, wanting to touch him and not giving in to it; he was too angry and full of self-recrimination to accept any kindnesses. "And how *were* you to know?" she asked tartly. "You told me yourself the Ihlini have been quiet for years . . . why would you be having a reason to think of Strahan now?"

"Precisely because it *has* been years." Niall leaned his brow against the stone. "Gods, Deirdre . . . *my sons*—"

"I know." Now she touched him. "I know, Niall. But you said yourself 'tis unlikely he'd want to *kill* them. Strahan's way is to use men instead."

"He wanted them twenty-two years ago . . . he nearly got them then. And now that he *has*—" Niall turned. "Oh, gods, I am so frightened. What sort of men will he make them?"

She sighed, knowing she could give him no answer. "When do you send the army to Valgaard?"

"In the morning." His hands rested on her shoulders. "Ian and I go with them."

Tight-faced, she nodded. "The gods grant—"

But whatever she desired the gods to grant was never stated. A servant, circumventing courtesy entirely, threw open the solar door. "My lord! *My lord!*"

"What is it?" Niall asked irritably.

Brennan stepped around the wide-eyed servant. "What he means to say, *jehan*, is that all of your sons are back." Kindly, Brennan moved the servant aside and held the door open himself as Hart and Corin and assorted *lir* made their way into the tower solar. The chamber was suddenly filled.

"All—" Niall said hoarsely.

"One, two, three." Hart grinned. "Unless Deirdre has contrived to add another in our absence."

"No," she said blankly. And then laughed aloud in joy.

Mute, Niall stared at his sons. One, two, three, as Hart had said. But they were not the sons he had sired and known for years. Something had changed each one, and profoundly. There was a tangible difference.

Brennan: much too gaunt and oddly haunted in yellow eyes, though his smile was genuine. His jerkin was soiled and crusted with countless unnamed things, and Niall had no desire to ask how it had become so; he had a good idea. His only desire was to see that Brennan was whole, and that was blatantly obvious. His hair was mostly clean, if too long, and he held himself with customary pride, but there was something about the way he moved that spoke of things unsaid even among his brothers.

Corin: bearded as an Erinnish brigand, looking less Cheysuli than ever, though there was, Niall noted, a subtle self-confidence Corin had always lacked, or was banished by bad temper. And though there was a tension in the way he moved, as if he waited for something, Niall saw no anger, no hostility, no reluctance to accept his place in the House of Homana. Clearly he had suffered; equally clearly, he had come to terms with himself.

And Hart, showing teeth in a familiar grin; showing something else in posture. All of them were clad in worn and dirty clothing, though clearly they had bathed a day or two before arrival, if only arms and faces; but there was more than a weary relief and elation in Hart's posture and attitude. He stood rigidly next to the door, left hand thrust behind his back as if he meant to hide something in it. Even as he stepped free of the door, letting it swing closed, he kept the forearm behind him.

But Niall would worry about them later. Now was the time for celebration and explanation. He expelled an eloquent breath of relief. "Oh, gods—all of my sons— *leijhana tu'sai*—"

"We have expressed similar sentiments repeatedly the last two weeks." Corin went to the nearest chair and collapsed into it, putting his feet up on a footstool. "I am footsore, hungry and weary, but I feel happy for it."

Brennan went straight to Niall and put out an arm to clasp his father's. But Niall ignored the arm altogether, instead jerking Brennan into a rough embrace. "You do not know how many times I petitioned the gods for the safe return of my sons."

Corin laughed. "Well, they must have grown weary of hearing it. All of us begged them, too."

Niall's good eye was wet as he released his oldest son. The patch hid the other from sight. There was more silver in his tawny hair and deeper lines in the contours of his face, but the smile banished the age worry had added. "You are well? All of you?" He wanted to hug Corin and Hart as he had hugged Brennan, but Corin was settled and obviously oblivious to the gesture; Hart's posture warded him against familiarity, even from his father.

"Well enough," Brennan said. "But first, let us swear to you that we are not Strahan's minions sent to do you harm. Because of Corin, we are nothing but ourselves, if a trifle worn." He glanced briefly at Hart, turned back and sought a chair.

Belatedly, Niall pushed one over. Deirdre beckoned Hart to take her own, but he shook his head and remained at his post beside the door. Or intended to. The door was abruptly shoved open; Hart, thrusting out arms to keep himself from being crushed between wall and wood, saw his father's face go white.

But Ian was in the room. "By the gods, it *is* true! All of you are back!"

Silence met his outburst. He stopped short, staring at his brother, then slowly turned to look at the Mujhar's middle son, his own personal favorite.

Hart's face was stark. "I meant to tell you later."

Niall summoned his voice. "*Strahan* did that to you?"

"No, *jehan*. My stupidity did this to me." Bitterness crept in. "A heavy price, but I pay it."

From the corridor came an urgent voice. "Corin? *Corin!*"

Corin sighed. And then Keely prodded her uncle aside to force her way into the solar past the bodies near the door.

"Corin—" But she broke it off, turning to look at Hart.

"Why not announce it?" he said unsteadily. "Why not say it and be done with it: *The Mujhar's son is kin-wrecked.*"

Abruptly, Brennan wrenched his eyes away to stare at the floor; he could not bear to see the pain in Hart's eyes.

"Come here," Niall said.

After a moment, Hart answered his father's bidding.

He was conscious of all the eyes, but looked only at the single blue one of his father. "*Jehan*—"

"If you think I will love you the less because you lack a hand, you have no wits at all," Niall said clearly. "If you think I cannot comprehend the pain—physical as well as emotional—that such a loss engenders, look again at my face."

Hart felt dizzy. He drew in a deep breath, wet his lips, did not avoid the topic. "No, *jehan*. But you are Mujhar; they dared not send you out of the clan."

"That had nothing to do with it," Niall said gently. "An eye lost, as Taliesin pointed out to me, is not a mark of physical weakness nor deformity of the spirit. I am no less a man because I have only one. And while it is true that the loss of an eye does not affect a warrior as much as the loss of a hand, I do understand what you feel."

Hart looked at the floor, thinking mutinous thoughts.

"I *do*," his father repeated.

After a moment, Hart nodded.

"Sit down," Niall told him. "Keely, will you send for wine? I think all of us could use it."

"*Usca*," Corin said, and grinned at her exaggerated curtsy just before she went out the door.

"So." Niall sat down in the last of Deirdre's chairs even as she settled herself on the stool nearest his feet. "I am ashamed," he said flatly. "Ashamed I did not realize sooner the scope of Strahan's intentions. But when Brennan and Rhiannon disappeared so soon on the heels of Teirnan's defection, I feared *a'saii* interference, not Ihlini. Not after so much time." Bleakly, he shook his head. "I spent weeks trying to trap Teirnan, and all I did was waste time and effort. Yet until a crofter's half-wit son at last had courage enough to come forward and tell me he had *seen* Rhiannon spirit Brennan away, I did not comprehend what was afoot."

"Nor did I," Ian said grimly. "Blind fools, all of us— and it gave Strahan the time he needed."

Niall glanced briefly at Ian, who had sired Rhiannon, than looked away from the bleak guilt in his brother's eyes. He sighed, rubbing at old scars. "I knew then he would want you all, *each* of my sons, and that further delay might result in your deaths, or worse. And so I readied an army to march on Valgaard itself." Niall's smile was twisted. "We were to leave in the morning . . . but I think I may cancel the duty."

"Unless you wish to engage Strahan once and for all." Brennan shook his head. "A formidable foe, *jehan*. He needs killing, but I think it will take more than an army. Even of Cheysuli."

"Or less," Ian remarked. "Perhaps a single man, in place of that army."

"No," Niall said promptly. "For now I want none of my family anywhere near Valgaard or the Ihlini. We are together again for the first time in nearly a year, and I would prefer to enjoy it."

"Nearly a year?" Corin grinned. "Our banishment is incomplete, then . . . do you intend to send Hart and me away again?" He slanted a glance at his middle brother, who merely shrugged one shoulder and smiled vaguely.

Keely returned. "The wine is coming," she said, moving to stand behind Corin's chair. "*And,* my lord Mujhar, if you intend to send Corin—or Hart—*anywhere,* you will have to contend with *me.*"

Niall's smile was crooked. "Aye, aye, so I see. And no, I do not intend to send them anywhere, unless they want to go." He lifted a tawny brow in Keely's direction. "Did you tell Aileen Brennan is home at last?"

In his chair, Corin froze. He felt Keely's hands on his shoulders, pressing gently, as if to offer support. "She knows," Keely said briefly. "Everyone in the palace knows."

Ian nodded. "I sent Tasha to Clankeep with the news, so you may expect Maeve home by evening."

"Maeve is at Clankeep?" Brennan asked in surprise.

Niall frowned a little. "She wished to see the *shar tahl.* She swore the vows of a *meijha*, Brennan, in good faith, even if in poor judgment. Now that Teir has renounced his clan, she wishes to formally renounce the vows."

"Teir is a fool," Hart declared.

"Teir is more than that," Keely said grimly. "He is *kin-wrecked*—proscribed by the *shar tahl*, by the clan-leader . . . he is forbidden Clankeep, Mujhara—not that he would wish to come here anyway—and all the other clans." She grimaced. "Though he goes where he will, in truth, gathering other warriors."

"How many?" Brennan asked bleakly.

"Unknown." Ian moved aside as a servant came in with wine and goblets. He took them from him, dismissed the man, set everything on a table and began to pour, handing out the cups. "There are rumors one day he has seven men, the next day seventy."

"He is shrewd," Niall said. "Much smarter than I believed. But Ceinn has suckled him on tales of the old days, when the race was exquisitely pure . . . Teirnan is now dedicated to the restoration of the old ways without benefit of the prophecy."

Brennan shook his head as he leaned forward to take the cup from Ian. "How can a warrior who has been raised to respect the prophecy turn his back on it? I admit that I am less than enamored of the need to cohabit with Ihlini, but to deny myself the afterworld? No." Brennan shook his head. "Teirnan must be mad."

"Not mad." Ian carried the requested *usca* to Corin. "Determined. We have been blessed, as a race, with a consuming dedication—to the exclusion of all else—to fulfillment of the prophecy. We have been accused, on more than one occasion, of being blind and deaf to the truth, locking ourselves away in insular arrogance, believing we know the only way." He looked at his brother. "*Some* might name us cursed."

Niall nodded thoughtfully. "Once, we believed no Ihlini could intend anything but harm to us. We learned differently from an old woman, an old *Ihlini* woman, who lived in Homana out of choice. And from an ageless harper, who showed me that an Ihlini formerly sworn to the Seker could renounce that allegiance in the name of peace and coexistence, and actually work *for* the prophecy."

"And still does so." Hart reached for wine with his left

hand, stopped rigidly, put out his right. "It was Taliesin who gave us refuge from Strahan."

"And Taliesan, with Carollan, who gave us back our youngest *rujholli*." Brennan smiled at Corin. "If you do not tell him all that you accomplished, even in front of Strahan, I *will*."

Corin shrugged. "Another time."

Niall smiled. "That, too, has changed." His eyes glinted. "No more resentment of your oldest *rujholli*."

Corin stared. "You knew?"

Silvering brows rose. "How could I not? Do you think I am blind? I knew very well how much you wanted what Brennan had. As for now?" Niall smiled. "I think you have learned there are more important things to concern yourself with than what your *rujholli* has."

"Such as survival," Hart said dryly. "The gods know we could have died a dozen times."

"I did." Brennan's tone was hollow as, for the moment, he was back in the tiny cell. He shivered, rose abruptly, put his unfinished wine down. "*Jehan*, there is more to tell you. But I think it will wait for another time." He straightened his jerkin. "There is something I must do . . . someone I must come to terms with."

Corin, thinking of Aileen, thrust himself to his feet. And checked as Brennan turned to look at him. Uncomfortable, he shrugged. "I—I intend to have a bath. I am filthy."

"'So are we all." Hart rose as well, sucking down the last of the wine in his cup. "I think I will catch up on lost sleep."

In silence, Niall's sons filed slowly out of the solar, automatically sending *lir* ahead to bedchambers. Intent upon their thoughts, they paid no attention to one another. Not even Corin to Brennan, as much as he wanted to. Like Hart, he turned away, and Brennan went on alone.

It was midmorning. Sunlight spilled through stained-glass casements and painted the Great Hall a mass of liquid colors. But Brennan ignored the light, ignored the

Lion, moving instead to the end of the firepit. He cleared wood and ashes, gripped the iron handle, peeled back the lid.

He stared down into the hole, watching the stairs fall away into darkness. One hundred and two of them. Far fewer than in Valgaard on the way to the Gate of the god.

Time enough for such foolish fear as I have known . . . never again will I give over such a weapon to the enemy.

But sunlight, however bright, did not touch the darkness. And so Brennan turned away, intending to light a torch, and saw her standing inside the hammered doors.

Red-haired. Green-eyed. Supple as a willow. She carried her head high on a slender neck; brilliant hair fell to curl around her hips.

"They were saying you were back." He heard Erinn in her voice, far more lilting than Deirdre's accent.

This woman, this girl, whom I am to wed, nearly cost all of us our sanity, because of Corin.

But he could not tell her that. Not yet. Perhaps not ever; too much, at this moment, lay between them. Because of Corin. "Back," he said. "Aye." Not knowing what else to say.

"And safe."

"Aye," he agreed, "and safe." Then, giving in to it, "So is my youngest *rujholli.*"

She did not flinch, though clearly she had heard him. Nor did she answer, though she calmly walked the length of the hall from doors to firepit. And then she stood before him, considerably shorter than he, and he found, oddly, he wanted to apologize to her. Corin had said little enough of Aileen on the journey home from Solinde, shying away from the topic as if fearing Brennan might be further insulted by his words.

But Brennan was not insulted. At this moment, facing the stranger he would marry, he did not know what he was.

He drew in a breath. "You are in love with Corin."

"Aye," was all she said.

"And he in love with you."

Her lips tightened minutely. "Once," she said quietly. "I'm not knowing how long it lasted."

Resentment rose, then faded. Brennan smiled wryly. "It lasted," he told her sardonically. "I can assure you of that."

She said nothing. She was no beauty, he saw, and certainly not the kind of woman Corin generally sought for companionship. What she *was,* he realized, looking at her without benefit of prejudice, was proud as a Cheysuli, with a spirit that blazed as brightly. And he knew, seeing that pride, that spirit, Aileen of Erinn was as trapped by circumstances as the Prince of Homana himself.

How do I deal with this?

But there was no answer, not in her face. Nor, he knew, in his own.

Brennan sighed. "Corin is different," he said. "I saw it at once, when I coud see again, but I did not recognize it. The circumstances did not, quite, lend themselves to contemplation." She gazed at him steadily, hands folded primly in the folds of her gown. And yet, somehow, he knew better. This was not Aileen he faced, but another woman entirely. A woman who knew how she felt no more than he himself did. "Different," he repeated. "Not all of it, I think, is from imprisonment. I think most of it is from you. And so, in the end, instead of blame, I must offer gratitude; it was what saved our lives."

She did not avoid his eyes. "It was not intended, none of it. I was meaning it no more than Corin. It—" she checked, sighed, went on quietly, "—just *happened.*"

Brennan thought of Rhiannon. None of that had 'just happened,' being carefully designed, but he understood what Aileen meant. And knew he could lay no blame. "I admire your honesty," he said abruptly. "I have had little of that, of late, from women." He paused. "You do know the story."

"Aye. Keely told me."

Trust Keely— But now was not the time. Now was the time for honesty. "Aileen—I cannot promise it will be easy. Arranged marriages are difficult enough, particularly cradle-betrothals, but now, with *this*—"

Her cool voice interrupted. "I'm knowing it as well as you, Brennan. D'ye think I've not spent my nights thinking about it, wondering what I would do when you and Corin came home?" A trace of inner fire lighted Erinnish eyes—green as emeralds, he thought—and he saw a hint of Aileen's passion. " 'Twill be as hard as we make it, I think."

Brennan did not couch his words in diplomacy. "And if Corin stays here? What then? Am I expected to *share?*"

The fire caught and burned, blazing in her eyes. " 'Tis between Corin and me, I'm thinking."

He laughed once, incredulously, on a gust of air. "Is it? Am I discounted so easily?"

Her skin was very fair, and he saw the bloom of color in her cheeks. Bright scarlet, competing with the brilliance of her hair. "He left me," she said. "He *left* me, my lord husband-to-be, because he would not steal his brother's betrothed. An honorable man, your brother; d'ye think he'd discard that honor *here?*"

It was a new light she cast on Corin. A few weeks before Brennan might have protested she did him too much credit; now, he did not think so. He had seen Corin's unexpected sense of honor on dramatic display in Valgaard.

"No," he said quietly. "No, I was wrong to imply it."

Some of her vitality drained away. "Were you? No. I'm thinking not. You believed what any man might, faced with such a coil." Aileen shook her head, wide mouth twisted. " 'Tis sorry I am, Brennan. We none of us asked for it, but it has all been spilled into our laps by your gods . . . by your capricious Cheysuli *destiny*." She sighed. "Keely told me you are a good man, if a trifle unimaginative."

He considered it thoughtfully a moment. Discarded the idea; he was whatever he was. "And did she tell you of my fear? The flaw in the Prince of Homana?"

Aileen stared back at him. And then she smiled a little. "If you're meaning he could put a cask of hot water and scent to good use, then aye, I see—*smell*—a flaw. But otherwise—no. Keely said nothing of a flaw. Nothing of a *fear*."

"Then I should tell you of it." He went to the wall, took a torch from the bracket, lighted it from a candle and returned to the firepit. "Come down with me," he said. "Come down with me, *meijhana*, and tell me how it was a bad-tempered, impetuous Cheysuli princeling won the heart of Aileen of Erinn." He smiled. "And I will tell you how it is Corin's oldest *rujholli* means to face his fear and destroy it."

Green eyes widened in surprise. "Are you really wanting to know?"

"No," he said truthfully, "but it will give me something to listen to instead of chattering teeth."

She frowned. "My teeth are not much for chattering."

"Mine are." He took the first step into the stairway. Turned to look back at the woman his brother loved, knowing, one day, he might learn to feel the same. "Will you come, Aileen?"

After a moment, she did.

Corin sprawled on his back in the center of his bed. It felt odd to be in it after so many months, smelling familiar smells, feeling familiar warmth and the softness of the mattress. He had known so little warmth and softness in Strahan's glassy fortress.

He sought Kiri with one hand, found her, lost himself in silent communion. It remained unbroken until his sister came into the chamber.

"Corin?"

He turned his head.

"You mean to go back to Atvia."

It was a statement, not inquiry. He thought about it a moment, then nodded. "I think so."

Keely moved closer to the bed. "And if I asked you to stay?"

The wall of his belly clenched. "Do you know *what* you ask?"

"I know." She stood rigidly beside the bed. "Aileen has confided in me." She shrugged a little, clearly tense.

"We became close, Corin, being somewhat alike . . . she told me what had happened, and how." Abruptly she sat down. "Gods, *rujho,* I know how you must feel! But if you go to Atvia you will leave me all alone."

"I went to Atvia before."

"That was for a *year.* You would come home, I knew it—but now, *now*—" She sighed, shaking her head; the tawny braid shook itself. "You will go, and never come home again."

He stroked Kiri with resolution, locked away in silence. Keely's tone altered. "You are *afraid.* I see it."

"Aye." He did not shirk the admission.

"You, Corin?"

"I have cause." He threaded fingers in Kiri's pelt. "Alaric is dead. Atvia lies open to whatever influence Lillith wields, and Strahan. And *jehana* also is there— witless, twisted *jehana.*" He rolled his head against the bedclothes. "Someone must go, Keely . . . and Atvia is mine."

"Leave it to someone else."

"No."

"Corin—"

"I will not run from responsibility, nor bewail it. I have something of my own at last, something no one else may hold; Atvia is *mine.* It is for me to put the realm into order again, *my* task, to put light in place of darkness. It is for *me* to do; not Brennan, not Hart, not you." He shook his head again. "One day, Keely, you will learn that saying no is not always the answer. Nor is turning your back."

"Then you *will* go."

Corin sighed. "Aye."

Keely's tone was bitter. "Because the prophecy requires it."

"As much as it requires service of you. And you *will* serve it, Keely; no matter how difficult, how demanding, how much sacrifice is asked. You are not like Teirnan." Corin sat up and turned, swinging his legs over the edge of the bed. He still wore his boots; he did not care that he had soiled his bedclothes. "Be what *you* must, Keely, but let me do what *I* must."

She leaned against him slightly. "Then do it. I will not gainsay you; I am not such a fool as to say no to you now, after such a pretty speech. But *you* are a fool if you think I will not curse you for such newfound resolution."

"I am not a fool; I know you will." He flipped her braid behind her back.

Keely drew in a breath. "Will you see her before you go?"

"I thought to do so now."

She opened her mouth, then shut it, and would not meet his eyes.

After a moment, he nodded. "She has gone to Brennan."

"They—she said there are things to be settled between them, things Brennan must know of her, and things she must learn of him. She said if she left it until after she had seen you—" She broke off, plainly uncomfortable. "Oh, Corin—"

"Later, then; we will both of us be better prepared to say good-bye." Corin nodded; his "newfound resolve" was firm at last, and something he could live with. "And now, if you do not mind, I would like to take a bath." He bent over and tugged off his boots, one by one, welcoming the activity. And then, distracted, he looked at his sister in startled comprehension. "Oh, gods, Keely— one-handed, Hart cannot even do *this!*"

Keely turned her face against his shoulder in unspoken grief for lost hands and lost brothers, not knowing, for her, which was worse, or would be.

Hart pushed open his chamber door, leaned against it in weary numbness, at last moved aside and shut it. As always, he looked for Rael. As always, the hawk was on his perch, wings folded, perfectly groomed, content to wait in silence.

He sighed. He wandered aimlessly to the bed, sat down on the edge, stared blankly at the floor. He wondered vaguely if he was ill; depression was foreign to him.

"Gods," he said aloud; it seemed a most eloquent comment. Wearily he bent forward, reached to grab his boots, realized abruptly he no longer had the freedom to undress himself at his leisure.

It stunned him. But then for longer than he could remember, he had not been *required* to change clothing or boots. In Valgaard, there had been no need, and there had been no time on the journey from Taliesin's cottage to Mujhara except to dip head in a bucket and scrub face and hands—*hand*—clean.

Hart stared at his boot. At his hand. And at the hand that no longer existed. *"Gods—"* he said; he choked, and covered his head with his arms.

"Let me," the woman said, and he jerked arms away in shock.

Ilsa. He gaped at her like a fool.

Ilsa. In his room.

"Let me," she repeated, and knelt to remove his boot.

Awkwardly, Hart scrambled away. He found himself standing some ten feet from her, still staring, still made mute by her presence; filled with abject humiliation, that she had seen his helplessness.

And then anger began to replace it. "Go," he said curtly.

Ilsa rose. The incandescence of her beauty had not faded, and he felt renewed astonishment at the magnitude of it. "Hart," she said, "it does not matter to me."

He was shaking. "You knew."

"Dar told me what he had done." She was pale as death. "He thought I would approve."

"And you did *not?*"

"I was appalled." Her tone was even. At first he thought she spoke by rote, not caring what she said; beneath the tone he sensed a wire stretched to breaking. "I swear, I did not know what he intended. I did not know he would go so far."

"But you did not tell the Mujhar." He recalled too clearly his father's shock.

Even her lips were pale. "I could not find the words. Not after I learned how he lost his eye. To tell him his son had also been maimed by Ihlini treachery—?" White-faced, Ilsa shook her head. "I could not do it. I thought it better left to you."

He thought again of Dar. "You were in the house." As he intended, his tone accused.

Ilsa drew in a breath. Slender fingers shredded the gray-blue silk of her gown. "Dar came," she said. "We drank wine. We spoke of you. I told him I wanted no harm to come to you, nor to him, nor to Solinde. And he laughed, and said it would not; that the wager was merely a game." Her tone wavered minutely; she steadied it and went on. "I looked into his eyes, and knew he lied to me. But by then it was too late. The wine was drugged. I—slept." Color touched her cheeks; the glacial eyes were angry. "In the morning, he came in triumph, saying the enemy was removed. And he told me what he had done."

Hart longed to believe her. "Did he tell you all of it?"

"Aye." She did not look away as he displayed the handless arm before her. "He told me quite clearly, in his perversity, knowing I would be sickened, and seeking pleasure from it." Ilsa drew in a trembling breath. "I swear, *I swear,* I had nothing to do with it."

His eyes narrowed. "Why are you here? What did you tell my *jehan* so he would let you stay?"

Her eyes were startled. "The truth. That I desire you to come home."

"Home?"

Fingers twitched in a gesture of arrested acknowledgement. "To Solinde," she amended.

He nodded grimly. "Dar should like that."

"Dar should not," she said quietly, "knowing he will be executed."

That startled him out of his bitterness. He stared at her and saw the grief in her eyes, that she tried to hide and could not. "I am not dead. It was a *hand,* not my head." And he knew, as he said it, the first seeds Taliesin had so carefully planted were beginning to take root.

"It was treason," she said steadily. "He attacked the Prince of Solinde and otherwise threatened his person. I had no other choice but to petition the regent for Dar's arrest, and I did so immediately." She paused awkwardly. "It is for you to give the order, when the trial is completed."

"Me?"

"You are the Prince of Solinde."

He did not deny it. "Why a trial, Ilsa? So that others might argue in Dar's behalf? I should think the Solindish might prefer to be rid of me, regardless of circumstances."

"Some, aye," she agreed, "but not all."

"What of you?" he asked. "What of the last of Bellam's line?"

Ilsa drew in a breath. "I came here to bring you home—" quickly, she caught herself, "—to *Solinde*. I came to tell you that we are in need of a prince of the blood." Her smile was slight, but wry. "A prince not *entirely* of our blood, perhaps, but there is some. Electra was your kinswoman as well as mine, though we tend to overlook it; I am *not* the sole bearer of the blood of Bellam's House. It should, in the end, please those who argue against you." Briefly, Ilsa looked down at closed hands, "I came here to tell you I had chosen even *before* Dar arrived—it was why I sent the messenger—and that you were the one I chose."

"Did you?" It was rhetorical; he was not certain he believed her.

"Aye," she told him evenly, and held out her closed right hand.

After a moment, he accepted what she gave him. Heavy rings chimed. He looked down at the Third Seal. At the Second, which Tarron had held. And the First, that had been in Niall's keeping.

"The Trey," Ilsa said.

"I know what it is." He felt empty. "I do not think I can."

"There is also this." Ilsa held out her other hand. When he did not move to accept what she offered, she turned over her hand and opened it. Against her palm the sapphire glowed.

"My signet," he blurted, startled.

"I got it from the wine-girl after Dar told me she had it."

He smiled wryly. "She would not sell to me."

"She did not sell to *me*." Ilsa answered his smile. "I won it from her, Hart."

He stared at her in shock. And then began to laugh.

Ilsa smiled also, but the amusement faded quickly. "Will you come, Hart? Solinde has need of you."

"To give the order for a patriot's execution."

Her gaze did not waver. "If you would prefer—if it is a *test*—I will do it myself."

"As you would have put down my broken-legged horse."

Her chin rose minutely. "I do what must be done. There are requirements of state."

His eyes were oddly intent. "I have been told," he said slowly, "that in Solinde the customs are different."

"Aye." Her tone was guarded.

"I am told that *in Solinde,* it does not matter so much that a man lacks a hand. That a *king* lacks a hand."

Comprehension lighted her eyes. "My lord, in Solinde all that matters—*in kings*—is that they do not lack the wherewithal to sire children on their wives."

Hart smiled crookedly. "No," he said, "I do not."

She lifted a delicate chin. "Then will you come home with me?"

He studied her a long moment. And then he turned and set the Trey of Solinde down onto a table, and stepped closer to the woman. He took the sapphire signet from her palm and slipped it onto her thumb, knowing it too large for any of her fingers.

He did not smile. "Only if you wear this."

"The requirements of state." But there was laughter in her eyes.

Niall sat slumped in his chair. Nearly all of them were gone; his sons, his daughter, his brother. Only his *meijha* remained.

Deirdre stood behind his chair. She leaned down, caught his neck in both arms, hugged briefly. "*All* of them," she said; nothing more was needed.

"All of them," he echoed. "But *gods*, how changed they are."

"Were you expecting something else?" She asked it gently, knowing it would hurt him. "You, who lost an eye to the Ihlini?"

He sighed, reached up to catch her arms beneath his chin, held them. "Each," he said, "so changed. Corin, I think for the better, though there is pain in him; I saw it. And Brennan—something in his eyes, *something*—" He shivered. "And *Hart*—" Abruptly, Niall checked, took his left hand from Deirdre's arm and stared at it, studying palm, fingers, thumb. "Gone," he said hollowly, then dropped it to his thigh. "He will not stop, *meijhana*. I know him and his kind too well . . . the Ihlini will not stop."

She moved around the chair to stand close beside him, one hand stroking back silvering hair. "No."

"He will seek them out again, or me, or Ian, or someone else of the *proper* blood . . . he will seek them out, and take them, and do his best to twist them to his needs . . . to fulfill his god's desires."

"I know."

"Strahan *does not* give up."

"No." Deirdre knelt beside the chair and locked her hands around his forearm, feeling the tension in the sinew beneath the bare flesh. On his arms, *lir*-gold glowed. "But neither do the Cheysuli. Neither did your sons."

"No." Niall closed one of her hands in his. "*Leijhana tu'suai* for that." He sighed. Looked at the folds of yarn and tapestry. Studied it absently. And slowly, some of the tension drained away; amusement crept in to replace it. "*Which* lion did you say was me?"

Deirdre laughed, and showed him.

Epilogue

She walked steadily through the corridor of spiraling columns, passing beneath tier upon tier of glass forming interlocked arches above her head. So lovely, all of it, in its glassy magnificence; in its sharp-edged, threatening beauty. Much like her brother, she thought.

She saw him, then, where he had spent the entirety of the night, and all of the following day. It was night now again, although within the heart of Valgaard it was difficult to tell. When one wanted light, one needed only to summon the *godfire*.

Lillith did not. In darkness she walked to the Gate. There she paused, and waited.

He did not look up. He did not, in any way, acknowledge her presence. He sat cross-legged by the lip of the Gate, head bowed, staring fixedly into the hole. Black hair spilled over his shoulders. The glow of *godfire* touched the circlet and set it ablaze in the heavy darkness.

"So," she said, "they are gone. You have lost them yet again."

Strahan did not answer.

"Brooding will not help."

"I am thinking, hardly brooding . . . there *is* a decided difference."

She was relieved. He sounded normal. "Aye," she agreed, "there is, and I am glad you know it."

Strahan sighed. "What do you want, Lillith?"

"To offer condolences, if you want them; encouragement, if you need it."

"No and no." One pale, slender hand brushed nonexistent dust from a knee.

Lillith waited. He said nothing more. Perhaps he *was* brooding. "Strahan." She knelt down, spreading blood-red skirts, and looked at his face across the Gate. It was a mask in the glare, lacking definition. "You did try."

After a moment, he nodded. "And I will try again. Perhaps *this* time I will succeed . . . already I have a plan."

A plan. Lillith smiled. She felt anticipation.

At last he looked at her. "It does not matter: *time*."

She lifted winged brows. His face was so like hers, except for the mismatched eyes.

Casually, he said: "I have all the days of forever."

THE HOUSE OF HOMANA

CHEYSULI/OLD TONGUE GLOSSARY
(with pronunciation guide)

a'saii (uh-SIGH) — Cheysuli zealots dedicated to pure
  line of descent.
bu'lasa (boo-LAH-suh) — grandson
bu'sala (boo-SAH-luh) — foster-son
cheysu (chay-SOO) — man/woman; neuter; used within
  phrases.
cheysul (chay-SOOL) — husband
cheysula (chay-SOO-luh) — wife
Cheysuli (chay-SOO-lee) –- (*literal translation*): children
  of the gods.
Cheysuli i'halla shansu (chay-SOO-lee ih-HALLA shan-
  SOO) — (*lit.*): May there be Cheysuli peace upon
  you.
godfire (god-fire) — common manifestation of Ihlini power;
  cold, lurid flame; purple tones.
harana (huh-RAH-na) — niece
harani (huh-RAH-nee) — nephew
homana (ho-MAH-na) — literal translation: of all blood.
i'halla (ih-HALL-uh) — upon you: used within phrases.
i'toshaa-ni (ih-tosha-NEE) — Cheysuli cleansing ceremony;
  atonement ritual.
ja'hai ([French *j*] zshuh-HIGH) — accept

ja'hai-na (zshuh-HIGH-nuh) — accepted

jehan (zsheh-HAHN) — father

jehana (zsheh-HAH-na) — mother

ku'reshtin (koo-RESH-tin) — epithet; name-calling

leijhana tu'sai (lay-HAHN-uh too-SIGH) — (*lit.*): thank you very much.

lir (leer) — magical animal(s) linked to individual Cheysuli; title used indiscriminately between *lir* and warriors.

meijha (MEE-hah) — Cheysuli light woman; (*lit.*): mistress.

meijhana (mee-HAH-na) — slang: pretty one

Mujhar (moo-HAR) — king

qu'mahlin (koo-MAH-lin) — purge; extermination

Resh'ta-ni (resh-tah-NEE) — (*lit.*): As you would have it.

rujho (ROO-ho) — slang: brother (diminutive)

rujholla (roo-HALL-uh) — sister (formal)

rujholli (roo-HALL-ee) — brother (formal)

ru'maii (roo-MY-ee) — (*lit.*): in the name of

ru'shalla-tu (roo-SHAWL-uh TOO) — (*lit.*): May it be so.

Seker (Sek-AIR) — formal title: god of the netherworld.

shansu (shan-SOO) — peace

shar tahl (shar TAHL) — priest-historian; keeper of the prophecy.

shu'maii (shoo-MY-ee) — sponsor

su'fala (soo-FALL-uh) — aunt

su'fali (soo-FALL-ee) — uncle

sul'harai (sool-hah-RYE) — moment of greatest satisfaction in union of man and woman; describes shapechange.

tahlmorra (tall-MORE-uh) — fate; destiny; kismet.

Tahlmorra lujhala mei wiccan, cheysu (tall-MORE-uh loo-HALLA may WICK-un, chay-SOO) — (*lit.*): The fate of a man rests always within the hands of the gods.

tetsu (tet-SOO) — poisonous root given to allay great pain; addictive, eventually fatal.

tu'halla dei (too-HALLA-day-EE) — (*lit.*): Lord to liege man.

usca (OOIS-kuh) — powerful liquor from the Steppes.

y'ja'hai (EE-zshuh-HIGH) — (*lit.*): I accept.

Coming soon . . .

DAUGHTER OF THE LION

BY JENNIFER ROBERSON

She is Keely, twin sister to Corin, and daughter of Niall, the ruler of Homana, and she alone has the power to shapechange into any form, a power akin to that of the Firstborn. And like her brothers, Keely has been chosen to play a crucial part in the Firstborn's prophecy. Yet Keely, a true daughter of the Lion, is no weak pawn to be used in men's games of power and diplomacy. Trained alongside her brothers in the art of war, gifted with more of the old magic than most of her close kin, she will not easily give way even to Niall's commands, nor be forced against her will into an arranged marriage. But others besides Keely's father have plans for her future. Strahan, the most powerful Ihlini sorcerer, is already preparing a trap from which even one as magic-gifted as Keely may find no escape. And in the deepwood, another waits to challenge Keely, an outlaw fully as dangerous to her future freedom as Strahan is to her life . . .

0 552 13123 7

DRAGONSDAWN

BY Anne McCaffrey

Before Thread, before the Dragons, before the Holds and the Weyrs and the elite Dragonriders of Pern, was just the great ship gliding through space with nearly three thousand colonists prepared to tackle the mighty task of beginning a new world on a strange planet.

It was a jewel of a planet – with rivers and seas and mountains, and breathable air and growing things. Then came the terror.

The strange, unidentifiable circles in the grass suddenly revealed a meaning, and every living thing was at risk. Many died – a horrible and consuming death. All resources, every man, woman and child had to fight the horrible nightmare of Thread.

But a new creature was about to save the planet. From the delicate fire lizards a new life was born – a new symbiosis between man and beast.

0 552 13098 2

A SELECTION OF SCIENCE FICTION & FANTASY TITLES AVAILABLE FROM CORGI BOOKS

☐ 13017 6	MALLOREON 1: GUARDIANS OF THE WEST	David Eddings	£3.50
☐ 13018 4	MALLOREON 2: KING OF THE MURGOS	David Eddings	£3.99
☐ 12284 X	BOOK ONE OF THE BELGARIAD: PAWN OF PROPHECY	David Eddings	£2.99
☐ 12348 X	BOOK TWO OF THE BELGARIAD: QUEEN OF SORCERY	David Eddings	£2.99
☐ 12382 X	BOOK THREE OF THE BELGARIAD: MAGICIAN'S GAMBIT	David Eddings	£2.99
☐ 12435 4	BOOK FOUR OF THE BELGARIAD: CASTLE OF WIZARDRY	David Eddings	£2.99
☐ 12447 8	BOOK FIVE OF THE BELGARIAD: ENCHANTERS' END GAME	David Eddings	£3.50
☐ 08453 0	DRAGONFLIGHT	Anne McCaffrey	£2.99
☐ 11635 1	DRAGONQUEST	Anne McCaffrey	£3.50
☐ 11313 1	THE WHITE DRAGON	Anne McCaffrey	£3.99
☐ 10661 5	DRAGONSONG	Anne McCaffrey	£2.50
☐ 10881 2	DRAGONSINGER: HARPER OF PERN	Anne McCaffrey	£2.99
☐ 11804 4	DRAGONDRUMS	Anne McCaffrey	£2.50
☐ 12499 0	MORETA – DRAGONLADY OF PERN	Anne McCaffrey	£3.50
☐ 12817 1	NERILKA'S STORY & THE COELURA	Anne McCaffrey	£1.95
☐ 13098 2	DRAGONSDAWN	Anne McCaffrey	£3.99
☐ 10965 7	GET OFF THE UNICORN	Anne McCaffrey	£2.99
☐ 12097 9	THE CRYSTAL SINGER	Anne McCaffrey	£2.95
☐ 12556 3	KILLASHANDRA	Anne McCaffrey	£2.99
☐ 08661 4	DECISION AT DOONA	Anne McCaffrey	£2.50
☐ 08344 5	RESTOREE	Anne McCaffrey	£2.75
☐ 09115 4	THE SHIP WHO SANG	Anne McCaffrey	£2.50
☐ 12497 4	STITCH IN SNOW	Anne McCaffrey	£1.75
☐ 13118 0	CHRONICLES OF THE CHEYSULI 1: SHAPECHANGERS	Jennifer Roberson	£2.99
☐ 13119 9	CHRONICLES OF THE CHEYSULI 2: SONG OF HOMANA	Jennifer Roberson	£3.99
☐ 13120 2	CHRONICLES OF THE CHEYSULI 3: LEGACY OF THE SWORD	Jennifer Roberson	£3.99
☐ 13121 0	CHRONICLES OF THE CHEYSULI 4: TRACK OF THE WHITE WOLF	Jennifer Roberson	£3.99
☐ 13101 6	SERVANTS OF ARK 1: THE FIRST NAMED	Jonathan Wylie	£3.50
☐ 13134 2	SERVANTS OF ARK II: THE CENTRE OF THE CIRCLE	Jonathan Wylie	£2.99
☐ 13161 X	SERVANTS OF ARK III: THE MAGE-BORN CHILD	Jonathan Wylie	£3.50
☐ 13416 3	THE UNBALANCED EARTH 1: DREAMS OF STONE	Jonathan Wylie	£2.99
☐ 13417 1	THE UNBALANCED EARTH 2: THE LIGHTLESS KINGDOM	Jonathan Wylie	£2.99